THE KEY TO LOVE

THE KEY TO LOVE

BETSY ST. AMANT

THORNDIKE PRESS
A part of Gale, a Cengage Company

Copyright © 2020 by Betsy St. Amant.
Thorndike Press, a part of Gale, a Cengage Company.

Thorndike Press® Large Print Christian Romance.
The text of this Large Print edition is unabridged.
Other aspects of the book may vary from the original edition.
Set in 16 pt. Plantin.

**LIBRARY OF CONGRESS CIP DATA ON FILE.
CATALOGUING IN PUBLICATION FOR THIS BOOK
IS AVAILABLE FROM THE LIBRARY OF CONGRESS.**

ISBN-13: 978-1-4328-8592-2 (hardcover alk. paper)

Published in 2021 by arrangement with Revell Books, a division of Baker Publishing Group, Inc.

Printed in Mexico
Print Number: 01   Print Year: 2021

To my precious grandmother, Betty Jo McLemore, and to the love story you had with my dear grandfather, "Mr. Mac." Now both of you are swallowed up in heaven, experiencing the greatest love ever known. Thanks for always being one of my biggest fans.

CHAPTER ONE

The only thing Bri Duval loved more than romance was a perfectly executed French macaron.

Fortunately, at least one of the two was within reach.

She nudged the pastel-purple, lavender-honey macaron into position on the paper-layered tray and carefully slid it into the display case next to the petit fours. Well, maybe both were in reach — just not for her.

Casey, a single mom and one of her regular customers at the Pastry Puff, would be in shortly, per her usual Tuesday routine, seeking a dessert and a latte after dropping her two toddlers at Mother's Day Out.

If Mabel and Agnes's plan was as perfectly executed as Bri's macarons, then local fireman Nathan should be right behind her for his midmorning cinnamon coffee.

"Is she here yet?" Mabel rushed through

the swinging door of the kitchen, out of breath, her attempt at contouring her makeup that morning smeared across her droopy cheekbones. But her blue eyes sparkled beneath white eyebrows, as they always did when she got a chance to play Cupid.

The winged legend didn't stand much of a chance against Mabel and Agnes. The seventy-something co-owners of the Pastry Puff might too frequently blur the line between matchmaking and meddling, but they had proof of their success. And that proof was locked up tight in the bakery's backyard.

Literally.

Bri brushed off the front of her apron even though it was already clean. It'd been a slow morning. "Don't panic, Mabel. She's not here yet." She glanced at the clock ticking on the wall above the display case, its numbers black and bold against the pale pink paint.

Casey had no idea what was teaming up against her. Everyone knew and adored Casey, and the poor thing had survived more than one blind date set up by a well-meaning neighbor — hazards of a Midwest small town — but Mabel and Agnes were convinced Nathan was "the one" for Casey.

And when those two were convinced of something, it was best to back out of the way — or better yet, pull up a chair and watch.

Bri was more than happy to have a front-row seat to the shenanigans. She only wished she could have been there when the arrows had flown into her parents' hearts outside a tiny Parisian bakery decades ago. Talk about the match of the century.

The chimes above the front door jingled as Casey bustled inside, early autumn leaves blowing in on the heels of her sleek brown boots. She always looked put together in public — part of her real estate agent persona — though Bri had seen Casey more than once on her front porch swing in sweats, surrounded by tissues. She couldn't imagine what it would be like to raise two babies alone.

Or to just be a mom.

Bri batted away the discouragement before it could nest. Love couldn't be rushed. Had her parents taught her nothing? She was only twenty-seven. Some things were worth the wait. And if waiting guaranteed a love like her parents', then she could chill out and watch Mabel and Agnes matchmake around her — and possibly keep picking up a lot of "what not to do" tips.

9

Mabel clutched Bri's arm in excitement. "She's here!" She coughed twice, in what she often attempted to be a secret signal that her sister never seemed to catch. "Agnes, get out here!" The familiar hiss of Mabel's failed whisper wafted through the bakery.

Casey politely averted her gaze to the ceiling, as if pretending not to notice the obvious as Agnes barreled through the swinging door behind the counter.

"What? Where!" Agnes's voice, three times deeper than her sister's, barked her confusion. She caught sight of Casey, adjusted her wire-rimmed glasses, and patted her no-nonsense, brown-and-gray-speckled hair, as if it had somehow dared move out of place.

It wouldn't dare. No one crossed Agnes.

The two elderly sisters were opposites, to say the least. Agnes was about as subtle and gentle as an elephant, stoic and sensible, always rotating through the same variety of dress slacks and blouses, while Mabel, wild at heart and dramatic, experimented with new lipsticks regularly and thought Bri was still the elementary-school girl who used to fall out of the oak tree in her front yard. Agnes would lecture her on climbing too high in the first place; Mabel would rush out with ice packs and homemade chocolate

10

chip cookies. The sisters had been like great-aunts to Bri growing up, even more so after her parents died in a car wreck when she was eighteen.

Bri smiled calmly at Casey, ignoring the two living, breathing cartoon characters behind her. The sisters might be successful at matchmaking, but they failed miserably in the art of subtlety. She reached for one of the macarons with the dainty tongs she'd convinced Agnes to buy for just that reason. "The usual?"

Casey nodded. "Please." Now that she was closer, Bri noticed the stress behind the young mom's brown eyes. Casey fought back a yawn as she riffled through her coin purse. "It's four twenty-seven with the latte, right?"

Actually, it was five thirty-nine, but . . . "On the house today." How much real estate could Casey possibly turn around in a town like Story?

Bri felt both Mabel's approving smile and Agnes's disapproving glare on her back at the same time. She couldn't help it. The woman needed coffee, and her kids probably needed new coats this winter. They grew like weeds. Every penny helped.

The bell chimed again. An extra bunch of leaves skittered across the floor, one making its way to Casey's feet. She looked down slowly, then turned.

Nathan approached in his standard department-issued black polo and utility pants. He offered a quick nod to all the ladies, then did a double take at Mabel and Agnes beaming at him. His easy smile faded into the all-too-familiar deer-in-the-headlights look Bri had witnessed many times from her side of the counter. Poor guy.

The elderly sisters shouted in unison. "Congratulations!"

Nathan blinked twice, one hand frozen in place halfway to his wallet. "Huh?"

Mabel nudged Agnes, who shook her head. Mabel nudged harder, and with a sigh and a resigned roll of her eyes, Agnes pulled a tiny contraption from her pocket and yanked on the top.

Confetti shot across the counter, tangling in Bri's hair and landing on the sleeve of Casey's corduroy jacket. It fell a foot short of its intended target, who looked as if he wasn't sure his cinnamon coffee was worth this madness.

Casey, cheeks flushing, brushed the miniature colored streamers off her arm. Nathan pulled one out of her shoulder-length curls. "Got it."

"*Yeah* he does."

Now it was Agnes's turn to elbow Mabel into silence.

Mabel cleared her throat, a hearty pink blush working its way across her overly made-up face. "I mean, congratulations! You're our twenty-fifth customer of the day."

He wasn't. More like the sixth, maybe. If he'd actually been the twenty-fifth, then maybe Charles Richmond wouldn't be sniffing around all the time, half joking about purchasing the place.

Nathan blinked again. "I am?" He shot Bri a glance that begged for interpretation. She hid a grin behind her hand and cleared her throat.

"Which *means,* you win free coffee." Agnes shot Mabel a pointed glare, as if to get her sister to the point faster.

"Right! Free coffee." Mabel's eyes darted to the display case. "And, uh, and macarons! Which means, obviously, you'll need help carrying them."

Nathan took the coffee Bri had already poured for him and gestured to the sack Agnes was preparing with the pastries. "That's really nice of you ladies. But I can manage one cup and a bag."

Bri gave him mental props for not punctuating that last statement with the "duh" it deserved.

He reached for his prizewinnings with the air of a man who'd rather be fighting a wildfire. "Thank you."

Mabel grabbed Agnes's arm, yanking the bag out of his reach just in time. "No, no, you don't understand." Her frantic gaze landed on Casey, who stood there sipping her latte and absently brushing more confetti onto the floor. "I meant, it's free coffee — for the *entire* department."

"Trust me, Nathan." Agnes handed the sack back over. "You need help."

Bri snorted, turning it into a cough. Agnes glared, and Mabel ignored them both.

Casey shrugged, finally zoning in on the opportunity. She straightened a little, shifting her coffee cup to her other hand. "I could help you. I don't mind."

Nathan's gaze finally rested on Casey, and he tilted his head, as if seeing her for the first time. "You sure?"

"Of course she's sure." Mabel clasped her hands under her chin, which boasted a darker streak than the rest of her face.

Bri didn't try to hide her smile this time. She should have gotten this on video. The Pastry Puff would have gone viral on You-Tube in an hour — which, honestly, would be great for business. And would serve as a reminder to Charles to back off.

A few minutes later, Casey and Nathan strolled out of the bakery together, juggling the multiple cups of coffee and bags of macarons and laughing. At their matchmakers, no doubt, but laughing all the same.

"And that's how it's done." Agnes released a curt nod, the most excitement she ever allowed herself to show.

Mabel, however, sagged across the counter, fanning her flushed cheeks with her wrinkled hand. "Oh, my stars, did you see the way she stared at him in that uniform?"

"I saw the way you did." Bri grinned and plucked a macaron from the display. They'd already given away a dozen. What was one more on the house?

"It's your turn next, missy." Mabel straightened, taking Bri in with her sparkling eyes that always seemed to see more than the average person. "Don't think I've forgotten you."

"Give it a rest, Mabel." Bri bit into her macaron, relishing the rich flavors. She'd nailed it that time — maybe it was the extra dash of almond powder she'd sprinkled in at the last minute. Still, it wasn't the missing secret ingredient to her mom's recipe that she'd been trying to perfect for years.

"You've already ruled out the entire fire department, half the police force, the coffee shop barista on Main, and the gas station attendant."

"Don't forget the hardware store owner's son. And Mrs. Beeker's grandson, who helps her at the B&B. Oh, and that guy who likes to pretend he's a cowboy." Agnes pursed her lips. "Closest thing he owned to a horse was that giant dog of his."

Oh, the memories. "The one who slobbered all over me?"

"Hey, at least the dog slobbered, and not the guy." Mabel chortled.

Bri winced. "You didn't see the last half of our date." Their first date, and their last. Story of her life. Then again, her standards were pretty high — she wasn't convinced she'd ever find a romance equivalent to her parents'.

But she'd much rather wait for her fairy-tale ending than waste time kissing frogs.

"At least you're out of that horrid relationship with that lawyer." Agnes shuddered. "I couldn't imagine a duller marriage than one to Charles Richmond."

Bri shuddered. "He was pretty bad." Definitely more sidekick than hero — he'd ironed his socks. He needed a woman less romantic than Bri, someone with an equally

16

law-obsessed head on her shoulders. And she needed someone who could kiss her and make her foot pop like in the black-and-white movies.

The only thing Charles made pop was her bubble of expectations.

"Mark my words, Abrielle, I'm going to place your love lock on that gate outside one of these days." Mabel's gaze pierced into Bri's, and she believed her.

Somewhere, he was out there. Apparently not at the firehouse or the police station or Johnson's General, but somewhere, he was there — a man with zero froggy intentions and a heart as romantic as hers.

CHAPTER TWO

The only thing Gerard Fortier possibly hated more than romance was writing about it.

He shoved his fingers through his thick dark hair, wishing he could shove Peter's smug grin where the sun didn't shine. "You've got to be kidding, man."

But he'd known Peter long enough — even before those silver streaks appeared on his supervisor's temples — to know this assignment wasn't a joke.

They started out as buddies, and usually maintained that relationship, but Peter was all too quick to play the managing editor card when needed. Work first, poker games second. He had a knack for keeping his business and his personal life separate, which was a plus around *Trek Magazine*'s Chicago headquarters *and* around the bar. But the man was a bull when it came to teaching stubborn.

And right now, Peter might as well have had his head down and nostrils flared.

"Hey, now, all I've heard from you for the past nine months is how badly you want to write about 'what matters.' " Peter crossed his arms over his snug-fitting polo, the one everyone knew he bought a size too small on purpose, and grinned, propping one foot up against the side of the mahogany desk. "What matters more than love?"

If Gerard had a dart gun, he'd have shot his boss in the loafer.

"Not exactly what I had in mind when I said that." Gerard leaned against the doorframe, grateful he hadn't accepted the invitation to sit in the leather chair opposite Peter's desk and be looked down on literally, as well as figuratively. Everyone at *Trek Magazine* — thanks to Keurig-fueled chatter, a few scorned sweaters, and one too many rounds at coworker happy hour — knew how Gerard felt about love.

They didn't know why, and he'd keep it that way. Except Peter. Peter knew, and he was baiting him — but why?

His boss spread his arms wide. "You want the assignment or not?"

"Not." Gerard boldly met his gaze, hoping Peter could see he was just as determined not to take the task as Peter was to

give it to him. This was crossing the line —
he could write plenty of other pieces for the
upcoming issue.

But the bull hadn't gotten that way by
turning soft. Peter straightened his shoulders, one eyebrow raised in a way Gerard
knew from experience meant he was inch-
ing closer to an invisible line he shouldn't
cross.

Gerard stood taller, even though he already had two inches on Peter. And even
though he knew it was impossible to intimi-
date the man. "Don't you have something
— anything — more appealing? You know,
like maybe a month's stay in the snake-
infested South African bush?"

He was joking. Sort of. Their readers
would prefer to hear a firsthand account of
a jungle adventure than read a boring piece
on some European-style café in Nowheres-
ville, USA, right?

And he'd much rather write it.

Peter grabbed a golf ball from the stand
on his desk and tossed it casually from one
hand to the other. "I told you, this little
French-themed hole-in-the-wall in Kansas
is going viral, thanks to some YouTube
matchmaking videos and the cute blonde
who works there."

Hopefully he hid the eye roll threatening

to break free. It was always a blonde with Peter. Gerard preferred brunettes.

Minus the last one, anyway.

"Bakeries are a dime a dozen in the Midwest, man. What makes this one so special?" Gerard didn't really want to know; he wanted to stall. But Peter would tell him anyway.

"I mentioned the blonde."

Gerard glared. "Not interested." They couldn't all have perfect marriages like Peter and his wife, Cynthia. She was a rare find, and Peter knew it. At least they were proof that all marriages weren't doomed.

Just most.

"I'm kidding." Peter set the ball back on his desk, then shifted his weight against the side of it. "It's like this. Apparently the feedback from our last few issues wasn't stellar. Sales are down — significantly down."

"Is *Trek* in trouble?" His heart stammered a beat. If that was true, he might have more pressing problems on his plate than dealing with some silly old women in small-town America.

"Not yet."

Gerard sank into the chair by Peter's desk, knowing the movement indicated a white flag on his part, but he couldn't muster the

21

fight any longer.

He ran his hand down the length of his face. His stubble scrubbed his palm, which was still calloused from that mountain bike excursion he'd written about two weeks ago. Racing bikes on a Pacific cliff required a death grip on the handlebars.

He'd rather do that again, blind and barefoot, than write about some old ladies playing Cupid.

Which reminded him . . . "Did you really refer to the bakery women earlier as love angels?" He winced.

"That's the YouTube commentary, not mine." Peter grinned.

"How bad is the magazine doing, for real?" He needed to know, needed to send his mom another check at the end of the month. "Just between us."

Peter met his eyes, which let Gerard know he was telling the truth. His friend — and boss — had zero poker face and never, ever bluffed. "The magazine is holding its own, and our digital sales are still trending up. But there was enough of a sales dip last quarter, combined with the reader feedback, that corporate was prompted to make some suggestions. They say readers want 'relatable.' " Peter leaned forward, bracing his elbows on his knees. "And, unfortunately, most readers can't relate to racing bicycles around cliffs or skydiving in the Amazon or deep-sea fishing in Alaska."

All recent stories Gerard had written. "I see what you did there."

"Look, this isn't about a bakery in Kansas." Peter leaned forward. "I'm trying to help you out, man."

Gerard set his jaw, wanting to believe that. Peter knew him better than anyone else outside of his family. Knew about his mom. And knew how Kelsey ripped his heart out in her cold, manicured hands three years ago. He also knew that it had taken Gerard a year of extra assignments to pay off the ring she never wore but decided to keep anyway. "How is that, exactly?"

"By giving you a chance. If the big, exotic stories aren't selling, and you're the one writing the big, exotic stories . . ." Peter's voice trailed off, and he leveled his gaze at Gerard. "If you won't write this feature on the love-lock wall in Kansas, then I'll find someone who will."

CHAPTER THREE

"I still can't believe we're getting featured in a global magazine." Mabel poured her second cup of coffee, then surrendered the carafe to Bri's waiting hand. "Who would have thought? Little ol' Story, Kansas!"

Bri poured the steaming brew into her favorite mug, the one with the pink Eiffel Towers. "Not just Story, Mabel — the Pastry Puff, specifically. *Us.*" *Unbelievable* didn't quite cover it, although she supposed less worthy causes had gone viral on the internet before. It only took a few cat videos to realize that.

"What's that thing they discovered us on, again?" Agnes stirred creamer into her mug, then tapped the spoon twice against the side as she always did before sitting down at one of the black iron tables. "View-a-Tube?"

Bri tried to hide her laugh. "It's YouTube, Agnes." A week after Casey and Nathan had strolled out of the Pastry Puff, loaded down with macarons and cinnamon coffee, little cartoon hearts pulsing between them, Mabel made a comment about wishing she could have been a fly on the wall on their first date. Bri remembered her earlier thought about how if she'd filmed the sisters' match-making tactics, they'd have been an internet sensation. So, she got permission from Casey to document her and Nathan's developing story.

That led to going back and getting quotes from all the couples Mabel and Agnes had successfully matched over the years and filming them standing by their love locks that hung all around the gate in the café's backyard — the gate Bri had incorporated at the bakery years ago, before city officials had shut down the famous love-lock bridge in Paris.

Her plan to generate more business for the bakery and dissuade Charles's annoying requests for the sisters to sell had worked like a charm. Business had picked up the past few weeks — along with the match-making requests. They had been approached by everyone from mothers dragging their gamer sons in by the ear to ol' Mr. Hansen, who until now rarely left his perch at the checker table outside Johnson's General. But he'd bought six petit fours in three days and kept eyeballing Agnes like she was the next dessert on the menu.

Bri took her cup to Agnes's table and pulled up a chair. Mabel joined them, and they all stared into their mugs, processing the impossible. Bri wished her parents were there to see her success. They'd been gone almost a decade, but on days like this, it felt like mere weeks. The pain pinched fresh. Her mom got her start at the Pastry Puff, too, and she'd have been so delighted to see what had developed on her home turf.

"When is the reporter supposed to come?" Mabel asked.

Good question. They hadn't been given much information on the phone, and Bri had been so blown away, she hadn't thought to ask for any additional specifics. "The editor from *Trek* only said he was sending someone this week."

"Well, I hope she's nice." Mabel propped up her chin in one hand, pursing her hot-pink lips.

Bri eyed their overflowing display case. "I hope she likes macarons."

"I just hope she's a good writer." Agnes frowned. "This could go south on us if she's not."

"Come on, now. Haven't you ever heard there's no such thing as bad publicity?" Bri

26

playfully tapped her arm. "What could go wrong?"

Mabel agreed. "She's right, Agnes. I doubt they're sending a reporter all this way just to say bad things about us."

"I beg to differ." Agnes lifted her chin, raising her voice to be heard over the sound of a motorcycle revving past the bakery. "We have no idea of their agenda. The media can be very shady."

The motorcycle revved louder.

"Media? It's a travel magazine." Bri grinned. "Hey, I bet Mr. Hansen will read the feature."

Agnes bristled, a deep red working its way up her throat. "I wouldn't know anything about his reading habits."

The door chimed, and Bri swallowed back the next tease threatening to leave her lips. The bubbling laugh died in her throat as a tall, dark-haired man stepped into the bakery, sober-faced, his broad shoulders stretching taut the fabric of a navy T-shirt. He had a leather bomber jacket draped over his arm and a tan backpack hitched on the opposite shoulder. A tattoo crawled out of the sleeve of his shirt and stretched halfway down his arm.

Definitely not the average Story tourist. At least that explained the motorcycle cacophony.

"Afternoon, sir." Agnes pinned him with a stare that clearly expressed how she expected him to ride his motorcycle through the front door — and that she was absolutely not okay with it. "You needing directions?"

Surely. No way was he there for a petit four. Still, maybe they could sell him something before he hit the street again. She stood, attempting to soften Agnes's words with her best smile. "Or maybe a cup of coffee?"

His dark eyes darted between the two of them, and he set his backpack in an empty chair a few tables away. "Maybe. Is it any good?"

Bri's smile faltered. "I like to think so."

"Just you?" He laid the jacket on top of his pack, and Bri felt her mouth threaten to unhinge.

She crossed her arms over her apron instead, gathering her composure. "No, not just me. Apparently so do the other customers who have tried it."

"Ah." His voice held a trace of an accent, but not one Bri could immediately place. A little bit of Yankee, a little bit of southern drawl . . . where was this guy from? "I can see business is booming." He cast a doubtful glance around the empty establishment.

28

Bri lifted her chin, her need to defend the bakery burning strong. "It has been. Perhaps you've heard of the Pastry Puff Matchmakers on YouTube?"

"That's right. We went virus." Mabel beamed proudly, seemingly oblivious to their customer's rudeness.

"Viral. We went *viral.*" Agnes barked the correction with a shake of her head. "She hasn't gotten that right a single time yet. Though I still don't fully understand the doohickey on the computer myself."

"Viral, virus, tomay-to, tomah-to." Mabel waved her hand dismissively. Then her eyes widened. She reached toward the stranger, who took an automatic step back. "We're not sick, though, don't worry."

He raised one eyebrow.

Mabel gestured eagerly between her and Agnes. "We're the love angels."

"Stop it." Agnes pushed her sister's hand down with a huff. "I told you that was a ridiculous name."

Mabel sniffed. "It is not. It's cute. And catchy."

"I've heard of you." His deep baritone interrupted the pending argument.

Mabel stuck out her tongue at her sister. "See?"

Bri, mind racing, reached for the still-warm carafe. He'd actually heard of their café? He didn't seem the type to sit around watching videos about small-town romance. But hey, he was still a guy — maybe he just really liked baked goods.

She tried to start over, ignore his sarcasm. "So, coffee?"

"I guess."

She hesitated, looking up for confirmation. He was edging closer to the display counter, and the closer he came, the taller she realized he was. At least six-two, maybe six-three. And those muscles.

His dark eyes met hers, and she gripped the handle of the carafe tighter as a blush heated her throat. Hopefully he hadn't read her thoughts.

She stammered to get them back on the matter at hand. She lifted the carafe. "How do you take your coffee? If you'd rather, I can whip you up a latte or a cappuccino or a cinnamon mocha —"

"Black."

Of course he drank it black. She had half a mind to pour some sugar in it when he wasn't looking, just to see if it would sweeten him up a bit.

Her shoulders stiffened. It wasn't often people didn't respond to her friendliness with friendliness in return. The often-cranky

Mayor Hawthorne always cheered up when she presented him with a smile and a macaron after stressful town meetings. And once when Charles's ex-girlfriend came into the bakery in a jealous fit over a misunderstanding, Bri had talked her down with a latte and a hot mini-donut.

Her half-fake smile went into full façade. "For here, or to go?" Hopefully to go. She really didn't see any reason for him to hang around, not with that attitude. She automatically reached for the stack of paper to-go cups.

"For here."

She yanked her hand back, and the stack of cups tumbled and fell in a heap on the counter. *"Really?"* The word blurted from her lips before she could censor it, and she quickly pressed her glossed lips together as she gathered the spilled cups.

"You love angels always this friendly to your customers?" A smirk lifted one corner of his mouth, which she couldn't help but notice was surrounded by what seemed to be a permanent five-o'clock shadow. As if even his facial hair had a stubborn will of its own.

She straightened the stack of cups. "I'm not a love angel." That was Mabel and Agnes's self-proclaimed title — she was no matchmaker. But she sort of had a feeling clarification wasn't what this stranger was after.

"That's for sure." His first smile since he'd walked in the room.

"What is that supposed to mean?" She set the carafe down harder than she'd intended, and coffee splashed onto the counter. She reached for a paper napkin.

"Hey." He tapped two fingers on the counter. "You're wearing an apron."

She tossed the soiled napkin into the trash can under the counter and smoothed the front of her pink, lacy apron. "I'm aware." Captain Obvious. She felt proud that the term didn't verbally dart from her mouth. At least she still had some self-control in front of this sullen stranger.

"Are you?" He leaned one elbow against the glass countertop, the one she'd just cleaned a few hours ago, and drew closer. The scent of evergreen wafted over her. "Then why didn't you use it for the spill?"

That was such a man thing to say. "Why on earth would I use my apron when there's a perfectly good napkin right beside me?"

"So, it's a costume, not a functioning apron." He tilted his head, dark eyes narrowing as they assessed her. "That doesn't make me very confident in the quality of your coffee."

Her cheeks flushed hot. "Then why are you still standing here? Go drink it and find out for yourself."

"You still haven't given me any."

Oh, for the love of —

She poured his coffee into a mug, purposefully choosing the one with red hearts just to irk him, and set down the carafe. "There," she said, sliding the mug across the counter.

"How much do I owe you?" He reached into the pocket of his jeans and pulled out a wad of bills.

She fought the urge to roll her eyes. Not shocking that Mr. Motorcycle didn't carry a wallet like a grown-up but instead fisted Hamiltons in his pocket like a teenager with lawn-mowing money. "It's on the house. In fact, it's on *that* end of the house, to be exact."

She pointed to the table farthest away from her, throwing a quick glance at Mabel and Agnes. Couldn't they see she was desperate for backup here? Agnes especially had to be steaming right now at his demeaning attitude . . .

Nope. Both women were staring with wide eyes and cat-ate-the-canary grins, chins braced on their palms. Mabel whispered something to Agnes, who nodded intently and murmured back.

Oh *no.* No way. She knew that look.

Mr. Motorcycle slowly backed away from the counter and raised one eyebrow again. She hated how much the feat impressed her. "You trying to get rid of me?"

"Finally, we're speaking the same language." Bri folded her arms around her middle, determined to get her message across to both this rude customer and the love angels. *Back off.* In fact, she'd step it up a notch, for all their sakes. "And for the record, if you're trying to flirt with me, you're doing a horrible job."

Mabel gasped. Agnes's mouth dropped open.

The corners of Mr. Motorcycle's lips twitched. "Glad to hear it." He glanced down at the counter and nodded twice, as if processing her proclamation. "I appreciate the clarification. That'll certainly make writing this article easier." He picked up his coffee.

Her heart slid down into her stomach. "Article?"

He smiled, revealing even, white teeth. "Perhaps you've heard of *Trek Magazine*?"

Her stomach began to churn into her sinking heart. This wasn't happening. No. This was a dream.

She closed her eyes, hoping all of this had been a really bad nightmare, and she would open her eyes, and there'd be a nice woman in a pencil skirt and really cute shoes breaking apart a petit four and gushing over how adorable the café was.

Three, two, one . . .

But no. She opened her eyes, and there he was, their feature writer — the one she'd just insulted in about ten different ways — saluting her with his heart-decorated mug. "Cheers."

CHAPTER FOUR

Gerard had worked with — and dated, before realizing it wasn't worth it — his share of women over the years. But never had he seen one pale to the point of making Casper look tan.

When Bri had realized who he was, she'd stammered some strange apology, something about free petit fours and pencil skirts that he hadn't quite grasped, before finally offering her name and another cup of that awful coffee.

It would have been humorous if this whole assignment wasn't still so grating. He'd tell Peter and have a good laugh — later, anyway, after this initial annoyance wore off.

Assuming it did.

He flipped his kickstand down and hiked his duffel on his shoulder as he peered up dubiously at the three-story frame house before him, covered in stretching vines and trimmed in gingerbread. Dainty flower boxes lined each window, while wooden stakes decorated to look like lollipops peeked out of the landscaping. A swinging sign on the picket fence boasted the name of the bed and breakfast in elaborate pink cursive.

The Gingerbread House.

He was going to kill Peter.

When his boss assured him the lodging in Story was sufficient for the assignment and his assistant would handle it, Gerard assumed he'd meant clean sheets and free continental breakfast. Not a B&B torn from the pages of a children's book.

He glanced back at his bike. He could leave now — roar away, forget the love angels and their mediocre coffee and this silly love-lock wall. Forget the assignment altogether.

An image of Bri's welcoming smile filled his mind, and he shoved it away. He could forget that too. Pretty blondes were a dime a dozen.

And she *was* pretty, he'd give Peter that one.

He didn't, however, want to forget the paycheck or his one opportunity to become a lead writer at the magazine's sister publication, *Traipse Horizon.* Everything in him needed to provide content beyond summer vacation prospects. He wanted to write about the government's dealings in Pakistan and the latest drug raid in Colombia and the economic statistics in Guam. He wanted to write something that mattered — a byline he could be proud of. That his mom could be proud of.

And maybe one day, his father too — if he ever bothered to pick up a magazine. Or even remembered Gerard's name.

So, into the witch's house it was.

He grabbed his duffel, pushed open the picket gate that matched the swinging sign, and plodded up the three stairs to the front door.

His black leather boot cracked through the second step and he lunged forward, catching himself on the splintered railing. A wood chip dug into his palm just as his duffel hit the dusty porch floor with a thump. His backpack swung off his shoulder and smacked him in the face.

Welcome to Story.

"Oh, my cheese and crackers!" The screen door opened, nearly nailing him in the head, and a red-haired, spectacled woman rushed outside, an apron tied around her ample waist. Her hands fluttered like she was shooing birds. Or perhaps trying to fly herself. "Are you okay, sir?"

"Yep." Gerard straightened, tugging his boot from the step. He'd probably be a little sore from the sudden lunge, but there was no need to point that out. "Looks like that stair needs repairing."

"They've been rotted for a while now." The woman leaned over and winked dramatically at him. "Don't tell my insurance agent."

Right. "Your secret's safe." He adjusted his backpack, just as she handed him his duffel. Thankfully his laptop was in a padded case inside. He never traveled on his bike without the extra protection.

"Hopefully the rest of your stay at the Gingerbread House will be top-notch." She extended her hand. Up close, he could tell now her red hair was from a bottle. Judging by the laugh lines around her overly plucked brows, she must be in her late sixties.

"I'm Mrs. Beeker, proud owner. And housekeeper, and chef." She laughed. "I would do the books too, but I can't add to save my life. I leave that to my grandson."

Noted. He shook her hand. "Pleasure is mine."

"It's not every day we get a traveler like yourself from the Rainy City."

Close. "It's Windy."

"Is it?" She licked her finger and held it

up, squinting. "I hadn't noticed."

"No, I meant —" Never mind. Time to switch gears so he could get to his room and write out his initial impressions of the Pastry Puff. Another image of Bri in her apron filled his mind, and he shook it away. "I'd love to see my room. It's such a charming establishment you have here." It wasn't a blatant lie. Someone would find it charming. Just not him.

"Oh, you're too much!" Mrs. Beeker swatted in his direction as a pink flush dotted her cheeks. "I do hope you'll leave us a good review on the World Wide Web. Business has been booming since the love-lock wall got so much publicity."

She should probably fix that stair, then.

Gerard followed her inside, catching the screen door she forgot to hold open in her excitement before it hit for the second time. This woman was like a redheaded tornado.

The foyer looked normal enough, with dark wood and old floral wallpaper. Outdated but harmless. And no candy decorations. He relaxed an iota. Maybe she just hadn't taken down her Christmas decorations outside.

Mrs. Beeker rounded the corner of the front desk. "People want to come see it, you know."

40

He dropped his bags at his feet and dug in his wallet for his company credit card. If this place had room service, he'd order it, just to get back at Peter. "It?"

"The love-lock wall, of course. They want to hang their lock on the fence and fall in love." Mrs. Beeker sighed and batted her eyes. "Every single one of them."

"Is that how it works? You hang a lock and fall in love?" He handed her the card.

"Oh, my cheese and crackers, no. You have to fall in love first. The lock is the symbol of your commitment."

"I see." So, it was sort of like prison. Fitting.

"Is that why you're here?" She wiggled her eyebrows.

"Heck no." He caught himself. "Well, sort of. It's related. But I can assure you, it's not because I'm in love."

"Never say never, dear."

Technically, he hadn't said never. He opened his mouth, then bit back the argument. "Yes, ma'am." He waited for her to pull up his reservation in the computer, then realized there wasn't one. She had a notebook — and a pencil.

Mrs. Beeker flipped open the thin calendar book and placed a checkmark next to his name. Elaborate system. "Well, I can't run

41

the card until my grandson gets here later this evening. I just don't know how, dear. But don't worry, I know where to find you." She gave him back the card and dangled a room key from her other hand. "Room three."

That didn't sound so bad. After seeing the outside of the establishment, he'd half expected the rooms to be called Gumdrop Fantasy or something equally nausea-inducing. "Thank you." He reached for the key.

She didn't relinquish it. "That's the third floor."

"Right." He held out his hand, waiting.

She pulled the key back and peered at him over the top of her glasses. "The color red doesn't give you anxiety, does it?"

"Not that I've noticed." Except it might now, after looking at her hair this long.

"Good." She grinned, and her gold hoop earrings swung. "Then, here you go."

He was definitely edging up on the anxiety now. He nodded with a brief smile, grabbed his bags, and headed toward the winding wooden staircase. Third floor. Apparently he wouldn't be getting too big a break from his gym regimen on this trip, after all.

He needed to keep up the endorphins anyway. He was already grumpy. He just needed to do his job, write this silly article, and get out of Dodge.

Besides, the more miserable he was, the more Peter would gloat.

He creaked his way upstairs and stopped at the top of a short hallway leading to the door with a gold-scripted 3 on the front. He inserted the key, turned the knob, eased the door open — and saw red.

Literally. Red everywhere.

He took a step back, his eyes trying to process the red floor rugs, the red rose wallpaper climbing above the white wainscoting, the red floral bedspread draped over the queen-sized frame. The red vases holding faux red flowers on the small desk shoved under the window.

It was as if the color had vomited over the entire room. And if that wasn't enough, a short Christmas tree stood guard in the corner of the room, decorated with red candy ornaments.

He was going to kill Peter.

"I didn't know I could ruin something so thoroughly, so quickly." Bri tossed a lacy oven mitt out of the way on the counter and leaned over the glass, not even caring about the smudges sure to follow. She couldn't stop replaying that morning's encounter

with Gerard in her mind. Gerard Fortier —
travel writer, insult doler, and sarcastic guru.

Figured he'd have a French surname. The
Lord's sense of humor never failed her.

"Well, I always thought you were part
superhero, if that helps." Casey grinned as
she popped a pinch of macaron in her
mouth. She'd been patiently listening to Bri
bemoan her first impression with the *Trek*
writer for the past half hour. They'd become
closer friends since the viral video — one
more pro that had sprung from the debut.
Hopefully this travel feature wouldn't
become a con.

"Superhero?" Bri raised her eyebrows.

"Sure. You know — capable of anything?"

"In the kitchen, maybe." Bri rolled her
eyes. "And apparently I have mad skills in
messing up what could be the bakery's only
chance at deterring Charles's bullheaded
offers."

"Charles is no bull." Casey took another
bite of macaron. "Bulldog, maybe. He just
tries to act tough. He's all bark, no bite."

Still, his persistence made Bri nervous. So
far Mabel and Agnes weren't taking his offers seriously, but she recognized that
determinedness in his eyes. It was the same
characteristic that helped him pass the bar.
She just didn't know why he was so obsessed

with the Pastry Puff. Why not use any of the buildings for sale farther down the street for his next venture? There were two perfectly good properties closer to Johnson's General.

Casey shrugged. "Besides, you didn't ruin anything. The reporter probably thought it was funny."

Hmm. Gerard *had* smiled when he saluted her. But that was probably because of her shocked response. What had she even said to him afterward? She moaned as she remembered. "Casey, I rambled to him about pencil skirts. Trust me. It's ruined."

The pretty brunette tossed her head back and laughed. "Classic." Gone were the bags under her eyes, which Casey attributed to a new concealer, but Bri knew the truth. Now she had help — and someone to love her. What girl wouldn't be smiling about that?

"Do you care?" Casey eased forward, eyebrows furrowing together and a half smile playing on her lips.

Bri frowned. "Of course I care. This is the bakery's one big chance and I ruined —"

Casey waved her hand. "Not because of the bakery, silly. I'm sensing there might be a little bit of embarrassment for other reasons. You know. *Personal* ones." Her eyebrows wiggled up and down now in a suggestive dance.

Heat cloaked Bri's chest. "Hardly."

"Oh, come on. I googled him. He's not exactly hard to look at. You're single . . . and he's got to be, with a personality like the one you've described." Casey's cheeks dimpled as she grinned.

The heat cranked up a notch, and she tugged at the neckline of her shirt to cover it. "Definitely none of that."

Casey sighed. "Whatever. Listen, regardless, I'm sure it's not as bad as you think. You worry too much. And trust me, I'm an expert at worry, so I recognize it a mile away." She crumpled her napkin into a ball, then pointed at Bri. "Nathan's helped me chill a lot. Now I'm going to help you."

"Do you have a pill for that or something?" Bri was kidding. Sort of.

"Better." Casey winked. "It's called love. I'm going to help Mabel and Agnes set you up."

Oh no. She'd drunk the Kool-Aid. Panic flared. "I just said Gerard —"

"It doesn't have to be him." Casey shrugged. "Just, you know. Love in general."

Bri shook her head. "I'll have my turn one day, I'm sure. But for now, I've got bigger cakes to bake. Like saving the Puff." She forced a smile that hopefully looked cheerier than she felt. "Besides, I'm sort of picky, and you just snatched up the last decent man in Story."

"No way! There are some great guys at the fire department." Casey tilted her head, rolling in her bottom lip. "Well, two. Okay, one, because the other guy is dating that girl in Missouri now. But the one left is pretty great!"

"If he's single and breathing, it's already been attempted around here, trust me." Bri straightened and moved away from the display before she was tempted to take another petit four out of the case. The last thing she needed right now was to stress eat. "Some things can't be forced."

"I understand. But if you change your mind . . ." Casey's voice trailed off as she stood and threw away her trash. "Come to the station and ask for Kyle."

"Sure. Tell Nathan I said hey." Bri waved as her friend headed to the door, appreciating her good intentions but knowing she'd never contact Kyle. She was sure he was a perfectly nice guy, but she hadn't waited around this long for nice. She was waiting for a prince. Charles had been nice, and Charles was no prince.

There was a difference. She wanted a love like her parents'. A love that stood the test

47

of time. A love to write home about — literally, as the letters in her mom's trunk demonstrated.

The bakery door swung open from the outside just as Casey pushed against it.

Speaking of non-princes.

Bri straightened as Gerard stepped back on the sidewalk, allowing Casey sufficient room to exit. His averted gaze as he held the door gave Bri the opportunity to reluctantly notice two things: one, his firm jawline, still stubbled over, and two, the wide eyes and "wow" Casey mouthed behind her hand to Bri.

Bri widened hers back at Casey in warning just as Gerard stepped inside. Casey plastered herself against the door behind him, pointing and wiggling her eyebrows again.

Bri attempted to wave Casey away, just as Gerard looked up and made eye contact. She quickly patted her hair, as if she'd been fixing it the entire time. "Welcome back." She wasn't going to stop and evaluate why she suddenly felt out of breath. Probably just from the looming embarrassment of Casey's antics.

Surely not because of the way Gerard strode purposefully toward her, still clad in that leather jacket and those distressed jeans.

"Before you even ask, no petit fours. Just coffee." He leaned against the glass countertop that Bri had just vacated.

She hadn't intended to ask. Why waste a perfectly good petit four on someone so grumpy? "Coming right up." Funny how the moment he opened his mouth, it became much easier to breathe normally.

She had to be nice now, though. No more barbs or sarcastic impulses. She had to remember this was their feature writer, not just a jerk with a chip on his shoulder. This was someone to impress — for a good cause.

She couldn't let Charles have the bakery. Now, or ever.

Gerard rapped his knuckles lightly on the display as she reached for a mug. "Your town sure likes its sweets."

"Is that a bad thing?" Who didn't love fresh-baked desserts? It sounded like he was already tired of them. But wait. That could only mean one thing. "Let me guess. You're staying at the Gingerbread House?"

His eyebrow rose. "You mean there's another option?"

She picked up the carafe of black coffee, trying to hide her smile. It wasn't polite to gloat, even at irony. "Not unless you go about thirty miles north of town."

He narrowed his eyes, as if debating the potential commute.

Which meant one other thing. She reached for a mug to serve him. "Red room?"

He nodded, jaw tightening.

Bless Mrs. Beeker and her quirks. "It could be worse. It could be pink." She casually poured his coffee into a pink polka-dotted mug and slid it toward him.

Gerard cradled the mug between his hands. "You enjoy this, don't you?"

"Hey, a town that loves sweets is good for business. You might as well jump on board." Bri placed the carafe back on the warmer. In fact, he needed to be completely on board, or this entire feature would tank. And when sales generated from the viral video tapered off, there wouldn't be enough momentum to keep Charles from sniffing around with his briefcase and lowball offers.

She reached for Gerard's mug again. "On second thought, let me put that in a to-go cup. There's something you need to see."

"Let me guess. The love-lock wall?"

Bri poured his coffee into a to-go cup and snapped the lid on tight. "Isn't that why you're here?"

"Well, I'm not here to drink the coffee, if

50

that's what you're asking."

She stiffened. "If you'd just sweeten up a little, it wouldn't be so bad."

"Did you mean sweeten *it* up?"

"That's what I said." Should have said, anyway. She sighed in an effort to relieve some frustration. "Try it with some cream or sugar."

"That's going to be the opening line of the feature." Gerard framed the imaginary headline with his fingers. *"Just a spoonful of sugar helps the coffee go down."*

"It's not that bad." She slid the cup toward him and reached to untie her apron. His eyes followed her hand movements, and she remembered his teasing earlier about wearing the allegedly useless garment. Her chest heated. "And don't you start on my apron again."

"Wouldn't dream of it." He half managed to cover his grin with his coffee cup.

She wanted to swat him with said apron, but with her luck, Mabel and Agnes would return from the store before she could and start giving her that look again. Besides, swatting was definitely on the list of things she shouldn't do to their feature writer.

Running her fingers through his waves of dark hair to straighten it out was also on that list.

She tossed the apron on a clean part of the counter, next to her favorite *Wanderlust* pallet sign, then stepped through the waist-high swinging door that separated the behind-the-counter area from the shop. "Come on. It's not so bad."

Gerard straightened. "The coffee or the love-lock wall?"

"Both."

"You're going to have to sell me."

"Your coffee is already free."

"I meant on the wall." Gerard followed her outside, his begrudging presence heavy on her heels as they crunched through the leaves. "What's the big deal about it, anyway?"

She stopped and turned so quickly that he stumbled not to run into her. "Am I trying to convince you or your readers?"

He took a sip from his paper cup and winced. "Both."

"You're incorrigible."

"Now, Ms. Duval, you haven't known me long enough to make that declaration."

She held up her hand to shade her eyes from the setting sun. A crimson leaf blew from a nearby maple and drifted down between them. "How do you know it's not Mrs.?"

He opened his mouth, then immediately

pressed his lips together, as if changing his words mid-verse. "My editor did his research."

Wait a minute. "How is my relationship status part of the feature?"

"It might not be, but you know how it goes. A cute, single blonde sells copies a heck of a lot better than a cute, married one."

He thought she was cute.

And now she couldn't remember a single thing about the love locks.

CHAPTER FIVE

This chick needed a hobby.

Gerard considered clicking off his recorder for the third time since she'd started rambling about the love locks. She stood in those cream high heels on a crimson carpet of leaves, gesturing toward each lock like a tour guide. And doggone it, she remembered the individual story behind most of them.

The wall, which was really a black wrought-iron fence wrapped around a stone fountain, held more than a hundred padlocks, some piled on top of each other on the same rod, others stacked on the bottom and waiting for a lock to fall on top of it. Some silver. Some black. Some chrome. A few spray-painted a bright color for easy recognition.

This entire feature was already grating on his nerves more than he'd anticipated — and that'd been a lot. "Just stop." He needed a minute. Needed a breath. Needed her to take one, and stop babbling like a lunatic about some crazy matchmaking ideas she kept trying to make French.

Bri paused on her amble along the stepping-stone pathway and blinked, as if coming out of her host trance. The next step in front of her fancy shoe read *Wanderlust,* just like some of the décor he'd noticed inside the bakery.

For some reason, that annoyed him even more.

She blinked up at him. "I'm sorry, do I need to repeat something? Was I talking too fast?"

Heck no. And yes. But that wasn't the problem. Gerard ran his fingers through his hair, trying to pinpoint the wave of frustration rising. "First of all, the name is ridiculous. *Love locks.* What even is that?"

Bri shrugged. "Take it up with Paris. They started it."

There she went again. "And hated it, hence why they shut it down."

"Oh, come on. Now you sound like Charles."

Gerard clicked the recorder back on. "Who's Charles?"

"This local lawyer who wants to buy the property from Mabel and Agnes."

"Trying to find his match made in heaven?"

The breeze stirred her long blonde hair off her shoulders. "No, trying to tear it down and build something else. Probably some overpriced, corporate coffee chain."

He sort of liked Charles already.

Bri crossed her arms over her pink sweater. "Why are you writing this feature, anyway? You don't seem like the romantic type."

Good eye. He shut off the recorder. "What type am I, then?"

"Well, look at you. I'd much sooner expect an article with your byline in something like *Mechanics Weekly.*" Bri slapped her hand over her mouth. "Ugh. I don't know why you make me do that."

He held out both hands. "Do what? I'm just standing here. Not insulting you, by the way."

"I know." She groaned and shoved her hands into the pockets of her sweater. "You just make it so easy."

"To insult me?"

She straightened, as if she'd found her propriety somewhere in those pockets. "You bring out my sarcastic side. I'm sorry."

He liked seeing her rattled. Between her perfect hair and that flawless apron, she could use some mellowing. "Don't be. You seem like you need toughening up."

"What do you mean?" She bristled.

He pointed to her tense posture. "That, right there. Everything offends you, doesn't it? You keep your heart on your sleeve but get upset when someone bumps it."

"Sure you're not a reporter from *Psychoanalyze Weekly*?"

"You do know that not all magazines have the word *weekly* in them, right?"

"There I go again. And there *you* go again." She turned away from him and started walking toward the stone fountain.

"Okay, okay. Truce?" He caught up to her and touched her shoulder. She ducked out of the gesture but plastered on a polite smile as fake as Mrs. Beeker's hair color.

"There's no need for a truce, Mr. Fortier." She lifted her chin. "You're a professional writer researching for an article, and I'm a professional baker providing said research."

Apparently she'd found a "How to Be Formal" manual in that pocket too. As much as her gushing romantic vibe bugged him, this stilted professional act was much worse.

He clicked the recorder back on and braced himself. "Tell me about the fountain."

A slight smile flickered across her glossed lips. Truce accepted. "In Paris, lovers would throw their key into the Seine after securing their lock on the fence. It was a symbol of their everlasting commitment."

He knew that already. He'd been there nine years ago. Had stood near the fence and met his hero, a famous travel photographer named Remy, and had a potent conversation about the trappings of love. He'd seen the locks, touched them. Watched Remy scoff at them.

Remy had been right. *Just chase after the story, son. Don't let it catch you.* Love didn't last, whether or not you threw away the key. Some keys floated right back up and had no trouble clicking open metal. He'd witnessed it a dozen times in his mom's life, had experienced it once himself with Kelsey, and didn't need further proof. Love was a sham, and this pitiful impersonation of the Parisian love-lock bridge here in Kansas was feeding into the illusion.

But what else could he expect from these locals, with their obsession for petit fours and themed hotels and all things fantasy? They wanted to stay in their illusion. Unfortunately, it was his job to make it sound good enough that people would travel to come taste it for themselves.

And the way Bri lit up when she talked about this stuff might mean she was the most disillusioned of them all.

He held the recorder closer. "And then what?"

She glanced down at the little black box, then at him. Confusion danced in her eyes. "What do you mean?"

"After they lock it and throw away the key — then what? They live happily ever after?"

Her brow furrowed. "I like to think so."

He knew better. After the commitment came too much reality. Food preference arguments that led to financial fights that led to spiritual differences. Shouting matches and slammed doors and holes in the Sheetrock. Rubber marks on the driveways from squealing tires. Missed calls and sleepless nights and unfamiliar men's colognes.

After the commitment came pain. Not a fairy tale.

"I know family law. And I can confirm there are not a lot of happily ever afters out there." An unfamiliar male voice broke the pulsing silence between them.

Gerard turned. A thin man with wire-rimmed glasses walked toward them, stepping carefully across the grass in what looked to be new loafers. A brown suit jacket was draped over one arm of his perfectly pressed dress shirt.

Bri sighed. "What are you doing here, Charles?"

Charles. As in, the Charles wanting to open a corporate chain? He stopped passing judgment on the guy's stuffy suit and held out his hand. "Gerard Fortier."

Charles shook it with a grip firmer than he'd expected. "Charles Richmond. You must be that feature writer from up north."

"That would be me."

"Pleasure." Charles released his hand and tucked his back under his draped jacket. His expression hardened as he looked back to Bri. "And to answer your question, I'm here to talk business with the owners."

"Mabel and Agnes are still at the store." Bri stepped toward Charles and pressed on his elbow, turning him toward the parking lot. "I'll make sure to tell them you came by."

"Eyesore, isn't it?" Charles ignored her attempt, turning back to Gerard.

He clearly wasn't taking Bri's hint to leave. Gerard hated that type of personality — he'd seen men do that to his mom over the years and it had rubbed him wrong ever since. That sense of entitled arrogance — and from the looks of Charles's wardrobe, the man had money. That typically made it worse.

"The wall." Charles pointed to the locks, as if taking his silence for confusion.

Gerard shrugged. "Beauty is in the eye of the beholder." Yes, it was an eyesore. He'd give him that, but he couldn't say so outright in front of Bri — that wasn't exactly professional. He was a feature writer, not a critic. Still . . . there could be a game to play here.

He crossed his arms and regarded Charles. "What would you put in its place?"

"Something the town could appreciate. Who wants a reminder of an outdated historic icon in another country?" Charles scoffed. "They tore it down in Paris for a reason."

Bri glowered. "If you're done eavesdropping on our conversation, the parking lot is that way."

Apparently Gerard wasn't the only one to bring out the aggression in Bri. He held back his grin. The guy was a complete tool, though, to ignore her the way he did. It seemed like their war for the bakery went deeper than Bri had initially let on.

And the device in his hand was still recording. "I'm guessing from your reaction that you don't have a lock on that wall?"

Bri snickered, then tried to cover it with a cough.

Charles cut his eyes toward her, then smiled at Gerard — a cool, polite smile that hinted at something much more tumultuous beneath the surface. "I do not. And soon enough, no one else will have to worry about that pitiful display either."

"I'll be sure to tell Mabel and Agnes you stopped by. Uninvited. Again." Bri's cheeks flushed.

"That would be lovely. Please do." Charles nodded calmly, which just seemed to make Bri madder. Her small hands clenched into fists at her sides.

Gerard wished he had popcorn. What was the deal between these two? Did she really just want to hang on to the crazy old ladies' bakery that badly? It wasn't like Bri couldn't find a job elsewhere. Heck, Peter could probably get her a modeling gig up north with a single phone call. And why did Charles act like the love-lock wall personally offended him?

No one was saying what they meant.

Gerard opened his palm around the recorder so as not to muffle the sound. "What's so bad about the love locks? Besides the eyesore element."

Charles started to respond, then glanced

down. His eyes lingered on the recorder, and he shifted his jacket to his other arm. "I believe I've overstayed my welcome. Good day, Mr. Fortier."

Then he nodded at Bri, just enough to say he did it if accused otherwise but not overtly enough to encourage friendly thoughts. Gerard should know — he'd mastered that particular nod over the years.

Bri watched him go, a mixture of worry and disdain coating her expression. "You missed your quote opportunity."

"I sort of gather he'll be back."

"Unfortunately."

He watched her. "Not your favorite person?"

"He can't buy the bakery." She said it so matter-of-factly, Gerard almost wondered if he'd misread the concern a moment ago.

"What's the big deal if he does?"

Bri's eyes narrowed. "I thought you were here to bring publicity to the Pastry Puff — *positive* publicity."

"Honest publicity." Gerard slid the recorder into his pocket. "But hey, I'm just asking questions to get the whole story. It's called being interviewed."

"Then ask better questions."

He shook his head as she strolled off ahead of him, back to the bakery. She was toughening up, that was for sure. He just wasn't sure if he — or Charles — had inspired the sudden burst of fortitude.

A flicker of an unfamiliar emotion rolled through his stomach.

Jealousy? No. Impossible. He'd never been jealous a day in his life, and he wasn't about to start now over some starched suit and a woman he'd known for less than twenty-four hours.

He started to head inside after her, then detoured to his car instead. He would start fresh at the bakery in the morning, after everyone had a good night's sleep and Bri had some distance from her encounter with Charles.

At this point, even the red room felt more appealing than dealing with her.

The man was infuriating. Both of them, actually.

Bri's frustration welled up and over. How dare Gerard act so cocky about something he knew nothing about. And how dare Charles waltz onto property she'd practically been raised on and dismiss her so casually — in front of a stranger, no less.

She groaned as she slid Mabel the money bag of the day's cash and receipts across the counter. "I really don't know who's worse."

Agnes intercepted the bag with a frown and unzipped it, rummaging inside as Mabel patted Bri's hand atop the glass display. "I know, dear, it's a tough call."

The sisters had finally returned from the store, and they'd just put away tomorrow's baking supplies and were having their evening ritual of coffee and conversation before locking up for the night.

"Tough call, indeed." Mabel sighed and shook her head as if commiserating with her. "Both men are pretty handsome."

"Ugh, no." She needed more coffee. Or one of those petit fours, after all. She cast a sidelong glance at the leftover desserts from the day. "Charles is *not* handsome."

Agnes mumbled her agreement as she counted out fives.

Mabel adjusted the purple shawl she always wore to the grocery store, year-round. "Well, he wasn't too hard to look at, or you'd never have dated him."

"Can we just forget I ever did?"

Agnes nodded. "Hear, hear."

"By the way, Mr. Hansen came in earlier while you were out." Bri tapped the stack of ones Agnes had just counted. "He left a big tip."

Agnes huffed. "Now I have to start over with my counting." But her flustered smile gave her away.

"Quit counting, Agnes. You missed it." Mabel pointed a manicured nail at Bri. "She just admitted that Gerard was handsome."

Bri's head jerked up. "What? When?"

"Just a moment ago." Mabel kept pointing, nearly blinding Bri with her big *aha* grin. "You argued that Charles wasn't. You didn't argue about Gerard."

Oh, forget it. She was getting a petit four. Bri plucked the one with the biggest flower petal from the display tray, then shoved half of it in her mouth.

Mabel beamed at her while Agnes shook her head with a *tsk.* "Now she's stress eating. Just like her mom used to do."

The mention of her mom settled Bri's stomach. She set the petit four on its wrapper and licked a remnant of green icing from her thumb, suddenly feeling much calmer. Talking about her mom always tended to do that to her — especially with the two ladies who had known her better than Bri had. "What was her favorite dessert when she worked here?"

"Macarons." Mabel and Agnes answered at the same time.

Mabel winked at her. "She'd have loved your new recipe tweak, adding that extra dash of almond powder."

66

Bri paused. "How'd you know I used extra —"

"My taste buds aren't as dull as my eyes, dear."

Guess not. Bri braced one hip against the counter, chewing slowly on the remainder of her petit four. "I still can't figure out her exact recipe, though." She was missing an ingredient, something vivid she remembered from the past, something Mabel and Agnes never knew either but confirmed was just a little different in her mom's recipe. She was determined to master it one day.

"But think of all the great new recipes you've invented from trying."

Bless Mabel and her encouraging heart. Bri shot her a grateful smile. Charles couldn't buy the bakery — because Bri couldn't lose this. This physical connection to her mom. Her eyes darted around the shop, taking in its tiled floors and tiny tables meant for two, the little vases boasting fresh flowers and pink napkin holders with the Pastry Puff's signature cursive print scrawled across the front.

Her mom had learned to bake here. And while the shop had been updated over the years, the building carried a permanent piece of her mom's presence. That was the same counter she used to stir at, the same giant metal mixing bowl she used to dump ingredients into. Just like Bri had that morning.

And Gerard had asked what the big deal was. Fresh irritation blossomed. He probably didn't have a sentimental bone in his body. The sooner this feature was written and he rode off into the sunset on his motorcycle, the better.

Mabel began packing the few remaining petit fours, macarons, and cookies into a to-go box. Bri brushed the petit four crumbs off the counter and into her hand and dusted them over the nearby trash can. "Where are they going today?"

Every evening, the sisters alternated where they sent leftover food. Sometimes they took the desserts to the fire station, sometimes they split them up to take home themselves, and more frequently than not, the sweets went to a local church for the staff to enjoy or hand out to someone in need.

Mabel tucked the cardboard corners neatly inside the box, her voice breezy and innocent. Too innocent. "Why don't you run these over to the B&B?"

"Oh no. No way." Bri held up her hands. "I don't need any more of your matchmaking schemes." She'd already had her daily dose of Gerard, thank you very much, and it was plenty.

"It's not matchmaking." Agnes huffed. "It's simply a crying shame to let these go to waste."

Nice try. Bri pushed the box across the counter toward Agnes. "Then why don't you take them to Mr. Hansen, like you did the other day?"

Agnes gasped.

"That's right. *My* eyes aren't dull at all." Bri winked at Mabel, who grinned behind her handkerchief.

"That's neither here nor there." Agnes pushed the box back toward Bri. "Think about it. That man is here to write a story about the bakery, and he hasn't eaten a blessed thing from it yet."

Bri started to protest, then stopped. Unfortunately, Agnes had a valid point. Gerard had been in the shop twice now — twice? Three times? It was starting to blur. And he had only drunk — and complained about — the coffee. Not exactly the best material for a headlining, save-the-bakery-from-Charles feature.

"Fine. I guess a little bribe never hurt anyone." She took the wide bakery box and balanced it on her hip. She pointed her finger at both of them in warning. "But don't get any ideas. I'm just doing this for publicity's sake."

"Of course, dear," Mabel cooed as she reached over and smoothed back a flyaway wisp of Bri's hair. "Do you want to try my new Sparkle Magic lipstick?"

Bri shooed Mabel's hand away and hurried for the door before she could offer perfume or a padded bra. "You're all incorrigible."

She'd go. But she'd stop by her home for a minute first. She needed a positive boost before she saw Mr. Anti-Romance Mechanic Weekly, and that boost was safely tucked away in her attic.

CHAPTER SIX

Gerard's feet hung off the red bed by two inches.

He rolled onto his side and shifted his cell phone to his other ear, simultaneously weary and hyped up. He definitely wasn't used to drinking that much coffee in one day. "You'd love this place, Mom. It's right up your alley. All home-cooked comfort food and desserts and obnoxiously decorated inns."

His mom's familiar voice, soft and permanently tired, filled his ear. "Maybe I'll come through town for a macaron one day."

Fat chance. His mom never traveled, despite his former attempts to help pay for her to do so over the years. He'd even tried to give her a free cruise he'd won once, and she'd refused. She'd never held a job with paid time off or many benefits, and she claimed it wasn't worth it to be out of money when she got home.

"Maybe I could mail you some. If the Pastry Puff ships." He'd have to check into that fact for the feature, regardless. Readers would want to know. He one-finger typed a note on the open document on his laptop. *FIND OUT ABOUT SHIPPING OPTIONS.* Mom would love those frilly-looking purple ones he'd glimpsed in the display earlier.

"That'd be nice. Always looking out for me." She coughed. "Son, you know I hate to ask, but . . ."

"You need money." Something he was short of until he got paid for this feature. The downside to freelance work — one had to be good with budgeting. And he'd splurged on his new laptop and sent his mom a pretty good-sized check just last month.

He wouldn't ask her where it went. He never did.

"I'm just a little behind. They cut my hours at the diner, but Frankie says they'll get me back on my regular schedule next month."

Frankie was her boss, and one of the biggest jerks Gerard had ever met. Well, excluding the men who'd dated his mom. He was overly gruff with his staff, including his mother. But Frankie was big, burly, and didn't take anything from anyone. Gerard had personally witnessed him grab a guy twice his size by the collar and haul him into the street when he'd gotten fresh with one of the other waitresses. It was the only reason he hadn't made his mom quit a long time ago — he knew she was safe.

He stretched out his legs, then pulled them back onto the bed. His ankle dangled over the edge of the mattress. "What'd you do to make them cut your hours? They catch you stealing apple pie?"

"Now, that was *one* time, and I thought it was leftover." Her voice pitched with defense.

Gerard pinched the bridge of his nose. "Mom, I'm kidding." Good grief. Had she actually done that?

"Oh." She let out a hoarse laugh. "No, they just said business slowed."

Her vague tone made him doubt the validity of that, but he wouldn't pry. He never did.

Gerard pulled his wallet from his pocket and flipped through the measly bills. He doubted those two soggy tens were going to help her for long.

She coughed again, muted this time, as if she'd tried to cover the phone. "If it's too much, son, don't worry about it. I'll be fine."

She really needed to quit smoking. "What time is your shift tomorrow?"

"Early." Her voice cracked and she paused, then swallowed, as if taking a sip of water. When she spoke again, it was a little clearer. "Six a.m."

Gerard squeezed his eyes shut. "Go get some rest, Mom. I'll figure something out, okay?"

"You always do." Tenderness filled her voice, and a band tightened around his heart. A band of obligation. Responsibility. Love.

No one had ever wanted to take care of her long-term. He was the only one.

He'd go to his grave making sure he did.

"Good night, Mom." He dropped his phone onto the bed, eyeing his depleted wallet, and sighed. There was only one thing to do, and he hated to do it even more than he hated the red dripping off the walls around him.

He was going to have to ask Peter for an advance.

The attic loft of her little townhouse smelled the same as it had when she first purchased it seven years ago — musty cedar and pine.

Bri dragged her mom's trunk from its revered designated spot by the tiny circular window overlooking the front yard. She used to consider keeping the chest in her bedroom, but it took up too much of the limited floor space. Besides, some days it made her sad to see it — a physical reminder of her official orphan status. She didn't need that greeting her first thing in the morning. Grief was raw and unpredictable enough.

So, in the attic the trunk remained. Besides, coming up here made reading the letters more of an event, like visiting with old friends. She got to peek into her parents' past with these crisp old notes — glimpse briefly into a time before she was born, where love reigned fresh and dripped in all things Parisian.

Unfortunately, her parents would never know the inspiration they were to her.

Outside, the dusky sky faded slowly from periwinkle to pewter. Faint stars began to peek through the evening curtain. Bri stared into the coming night. Maybe somehow, they did know. She liked to think they did.

She set her steaming mug of tea next to the faded beanbag chair she'd hauled up there last year and opened the cedar chest. The stack of letters, tied with a lavender ribbon, were on top of a stack of shoeboxes and quilts.

She gently picked them up. When had she come up here last? It'd probably been four months, at least. Maybe six.

The letters were scrawled in English with plenty of French endearments scattered throughout. French. She'd translated the French long ago and stuck a typed copy of the translations with the letters for quicker reading. Her father was born and raised French, her mother American. He'd learned English for her.

Was there anything more romantic?

Bri wasn't quite fluent yet, but she'd been practicing off and on over the last few years. She knew enough to get by for a vacation to Paris — if she ever made it there.

She pulled the next letter from the stack and tugged it free of its envelope.

Dearest love,

I can't wait to see you again. To tuck your hand into mine, to feel your slim fingers threaded through my rougher ones. To watch your joy as you gaze upon the Seine. To witness the wind caress your hair, each lock dancing to its own rhythm.

I miss dancing with you.

Your beauty takes my breath away.

Even when you are not with me, I feel you here, and that's enough. For now.

From Paris, with love

The words washed over her, a breath of fresh air from Gerard's bitterness and Charles's greed. There were good men in the world, men capable of love and chivalry, as evidenced by her father in these notes. It existed at one time, so surely it still did. Her prince would come.

Maybe he'd even have an accent.

She read the second letter in the stack, then the third. The words, familiar yet never old, soothed her weary heart like a balm. Somehow, connecting with her parents this way made her feel like things would be okay again. Charles wouldn't prevail over the bakery. The love-lock wall would live on, and the Pastry Puff would thrive. Mabel and Agnes would continue matchmaking and grocery shopping in shawls.

Nothing else would change.

She glanced at her watch. Almost 8:30, and she still had to deliver those desserts to the B&B. She reluctantly slid the last letter into its yellowed envelope, then tucked them back inside the trunk.

The nostalgia sat a little heavier tonight than usual as she climbed back down the attic stairs into the hallway. Or maybe it was just because she knew she was about to see Gerard again.

Maybe she could just leave the desserts with Mrs. Beeker at the front desk.

She picked up her keys and the box of pastries, a strange mixture of compassion and irritation welling inside. Irritation at Gerard's grumpiness and general apathy toward her favorite things — the Pastry Puff, romance, the love-lock wall — and compassion, because she'd learned over the years of peddling desserts and discounting coffee that people weren't permanently grumpy without reason. Even Disney villains had an old wound and a backstory.

What was Gerard's?

CHAPTER SEVEN

He'd been in this hole-in-the-wall town for one day and was already addicted to bad coffee.

Gerard opened his door and squinted down the hallway, lit only by an oddly shaped nightlight plugged into the wall. Surely Mrs. Beeker wasn't still downstairs in the front lobby . . . and surely some coffee was. He probably needed decaf — it was already almost nine o'clock — but he still felt oddly exhausted and wired. He couldn't get the Pastry Puff out of his mind. Or Bri.

Which meant he must be really tired.

The phone call with Peter hadn't helped.

Gerard rubbed his hand down his jaw, the stubble prickling his calloused palms. This particular writing gig wouldn't be calling for any fresh blisters, that was for sure. He missed the adrenaline rush of flying over a multi-terrain trail, parasailing over crystal-clear waves, taste testing exotic cuisine.

But if he didn't nail this assignment, boring as it was, then he wouldn't have the opportunity for any future blisters. Peter had made that clear on the phone twenty minutes ago.

Gerard bit back the frustration rising in his throat. He really shouldn't have asked, but he couldn't get his weary mother's voice out of his mind. He was almost thirty, and he hated that he wasn't able to help her the way he should be able to.

He peered down the hall. The last thing he wanted currently — or ever — was to get stuck making small talk with a stranger. Which begged the question — who else would be visiting Story in the first place? Another love-lock hopeful? A traveling tourist wanting to check the Pastry Puff off their bucket list? He *was,* unfortunately, going to need to interview a few locals to complete the piece.

He wondered if there was anyone those two goofy love angels had failed to set up successfully who might be bitter about it. That'd be one way to show Peter the "fresh angle" he demanded. Apparently the write-up they'd initially agreed on wasn't going to be sufficient. It was bad enough he had to write about this mess in the first place, but now he had to find an additional slant to make it more interesting.

The fact that Peter — or corporate, rather — was afraid it wasn't interesting enough should have told him something right there.

Gerard checked one more time in both directions. Mrs. Beeker was nowhere in sight. Come to think of it, a small, cottage-style house sat behind the main structure — he'd seen it from his window earlier. Maybe she lived out there.

Enough debating. Coffee won. He needed something to wash away the bitter taste Peter had left. He'd had the nerve to call Gerard a flight risk. No feature, no paycheck.

Then Peter made it worse by caving halfway and offering Gerard the advance once he turned in a solid rough draft. Better than nothing, maybe, but the worst part was realizing Peter didn't fully trust him with this one. So why had he even bothered to assign it to him? And why had he peppered him with so many useless questions about Bri?

Nothing about this assignment — this place, this town, this B&B — made sense.

And yes, that was a red candy cane-shaped nightlight shining in the hall. Of course it was.

He attempted to tread lightly down the

81

spiral stairs, but his anger built with each tentative step. Anger at Peter, for being practical instead of giving him this one as a friend. Anger at his father, for bailing on their family decades ago. Anger at the parade of men who had put his mom in this position in the first place, cosigning loans with her and leaving her with loads of debt and bad credit.

Anger at God, if he was honest, for the weariness his mother couldn't ever shake, for the joy that always seemed right out of her reach. She deserved love. Real love, not some love-lock fairy-tale mess, but someone who really wanted to be there for her.

He didn't need it, but she did. She always believed it was possible — as for him, he stopped looking the day Kelsey packed up her diamond and went home.

By the time he reached the end of the staircase, he was stomping much harder than he had initially intended. He winced at the consequent creak of wood and froze. This was his life now — creeping around some old B&B in middle America, avoiding talkative women with bad dye jobs, and begging his boss for money.

He flexed his blisters. Too bad he couldn't spike that coffee. He'd given up alcohol several years ago, for myriad reasons, but a

dash of whiskey wouldn't be entirely un-
welcomed right about now.

The door to the B&B was unlocked, like
most doors on any given night in Story.

Bri turned the handle, half expecting chip-
per Mrs. Beeker to greet her from the front
desk and half expecting a silent tomb of a
foyer.

She got the latter and breathed a sigh of
relief. If Mrs. Beeker wasn't at her post,
then Bri didn't have to explain why she was
there or risk any assumptions about Gerard.
That was the last thing she needed in the
midst of this love-lock feature — additional
small-town gossip. That was one perk to
having come so late. Now she could just
place these treats in the kitchen, write a
quick note of explanation, and wish them
all a happy breakfast the next morning.

Bri tucked the pastry box on her hip,
grabbed a yellow sticky note and pen from
the lobby desk, and headed into the kitchen.

She ran smack into a brick wall.

She grunted and jerked backward, fumbling with the dessert box to keep from
dropping it. A strong grip steadied her and
she gasped.

Nope, not a wall. She squinted into the
dim lighting as her eyes adjusted. A chest. A

broad chest, hard as a board — and belonging to one Gerard Fortier.

"What are you doing here?" she hissed, adrenaline spiking through her veins. She hated adrenaline. Hated roller coasters, hated horror movies, hated tripping over shoes in the middle of the night.

Hated that the memory of his touch would most likely be forever branded on her forearms.

Gerard let go of her and crossed his arms over his chest — the chest that had ricocheted her like a ping-pong ball and was currently covered in a soft-looking T-shirt. "I'm staying here, remember? The better question is, why are you breaking and entering?"

"First of all, it's technically impossible to break and enter anywhere in Story, since no one bothers to lock their doors." She set the box down on the kitchen island with a thud. "And second of all, I was bringing these to you."

"To me?"

That sounded way more personal and intimate than she'd intended. Probably exactly what Agnes had in mind. "I meant to the B&B." She flipped on the light. That would solve that problem. Hard to take anything intimately under fluorescent lighting.

Gerard blinked and scrunched his face at the sudden change. "At nine o'clock at night?"

"I got hung up."

"On what?"

She narrowed her eyes. "I thought you were a feature writer, not an investigative reporter."

"Zing." He drew a checkmark in the air with his finger and grinned. "You got me again."

Ugh. "Why do I keep doing that?" Good gravy, the man drove her to her last nerve. Her breath still caught from the scare, and she inhaled deeply to calm her racing heartbeat. "I just need a minute." He was in pajama pants. Black ones. She looked away.

"Not an adrenaline junkie, are you? Might want to rethink your crime spree then, Cupcake." Gerard casually opened the box on the island, then shut it and nudged it away.

Dismissed, just like that.

She glared. "Try one."

"Bossy."

"Try one?" She turned it into a question, biting back the second sarcastic remark begging for release. She had a mission here.

85

He crossed his arms, the sleeves of his T-shirt pulling taut. "I'm not hungry."

"People don't eat desserts because they're hungry, silly."

Gerard leveled a stare at her, one that clearly stated he had never been, and would never be, silly.

"Come on. One petit four won't kill you." She nudged the pastry toward him.

"I was coming down here for coffee." He pointed to the Keurig sitting on the counter by the sink. It wasn't even turned on.

"As it so happens, coffee and petit fours go perfectly together."

He leaned one hip against the island. "Maybe some coffees, anyway."

She leaned forward, bracing her elbows on the countertop by the box. He was just baiting her. She refused to bite. She scooted the box closer to him. "Try it. For the feature."

His gaze met hers, and she held it steady. Talk about an adrenaline rush. What was wrong with her stomach? Regardless, he wasn't budging. Stubborn.

Whatever. She wasn't going to beg. She straightened just as he leaned forward and snagged a petit four. "Fine. Just one."

He took a bite while she watched. Then he rolled his eyes. "Staring at me isn't awkward at all."

"Only if you chew with your mouth open." She grinned.

He pressed his lips together, green icing dotting the corner of his mouth.

She couldn't wait any longer. "So? How is it?"

"Better than your coffee." He wiped his mouth with his wrist.

Such a guy move. "I'll take that as a compliment." She searched through two of the cabinets by the fridge until they produced a mug — a solid black one. Peace treaty. She grabbed a pod of decaf and flipped on the machine.

She felt his eyes on her back as she worked, so intensely she had to cast a sidelong glance. He leaned against the counter, watching her.

There went her stomach again.

"Such service. And hey, with a smile too." He theatrically tapped his chin with his finger. "Too bad there's not a bakery around here that offers both of those."

And just like that, her butterflies ceased. She snapped shut the lid of the Keurig and faced him fully. "It wouldn't kill you to be genuine just once, you know."

"Wait, is this the Bri who can't help but insult me talking or the Pastry Puff chef determined to make a good impression talking?" He imitated writing on an invisible notepad. "I want to get my quotes straight."

"This is off the record."

"I'm not a reporter."

"Still applies."

He shrugged, as if she had a point. She had no idea if it actually applied, but she barreled on. "Our service is phenomenal. My coffee isn't gross. And my petit fours aren't just decent, they're amazing. You know how I know that?"

His lips twitched. "How?"

"My mother invented the recipe." She leaned back in satisfaction.

Gerard moved forward slightly, as if waiting for more.

Apparently her mic hadn't fully dropped after all.

He raised his eyebrows as the silence stretched on. Finally, he spoke. "What about your mother?"

It sounded rude but couldn't have been. He looked genuinely confused.

Bri's mouth opened, then closed as reality dawned. Gerard wasn't from here. He didn't know her mother like the majority of the town. He had no idea her mother had won the sweetheart pageants three years in a row in high school. Had no clue she'd learned to bake at the Pastry Puff and gone on to train at a prestigious school in Paris, where she'd met Bri's Frenchman father — the course instructor's son — and lived happily for years before moving to the States and starting a family. Had no idea she'd single-handedly set the standard for pastries in Story.

There was too much to say, and not nearly the right words to sum it up. To sum *her* up. Bri swallowed hard. "My mom was a treasure."

"Was?"

She nodded, emotion balling in her throat. She hadn't cried over her parents in a few years — that wound had long since scabbed over. After all, it'd been almost a decade now since the car accident. But reading their letters earlier that evening had stretched the scar.

Gerard's head dipped. "I'm sorry to hear that."

She nodded again and picked up a macaron, having zero appetite but needing something to do with her hands.

"Any woman whose kid can simply mention her and readily expect a listener to stand up and recognize must be something."

Understatement of the year. Her mother's patience, calmness, and steadiness toward

Bri's not-as-mild-mannered father had stood out over the years. Memory after memory of her mother's gentle touch on his shoulder, calming his churning anxiety or anger, filled her mind. Presenting him with a hot cup of coffee as he pored over the family bills, whispering words of comfort in his ear when the grief over losing his own father struck fresh and deep.

Tears pricked beneath the surface and Bri focused harder on the macaron, memorizing every crumb. Every ounce of the creamy center oozing between the sugar-dusted layers. Anything to not look at Gerard. His sudden, out-of-character tenderness was going to make her lose it completely.

Gerard reached over and took the macaron from her grip. "Why don't you let me try that one too. In her honor."

So much for trying not to cry. The tears slipped over her lids and dripped silently down her cheeks as she surrendered the dessert. Bless him. Gerard acted like he didn't notice as she frantically dabbed at her face.

"Was she French?"

"My dad was." Bri shook her head. "Is your mom?"

"My father. Third-generation, so I guess I'm a quarter." He bit into the macaron, a shadow crossing his face briefly before dissipating. "I'm pretty close to my mom too."

She didn't care in the slightest that he was talking with his mouth full. "I'm sure she appreciates that."

"And I'm sure yours would appreciate the way you describe her."

"Thank you." She studied him, the macaron crumbs on his shirt and the corded muscle in his forearm as he raised his coffee mug. Gerard Fortier might be more bark than bite, after all. Who would have thought the leather jacket–wearing, motorcycle-riding guy with a chip on his shoulder had a sensitive side?

And who would have ever thought she'd find it attractive?

He took another sip. "Thank you for sharing that with me."

Maybe it had been the emotional night, but a tiny piece of her defensive wall chiseled off and dropped to her feet. "You're welcome."

She instinctively moved a step closer to Gerard. Met his gaze. She didn't know what she wanted from him, but she knew she wanted to be closer. She took another step, edging around the island. Her stomach dipped again. Surely, he felt this too. This magnetic connection.

He nibbled another bite of the dessert, looking right into her eyes. "You should tell me more."

Bri's heart skipped. He cared. He was being genuine, for once — just like she'd wanted him to. And he was being genuine toward *her.* Inviting her in. Wanting to know more about her past and her family. "Yeah?"

"For sure." Gerard finished the macaron and dusted off his hands. "It'll be a great addition to the feature."

The feature.

Maybe not that genuine.

Her cheeks flushed, and she backed up several steps. "Of course. Anytime." She grabbed the bakery box, then remembered she'd meant to leave it. "But it's getting pretty late. I'll see you around, I'm sure."

She backpedaled toward the door, lifting one hand in acknowledgment, trying to ignore the confusion on Gerard's face as she hurried to escape, heated embarrassment spreading like poison ivy across her chest.

At least he liked the desserts.

CHAPTER EIGHT

The birds in Story apparently never got the memo that freelance writers didn't need to get up at dawn. They had started chirping on Gerard's third-story windowsill with the sun and unfortunately didn't come with a mute button.

Mrs. Beeker hadn't gotten the memo either. She'd knocked on Gerard's door at 6:30 sharp, hollering "yoo-hoo" when he didn't answer. He had thrown a pillow at the door, but the resounding thump neither confused nor deterred her. "Your breakfast is downstairs," she'd cooed. "And surprise — it looks like the dessert fairy came last night!"

Dessert fairy. That about summed up Bri.

What Mrs. Beeker didn't know was that he'd eaten half that box of leftover pastries last night while contemplating what was wrong with Bri to make her run off so quickly. They'd been having a good talk, one full of personal information he could actually use in the feature, and then she'd gotten this weird look on her face and vanished.

Gerard braced his arms on the sink and stared at his reflection in the bathroom mirror, attempting to get presentable before heading downstairs and facing the red-headed wonder. But all he could think about was Bri. Something had spooked her.

He turned off the running water, deciding to skip shaving. Another day of layered stubble wouldn't hurt anybody. Besides, the water wouldn't heat past lukewarm.

Kind of like Bri last night. She'd been so emotional about her mom — to the point he actually felt like maybe they'd connected a little, finally. She'd knocked the chip off her shoulder long enough to open up a little and give him a relatable angle for the article. Peter would love that mushy stuff.

Besides, Gerard could relate. He felt pretty fiercely about his mother too. But when he'd asked Bri to tell him more, she'd claimed the late hour and ducked out. If she wasn't going to talk more about her mom, then he couldn't use that to boost the article.

This was why women were so frustrating.

Well, partially why.

He threw on his leather jacket, grabbed his keys and laptop bag, and crept down the stairs, wondering if he could slip outside and bail on the obligatory breakfast. He definitely didn't want any more pastries — his stomach felt upset from the binge last night. He rarely ate sugar, but just like that, Bri had him munching down half his feelings. There must be some kind of spell on this town that made people vulnerable and emotional.

It was enough to drive a practical man on a paycheck-minded mission insane.

He successfully snuck outside, without Mrs. Beeker spotting him, and shut the door behind him with a relieved sigh. He'd find to-go caffeine elsewhere and maybe plug in at a local diner or coffee haunt and type up his notes. He needed to make a dent in that rough draft, adding what Bri had told him last night before he forgot the details.

He hesitated at the picket gate. Question was, where was the nearest coffee shop?

"I'm glad you're here."

Gerard turned at the sudden voice. Charles. He really wasn't up for dealing with this guy pre-caffeine. "Didn't you sneak up on me last time?"

"Better learn to watch your six, then." Charles grinned and held out his hand.

He didn't like the look of that grin, and he still didn't like Charles. But duty called. Gerard reluctantly shook it.

Charles redrew his hand and casually crossed his arms over his starched dress shirt. "I was in the neighborhood and thought I'd stop by. I wanted to speak to you privately."

"Privately?" Gerard hiked an eyebrow.

"As in, without Abrielle."

"Abrielle?" Now he felt like a parrot.

"Bri." A flicker of humor twitched in Charles's jaw. "She didn't tell you her real name?"

"It hasn't come up." He crossed his arms too, mimicking the guy's stance. He wasn't exactly a fan of Charles and the way he treated women — or smarted off at him, for that matter — but the man could be a source, so he hated to burn bridges too early. He'd learned over the years of digging up information that sometimes it was better to swallow pride and keep your cards close.

"No matter." Charles plastered on that smile again, the same one he'd worn when dismissing Bri yesterday. "You're writing the feature on the place, right?"

"Right."

"Where do you stand on it?"

"On what?"

Charles frowned. "The debate, of course."

"I'm afraid I'm not aware of a debate." Gerard played dumb and waited, intentionally not saying more. He wanted to see how much Charles was willing to verbalize.

"On whether or not I should buy out the bakery."

Gerard shrugged. "Has nothing to do with opinion, mine or otherwise. Either you will or you won't."

Gerard held Charles's inquisitive gaze without blinking. He might have been an attorney, but he was far from intimidating.

"Maybe." Charles looked away briefly, down the tree-lined street. A squirrel darted across the road, then back into the safety of a nearby leaf-dusted yard. "Or maybe not. Maybe you can help."

"You're going to have to be less cryptic if you want my help."

Charles chuckled. "It's simple. You have the power of the pen."

He wanted Gerard to slant the feature in a way that promoted the buyout of the bakery? That was ludicrous. He could just see Peter's face now. *Hey, boss, you know how I'm supposed to market this cozy little family-owned, Parisian bakery and convince readers to travel there? Wouldn't it be hilarious if it was torn down and replaced with a*

Starbucks by the time they arrived?

No dice.

Gerard hesitated. But what *was* interesting was the stand-down between the town's two influentials. Local beloved baker versus local successful lawyer. That was definitely an angle. If he could keep the feud fires burning, he could up the word count on the finished article — which meant more pay. More readers. More copies sold. He would be a shoo-in for the new position.

Not to mention the article angle would be a lot more tolerable than that lovey-dovey, matchmaking mess.

He squinted at Charles, who wore a self-satisfied smirk. The expression "the enemy of my enemy is my friend" rolled through his thoughts. Not that Bri was his enemy, but Charles was definitely hers, and that left the latter up in the air.

He adjusted his laptop bag on his shoulder. "I see what you're saying."

"Excellent. I thought you might." Charles clapped him on the shoulder, and Gerard shrugged out from under the touch. "I'll see you around."

"I'm sure you will." Gerard probably couldn't escape the slippery little manipulator if he tried, but that didn't matter. He'd work it to his advantage.

It would take some finagling to let Charles think he was on his side, without letting Bri catch wind of it. Honestly, he personally couldn't care less if the bakery was torn down, left as is, or shot up into space.

His mom needed his paycheck, and he'd do whatever he could to make it as big as possible. Get his promotion, write some pieces that would actually gain attention and respect, and move forward in his career. He certainly didn't need a father — or a wife — to bring him success. He'd do it on his own.

As he'd always done.

It was going to be a good day, and she had worn her favorite pink *Wanderlust* sweatshirt to ensure it.

Bri pushed up her sleeves and hummed to herself as she stirred the batter for her best cookie recipe. Every now and then, when she got a little antsy, she made a batch of simple tea-cake cookies and decorated them with seasonal icing. Today's theme was the Eiffel Tower, complete with piped red and orange leaves.

She wasn't going to let Gerard get to her. And she most certainly wasn't attracted to him. She'd had a moment of weakness last night, that was all. She'd been emotionally charged after going through her parents' letters, and Gerard had been in the right place at the right time.

Or rather, the wrong time, depending on how you looked at it.

And that's how she chose to look at it. Especially since he'd obviously been trying to connect with her for the sake of the article alone. She'd almost made a huge idiot of herself by assuming otherwise.

Thankfully, she'd gotten out of there before he could realize it.

She whisked faster. Besides, Gerard was the exact opposite of everything she'd held out for in a man. Cynical. Sarcastic. Goading. He didn't have a romantic bone in his body. Whatever heart-tipped arrows Mabel and Agnes had drawn back in their direction the other day better be a misfire — because she and Gerard were the last two people in the universe who made sense together.

The door chimed, and Bri sucked in her breath as she glanced up.

Casey strolled inside, high ponytail swinging. Her cheeks were flushed pink and her eyes sparkled. "Guess what?"

Bri wasn't disappointed it wasn't Gerard. No, that feeling flooding through her limbs surely was relief. She sprinkled in the sugar and reached for the almond powder. "You won the lottery?"

"Better." Casey leaned against the counter and grinned.

"You won an all-expense-paid vacation to Tahiti?"

Casey scrunched her nose. "Better."

Bri stirred in a capful of vanilla. "You found Justin Timberlake's home address?"

"Almost better." Casey winked and held up her left hand. "Nathan proposed."

"What?" Bri dropped the whisk and grabbed her friend's weighed-down ring finger. "That's so beautiful! Congratulations!" Bri tilted Casey's hand to inspect the ring at a different angle. The light hit the diamond and spiraled in tiny rainbow-tinted rays. "When did this happen?"

"Last night."

Bri let go of her hand and poured in the flour. "Tell me everything." She bet Nathan went all-out. There were probably hundreds of bouquets, a starlight sky, soft music, and twinkle lights.

Or maybe he took her to the pond behind Old Man Miller's farmhouse, where everyone had free access to his two paddleboats and left donations in a rusty tip jar on the dock, and proposed under a canopy of fireworks.

She began kneading the thickening dough. Or maybe he'd taken her to that popular steakhouse up north, where they drizzled dark-chocolate icing around the edges of the dessert plates. Nathan had probably buried the ring in a thick slice of triple chocolate cake and dropped to one knee while she gasped in surprise.

Casey tapped her finger on the parchment paper Bri was using to prepare the dough. "You have stars in your eyes right now."

"Well, you have little pulsing hearts in yours." Bri laughed as she reached for her marble rolling pin. "I can't help it. I love a good romantic story." Nothing could have topped her dad's proposal to her mom in Paris. But for Casey's sake, hopefully Nathan had tried. "So, tell me already."

Casey cupped her hands under her chin, her pale pink polish gleaming. "He came over last night for lasagna."

A home-cooked meal. Nice. "He made it?"

"No, I cooked. He had just gotten off a long shift." Casey grinned. "It's his favorite."

Hmm. "Go on." Bri started pressing her Eiffel Tower cookie cutter into the dough.

"We were eating with the girls. Evie had just smashed a fistful of tomato sauce into Lexi's hair, so Lexi threw her milk at Evie in revenge." Casey rolled her eyes. "Just your typical weeknight."

Bri could only imagine. She used to offer to babysit before Casey met Nathan, and Casey always resisted. Lately, after hearing so many of her mom stories, Bri understood why. Mental note for the future — ages two and three were apparently difficult ones.

"So, Nathan grabs this polka-dotted dish towel off the oven handle — my favorite one, which is the only one in the entire kitchen that has thus far avoided permanent stains — and begins wiping up the kids, red sauce and all." Casey shook her head. "I literally burst into tears."

Her eyes widened. "Oh no." She could relate. It was sort of how Gerard had expected her to use her favorite apron to clean up coffee.

How did he get into this story? She shoved away the thought. "What happened next?" This sounded more like a breakup story than a proposal story so far, but surely any minute now, Nathan would swoop in and knock Casey off her feet.

Hopefully not literally, the way this was going.

She peeled the excess dough away from the mini Eiffel Towers as Casey continued. "So, Nathan grabs a paper towel then, while I plop Evie, who is dripping milk, into the sink. But the roll snags and the stand falls over, so the entire stack unrolls across the floor. Lexi is screaming because tomato sauce is in her eyes. I'm still crying because I love that dish towel so stinkin' much and it's ruined."

By now Bri had stopped forming cookies and stood staring at Casey. The poor girl. A proposal was a once-in-a-lifetime experience. And he hadn't even hidden the ring in the lasagna?

"I just look at Nathan across the kitchen, tomato sauce smeared all over his jeans. I've got milk dripping down my arms, soggy paper towels draped everywhere. We both start cracking up."

Definitely a laugh or cry moment. Bri sort of wanted to cry just hearing the story.

"He says, 'You know what? We should get married.' And I think he's joking, because who wants to marry into this hot mess of my life, you know? But before I can advise him to run for the hills, he pulls this ring out of his pocket." Casey holds up her left hand. "The next thing I know, I'm yelling 'yes' while the girls are clapping, and then we're kissing while the sink overflows with water and floods the kitchen floor."

Bri's initial urge was to offer sympathy, but Casey rested her chin on her palm and all but swooned. "It was perfect."

Perfect? More like horrific. Disappointing, at best. How could she be content with that? Bri didn't consider herself a diva, but some things in life were worth holding out for. A beautiful, romantic proposal was one of them.

But she didn't want to burst Casey's bubble.

She began carefully placing the cutout Eiffel Towers on the baking sheet. "I'm so happy for you." And she was. Casey deserved happiness — and that was hers to determine, not Bri's.

"I love that he asked me, right in the middle of a mess." Casey picked up the discarded cookie cutter and absently ran her finger up the side of the tower. "I would have doubted his sincerity otherwise, you know? Especially since this is happening so quickly. I would have wondered if he really got it."

Bri's hands stilled on the cookies as Casey continued.

"I'm not exactly fairy-tale material. I'm complicated. I come with baggage — even if they are the cutest set of baggage in town."

"Definitely that." Bri smiled.

Casey's gaze drifted somewhere over Bri's shoulder, almost if she were speaking to

105

herself. Her voice softened. "But he didn't ask when everything was perfect. It's easy to love when life is shiny and looks its best — it's a lot harder when it's covered in tomato sauce and Pull-Ups."

"Easy to love when everything is perfect . . ." Casey's words ricocheted around Bri's heart, as if searching for a place to land. But that didn't fit with what she knew of love. She'd had it modeled to her over her first eighteen years of life, and it was hard to imagine any other image. Her parents' lives weren't actually perfect, so to speak — no one's was. After all, they had died tragically young in life.

But their love story was something out of a romance novel. Bri's childhood was filled with comfortable, secure memories of love and affection and teamwork. Her parents got aggravated sometimes, like when her mom would calm her father down while he stressed over finances, but who didn't worry over money?

If Bri hadn't had such a lucrative life insurance policy paid to her when her parents passed away, she'd be stressing over money every day too. But that policy had bought her townhome and her car and padded her savings so she could live off her small salary from the Pastry Puff. She still had to be careful, but she could afford to give, just like her parents had given to her, and just like Mabel and Agnes regularly gave to the people of the town.

Too bad it wasn't enough to buy out the Puff and hush Charles once and for all.

Casey's words pinged softly through Bri's thoughts as she readied the baking sheet for the oven. But that couldn't be right. When love was love, it had to at least *feel* pretty perfect. That was romance at its finest — not shallow but glossy. Not surface level but deep and still and peaceful. After all, her parents never fought. She always figured fighting was a sign of a damaged relationship and had broken up with more than one casual boyfriend in high school and college because of it.

No, Bri was right. She had to be — and she had a trunkful of letters to prove it.

She tossed her oven mitt aside. Her parents' love might have been rare, but clearly such love was possible. She was glad Casey had found her version of it with Nathan. He was a good guy — sweet, treated her right, took care of her kids, and clearly cared a lot about her if he was willing to dive into her "mess," as Casey put it. That was great.

But as for Bri, she would keep holding

out for the guy with the drizzled chocolate desserts and the hidden rings and the fireworks.

CHAPTER NINE

Gerard had worked on his article for about half an hour at a breakfast diner a few blocks from the Pastry Puff, and halfway through his plate of bacon, he found himself at a brick wall. He really needed more quotes to keep going, which meant more conversations with Bri.

Though, if he were honest with himself, he'd admit the writer's block wasn't because of a lack of quotes. It was because he didn't want to write this story.

But admitting that meant stopping long enough to process why, and he didn't want to stop. He never stopped. Hence his fascination with world travel. He was good at roaming.

He wasn't good at roots.

Gerard, laptop bag on his shoulder, hesitated on his way into the Pastry Puff. That same girl he almost ran over heading into the Puff yesterday was hanging out at the counter with Bri. He looked closer — she also appeared to be the same girl from the YouTube video Peter had made him watch that started this whole feature in the first place.

Maybe he could quote her next, give Bri a break a little longer. That would also give him time to work on Charles and figure out exactly where this new angle was going to take him — and how far he was willing to go to make sure it took him somewhere.

Gerard opened the door.

"Have you had any more luck with that secret ingredient?" the YouTube girl was asking.

Bri shook her head. "No, and I've tried everything. Extra vanilla. Extra almond extract. Lemon. Cinnamon."

"Morning, ladies."

Both girls straightened at his voice and turned his way. One offered a friendly smile, one quickly glanced away. He wasn't surprised which did which.

"Good morning." The YouTube star beamed, running her fingers through her long hair. She was pretty, in an athletic way. Long brown hair, naturally tan skin. Her eyes shone as if she'd just revealed a secret.

Yet for all her pretty, glowing happiness, he couldn't tear his eyes off Bri, who stood demurely behind the counter, eyes averted, blonde hair tucked behind her ears. That blasted apron covered the lower half of her sweatshirt, which read *Wanderlust,* the same word that was on the stepping-stone outside by the love-lock wall — and on the décor at the bakery counter.

Interesting. Or maybe annoying. He hated gimmicks.

He joined them at the counter. He probably needed to turn on the charm, get this girl to talk and give him the information he needed for the write-up. But a second glance at her bouncing on her heels and twisting a ring around her finger confirmed he wouldn't have to make much effort. This chick was about to burst with news.

"Coffee?" Bri asked politely from her side of the dessert display, but he could see in her eyes that she was guarded. So, she was still being weird from last night. Good to know.

"Please."

She filled a mug for him, not even noticing the smile he'd made sure to offer. She slid it across the counter to him and he took a sip. Horrible.

He set the cup down. "What's this about a secret ingredient?"

"Nothing." Bri pointed across the display

to the brunette. "You remember Casey? From the YouTube videos we made for the love-lock wall."

Not the most subtle subject change, but he'd roll with it for now. Gerard held out his hand. "I don't believe we met. I almost ran you over yesterday coming in here, though."

"No worries." She placed her left hand in his, but not in a shaking position. Rather, she held it out flat, like he was supposed to kiss it. He shook it anyway.

"She's showing you her ring." Bri pointed.

"I'm engaged!" Casey held her hand up higher, and the diamond flashed.

That made more sense than her believing she was the Queen of England. Gerard nodded. "It's beautiful."

"Thank you."

"My condolences."

"Thank y —" Casey's automatic response broke off and her smile faltered, confused. "Wait. What?"

Bri rolled her eyes as she opened the mini-fridge door and peered inside. "He's kidding."

"Am I, though?" He saluted with his coffee cup and smirked.

Casey crossed her arms, but the sparkle didn't leave her eyes. This girl had it bad over her engagement. She studied him. "I think he's serious."

"Now you don't believe in marriage?" The fridge door slammed shut as Bri turned back to face him. "Are you kidding me?"

He held up his hand in defense. "I didn't say I didn't believe in marriage." It existed — though it was becoming more and more extinct as the generations passed.

Casey leaned toward him, as if interested in hearing more. Funny, most women tuned him out at this point. Or left the table for him to pick up the check. One had thrown her tea in his face.

Both women here were empty-handed, so he continued. "I believe in marriage. I just don't believe it's guaranteed or that it lasts. It's a huge risk." Peter and Cynthia were the only exception, and they weren't typical.

Casey tilted her head, eyebrows arched. "Maybe. But some risks are worth taking."

He gestured with his coffee. "True. Vegas shovels in quite a bit of money on that belief."

"You're comparing romance and true love to a neon strip?"

"Why not?" He shrugged. "Both are full of smoke and mirrors."

Casey's eyebrows shot up on her forehead.

"That's right, ladies and gentlemen, this is what *Trek Magazine* sends as a romantic destination writer." Bri gestured to Gerard like a game-show host might demonstrate a prize, then rolled her eyes. "Must see it to believe it."

Casey leaned in even closer, crowding his space. A knowing spark lit her eyes. "Been burned before, Author Man?"

Time to redirect. "While you're currently feeling lucky in love, may I interview you for the magazine feature?"

"Sure. As long as you don't quote me as wearing a black dress down the aisle and ordering black roses for my bouquet." Casey pointed at him in warning. "And don't you dare use the word *condolences.*"

"I'll make it accurate. Email me." Gerard handed her his business card. "Although, your idea is probably more accurate in general."

"A wedding is *not* like a death." Bri crossed her arms and all but glowered at him. Gerard squinted. Nope, there was definite glowering. She was taking this personally.

"What's the deal, Cupcake? No one's raining on your parade." He pointed at Casey and grinned. "I'm raining on hers."

Casey still looked like she'd taken up

permanent residence on cloud nine. He wasn't fazing her in the least, which was part of what he'd wanted to find out. She beamed. "Hey, every good romance movie ends in the rain."

Bri smiled, but the glower returned when her gaze collided back with Gerard's. He slid his empty coffee mug to her. "The coffee was better today."

She snatched the cup off the counter. "Incorrigible."

"No, I said *better.*"

Casey coughed into her hand, but not before Gerard glimpsed the smile she covered. "I've got to go pick up the girls." She nodded at Gerard. "I'll be in touch." She waved at Bri. "See you later. Don't forget book club Thursday."

"I'll be there! And congratulations again." She stressed the congrats, as if she could make up for Gerard's sarcasm.

The second the door swung shut behind Casey, Bri turned to him with a fiery spark in her eyes. "Why do you do that?"

"Do what? Uncover the truth?"

She gestured in frustration. "Sprinkle your darkness dust everywhere."

"Darkness dust?" Harsh. And a little comical.

"You know what I mean." She fumbled

with an oven mitt, and for a moment he felt the urge to duck. "Wait. What do *you* mean by uncover the truth?"

"I was testing her. It's part of my interview process."

"What? To goad your contacts into submission?"

"To see how easily they can be persuaded to have a view opposite the one they started with."

Whatever it was she'd been about to say, she must have changed her mind. Her parted lips slowly clamped together. "So Casey passed."

"Of course she passed. She's in love." He tapped the display glass. "Why don't you calm down over there, Cupcake, and get me a petit four?"

A smile cracked the surface as she made her way to the display class. "Fine. But I'm charging you this time."

"I'd have been shocked otherwise."

"And you have to sit over there." She pointed to the table farthest from the counter.

"Sold." He slid a five-dollar bill across the counter. "Make that two." He'd have a stomachache again, but he needed a reason to linger.

And dang it, if those petit fours weren't

concocted of pure ambrosia.

He took the desserts — she'd given him two with pink icing, which at this point had to be on purpose, but he wouldn't give her the satisfaction of acknowledging it — to the table she'd indicated and pulled out his laptop.

The door chimed, and an elderly man shuffled in with a walker, maneuvering it over the doorstop with surprising ease. His beige jacket hung loose around his slight frame, and he purposed toward the counter as if in slow motion.

Bri turned at the chime, and her countenance brightened to rival the sun. "Mr. Mac! I haven't seen you in nearly two weeks. I was getting worried."

"I had a cold." His husky voice cracked as he fished in his pocket and removed a white handkerchief. "You know I can't stay away long. Betty has her expectations."

"And it's a good thing she does." Bri began bagging up something the man hadn't even ordered from the display. "The usual?"

"Of course." He coughed, then tucked his handkerchief back in his pocket. "She's waiting."

"Of course." Bri mirrored the expression with a voice so kind it soothed a nerve Gerard didn't know had been exposed. He watched as she came around the counter to bring Mr. Mac the bag of treats. The elderly man handed her a wadded-up bill, and she took it without looking at it. "How are you?"

"Just left the doctor. Same ol' stuff." He turned, and Gerard noticed his thick, wiry gray eyebrows.

"Is Jill outside?"

"You know she is. That old goose won't let me out of her sight." He laughed, and it turned into a rattling bark. Gerard flinched at the harsh sound, but Bri didn't turn away. Rather, she touched his shoulder as he finished the coughing fit. "Let me get you an iced coffee to go."

He started to protest.

"Don't worry, I'll make it decaf. Soy milk."

He clutched his to-go bag. "But I already paid."

"Good thing I know the manager, then." She winked at him as she whipped up his drink.

Betty. *And* Jill? Gerard couldn't figure it out, but he was intrigued — and even more mesmerized by the way Bri transformed while taking care of the man.

He opened his Word document and typed some notes, keeping a sporadic eye on the animated, beaming pastry chef behind the counter. Bri handed the man a to-go cup with a secured lid, and he thanked her with a slightly shaky voice that Gerard could tell used to bark with authority. He'd bet anything the man was former military.

Marine, by the way he held his shoulders.

Bri helped him tuck the pastry bag into his baggy jacket pocket. "Don't keep Betty waiting, now."

"I'd never dream of it. That Jill, though, you gotta watch her. She'll bite." Mr. Mac chuckled, and it turned into a cough.

Bri patted his back. "I'll see you next week, sir."

"Not if I see you first."

Gerard bit into a petit four by habit, not even desiring the sugar but finding it awakening something in him regardless. Somehow, being in Story — more specifically, watching Bri interact with her community — was like having a front-row seat to a play, one deserving of a snack and the full experience.

Bri carried Mr. Mac's coffee for him as he ambled out of the shop with his walker. Gerard's gaze followed them outside, where a round, gray-haired woman in blue scrubs opened the door to a silver Crown Victoria. Bri chatted with her for a moment, holding her hair back with one hand as the wind kept threatening to toss it in front of her face.

She could be on the cover of *Trek.*

Gerard looked quickly back down at his notes. What was wrong with him? Something about Bri made it hard for him to look away.

He better nip that in the bud. Remy had been right — that fateful conversation in Paris when he was twenty-one had left him starry-eyed in the presence of his media hero. The traveling photo journalist had won every award possible and was only in his forties at the time. He knew how to document life because he'd *lived* it. He'd turned traveling into an art form and inspired Gerard, a college student at the time, to write about it just as artistically. If not for Remy, Gerard wouldn't be where he was today.

Standing by the Seine, Remy had warned him not to fall in love, not to lock himself into a lifetime of regret and pain as he'd done.

"Chase after the story, son. Don't let it catch you."

Gerard had naively nodded, hanging on to every word he'd said. But a few years later, he met Kelsey and forgot everything his mentor had said that day. He'd gotten caught.

Gerard's inner defenses rose, effectively guarding the place Kelsey had left raw. The door swung shut behind Bri as she reentered the bakery. Jaw cocked, he leaned back in his chair. "So, who was that? The town bachelor?"

"Mr. Mac?" Bri rubbed her arms through her baggy sweatshirt sleeves as if chilled. The smile she'd had while visiting with the older man still lingered. "Hardly. He's the most devoted man I know."

"To who? Betty or Jill?" Gerard snorted.

"Betty. He's been married sixty-five years."

"Does Jill know?"

Bri's smile faded, and her eyes iced over. "She drives Mr. Mac to the graveyard to see Betty once a week."

Oh.

"So yeah, I'd say she knows." Bri crossed her arms. "Jill is Mr. Mac's nurse."

He swallowed. "I'm —"

"A jerk? Agreed."

He couldn't argue that at all.

Bri slowly walked the deposit bag of the day's receipts, checks, and cash to the bank, the late afternoon sun warm against her cheeks despite the November chill cutting through her jeans. She replayed that morning's conversation with Gerard over and over in her mind but was unable to come up with any explanation other than he was simply a bitter bachelor.

Permanent bachelor, she'd wager.

She waited in line for the next available teller, foot tapping an anxious rhythm on the tile floor as the hum of the heater filled the quiet lobby. Of all the bitter, negative approaches to life. First, he actually expressed his sympathies toward a newly engaged woman, then he had the audacity to assume the worst about the sweetest old man in the entire town. The faster Gerard Fortier wrote this feature and got out of Story, the better.

It still bugged her that he was French — even if it was only a quarter.

"Well, now, Bri Duval. I thought that was you!" The woman in front of her caught her eye and smiled with overly lined red lips, her dyed blonde hair coiffed to perfection.

Bri stiffened. Sandra Thompson, town gossip. Normally Bri wasn't one to label people, but Sandra had actually written the town gossip column when that was still a popular thing in the local paper, well over a decade ago. And it was still a thing — one

Sandra took seriously, even if it wasn't published anymore and she now ran a secondhand shop over on Fern. She knew everything about everyone in town, and still held a grudge toward Bri for breaking up with Charles.

"Hi, Sandra." Bri quickly turned off her negative thoughts toward Gerard. She didn't believe in mind reading, but Sandra had an uncanny radar. It wasn't worth the risk. "How are you?"

"Doing well, dear." She held up her bank bag and wiggled it. "Business is booming." Her eyes traveled down Bri's sweatshirt and faded jeans. "You really should come visit our boutique. I get new arrivals weekly, and I only accept things that aren't worn out."

She would never do that. "I'll have to do that."

"I meant to shop, of course, dear. I doubt you'd have anything to sell consignment."

"Of course." She'd learned a long time ago not to be offended. Sandra had two decades on her age-wise and thought of Charles like a brother. Her dumping him hadn't gone over well, and the woman hadn't grown to be gossip queen because she was quick to forgive and forget.

Sandra leaned in, like she was about to get a scoop. Except she didn't lower her voice, because she'd never been able to whisper. Her voice practically bounced around the lobby. "How's the feature going? Is he going to put Story on the map?"

It was a wonder she hadn't come sniffing around the Pastry Puff yet to get a glimpse of Gerard. Or maybe she already had. Bri wouldn't put it past Sandra to peer into windows after hours.

"I hope so." Though she wasn't sure how Gerard's pen could write anything positive about the Pastry Puff at this point. He had warmed up to the petit fours, at least.

Sandra persisted. "I heard he's incredibly handsome. Do you think so?"

"Um." Bri peered past Sandra to the front of the line, checking for the holdup. Oh no. It was Mr. Piper and his monthly coffee can full of coins to roll. She was trapped. "Is who handsome?" She stalled, wishing she could hide behind the row of potted plants to their left. Or maybe shove Sandra into one of the giant decorative urns over by the loan officers' cubicles.

Talk about a story.

"The magazine writer." Sandra's voice pitched with eagerness. "I heard he's a total McDreamy. Do you think so?"

"Of course she does."

The deep baritone startled Bri, and she

turned. Gerard stood behind her, so close she almost bumped into his chest — that frustratingly broad chest.

"What do you want?" She stepped back, irritation rising quicker than Sandra's penciled eyebrows.

"Oh my. You *must* be the writer." Sandra held out her hand, palm down like Casey had, except this time there was no ring to show off.

Gerard shook her hand, oblivious, just like he'd done before. "In the flesh."

"I'll say." Sandra's eyes skipped over him.

Gerard coughed.

"Look, Sandra, it's almost your turn. Mr. Piper is down to his last roll of quarters." Bri stepped between them, turning to face Gerard. She lowered her voice. "Are you following me now?"

"You can follow me if you'd like," Sandra piped up over her shoulder, her teeth extra white against her red lips. "I'll be going to the coffee shop after this. I'd love to get to know you more. Maybe tell you a little bit about my business. I'm sure there's plenty of room in the article for —"

"Next, please!" the teller called from the counter. Bri grabbed Sandra's dress suit–clad shoulders and spun her around. "Off you go. I'll make sure he knows everything he needs to know about Story."

Sandra reluctantly walked to the counter, winking at Gerard before finally handing over her deposit.

"I'm confused." Gerard stared after her, rubbing his chin with one hand. His stubble scratched against his palm. "Is she after me for my influence or for my body?"

"I'd guess both." Bri pinched the bridge of her nose between her fingers. What a disaster. There was no telling what Sandra would spread around Story now. The last thing she needed was rumors of her having any involvement with Gerard, outside of being the main source for the feature.

Was this article even worth it?

Yes. Saving the Pastry Puff was worth it. Making a claim to fame in honor of the home where her mother had learned to bake was worth it. Sticking up for the dozens of love stories represented on the wall was worth it.

Gerard shifted his weight, voice lowering much more successfully than Sandra's. "I wanted to say I'm sorry. I know I was pretty rude about your friend in there."

"Which one?" Bri crossed her arms, tucking the bank bag against her chest.

"Mr. Mac. But I guess judging by your tone, Casey too."

"Wow. You are smarter than you look."

Gerard's eyes widened a fraction, and he stepped back. "Nice shot."

Her heart sank. Here she was having just convinced herself this was all worth it, and she couldn't even be professionally polite. Something about Gerard turned her into the worst version of herself. "I'm sorry. I got defensive. Mr. Mac is the sweetest —"

"It's okay, really." Gerard smiled, but it didn't reach his eyes. "I just wanted to clear that up." He glanced at the lobby floor, then back up briefly as he stepped toward the front door. "I'll see you soon."

The door shut behind him, letting a bit of the warm lobby air escape. A chill — or maybe that was regret — rushed down her spine and into her toes. She glanced toward the front of the line, where Sandra stood facing her squarely, eyes wide and alert, lips parted.

Bri wanted to throw herself into an urn.

CHAPTER TEN

"You're reminding me more of your mother every day." Mabel patted Bri's arm as she turned off the mixer and tossed the beaters into the sink. "You know she cleaned up as she baked too?"

"As everyone should." Agnes sniffed as she dropped her purse on the nearest table.

They'd come in at 8:00 a.m. as usual, even though Bri had been baking since dawn. She didn't mind — it was part of her job. Besides, she loved the way the quiet shop echoed the hum of the mixer, the warmth radiating from the double oven as she waltzed back and forth between the prepping station and the industrial sink. The way the canned lights in the front of the shop shone tiny spotlights above the display, which was begging to be filled with daily treats.

Baking alone in the shop somehow made Bri feel more connected to her mom. She could imagine her at the same counter years prior, singing softly under her breath the way she used to when she cooked dinner at home. Or picture her swaying in tune with the mixing bowl, her apron flaring about her skirt — just like when her dad used to twirl her in the kitchen.

"I always told her not to worry about cleaning up. I wanted her to just enjoy the experience of baking." Mabel smiled, staring off at something past Bri's shoulder as she reached for the roll of paper towels. Her voice softened, seeming extra quiet next to the brightness of her electric-blue eyeshadow. "There's something therapeutic about creating amid the mess."

Creating amid the mess. It sounded nice. But Bri never made a mess. She liked life tidy. Neat. In her control.

"Did she take your advice?" Bri wiped the counter with a damp towel, gathering the last clumps of flour and smears of cream cheese from the smooth surface.

"No," Agnes piped up. "Thank goodness."

"I think after so long, the kitchen just knew to sparkle whether she actually cleaned up or not." Mabel chortled.

That sounded like the type of magic her mother had wielded. Bri smiled as she picked up her piping bag. She had no problem being just like her mom — neat, tidy, controlled. Life didn't have to be complicated. Baking in the Pastry Puff was simple and predictable, and that's where Bri wanted to stay.

Mabel's voice broke the cozy silence. "Charles called again last night."

Bri's hand tightened on the piping bag. "To discuss the weather, right?"

"Cloudy with a chance of ignorance." Agnes rolled her eyes.

Mabel swatted at her. "Agnes, he's just a dedicated businessman."

"No, he's a meddling lawyer."

"Who made us a very generous offer."

How generous? Bri's stomach dipped. Surely they weren't actually entertaining him.

"A generous offer from an annoying —"

"Now, Agnes, he's persistent. It's an admirable trait." Mabel pointed with a hot-pink nail. "Besides, business has slowed since that initial rush after the virus."

"Viral video," Bri and Agnes corrected at the same time.

Mabel waved her hand. "Po-tay-to, puh-tah-to."

"She has a point." Agnes pursed her lips. "I truly hate when that happens."

Bri had noticed the slowing business too

but had hoped it'd been her imagination. Unfortunately, it seemed like business was back to locals only, which before the video had barely been enough to sustain the shop. The sudden influx of customers helped a lot, as evidenced by the bank deposits, but how long would the sisters be willing to keep it going on a thread if everything returned to normal?

Her heart thumped louder in her chest. On top of that, Charles was upping the ante. Was her worst nightmare actually possible?

Mabel chimed back in, concern pitching her voice. "Bri, dear, I think that petit four is decorated enough now."

Bri glanced down at her angry grip, which had squeezed enough green icing to represent an entire forest, instead of the flower leaf she'd intended. Oops. She set the bag down on the counter, unable to meet Mabel's eyes.

She tried to keep her voice level, but it pitched anyway. Agnes's gaze bored into her cheek. "So, are you considering the offer?" She focused on the petit four in front of her, painstakingly swiping the excess icing with her finger and attempting to appear casual, as if her entire future didn't hang on Mabel's answer.

"When you're our age, honey, you consider everything." Mabel laughed and elbowed Agnes, who remained stoic. She didn't seem as tempted as Mabel to sell, which offered Bri a bit of hope.

No way could Charles win. He had no idea what the Pastry Puff meant to her — not really. No one could truly understand, except maybe Mabel and Agnes. But if they were mulling over his increasingly ludicrous offers, maybe they didn't fully get it either.

Charles definitely wouldn't listen to her — if anything, his bitterness over their failed relationship was egging him on out of spite. But Charles was too much of a professional to admit as much.

If coaxing him down wasn't an option . . . there weren't many left. She licked a clump of icing off her finger. She had to do something.

She hesitated. More like, Gerard had to do something. He might be her only hope — and she'd just publicly insulted her only hope in front of the town gossip and an entire lobby of people. It looked like there was only one solution. She stared at the lingering green stain on her finger.

The crow she was about to devour wasn't going to taste nearly as sweet.

He'd never admit it, but libraries had always

been comforting. When Gerard was younger and needed to hide from his mother's newest boyfriend, he'd escape to the rows of science fiction and spend hours poring over the graphic novels and the newest releases from his favorite authors — which were usually over a year old by the time the library picked them up.

The librarian who worked afternoons — he couldn't remember her name, but she smelled like the wildflowers that grew by the highway and had curled gray hair he would swear to this day was a wig — would always give him a free bookmark or soft peppermint. Looking back, he figured she knew something was up at home and was doing what she could to encourage him.

Back then, he just appreciated the free candy.

Gerard pulled open the heavy door to Story's library, a rush of warm air washing over him. He inhaled the scent of memories and felt a little bit of the stressful day chip off his back. With all his travels and writing, he didn't spend nearly enough time on his favorite pastime, reading. One more thing to add to the "after this feature is finished" list.

He figured he'd research the city's history to give his article the extra depth it was missing. Checking out the local library had sounded a lot more appealing than googling facts while hiding in his room from Mrs. Beeker. The woman stalked him almost nightly with her tray of "bedtime snacks," as she called them, which he knew were just a variety of Little Debbie snack cakes piled high on a silver platter. He'd better be careful or he'd be at risk of gaining a few pounds in this eccentric place, and the last thing he needed was to have to buy new jeans at the outlet strip on Honeysuckle Street.

The fact that he knew the outlet strip was on Honeysuckle Street unnerved him enough.

He really wanted to finish this project and get out of Story before he got pulled into the illusion any further. This town did something to people — sucked them into a sugarcoated reality, just like they literally sugarcoated everything else.

The thought of sugar reminded him of Bri. Just when he thought they might be making progress in their working relationship, he had to smart off about an old friend of hers. Mr. Mac was apparently a town favorite — or maybe Bri just treated him like that. Come to think of it, she treated everyone who wandered into the bakery like a VIP.

Except him, of course.

He hadn't meant to insult someone she cared about so deeply. Her defensive cut at the bank still throbbed a little. He'd pushed her too far, though, and he deserved it.

However, he wasn't sure anyone deserved that crazy, middle-aged blonde woman in the bank. He shuddered. What was her name . . . Sally? Sandra. That was it. The unfortunate reality, though, was that, in his experience, characters like that usually turned out to be pretty useful later. It was sort of like playing the game he was playing with Charles — keep a poker face and your cards flat on the table until you know how it's going to go.

He hadn't made it this far in his life — or career — by trusting everyone who crossed his path.

Gerard nodded his acknowledgment to the science fiction section, making a mental note to come back and browse after he accomplished some thorough word count the next day on his feature. It'd be his reward for dumping this story on paper and being one step closer to heading back to Chicago — with a check for his mom in one hand and a well-deserved promotion in the other.

Then he could write about politics and third-world finances and things that mattered.

He found a row of history books, not surprised at the small but overtly decorated endcap dedicated entirely to Story.

He scooped up the two books that looked semiuseful, blew a layer of dust off the first one, and tucked them under his arm. Maybe he could just stroll past the sci-fi real —

"I believe the theme of *Pride and Prejudice* was opposites attracting and producing a forever type of love." A soft — and familiar — voice grabbed Gerard's attention.

Bri?

He peered around another endcap featuring DIY home projects, not entirely sure why he cared whether it was her. And not sure why his heart raced at the idea that it might be. Probably wasn't, though. What were the odds she'd be in the library on a random Thursday night?

But it was definitely her. She was sitting in a leather armchair in an open nook slightly off the library's main floor. She had her legs pulled up under her, twirling one lock of hair around her finger as she spoke to a small, eclectic mix of people also in armchairs. Casey, the recently engaged friend, sat to Bri's left.

"It's like with my parents," Bri continued. "My mom was the dedicated, loyal caretaker of the relationship, just like Elizabeth. She never stopped pursuing love. And my dad was more like Mr. Darcy — a bit more cynical by nature but easy to come around and adjust for the right woman."

What? This was ridiculous.

A skinny guy in a plaid shirt and sandals adjusted his blue-framed glasses. "Yeah, I agree. Mr. Darcy was kind of harsh, and Elizabeth totally mellowed him out."

"Come on! Did you even read the book?" Gerard burst into the circle before fully processing the decision.

Six sets of eyes jerked his way, Bri's widening the most.

Bri stared at Gerard staring at her from the middle of the circle of chairs. He was like a pop-up book. Always at the bakery, then appearing at the bank . . . now he was intruding on book club?

She opened her mouth, then shut it, unsure which situation to address first — his accusation of her favorite novel or that he was there in the first place.

William didn't give her time before coming to her defense. "Of course she did. We all did."

"You, I can't even deal with right now." Gerard held up one hand to William before pointing at Bri. "You. Did you read the book?"

Bri stood to face him and crossed her arms to hide her shaking hands, her heart pounding a defensive rhythm. "I could *quote* the book."

"You read the book? In your native language?" Gerard still hadn't lowered his finger. "And you somehow still came away with that crazy theory?"

"I could have read it in French too." She narrowed her eyes. *"C'est une vérité universellement reconnue que —"*

He grabbed the books tucked against his side and crossed his arms to imitate her, interrupting with the rest of the novel's famous opening line. *"Un homme célibataire en possession d'une bonne fortune doit avoir besoin d'une femme."*

Bri gasped and her arms fell to her side. Gerard knew *Pride and Prejudice?*

"I'm a world traveler, Cupcake. You want to go Italian next?"

The library briefly tilted around her, and anger sparked in her chest. He had the nerve to invade her personal space and then call her out in front of her entire group? He was rude and unnecessary — this gesture perhaps the rudest of them all. Just because he came to try to smooth things over at the bank earlier didn't give him an open invitation into her life.

Especially if he was coming to commandeer it.

She glared. "Don't be ridiculous."

Next to her, Casey wiggled in her seat, grinning and turning to hang her legs over the side of her chair. She looked like all she needed was popcorn as her head turned back and forth between Bri and Gerard.

A brief warning signal flashed in the back of Bri's mind. *Abort. Abort.* So much for Bri's plan to save the bakery — she not only wasn't implementing said plan, but she was hard-core running in the other direction at this point. It was difficult to remember her motivation when he challenged her like this. What was it about Gerard that set her so on edge? Her frustration knew no limits when he goaded her. They had zero compatibility.

Sort of like Elizabeth and Mr. Darcy.

Bri flinched. No. That was totally different.

"I'm sorry. Who are you?" Their book club leader, Julie Thompson, smiled politely as she glanced up at Gerard. She looked unsure if she should offer to pull up a chair or run him off. "I'm Julie."

"Gerard Fortier. Pleasure." He nodded briskly, then turned back to Bri before Julie could respond. "Darcy wasn't a pushover, giving in to the whims of some wishy-washy woman. He was a man who stood his ground and spoke the truth."

"What? Elizabeth wasn't wishy-washy. She knew right away what she wanted — *who* she wanted, for that matter." A flush crawled up Bri's neck. He had the story completely wrong. Like he had their town — and the Pastry Puff — completely wrong.

"As for you." He pivoted toward William, tucking the two books back under his arm. "Darcy wasn't harsh. He was honest — which, by the way, is a refreshing and rare quality in a man today."

"You think?" William's eyebrows shot up so fast, his glasses slipped on his nose. "Honest, huh?" He nodded eagerly. "I can go with that."

Bri turned away so he wouldn't see her roll her eyes. Figured. William was definitely more Mr. Collins. He hadn't stood by a single opinion he'd offered in book club yet.

Gerard ran a hand down the length of his face before peering at Casey in her chair. "I suppose you think these two are right?"

"I actually haven't read the book." Casey grinned. "And who needs to now?"

140

Bri huffed. "Casey!"

"What?" She laughed, twisting back around in the chair so her feet dropped to the floor. "It's more fun this way. Besides, I'm planning a wedding. I don't have time for novels."

"But you have time for book club?" Bri shot her a pointed glance.

Gerard blew out a breath. "At least you're getting a glimpse of what real marriage is like with these Austen characters."

Finally, something they could agree on. "Exactly!" Bri reached back into her chair and grabbed her worn copy of *Pride and Prejudice*. "Romance, longsuffering, passion."

"Hardly." Gerard perched on the edge of the seat Bri had vacated. "More like arguing, stubbornness, and selfishness."

"Oh, I love a good fight scene." Casey flipped through her stiff new copy. "What page is that on?"

"Pick one. It's their entire relationship." Gerard shrugged. "I really don't see how this novel is a romance, anyway. More like a tragedy."

"Fascinating point." Julie leaned forward in her chair with a smile, smoothing her floral-print skirt over her lap. "I have to admit book club rarely gets this animated."

The rest of the group started chatting excitedly, considering other scenarios and themes. Even Casey joined in.

Bri watched a satisfied smirk slide across Gerard's face, and her grip tightened on the book in her hand, itching to wind it like a baseball and pitch it at his head. She narrowed her gaze at him, raising her voice to be heard over the chattering din of the club members. "How do you even know what marriage is like, anyway? Have *you* ever been married?"

The group fell silent at the same moment. Her loud question echoed through the small study nook.

Gerard's eyes locked with hers. "Almost. Once."

Bri's pounding heart tripped in its marathon rhythm, and her stomach flip-flopped. Regret at her brashness immediately flooded her senses, heating her chest and neck in a telltale flush she tried to cover with her hand. Despite wanting to sink into the ground, she absolutely couldn't walk past one detail. "Almost?"

Gerard slowly stood. "People break engagements every day, Cupcake. Just ask your buddies there." He gestured to the worn book in her hands. "Not all stories end in happily ever after."

Then he walked away, leaving the women swooning and William shaking his head in awe. "Wow," he said as he pushed his glasses up on his nose.

Bri rolled in her lower lip and looked away from his retreating form. Wow, indeed.

CHAPTER ELEVEN

He hadn't had a headache this bad — or swallowed back this much regret — since Spring Break 2009.

Gerard pecked aimlessly at his laptop keys. One of the library books lay open next to him on the table he'd wiped down with a napkin that he'd had to dip in his own water glass. Classy.

After tossing and turning all night, nauseated over the words he'd let slip to complete strangers — words he hadn't even said in front of his coworkers at *Trek* — he'd decided to shove aside reality and get some work done at the most inconspicuous place he could think of: Taylor's Sushi Barn, which boasted a full breakfast menu and the "town's best pizza" on their website.

More importantly, though, was that it was located on the opposite end of Story from the Pastry Puff. He'd drown his sorrows in black coffee and pancake syrup and try not to worry about where in the world Mr. Taylor secured his sushi and why he felt the need to sell it from a barn.

Temples throbbing from lack of sleep, Gerard stared at the words swimming on the computer screen before him. The library books so far hadn't helped much. Though it could be his fault for lack of focus. Always with the writer's block in this town.

Why had he blurted that out to Bri? *"Almost. Once."* He had hard rules about his personal life — as in, don't talk about it, at all, under any circumstances. Especially on a job. No one needed to know his business. Peter didn't even know the *whole* story about Kelsey, and here he was blabbering on in a library because of what? He was trying to prove a point about a classic novel? What was it about this town?

What was it about Bri?

He took a sip of coffee and winced. Apparently his waitress had topped it off when he wasn't looking. Now his tongue burned.

At least he could be fairly certain the morning couldn't get any worse.

"I heard about your commotion in the library last night." Charles slid into the booth across from him and saluted with his coffee mug. "Well played."

He was wrong.

Gerard shut his laptop. "Word gets around fast."

"That's Story." Charles took a slow sip, then smirked. "Plus, my friend Sandra was returning some DVDs and overheard the entire thing. I have to say, I'm impressed."

Sandra. Figured. Did that mean she'd heard the slip about having almost been married?

Gerard stayed silent, hoping for context before replying.

He didn't have to wait long.

"Not many people stand up to Abrielle Duval."

Who? Oh, right. Bri. He'd never get used to *Abrielle.* Bri was about the most American, partially French woman he'd ever met.

He shrugged. "It was just a book club discussion."

"Are you familiar with subtext, Mr. Fortier?" Charles rolled the saltshaker between his fingers. "The surface conversation might have been about the book. The undertone was a lot more. At least, according to Sandra."

He knew that woman was going to be trouble the moment he met her. Gerard leaned back in the booth, crossing his arms over his chest. "Yeah?"

Looking more than pleased with himself,

Charles adjusted the collar of his dress shirt. Yellow today, which didn't do his skin tone any favors. He looked extra pasty. Did the man ever dress down? This wasn't exactly Chicago. And good thing, because Chicago would eat this weasel alive in a minute. It was easy to play bigwig lawyer in a Midwestern town the size of a postage stamp.

He wished he could take this guy down a peg or two now. But the game wasn't over. There were still cards to deal, and Gerard couldn't take his chances on showing his hand yet. "What's your point?"

Charles returned the saltshaker to its cubby on the table. "I just made the Pastry Puff owners a new offer. One they'd be crazy to refuse." He shook his head. "Crazy even for them."

Gerard frowned. Mabel and Agnes were eccentric, for certain. But not crazy. If anything, Charles was the one with a few screws loose — striving and manipulating to purchase a property out of some kind of spite, when any other location in the city would serve just as well. "What's that got to do with me?"

"You can sway her. Bri is the only reason those sisters are holding out. If she were on board, they'd have taken my original offer. Who wants to run a bakery in their eighties?" Charles shook his head. "They'll see reason once Bri does. You're the man for the job. No one else can talk to Bri like you do."

Maybe so, but that didn't mean it did any good. If anything, he just kept shoving his foot in his mouth in front of her, to *his* detriment. Those figurative leather boots didn't taste great.

"I know you can do it." Charles tapped the table between them. "And don't forget what we discussed earlier."

About the power of the pen? Ha. Gerard glanced at his closed laptop. If Charles only knew how powerless those words currently were. At this rate, he wasn't going to convince anyone to come to the Pastry Puff — and not because of Charles's backhanded pleas.

But because he didn't want to be here himself.

The realization was suddenly so clear. His writer's block wasn't just typical writer's block. It was due to him not believing his own words. Usually he had no problem creating an artistic argument to lure fellow wanderers to experience his travels for themselves. It was easy to talk up nature's grandest opportunities and most scenic secrets.

But he didn't want to be in Story, and it was showing in his weak sentence structure and lackluster descriptions.

Charles slipped out of the booth, briefcase in hand. "So, we have an understanding?" He held out his free hand.

Gerard studied it for a moment. Something had to change. And unfortunately, it seemed the fastest way to do that was to take Charles's advice and try to talk Bri out of keeping the Pastry Puff. It was just like his reverse psychology attempts with Casey the other day — if he pushed, Bri would be sure to push back. He'd be able to see what made the bakery so special.

Then maybe he could finish this assignment once and for all. Besides, war sold. If the battle was still raging between the two when the feature was published, all the better.

He shook Charles's hand. "That we do."

Charles was ten feet away by the time Gerard realized the weasel had passed him two folded hundred-dollar bills.

Bri had a Friday tradition, one not even Mabel and Agnes knew about. On her midmorning break, she hoofed it down to Taylor's Sushi Barn and bought a slice of pepperoni pizza. She'd never worked up the nerve to try Taylor's sushi — come to think of it, she didn't even think he served it anymore. The man made weak coffee and stale banana muffins, but his extra-saucy pizza was to die for.

And after last night, she needed her secret Friday treat bad.

The scent of bacon and burned toast assaulted her senses as she hurried inside. She raised her voice over the clatter of silverware. "Morning, Taylor."

Taylor leaned backward from his post in the kitchen to see around the doorframe. He grinned as he flipped something in a skillet. "Morning, Ms. Bri." His apron was already stained with grease from the breakfast rush. "Is it Friday already?"

"You know it." She unzipped her pink coin purse and pulled out a few bills. "Pepperoni me, please."

"Coming right up." Something sizzled, and Taylor quickly popped back out of sight.

Bri glanced around the crowded diner — well, barn — and her stomach knotted. Taylor had a steady stream of customers, no doubt. It was like this every Friday. Did he ever get lulls too?

Or was it just the Puff?

Her gaze traveled over the patrons nestled in their booths — sharing pancakes, sipping coffee, munching bacon. One elderly woman had a slice of pizza on her plate, and Bri hid a smile. She hoped she was just like that when she reached that lady's age — still eating pizza on Friday mornings.

Then Charles strode purposefully across the restaurant toward the front door, briefcase in hand. She quickly ducked her head to hide behind her curtain of hair. He hadn't seen her, thankfully, or he'd have said something, for sure. He never missed an opportunity to goad her.

She peeked between the strands of her hair and noticed a lone figure sitting at the table Charles had just vacated. Someone had been forced to start his morning with Charles — poor guy.

Then her eyes narrowed as the lone figure shrugged into the sleeves of a leather jacket.

Any inkling of sympathy vanished. "You have got to be kidding me." It was official — Gerard was everywhere. Not even Taylor's Sushi Barn was safe now. How in the world had he figured out her Friday tradition?

"What's that, dear?" Taylor slid her pie across the counter on a scratched black plate.

"Nothing, Taylor." Bri forced a smile and handed him her cash. Better start faking it now. She couldn't repeat her mistake at the library last night and get hung up on the fact that Gerard was following her. She had to start implementing her plan to get his help, and quick, before Mabel convinced Agnes to take Charles's offer. That was all that mattered.

That, and the steaming, cheesy sustenance on her plate. She could do this. The Puff depended on it.

Her mother's memory depended on it.

She carried her pizza toward Gerard, hesitating by his table as he started to stand. He glanced up with a smirk. "You following me, Duval?"

She gritted her teeth. "I could ask the same."

"Actually, I was here first." He gestured to his laptop, which was sitting dangerously close to a sticky syrup stain on the table.

She set her plate on top of the stain and sat down in the booth. "I'm on my break."

"Slow down there, now. It's not even ten a.m." Gerard nodded toward the pepperoni she was picking off the top of her pizza. She always ate them first, separately. Except for the last one, which she left for the last bite of crust.

She started to snap back, something about not having judged his carb-loaded breakfast, then remembered the plan. She wouldn't let him derail her again. Seeing Charles had fortified her.

Instead, she laughed. "You're always so funny."

Gerard's eyes narrowed, as if he couldn't tell if she was being sarcastic. "Well, I was just leaving. Enjoy your plate of teenage rebellion, there."

He half slid out of the booth, waiting for her response, but she just kept smiling as she pulled another pepperoni off her pie and conjured happy thoughts. Puppies. The Eiffel Tower. The feel of plush new slippers.

She thought of Mabel ripping up a sales contract from Charles, and the smile turned a little more genuine. "You should stay."

"Stay?" His eyebrows rose. "Here?"

"Yes. Eat with me." She patted the table as if that could ease him back into the booth. "We can talk."

"Talk?"

She started to say something sarcastic about a parrot but restrained herself. Man, she was on a roll with the self-discipline today. Must be the joy from the pepperonis. "How's the red room treating you?"

Wait, that probably sounded sarcastic. She tried again before he could answer. "Is Mrs. Beeker harassing you too badly?" She plastered on what she hoped came across as a sympathetic smile. "I know she can be a little much at first."

"A little much? That's like saying a jet is a bit loud."

Bri's stomach tensed. Who did he think he was? Mrs. Beeker was a nice woman and a dedicated patron of the Pastry Puff. Sure, she was somewhat eccentric and her hair was hard to look directly at, but she truly cared about the residents of Story and —

Bri stopped. Swallowed hard. And attempted a fake yet genuine-sounding laugh. "You're so clever."

Gerard stared at her, eyes squinted, mouth half-open. "Okay, what's in that pie? Someone has clearly spiked your pizza."

Had the two of them gotten so bad, she couldn't even be decently nice without raising suspicion? She shook her head. "I'm just making conversation. Aren't you tired of arguing all the time?"

He leaned back in his seat, leveling his gaze at her. "Well, I wouldn't have to argue if you'd stop being wrong."

Her fingers tightened around her napkin. A million retorts danced through her mind, begging to be chosen. She clenched and unclenched her teeth. "Point taken."

Gerard leaned forward abruptly, crashing

154

into the table. "Okay, stop it right now. What is your problem?"

She fought to stay calm, wishing she had more pepperonis left. But she only had the one left for her last bite of crust. She tried to focus. "I don't have a problem. I'm being nice."

"Well, being nice is a problem. It's weird."

"So, I need to be mean, because that's what you're used to?"

"Yes."

"*No.* I'm turning over a new leaf, and you can't stop me."

They stared at each other across the table. Then Gerard reached over, plucked the last pepperoni from her slice, and popped it in his mouth.

She picked up her crust and threw it at him. It bounced off his nose, and he didn't even flinch.

Apparently her new leaf had withered.

"You're afraid I'm going to write something bad, aren't you? That's what this is about." He gestured between them.

That sounded bad. Like she was using him. But wasn't she? And why would he care, anyway? He didn't have a romantic bone in his skeletal structure — much less a heart.

His words from the library rolled through

her mind. *"Almost. Once."* A pinch of regret flitted through her chest. "I'm sorry I threw that."

"Well, I'm not sorry I ate it." He smacked his lips. "Taylor was right about having the best pizza in town. He'd give some places in Chicago a run for their money."

This was a pointless mission. "You're incorrigible."

"I'm not a reviewer, Cupcake. I'm going to make the feature good." A flash of something resembling doubt flickered in his eyes, but it was gone before she could fully decipher it. "The magazine isn't going to pay to publish something we're warning travelers against. That's a waste of time."

She'd never thought of it that way. "But you don't even like the Pastry Puff."

He shook his head. "I never said that."

"Yes, you did. Repeatedly, actually, about the coffee."

"Then it's a good thing the feature isn't on coffee." He wrinkled his nose. "Unfortunately, it's on romance and love locks and other wastes of time."

She rolled her eyes. "How are you going to make us shine when you don't even believe in what you're writing?"

He averted his gaze to the laptop in front of him, his expression sobering. "I'm working on that."

"Can you work faster? I've got a lawyer breathing down my neck." She dropped her wadded-up napkin on her empty plate. "The Pastry Puff needs this feature, Gerard. I need it."

He met her gaze, briefly. "I hear you."

"So, we have an understanding?"

There was that flicker again. He nodded once before she could ask. "The feature will be exactly what it should be."

Relief flooded through her.

He let out a dramatic shudder. "Just stop being fake nice to me."

"Deal." That'd be easy enough. She quirked an eyebrow at him. Speaking of lawyers . . . "What were you doing with Charles earlier?"

"The cha-cha?"

"Very funny."

"Hey, you said I was clever."

"I take it back."

He picked up his nearly empty mug and looked in it, as if debating the last lukewarm sip. "He was talking about the recent offer he made on the bakery."

To Gerard — a man he'd met one time at the love-lock wall? That was a new low, even for Charles. Was he getting that desperate for allies? The thought strangely comforted her. Maybe he wasn't as confident in the sales pitch as he wanted her to think. "What'd you say?"

"That he was lowballing. Should offer more."

"Whatever. Come on. Was he wanting you to write something about his part in this?"

He let out a long sigh. "I didn't want to tell you, but yes."

What? Bri's heart stammered. Charles was going after Gerard to slant his feature? But Gerard had just said he would make the Puff sound good. How could he do both?

Gerard continued soberly. "He begged me to write a haiku on the coffee. To which I, against all my deeply rooted beliefs about poetry, agreed."

Relief quickly doused the spark of emotion. "You did not."

"You're right." Gerard set his mug on the table. "We done here, Cupcake?"

"One more question."

"I don't believe you. I think you have at least fifteen left in that brain of yours."

She ignored him. "What do you think about my petit fours?"

He offered a casual shrug as he slid his laptop into his bag. "They're okay."

"Are they?" She leaned forward, ducking

her head slightly to catch his eye. "Just okay?"

He smirked. "Tolerable, but not handsome enough to tempt me."

Oh. She slapped her hand on the table. At least this time the quote wasn't in French. "Not fair — or accurate."

"Fine." He sighed. "They're amazing, okay? I wish the entire article could be just on those."

"Aha!" She knew it. She had her mother's touch, thanks to the Pastry Puff. Her resolve strengthened. This was going to work. Maybe not in the way she'd originally intended, but there was hope again. Gerard was on her side — as untraditional as it might look. But she'd gotten his word.

He stood, shouldering his bag. "See? I'm not too incorrigible."

She smiled up at him and mentally reached for a new quote from her arsenal. "Do not consider me now as an elegant female, intending to plague you, but as a rational creature, speaking the truth from her heart."

He squinted. "And what does that mean?"

"It means you definitely still are."

CHAPTER TWELVE

She was brilliant.

Or her idea was, anyway. Bri hooked her arm through Casey's and tugged her toward the china display in the local department store. Now to convince her friend of the same. "Let's look over here, Miss Bride-to-Be."

"Sure. I'm always up for a sale." Casey shrugged and tagged along behind her. They'd come to Johnson's General to price wedding favors during Bri's Saturday morning break from the bakery. "I still think I'd be better off ordering bubbles from Amazon in bulk, though."

"Probably. But buying local is important too." Something Bri hoped Story would keep in mind about the Pastry Puff. She ran her finger lightly over a floral-printed salad plate. "How's the rest of the wedding planning coming along?" Surely Casey would say yes to her idea. She had to.

"Not too bad, considering it's in two weeks." Casey picked up a polka-dotted teapot. "We're going to register for wedding gifts this weekend. This is pretty cute."

Bri couldn't even fathom Nathan — or any fireman, for that matter — using a teapot. Much less a polka-dot one. She hesitated. "Nathan would hate it."

"Exactly." Casey grinned. "Wish I had one of those scanner guns now."

She'd never understand their relationship dynamic. But at least her friend was happy. "Are the girls excited about the big day?"

"They don't fully get what's happening, but they know they get to wear pretty dresses, so that's enough for them." Casey moved toward the everyday dishes and stopped in front of the ones covered in roosters. "Oh my word, yes. I have to get these too."

Bri pulled her away. "What about the solid navy? Or the teal?" Any shade of blue or green was a good neutral — something a man could eat off of and not hate. Bri secretly preferred the pink ones with the gold trim, but she'd never expect Casey's fiancé to jump on board with that.

Her memories of handing Gerard all the pink mugs from the Puff jumped to the forefront of her mind, and she quickly tried to shove them out.

"Those are boring. Dinner should be *fun* — or at least interesting." Casey's lips twisted to the side in thought. "With my kids, though, that's probably never going to be an issue."

They were getting sidetracked. Bri led Casey away from the plates. "Let's go look for the bubbles. Maybe they have some bulk packages here."

"Good idea."

They browsed the toy aisle, which offered everything from old-fashioned Slinkies to the latest Avenger action figure. "What else is left to plan?"

"You're still doing my cake, right?"

"One three-tiered petit-four platter, coming up," Bri promised. "Did you decide on colors for the wedding?"

"Not yet. Maybe black and gold."

"That'll be pretty." Bri hesitated. "Of course, it sort of depends on where the venue is." She held her breath.

"True." Casey, wide-eyed, held up a pack of baseball cards. "Look! Did you know they even still made these?"

Off track again. Bri tried to redirect. "An Autumn wedding would be beautiful outside. It's the perfect weather right now. Just think, a crisp, sunny Saturday afternoon.

Gauzy sleeves. Lightweight suits."

Casey mumbled a noncommitted murmur as she thumbed through the various packs of cards. "Man. I don't know any of these players."

She was apparently being too subtle. "You know, a really lovely spot would be that gazebo behind the bakery. By the fountain." Bri casually cast a sidelong glance at Casey. "And the love-lock wall."

There. She'd said it.

Casey nodded as she tossed the cards back in the bin. "That would be pretty."

"So, you'll do it?" Bri clasped her hands in front of her. Had it really been that easy? All that worrying and scheming for nothing.

"Do what?"

Well, maybe not. Bri's hands lowered to her sides. "Get married at the love-lock wall." She held her breath.

Casey shrugged. "Sure. Why not? That's where it all started." She winked and nudged Bri in the ribs. "And it's free, right?"

"Of course." Relief and excitement vied for first place in her soaring emotions — along with a fresh dash of hope. "I'll even discount your petit fours."

"No way! They're already practically free. I know how much you're taking off for me."

"Then I'll take off another ten percent.

This is perfect!" Business would have to pick up once word spread of a wedding — the wedding of the famous love-lock couple, no less — happening in mere weeks. The Puff would be back in the news, which would generate another rush of sales.

And bonus — it would make Charles's attempt to buy out and tear down the love-lock wall look incredibly petty. Talk about poor timing for his repeated offers. He'd have to back off if he didn't want the bad publicity. And if she remembered anything about Charles Richmond, it was that image was everything. That had to be half the reason behind his grudge — she'd made him look bad by breaking up with him, the successful lawyer.

"Look! Bubbles." Casey held up a package of a dozen. "How many, do you think? Five packs?"

"Let's get them all." Bri handed Casey several more, then piled the remaining boxes in her own arms. She was feeling more than a little generous at the moment — and giddy. "Consider it one of your wedding gifts."

Now for phase two of her plan — ensuring Casey's wedding memories stayed intact.

"The love-lock couple is getting married at the love-lock wall?" KCUP producer Adam Sikes propped his sneakered feet up on the station's long conference table. "Tell me more."

"It's in two weeks." Bri handed him the details she'd typed out during the Pastry Puff's late afternoon lull. Or rather, the entire afternoon's lull. They'd been pretty dead for a Saturday. "The time is still tentative, but it'll be held outside the Pastry Puff at the gazebo, by the love-lock wall. The whole town is invited."

Adam pulled his skinny jeans–clad legs off the table to reach forward and accept the paper. He'd run the local news station for as long as Bri could remember yet rarely seemed to age. The whole town wondered if he snuck away annually for Botox injections. "We could run a quick promo for it. I assume you're doing the cake?"

"Petit-four tower."

"Well, I'm in." He grinned. "Put me down for a plus one."

"You'll want to do more than a promo, though. Trust me."

"We always do a Friday morning shout-out for weddings, anniversaries, happy birthdays, and the like." Adam nodded. "I can squeeze this in, no problem. Everyone loves Casey."

Bri pointed to the paper in his hands, fluttering slightly in the draft from the air vent above. "There *is* a problem, though."

His eyes skimmed over it for the first time, and his voice turned wary. "A 'I don't want to touch this' kind of problem or a 'This makes it juicy' kind of problem?"

"You tell me." Bri crossed her arms and leveled her gaze at him, trying to appear confident despite her pounding heart. "Local attorney seeks to destroy wedding destination."

Adam smirked. "This isn't a newspaper, doll. We don't do headlines — we do sound bites." He tilted his head. "But I kind of like it."

"You want this scoop, trust me."

He studied the sheet. "Who's the lawyer involved?"

"Charles Richmond."

Adam squinted at her beneath a shock of dark brown hair, also speculated to be dyed. "Didn't y'all used to date?"

"That's irrelevant."

"Is it, though?" Adam leaned across the table. "Maybe we have a different scoop here. Are you seeking revenge?"

Hardly. "I broke up with him."

"Oh. Then yeah, that's irrelevant." Adam flapped the sheet of paper in her direction. "We almost had something."

She was losing him. Bri sat up straighter, heart jump-starting in defense. "You still do. A prominent town figure is trying to buy — and *destroy* — a beloved city landmark."

"Landmark?" He raised a dubious eyebrow at her.

Too far. "Okay, maybe it's not that big, but a national travel magazine is doing a write-up on us. That's noteworthy."

"Indeed. I'll give you that." Adam nodded. "Who's the travel writer?"

Bri handed him another sheet of paper, on which she'd already written Gerard's name and the phone number to the B&B. "He'll help with anything you need."

He better, anyway. He promised.

"You've been busy. KCUP?" Gerard raised an eyebrow.

"It's the station's call letters. K-C-U-P." Bri shrugged as she shut the oven door. "Their morning broadcast is 'Wake Up with KCUP.' "

Gerard ran a hand down his face and groaned as he followed her from the kitchen back into the front of the bakery. "Now I've actually heard everything."

"Oh, come on." She rolled her eyes. "You've traveled the world — surely you've heard weirder."

"Weirder? Yes. Cornier, no. Not even close."

Bri pulled on a pair of plastic gloves and began stacking macarons in the bakery display. Her plan was working — convince Casey to get married at the love-lock wall, pitch it to the local news station, gain publicity for the cause . . . and watch Charles slink away in defeat with an unsigned contract. So far, she'd gained two and a half of the three.

Hopefully the news bite would generate the uproar she needed to make Charles back off for good.

She nestled a macaron in its place on the next row. Lavender, tangerine, and chocolate — the perfect Autumn lineup. "I can't believe he already called you."

"I can't believe you had him call me at all."

She met Gerard's gaze, which looked about as weary as she felt. This feature was getting to him too. "You said you were going to help. That the article was going to be all it needed to be."

"Right. The article will be. I never said anything about going on TV."

Uh-oh. Bri hesitated. "Adam asked you to be on the show?"

"Heck no." Gerard flinched. "I'm not going to lie on TV about love and romance."

Thank goodness. The last thing they needed was more of his darkness dust sprinkled over this entire event. "Then what do you mean?"

"I mean, he alluded to how me writing this feature was a large part of why he was going to broadcast anything at all. Apparently having *Trek* behind the scenes gives the Pastry Puff more value."

"That's ridiculous. The Puff is already invaluable."

Gerard shrugged. "To you, yes. But not necessarily to the entire town and beyond."

"Everyone loves us. Everyone loved my mom." Bri rolled in her lip to stop the stream of words threatening to burst forth. She hadn't meant to go there. But it was all so inexplicably mixed together. Like trying to separate dry ingredients once they already had been dumped into the bowl.

"Bri, you've got to stop taking everything so personally. It's okay if people don't love the Pastry Puff."

But they should. She swallowed and

stacked another macaron. He didn't get it. Mr. Big-City Travel Writer had no idea about roots and home and what went into a family business. He could grab the same giant slice of pizza at any Chicago joint and be just fine. She didn't want to live that way — nothing but chains on every corner.

"The Pastry Puff — and the love-lock wall — have history." Bri's hand shook as she carefully placed the next macaron. History was precious — something people needed to start appreciating again. If she could convince Gerard, she could convince anyone.

Fat chance.

"A lot of places have history. But just because something has sentimental value to you doesn't mean it will to everyone else."

She opened her mouth to argue, then stopped. He was right.

She really hated that.

She wiped a strand of hair out of her face with the back of her gloved hand and stubbornly held on to hope. "It won't matter. People flock to what's popular. Once I represent the Pastry Puff on the news and share what's going on, they'll start coming back like they did when that video of Casey and Nathan went viral."

"Maybe." Gerard nudged his coffee cup

170

across the counter. "Hint, hint."

Bri sighed and grabbed the carafe from the warmer. "You're going to float away on free coffee — that you don't even like."

"Maybe it's growing on me." His gaze caught hers and held, and her stomach flickered.

She had misinterpreted that look once before, and she wouldn't do it again.

She calmly topped off the coffee in his half-empty mug, ignoring the stirring in her chest from his proximity. She was probably just tired and needing a hug. Not from him, though. "Maybe. Or maybe your taste buds are finally growing up."

"Or maybe the bad coffee just made them give up completely."

Bri shot him a pointed glance. "They weren't giving up during those two macarons you just devoured."

He grinned over the rim of his cup. "Touché."

She turned around with the carafe. "Anyway, as I was saying, once the town hears my side, there's no way they'll stand for Charles tearing this place down."

"You seem to be forgetting a pretty big factor here."

She fumbled to replace the carafe on the coffeepot, her emotions still wadded up from that confusing, chemistry-laden moment. "What's that?"

"If they're going to interview you on the news, they're going to interview Charles too."

The carafe jerked into place with a bang and coffee spilled over the top. She stared at the drip forming on the counter, her heart sinking.

"It's called ethical journalism, Cupcake. They have to represent both sides of the argument."

He was right again, and it wasn't any less annoying this time. Despair nipped at the hope that had finally bloomed. How had she not thought of that?

She slowly turned to face Gerard.

He peered at her over the edge of his mug. "The town will hear your side — *and* his."

CHAPTER THIRTEEN

Three days later, Gerard edged his way across the small parking lot toward the Pastry Puff. A picketer wearing gloves and holding a to-go cup of coffee in her free hand pointed her sign at him. "We like fluff! Save the Puff!"

They really needed to work on their slogans.

He held up his hands. "Hey, I'm just visiting." He was Switzerland, as it were. At least as far as Bri and Charles were concerned.

The woman offered him a gloved high five, which he politely nodded at and slipped inside the bakery.

Bri wasn't behind the counter, as he'd expected. Nor had he expected the line of people fifteen deep stretching from the cash register to the door. Mabel and Agnes were steadily ringing up customers and bagging orders, uncharacteristically quiet as they worked.

Then he saw her — cheeks flushed with excitement and hair tucked behind her ears, making her look even younger than she was. She talked animatedly with a reporter, who scribbled in his notepad. He must be with the local newspaper.

Gerard ambled up behind him, hoping to stay off the radar but wanting to get close enough to hear the conversation.

"Ever since the news ran the interview the other day, business has been booming." Bri gestured around her. She was back in that *Wanderlust* sweatshirt of hers. "I think that's all the proof Charles needs that the people of Story love the bakery and want us to stay in business."

"What do you say to Mr. Richmond's counterargument that the love-lock wall is an eyesore?" The reporter waited, pen posed. His other hand held a tape recorder under the notepad.

Gerard frowned. Who used pen and paper anymore? Didn't the staff have tablets or some kind of electronic device to take notes on? It was a small town, but come on. And why both the recorder *and* the notepad?

"That's just his opinion." Bri's chin lifted slightly. "And I happen to think he's wrong."

The reporter shifted his weight to his other leg, glancing over his shoulder before continuing. "Does the fact that Paris removed the original love-lock bridge by the Seine give Mr. Richmond's argument any merit?"

"Not to me." Bri crossed her arms. "Just because some people in France made a decision doesn't mean we have to make the same decision here. Besides, it's a totally different scale."

The reporter tilted his head. "So, you're saying that you would never imitate the French?"

Her arms fell to her side. "What? I didn't say that."

"Because you *did* imitate the French, by creating the wall in the first place. A wall they deigned worthy to remove. Are you saying you disagree with French policies?"

Bri's brow furrowed. "I love France. What are you talking about?"

"So, you confirm that you are trying to imitate a foreign country."

She shook her head. "I'm not conf —"

"You don't even love America anymore?"

Oh, for the love of —

Gerard reached out and tapped the reporter firmly on the shoulder.

Charles was behind this goof. Had to be. This guy didn't even have a badge. "Hey, Skippy. What newspaper are you with?"

The guy straightened, fumbling with the device in his hands. He had to be nineteen years old, max. Maybe twenty. He swallowed. *"The Story Press."*

Gerard crossed his arms over his chest and leveled his gaze. "What's your name?"

The kid squirmed. "Dalton Edwards."

"How long have you worked at *The Story Press*?"

"Nine months."

"Who's your boss?"

"Charles Richmond." His eyes widened. "I mean —"

Bri gasped.

Gerard nodded. "Exactly. Beat it."

Dalton's face fell, and he started to push past Gerard. "Fine."

He sidestepped to block him. "Notepad."

The kid handed it over without argument, and Gerard ripped the notated sheets from the pad before slapping it back against the guy's chest. "Recorder."

"Hey —"

"I didn't stutter." He straightened, even though he already had two to three inches on the kid.

Dalton slapped it into Gerard's open palm with a sigh.

"Let me guess. Intern?"

He nodded, edging away step by step.

Bri's eyes narrowed. "Of all the —"

"Here's some advice." Gerard leaned in close before Bri could finish her thought or the guy could bolt. "Get a real job — one where they pay you *and* where you don't have to lie and hide."

"Yes sir." Then he was gone, pushing through the line of people eager for coffee and baked goods. Gerard shook his head. Charles was retaliating for the interview, which, although it had shared his side as well, definitely didn't go over as Charles must have hoped. KCUP gave a fair representation, but the facts tilted sympathy toward Bri's side. If given the choice, what average small-town citizen wouldn't want a local, family-owned, themed bakery in place of a corporate chain?

The unfortunate fact for Bri was, there wasn't a choice here. What Bri didn't seem to realize at this point was that Charles could buy whatever he wanted as long as he had a seller. She wasn't trying to convince the town of the bakery's long-lasting merit.

She was trying to convince the two exhausted old women behind the counter.

Bri's voice jolted him back to the conversation. "How could you tell he wasn't really with the newspaper?"

"Experience." He lightly grasped Bri's

elbow and tugged her toward a free table. "You should be a little more on guard there, Cupcake. Charles isn't playing around."

She sank into an open chair and sighed. "I don't know why you call me that."

Because it fit. Because she was naive and sugary and sickeningly sweet — well, until she started verbally berating him, anyway. Then she turned spicy and savory and became much more appealing.

Not that she was appealing. Well, appealing, yes — but not tempting. His coworkers bought him a gag gift last Christmas — a T-shirt that read, *I didn't choose the Bachelor life, the Bachelor life chose me.*

He sort of wished he had it on now.

"I can't believe he sent a minion to spy on me." Bri stared over Gerard's shoulder at the front of the bakery, then shook her head. "I guess it doesn't matter."

"Be careful with whoever interviews you next. Charles isn't going to take this publicity stunt you started lightly. You can see how he's trying to twist what you say to use against you."

"Thanks for the warning. I've never done anything like this." Bri rolled in her bottom lip. "I've never had to convince someone else of something this important to me."

Gerard sat in the chair across from her,

suddenly wondering if he'd warned her of too much. He had to play both sides, or Charles would figure out he'd helped her and he'd lose the upper hand. "What would be so bad if Charles did end up buying the bakery? Other than losing your job, of course."

"I don't need the job." Fire sparked in Bri's eyes. "But it would be devastating. My mother baked here."

He could see that being important to Bri, sentimental as she was, but . . .

"Didn't she bake at home too?"

"Of course, all the time."

"And you grew up here, in Story, right?"

She nodded.

"Did you fight to save the house you grew up in?"

Bri averted her gaze and her smile faded. "No." Her soft voice trailed off, as if she'd never thought of that. "It was part of the estate. I needed to sell it — it was too much for just me to live in alone."

He waited to let the point sink in. Then he realized what she'd said before. "What do you mean you don't need the job?"

"Well, I need a job, to supplement, but I don't make that much money working here. I have inheritance money that supports me. I just work here because of my mom — and

179

because I love it." Bri shrugged. "It's who I am."

Something didn't ring true about that. He leaned forward. "Do you really think this is who you —"

He stopped. Someone was watching them. Had Dalton returned to spy? He glanced to his right just as those two white-haired love angels behind the counter stopped whispering behind their hands and snickered.

He narrowed his eyes.

They smiled.

He glared.

They beamed, their gaze bouncing back and forth between him and Bri. Then they leaned in and whispered again.

Crap.

"It's heating up, man. Sales are booming over here." He'd leave out the part about the love angels setting their sights on him and Bri. Peter would never let him live it down. At least the sisters wouldn't have time to put any Cupid-inspired plan into action. He'd be leaving in a day or two.

Not that it'd work anyway if they tried.

He'd left the bakery in a rush earlier, mumbling something to Bri about meeting his deadline. Truth was, he was spooked after that look from Mabel and Agnes. The last thing he needed was for their old-lady magic to convince Bri that he was someone she could get involved with. If she'd noticed their whisperings and winks . . .

A pen clicked on and off from the other end of the line. Peter must be editing, which he always did with a red pen instead of on his computer. Any excuse to be in his recliner — and the man always did like pointing out the errors of others. "Tell me more about this news broadcast."

Gladly, since Peter had kept steering the conversation to Bri in the moments prior.

Gerard shifted position on the B&B's porch swing, keeping his voice low and a constant eye on his surroundings. He couldn't bear to sit in that horrible red room any longer, so he'd brought his laptop to the porch to work. "Bri's on a mission — this local lawyer wants to tear down the bakery and replace it with a chain of some sort. A high-end coffee bar, or whatever."

"Really?"

He adjusted one of the sentences in his story. "Yeah, so she went to the media and stirred up the town. There are picket signs outside the bakery and the lawyer's office. She generated a big stream of sales after her TV interview."

"This is perfect."

181

Gerard's fingers froze over the keyboard. "How so?"

Peter's recliner squeaked. "I want you to stay on at least another week, get the full scoop."

Gerard's stomach clenched as if someone had punched him. "Excuse me?" A breeze rifted across the porch, but the welcome rush of cool air did little to calm the sudden heat flooding his neck.

"Maybe longer. Two weeks, max. Well, that might be extensive, but whatever it takes to see how this plays out. The feature will be all the better for it."

His heart thudded, and adrenaline shoved through his veins. He flexed his fingers. "You've got to be kidding." His frustration spiked. "You promised me —"

"Go ahead and send me what you have, ending on a hook. We'll make this a series. Corporate will love it." Peter spoke faster as his diabolical plan unfolded. "You can write part two when you see how it lands. Either way, people will flock to visit the bakery. Be it victorious — or one more time before it's demolished. Doesn't matter to me."

To him either. Except now he was stuck in the red room for another week or longer. Stuck in Story with macarons shoved down his throat every fifteen minutes and

Charles's stalking and Bri's sugary sweetness and naiveté. How had he turned into Bri's babysitter, anyway? She couldn't even handle herself with a reporter, for crying out loud.

And she did things to him . . . things that made him want to forget Remy's word of warning that day in Paris.

He was done here. His fist tightened. "Peter, I'm not —"

"I'm writing your advance on the first draft now, as promised." The pen clicked again. "Plus, an extra seventy-five."

Gerard clenched his teeth. "Ten days. Max."

"Send me the first draft by noon tomorrow."

He'd do it by midnight — just to have the final word.

CHAPTER FOURTEEN

Mabel was making Bri take the leftovers to the B&B again.

She tucked the pastry box on her hip and made her way up the stone-lined path toward the cottage. The Gingerbread House sign swung in the breeze that also ruffled her hair. If this autumn air kept up, Casey was going to have the perfect weather for her wedding the following Saturday.

She stepped carefully over the stones, so not to turn the low heel of her ankle boot in the dim evening light. Bri couldn't believe the wedding was happening so soon — and she was the town's romantic.

So why wasn't she happier for Casey?

She shifted the box to her other hip as she maneuvered the three steps to the porch. Probably because she was still a little wary of their not-so-romantic romance. She couldn't get past their proposal story — but if Casey was happy, that's all that should matter. Besides, Casey had agreed to get married at the love-lock wall, which was a crucial piece of the puzzle to save the Pastry Puff. Bri couldn't complain.

She hesitated before knocking lightly on the front door. Hopefully she could drop the pastries off with minimal small talk and leave.

And yet a tiny part of her hoped Gerard might be in the kitchen again.

He'd left so quickly earlier that afternoon after helping her out with the fake reporter. He'd said something about needing to work on the article, which seemed legit. But then he'd turned white as meringue and ran off before she could thank him for helping her with Charles's minion.

On top of that, Mabel and Agnes had been quiet all afternoon with the customers, while Bri handled the press — which didn't bode well. She couldn't even remember the last time Mabel was quiet. Maybe everyone was just having an off day. She knew she could use some extra sleep after this last whirlwind of a week.

Bri turned the doorknob.

"You can just bring those over here." The sudden male voice echoed across the porch, slicing through the silence.

Bri shrieked and dropped the dessert box.

It hit the porch floor with a thud and two petit fours turned over at her feet.

She clutched her hand to her chest to keep her pounding heart inside her rib cage and squinted toward the dusty shadows. "What in the world?"

"Geez, Cupcake, it's not like I jumped out of the bushes with a knife."

She finally made out his still form on the porch swing and took a deep breath to steady her nerves. There he went with that nickname again. She couldn't tell if she found it endearing or annoying. "You could have said something."

"I did. And you freaked."

True. She bent and picked up the bakery box. Only two had bit the dust — thankfully, the rest of the box was intact. She tucked in the cardboard flaps and straightened. "You're finally admitting you're addicted to these?"

"I'm a lot of things, but a liar isn't one of them." Gerard held out his arms and for a split second, she thought he wanted a hug. Then she snapped back to reality — the reality of her holding his new favorite food.

What was wrong with her?

She set the box in his outstretched hands and stepped to the side, away from whatever odd temptation had swooped down and

186

threatened to take her logic captive.

"Thanks." He opened the box and took a big bite of the first thing he grabbed. Icing smeared across the stubble on his chin. He either didn't notice or didn't care.

She shook her head. And to think she'd almost dove into his arms. She must be more tired than she thought. Though Gerard had been extra nice to her earlier, saving her from Charles's latest trick and giving her advice. She probably was just riding the emotional wave from that. It was rare that someone ever tried to take care of her — besides Mabel and Agnes, of course.

She leaned against the porch railing as Gerard bit into a second dessert. Macaron, this time. She still wasn't sure how she felt about his point regarding her parents' old house. She hadn't thought of that house in years — it wasn't on her radar anymore. Most of the essence of her parents was locked up in their trunk in her townhouse attic.

But the Puff . . . that was different. The bakery still carried a portion of her mother's soul. Not literally — she knew where her mother was, knew that her faith in the Lord had been real and solid, and she was with Jesus now. But her history was so tangible at the bakery. Her mom hadn't baked at the

Puff in years, but Bri could feel her presence there, much more so than anywhere else in town.

"You can sit. I don't bite." He scooted over an inch, gesturing with his half-eaten macaron. He had finally swiped off the smudge of icing.

"You can't say that to the leftovers." She eased down onto the wooden slats, careful not to touch him. She didn't trust that emotional side of her, the part that still wanted a hug and appreciated his chivalry in the bakery. Leaning against that broad, solid side of his would possibly do her in.

"I'll be honest. You've got a ways to go with the coffee. But these —" He finished the macaron. "These have officially arrived."

She didn't have the strength to argue the coffee comment. She'd just take the compliment on the other. "As long as you write the latter in the feature."

"I'll see what I can do." Gerard brushed crumbs off his dark T-shirt. Mid-November, and here he was sitting outside in short sleeves while her sweatshirt was barely warm enough to keep her comfortable.

She fought back a shiver. "How long have you been out here?"

"A few hours." He pointed to a laptop sitting on the wicker end table under the window. "Ran out of battery."

"Did you finish?" She pushed off with her feet to move the swing. Gerard lifted his boots to allow the movement.

"I've got the ending to iron out." He tilted his head back to rest against the swing's top rung. "Just wasn't ready to give up the fresh air yet."

She looked away from his strong profile and chiseled, stubbled jaw, focusing instead on the wicker strands making up the table under his computer. "I'm surprised you haven't painted the red room blue yet."

"I've debated hunter green, actually."

She laughed. "Mrs. Beeker would kill you."

"Some risks are worth taking."

She nodded slowly. "Some." Others, not so much. Change was overrated, while comfortable and safe were way underrated. Familiar was much better.

But she had a feeling the traveling man next to her wouldn't agree.

He turned his head to glance at her, still reclined back against the swing. "What risks have you taken?"

"Lately? Not many." Bri shrugged. "Been busy with the bakery." Not to mention avoiding risks in general.

"Well, you've traveled a bunch, I'm sure.

Ms. Wanderlust." He nudged her, and his elbow in her ribs sent a jolt of electricity that immediately warmed her to her core. "Let me guess. Favorite sweatshirt?"

"It is." She wasn't entirely sure how she felt about him noticing — yet she found herself slowly relaxing against his elbow, still slightly resting against her side. The warmth of his arm through her shirt spread across her torso. "But I really haven't gone anywhere."

Yet. She'd make it to Paris. Eventually.

"Why not? Money?" He sat up straighter on the swing, shifting to face her. She immediately missed his warmth. "I've got some articles in my archives I could send you about traveling on a budget." He smirked. "It's not like *Trek* sends me out with an unlimited credit card."

She shook her head. "It's not the money." She had plenty of funds to travel with, if she wanted. She just wasn't ready. She grabbed a petit four from the open box on his lap, hoping for a change in subject.

No such luck.

"Then what? Everything in your life says wanderlust. Your shirt." He pointed. "The stones outside the bakery by the fountain. That plaque on the counter by the cash register."

190

She should have taken the financial excuse and let him assume. "Just haven't had the chance to go anywhere yet." It was more than that. But he wouldn't get it. She bit into the petit four, relishing the familiar taste. Predictable.

Exactly as it should be.

"Wait a minute. You mean, you haven't been anywhere?" His voice pitched in surprise.

Her defenses spiked. "I've been to Nashville." Which was only a few hours away by plane. "It was pretty cool." A little too loud and neon for her more reserved taste, but she'd never admit that to Mr. Motorcycle.

He opened his mouth, then shut it. Then he held up one hand. "I'll probably regret this, Cupcake, but I don't get it. You're young. You're single. No baggage. You have money, and you seem more than a little obsessed with Paris. You should have gone half a dozen times already."

Her defenses grew, forming a wall. She crossed her arms over her chest. "I really don't see how this is your business."

"Probably for the best." He rested back against the swing. "You wouldn't like Paris anyway."

"What do you mean?" She sat up straight, knocking the swing off its rhythm. "Of course I'm going one day. When the time is right." She thought she'd have gone by now too. But it still held her back every time she tossed around the idea — that old rush of anxiety that took over every time she pictured herself actually flying away from Story. Pictured herself actually trading the familiar for the unknown.

She always thought she'd have a husband by now — someone to travel *with,* to help take care of her, to safely adventure with, to live out a love story like her parents'.

It didn't seem right to go to the city of love single.

"Okay, whatever." Gerard reached over and set the almost-empty bakery box on the table by his computer. "Just be ready."

She blinked at him. "Ready for what?"

"I'm telling you, you're not going to like it. You're expecting the Americanized version of Paris."

He was so arrogant. And yet . . . she had to know. "What do you mean?"

He braced one foot on the ground. "What's the first thing you'd do once you got off the plane?"

That was easy. She opened her mouth, but he quickly interrupted. "I mean, after checking in to your hotel and unpacking and ironing, because you know you were going to say that first."

She'd never have admitted it, but he was dead-on. Except for one thing. "I wouldn't iron." Not on vacation. She'd iron beforehand, of course — and hang everything in her garment bag between those wrinkle-resistant sheets she'd seen on a late-night commercial so she wouldn't have to worry about it when she got there.

"Good for you, then. No ironing. What's the first thing you'd go see?"

"The Eiffel Tower." They said it at the same time, and he shot her a pointed glance. "After that?"

She thought for a second, though she really had no hesitation. She'd mapped out her itinerary a dozen times but had never actually clicked "add to cart" on the airline website. "The love-lock wall."

"Former wall," he corrected.

"Well, yeah." The city had replaced the links with glass. No matter. She still wanted to walk in that spot, where countless of other lovers had walked. Where her parents had walked.

"See the Seine."

She nodded.

"Then let me guess? The Louvre?"

Had he snuck a peek at her list?

"Then the *Champs-Élysées*?" He snapped

his fingers. "No, wait. Next for you would be *Notre-Dame.* Church before shopping."

He was ruining this. "You think you have me all figured out."

"I do." He said it so matter-of-factly, it grated across every raw, emotional nerve the busy day — and his presence and proximity — had exposed. "You've probably never even heard of the *Parc des Buttes-Chaumont.* Or the terrace at the Printemps department store? Or the Montmartre vineyards?"

She hadn't. And she hated he was right.

"People tend to have no idea about the real heart of the city. Forget the overcrowded tourist traps — Paris is so more than just the Eiffel Tower." Gerard sighed. "It's the 59 Rivoli art district. It's the Latin quarter, the *Rue Mouffetard.* It's the one hundred and thirty-five Arago medallions scattered across the city floor."

He kept on, but she tuned him out. Why was he rubbing this in her face? He didn't understand about her mom or the bakery or even what this fight with Charles was really about.

Her irritation intensified. He just thought he could roar into Story on his motorcycle, judge everyone — and her beloved town — for being different, and psychoanalyze her along the way? All while bragging about what he'd seen and done that was so much better?

She stood abruptly. "Look, maybe I haven't traveled anywhere yet. Maybe I haven't checked off my bucket list or heard of all these secret spots in Europe. But at least I have roots." She pointed. "You're the one running, Mr. Travel Writer."

He didn't answer. And it irked her further.

"You think the traveling bachelor life makes you so cool. Makes you better than everyone here with their quirky hair and bad coffee and eccentric hobbies. So what? We're unique. And we're a town family."

He started rocking the swing, silently, still refusing to answer.

"Everyone here was there for me when my parents died. That's worth holding on to." The words tumbled faster, building with indignation. "Who cares if I haven't made it to Paris yet? At least I'm not afraid to stay in one spot."

Silence.

She straightened the hem of her sweat-shirt, pulling it taut so the words were evident. "Maybe you should wear this shirt. What are you running from anyway? The police?"

He rolled his eyes.

"Debt?"

He ignored her.

"Love."

He met her gaze then, jaw tight. "You done yet, Cupcake?"

"Almost. Once." She'd done it again — thrown something hurtful in his face because of carelessness. Because of frustration.

Regret threatened her indignation, and she shoved it aside. It wasn't fair. She shouldn't have to feel bad for Gerard's probing comments into her life. He'd started it, pushing her to talk about private heart issues and her past.

If he didn't want to take it, he shouldn't dish it out. He was like Mr. Darcy, pre-redemption.

"Yeah, trust me. I'm done." Done with his incorrigibility and stubbornness and arrogance. Done with her wishing he'd notice her — *really* notice her — and hating the fact that she wanted him to. Her small town wasn't enough for his wanderlust, and never would be.

She gestured toward his laptop. "You said your feature is almost done. So, congrats. Soon you can head out on your next reality-denying adventure and forget you ever met us."

She pressed her lips together, but the words had already escaped. It was like she got in his presence and was immediately overcome with word vomit. No one had ever stirred her ire like that.

But he'd be gone soon, and it wouldn't matter anymore.

"I actually just got asked today to turn the feature into a two-part series." Gerard's quiet voice broke the stillness and interrupted the pounding of her heart. "I'm here for another week or so."

He was right.

The clock inched toward midnight as Bri clicked slowly through the Parisian images on the computer screen. Everything that appealed to her was just as Gerard had predicted. The art museums. The churches. The bicycling paths and the Eiffel Tower. It was all the stereotypical, American view of Paris.

After all her reading and dreaming, she'd prided herself an expert on the city by now. But as she clicked through the happy faces taking selfies in front of the various popular landmarks, she realized the truth — she didn't know a thing about the real city of love. What had Gerard mentioned? The *Parc des Buttes-Chaumont* and a terrace at some department store?

She'd never even heard of those places.

She soaked in the photos before her — of lush green parks and wildflowers, of bronze medallions and statues, of captivating fountains and funky graffitied walls, of elegant rooftop bars and restaurants — and felt like she was staring at a stranger.

What else had she assumed incorrectly? She'd been naive to the reporter at the Puff. Maybe she'd been blind to other things along the way too. Was that how Gerard saw her? Incapable, boring, ignorant?

Why did she even care what he thought?

She pressed her fingers against her forehead. Maybe it was the late hour, or the boiling mix of emotions hovering below the surface, but regardless, regret started a slow seep into her heart.

Ten more days.

Ten more days of Gerard's confusing invasion in her town. Yet wasn't he doing her a favor? Just hours ago, she'd been so grateful for his help. He was writing favorably about her favorite place on earth. Just because he wasn't sold on it personally didn't mean the feature wouldn't be lifesaving for the bakery. He had promised he'd do a good job. And just because he had his arrogant moments didn't give her any reason to assume he'd go back on his word.

The seep of regret morphed into an all-out flow.

Gerard couldn't have intended to be cruel earlier on the swing. He just had no idea how much she longed to be like her mother. How she wished she could be brave and leave everything to pursue a dream and see what blessings waited on the other side — like when her mom left Story to learn how to bake in Paris and met her dad.

And then she did it again when she left Paris and moved back to Story after learning she was pregnant with Bri, trading the familiar and safe for adventure and risk.

Bri had never been anywhere but Nashville. The biggest risk she took was wearing peep-toe shoes in October. She couldn't even figure out a simple secret ingredient to an age-old recipe that was supposed to be in her DNA.

Tears pricked her eyes, and she abruptly shut down her computer.

Maybe she was nothing like her mom after all.

CHAPTER FIFTEEN

Bri's skin was so thin, it was a wonder she wasn't see-through.

Gerard lowered the kickstand on his bike, then pulled the books he'd checked out on Story from his backpack and started across the library parking lot to the outside return chute.

It'd been two days since his encounter on the porch with Bri. In those two days, he'd sent Peter his first draft, received an overnighted check, sent his mom her portion through PayPal, and thought nonstop about Bri's reaction to his comments. He'd just been making small talk. Then when she brought up how she'd never gone anywhere, well — it was worth asking about. How could someone in her position *not* travel? It was downright ludicrous.

Her comments about him running and avoiding roots was beside the point.

He wondered if she was still upset with

him. Had she cooled down in the last two days? Gotten over her shock at his hanging around for another week? Or had she just taken the time to stew?

Regardless, he had to finish this second part of the feature or he could kiss his desired promotion at *Trek* goodbye — which was *not* an option. He wanted to write things that mattered. It was fine boasting about exotic locales and challenging others to eat spicy cuisine and go ziplining over rapids for now, but he had things to say that counted for something.

And no one to hear them.

Gerard glanced both ways across the parking lot, pausing to let a minivan pass before closing the distance to the drop-off chute. This feature could go either way at this point — the love-lock wall saves the bakery, love conquers all, and Casey's on-site wedding serves as a victorious, happily ever after or Charles dishes out enough dough to convince the sisters to sell, leaving the second half of the series to serve as a farewell to an outdated, once-beloved concept.

Sort of like marriage, if he thought about it.

Charles had been laying low as far as he could tell since sending his poser intern to trip up Bri. But backing off seemed way out of character for him. He probably had more calculated tricks up his sleeve — the question was, what exactly did he expect in exchange for that money he slipped Gerard at Taylor's? If Bri could be talked out of the entire ordeal, she would have been by now by Charles himself. Besides, Gerard didn't take underhanded bribes by anyone — especially not weasel lawyers in small towns.

It really didn't matter what Charles intended, though. Tempting as it was to send that money to his mom, Gerard planned to give it back — as soon as he could swing by the guy's office.

He shoved the books through the dropbox chute, then realized about three seconds too late that he'd sent the keys to his motorcycle down with them.

Figured. Now he'd have to go inside the library, swallow some crow, and ask the librarian to dig his keys from the drop box. Perfect.

He set his helmet on his bike seat, hiked his backpack onto his shoulder, and headed inside.

A rush of warm air greeted him as he entered through the automatic doors. There was a line at the front desk — a mom with a handful of kids, an elderly man wearing an argyle sweater, and two college-aged students loaded down with textbooks.

He tried to slip up to the front of the line. "Ma'am? I really need —"

"It'll be just a moment." The librarian didn't even look at him as she continued pecking at the keyboard.

Oh well. Might as well check out the sci-fi section that he never made it to last time. He ambled toward the novels, dodging a kid in a backward ball cap who had barreled out of the children's section.

He'd just picked up an older novel by his favorite author when her voice carried over the rows.

Bri.

He snapped the book shut and checked his watch. Thursday night.

Book club.

Who did book club every week? These people were serious. He bit back a groan. He'd have to face Bri sooner or later — after all, he was stuck in Story for part two.

He cocked his head, listening. Surely they were off *Pride and Prejudice* by now. But it wasn't the book club — it sounded more like a one-on-one conversation.

Bri's voice, lower this time, sounded again from around the corner. "Have you tried surprising him? You know, with his favorite meal or a date night?"

The second voice murmured quieter, the first half of her response muted. The last part he heard loud and clear. ". . . but he doesn't seem interested anymore. He just wants to work all the time."

"I wouldn't worry about it. You probably just need some romance." Bri's soft voice turned consoling.

Gerard frowned. Hardly. If a husband was staying at work all the time, it was for more than just a lack of romance. They probably needed a counselor — or at least some healthy conversation and hard truth.

Bri pushed further. "I bet there's a book here with some ideas for couples. Or hey, I could make his favorite cake and you could take it home to decorate for him."

"Thanks, Bri. You always know what to say. That's a great idea." The second voice muffled as if they'd hugged. "I'll see you next week." A few more muted comments, then footsteps drifted away.

Relief flooded him. At least Bri had left. Now he wouldn't have to point out what a ridiculous —

Bri suddenly rounded the bookshelf corner, a smile on her face. Then her gaze collided with his and her contented smile quickly vanished. "Gerard?"

He shouldn't. But he couldn't help it. "That's a horrible idea."

Her lips — glossy pink — parted. "That was a private conversation. What are you doing here?"

"Technically, the cake idea itself isn't that horrible." Gerard braced one arm on the bookshelf, ignoring the obvious. "Any guy would eat it and appreciate it, more than likely."

"What are you even talking about?" She blinked hard, as if that could make him go away. That answered his question as to whether she was still upset with him.

This conversation probably wasn't helping. But she was so wrong — and she was going to drag the women of Story down with her fairy-dust illusions of reality. "Listen to me. No man is going to take a cake as a sign of trying to fix a relationship."

She lifted her chin, stubbornness personified. "Sure he will."

"I'm a man, Cupcake. I'm telling you, never in a million years."

"Right. Mr. Expert on romance, here. Flowers wilt when you walk past." Bri crossed her arms over her pale peach top. "What do you suggest, then?"

"Do you really think everything is so easily fixed with romance? With a lock on a wall or a surprise date?" Gerard pointed toward where Bri had been talking to the anonymous woman. "They need solid counseling. There's a reason he's MIA."

"Not necessarily. They just lost the spark." Bri shrugged. "They've been married several years. It happens."

"And you know this from experience?"

She averted her eyes. "I've heard."

"It can happen, sure." Gerard caught her gaze. "But I *know.*"

Boy, did he know. Kelsey's inattentiveness had led him to make choices — bad ones. Not the same as hers, but unfair ones, nonetheless. If she would have talked to him instead of reaching out elsewhere . . . "Men are intentional, Bri. He's not working more because he loves his job so much."

"Maybe they need more money?"

He raised his eyebrows at her. "Do they?"

She shook her head slowly, tucking her hair behind her ear. "Why are you even telling me this?"

"Because you steered your friend wrong. She needs to have a real conversation with this guy, not cater to him with his favorite toys. If he's staying away, there's an issue that needs to be dealt with. Hopefully a minor one."

She opened her mouth, the familiar fire

from last night once again lighting her eyes. Then something flickered across her expression so fast that he almost wondered if he'd imagined it. She snapped her mouth shut and nodded. "Okay."

"Okay?" Wait a minute. That was easy — too easy. He narrowed his eyes. "What do you mean, okay?"

She adjusted the strap on her purse. "I mean, okay. I hear you. Maybe you're right."

He was right. But her realizing that so readily seemed wrong.

Bri swung back by the bakery after leaving the library. Mabel had texted in her clumsy, not-so-tech-savvy way full of typos and misused emojis, and asked her to make sure she and Agnes had locked up. The older woman couldn't remember if they had done it before they'd left for the night an hour or so earlier, and they worried about a break-in.

Highly unlikely in Story. No one locked any doors, and besides, they didn't even leave any desserts in the display overnight, much less cash in the register. What could anyone want?

Regardless, she'd appease Mabel. Whatever gave her peace of mind.

For a moment, Bri hesitated. Was this a

sign of the sisters getting ready to sell? Were their memories slipping? They were in great health for their ages, but Bri knew they couldn't go on full speed forever. Still, somehow, in the back of her mind, she had always assumed she'd just take over when that unfortunate day came. Surely they'd leave the Puff to Bri in their will.

But if they were considering Charles's offer, was that truly the case?

Bri pulled into the bakery parking lot and cut the engine. Crickets chirped in the sudden stillness, and she momentarily rested her head against the seat, exhausted from the mental debate. The night's events played vividly like slides on a projector screen.

She'd wanted to ream Gerard at the library for eavesdropping and offering his unwanted two cents — but something about the look in his eyes when he said he *knew* stole the pending indignation right from her lips. She couldn't help but think of his earlier comments, about how he must have been burned at some point, and she just couldn't bring herself to prove his opinion about women and love and romance correct by spewing back.

So, she'd swallowed her pride — and her gum, on accident — and taken the high road. Accepted his unsolicited advice and calmly walked away.

Then she frantically called her friend's cell to encourage counseling, because what if he really did know? It still irked her that he'd been right about her expectations of Paris. What else was he right about?

It was all just too much to think about right now. She wanted to go home, take a hot bath, and read their latest book club find in bed — and forget all about Gerard Fortier.

Bri opened her car door and headed for the front door of the bakery just as headlights cut through the darkness. She squinted. Make that one headlight.

She turned at the door of the bakery and shielded her eyes from the sudden brightness. The vehicle turned a tight donut and parked next to hers, tires skidding.

But it wasn't a car. It was a motorcycle. A dark figure emerged from the back of it — Gerard.

"Are you okay?" He rushed toward her, one hand resting on his back pocket.

She blinked, but the image charging directly at her didn't change. "Are you kidding me?" Bri, heart racing with fury and frustration, planted her hands on her hips. He was everywhere — literally everywhere. "What in the world are you —"

He stretched out one arm and used it to quickly flatten her against the wall, just to the left of the bakery door. He pressed his back against the wall beside her, his breath tight. The dim porch bulb highlighted his tense expression, and a muscle in his jaw twitched. "Did you see anyone?" His other hand still rested cautiously behind him, his gaze flickering to the right and left.

"Is that a gun?" Her eyes widened.

"Shh."

That was it. He'd lost it — everyone had lost it. Had she somehow made a left turn and accidentally fallen down Alice's rabbit hole?

She shoved his arm away. "*Shh,* or what — the crickets will call the cops? There's no one here. Are you even allowed to have that thing?"

"Yes," he hissed. "Now, shut up. We don't know if the intruder is gone."

"What intruder?" Her heart rate quickened. Irony of ironies. Of all the nights for Mabel to be unsure of the door. "Someone really did break into the bakery?" She couldn't believe it. She pressed back against the wall, straining to hear evidence.

But there was only silence — plus a cricket choir and the sound of Gerard chewing gum.

"I don't know." He was still whispering. "Mabel called and said she thought some-one was prowling around and asked if I'd come check it out. Said she was worried about the media having stirred up negative attention."

Negative attention . . . Bri frowned. That didn't sound like Mabel. She had been more concerned about what lipstick color she wore for her TV debut than about something bad happening as a result of the publicity. That almost sounded more like Agnes.

Wait a minute.

Bri reached over and tested the bakery door.

Locked. Of course.

The love angels had struck again.

Bri groaned as reality dawned. "It was me."

"Huh?" Gerard still had one hand in his back pocket.

Bri swatted at his wrist. "Stop it with that thing. *I'm* the prowler."

He frowned. "You have keys. And you work here. What are you talking about?"

"I meant, we've been set up. Mabel told me to come and make sure she'd locked up for the night."

"She lied? To get me to come here too?"

Bri waited.

Understanding finally dawned in his eyes, and his hand slipped empty to his side. "Nice. Clever ol' love angels." He shook his head. "I wondered why she didn't just call the police."

"Why would she, when she has a willing Robo Cop right down the street at the B&B?" Bri snorted. "This is a new extreme, even for them." She wasn't sure if she was offended or impressed. Maybe both. Definitely impressed at the way Gerard had come ready for a fight — for her sake. Well, for Mabel's, anyway.

Maybe both?

"I guess I don't need this." He patted his back pocket.

She tucked her hair behind her ears, willing her adrenaline to come back down — and her thoughts of chivalrous Gerard to chill out. "Why do you even have that thing?"

He shrugged. "I got my conceal and carry license a few years ago, did some training courses. It comes in handy when traveling the world and getting yourself into various situations."

She smirked. "Like ticking off various people with your explicit honesty?"

"That too."

Bri pulled out her keys and held up the one to the bakery door. "While we're here . . . macaron?"

He raised his eyebrows. "I thought you didn't leave desserts in the bakery overnight — that's why you're always delivering to the B&B."

"We don't. But I have a few in the fridge from this morning, from my experimental batch." Failed batch, but they would be edible.

Gerard nodded. "Why not? I think we've earned it."

She unlocked the door, then hesitated before opening it fully. "Put the gun away while I get the macarons ready?"

He looked like he might argue but didn't. Miracle.

"Deal."

Gerard met Bri back inside just as she arranged the colorful macarons on a paper napkin at one of the bakery tables. "What, is all the hot-pink china dirty?"

She smiled, a real smile, and he couldn't ignore the jittery feeling that ricocheted through him at the sight of it. Very unexpected and unwanted. Must be the adrenaline still coming down from the alleged intruder scare.

He sank into the nearest chair. "Is this a peace offering, or are you still mad at me?"

"It's hard to be mad at someone who galloped up on a metal steed to rescue me."

"Chrome. Chrome steed."

"Whatever." She wrinkled her nose. "Plus, the longer I think about it, the more I realize that, in your own twisted way, you were just trying to help my friend at the library."

"Something like that." That, along with correcting Bri's misguided views. It was only going to hurt her in the long run. She didn't deserve that.

He took a bite of macaron, paused, then took another. "This is different than last time." Not worse. But different.

He took a third bite. But maybe not better.

"Cinnamon in that one. No almond this time." She tilted her head. "And I think a dash of raspberry."

"Interesting."

"Is it good?"

He nodded, his mouth full.

"Not good enough, though." She took a frustrated bite of a yellow macaron on the napkin. "It still isn't right."

He'd be happy to take all the wrong ones, then. "What did you mean by 'experimental'?"

"I've been trying to find a missing ingredient my mom used — a secret recipe." She pointed to the pink macaron that was next in line. "That one has a bit of rosewater."

On second thought, maybe not *all* the wrong ones. He skipped over it and picked up the brown one. "Chocolate?"

"Ganache. That one was just for fun."

He liked that one. He finished it in two bites. "What's the deal with the secret recipe?"

"My mother's macarons were luscious. Downright legendary." Bri closed her eyes. "I can remember them like yesterday. But I can't place the missing ingredient. It's savory, and light, and not chocolate — but sort of like chocolate's cousin."

It sounded amazing. He could almost taste it too, the way she was describing it.

"They were comforting." Bri opened her eyes, defeat shadowing her expression. "I've researched off and on for years, playing around with different recipes, googling. Nothing. I might never know what it was."

"Nah, you'll get it. Just keep trying. And who knows what yummy mistakes you might create along the way?" He pointed to the rose macaron. "But hey, some mistakes are actually just mistakes. Remember that."

"Very funny."

He wasn't joking, but he'd let that one go. "What's in the darker pink one?"

She stared at it. "Honestly, I can't remember. But I know it wasn't right."

Was she a perfectionist with everything in her life, or just the things that had to do with her mom? He suddenly really, really wanted to know. But prying into her life hadn't gone so well the last few times he'd tried it, and he didn't want to throw off this truce vibe they had going.

"Did your mom ever bake?" Her eyes met his, the question slicing through his childhood like a carving knife through a turkey.

He swallowed. "No."

"Why not?"

So much for the subtle don't-pry messages. She apparently wasn't going to return the favor. His mouth went dry, and he suddenly wished he had coffee — even the Puff's bitter version. "I don't know."

But he did know. She didn't have time to be a Pinterest mom, or whatever version of that existed in the early 1990s. She worked her rear off to provide for him, countless hours at the diner or cleaning houses on the side, for minimum wage and meager tips — and spent the rest of the time trying to find him a replacement dad. When that hadn't worked, and she kept getting older and more exhausted, she defaulted to simply trying to find someone to care about her. Long nights turned into overnights and bruises on her cheekbones and alcohol-laced, pleading excuses for him to forgive her absence.

Not exactly prime opportunity to roll out some cookie dough from scratch.

Bri leaned forward slightly and squinted at him, her long hair falling across her slim shoulders. "You don't lie very well."

His jaw tightened. "Good."

She tilted her head. "That's a good trait to have, I suppose."

"No, I was correcting you. You should have said, 'You don't lie good.' Not 'well.' "

"Whatever!"

"It's true."

"You should know basic grammar, Mr. Travel Writer."

"Why? From my subscription to *Grammar Weekly*?"

She swatted at him. "Look it up."

"You look it up." He leaned back in his chair, casually raking the crumbs from the table onto the floor. Bri was right, of course, and from the way she eagerly pressed buttons into her phone, she would have visible proof here in about fifteen seconds.

No worries. His shoulder tension eased.

He'd gladly sacrifice being right for the invaluable gift of a subject change.

That particular subject change brought three more in its wake, and by the time midnight rolled through and they reluctantly locked up the bakery, Gerard felt the faint remains of a fairy tale hovering over him the entire way to his motorcycle. Okay, so maybe more like a Brothers Grimm tale. A little darker and edgier than the current stuff. But something — *something* — was happening between him and Bri, quicker than he cared to admit. Like worn pages of a book, flipping faster and faster. He wanted to shove a bookmark in place and yell, "Wait!"

He also wanted to see how it ended.

Gerard straddled his bike and lifted one hand in a wave as Bri climbed into her car. Was she on the same page? Did it even matter? Regret lightly tapped his shoulder. When was the last time he'd openly shared about his mother to a woman he cared about?

Cared about?

Crap.

He waited until Bri's headlights faded from view before cranking his engine. His stomach knotted. This was such a bad idea, this thing between them, however developing it might be. He was messy. His background. His mom. His current situation. All messy. Even for the Brothers Grimm.

He gripped the handlebars of his bike and eased toward the road, swallowing hard. Whatever story he thought he might be reading, best to shut the book now. Before someone got hurt.

Again.

Before he got hurt again.

CHAPTER SIXTEEN

Bri couldn't sleep.

She crept across the attic loft toward the trunk, drawn as always by the late hour and the insatiable thirst for something emotionally solid, sturdy.

Gerard — well, he was getting harder to read by the moment. First, he kept invading her space, offering his unsolicited advice and generally butting into her business and acting like she was such a burden to him.

Then he was the first to rush to her rescue — however unnecessary it'd been — to protect her and her favorite place on earth. All that just days after having made fun of her for never traveling and basically declaring it didn't matter whether Charles bought the bakery.

If he were a book, he'd be written in a foreign language — and most definitely not French.

But some things *were* dependable — like

her parents' romance. She'd just focus on that for a bit until she felt more centered. It'd always worked before, after a breakup or a bad date or lonely nights wondering if her prince would ever come. Of course, prayer helped too. But sometimes it was nice to hold a tangible reminder that her story wasn't over yet.

Bri pulled the stack of letters free of the trunk. She shut the lid, nestled into her beanbag chair, and decided to mix it up a bit. This time she grabbed a letter toward the middle of the stack.

She tugged it from the others, smiling at the letter's seeming resistance to let go, and gently opened the creased fold.

Fairest love,

Your beauty is like the Seine. Steady, constant, fluid. I can't wait to walk beside you once again, to appreciate your beauty up close. I miss you tremendously. You are the breath in my lungs that keeps me alive. Without the hope of your love, I would cease to exist.

Until we meet again.

From Paris, with love

Bri tucked the letter back into place and pulled another one free. Letter after letter, she read, absorbing the love that flowed from her father to her mother, the poetic rhythm of the words that pulsed directly from his heart. Her father had such a sweet, sensitive side she rarely got to witness firsthand, but knowing these letters existed had reminded her, since his death, how deep still waters could be. How everyone had multiple layers to their soul, despite a gruffer exterior.

Her thoughts flitted to Gerard, and she quickly focused back on the letter.

Her father had really pined for her mother. He clearly missed her badly while he was gone to France. The inheritance settlement from his dad's passing had taken almost a year to come through, from what she remembered her mom talking about when she was younger. It must have been a tough time for her mother — to be back in America alone with a toddler to raise, unable to comfort her husband mourning his father's death in another country.

They were so brave. Young, in love, and courageous against all odds. It was a love worth holding out for. Surely it could exist again, in its own form, for her story.

Surely.

Bri kept reading, then yawned, covering her mouth with her hand. One more letter, then she really needed to go to bed. She'd regret this late-night cram session in the morning if she didn't stop.

She pulled another one from the back half of the pile.

My dearest flower,

It's been too long since our last memory. Yet I'll never stop writing to you. I'll never stop dreaming, or remembering. Time can steal a lot of things, but it cannot — will not — steal my love. That is timeless.

I'll never forget you or our last night together. It's permanently embedded in my heart, as are you. Never doubt your position there, my Queen.

Always yours.

From Paris, with love

She studied the letter — the loops and tucks of the scrawled, familiar handwriting — and sighed. Such passion. They couldn't afford in those early years of marriage to travel back and forth, or she'd have bet her father would have been racking up the frequent flyer miles that year.

But they'd made it, and clearly absence had made their hearts grow fonder.

Gerard was leaving in a week.

Not that she would miss him.

Why had she even thought that?

She quickly closed the letter and dropped it in her distracted haste. It fluttered a foot away, and with a sigh, she bent over to retrieve it from her beanbag throne. The beans shifted as she leaned, as if giving her an extra boost toward her goal.

The letter lay on the dusty attic floor, closed, the crease slightly off center. The bottom half of the page hung slightly ajar from the top, underlining the signature — her favorite part of her father's letters. The consistent "from Paris, with love" brought feelings of comfort and security.

Some things never changed, and that was one of them.

She ran her fingers over the familiar phrase. Then she frowned and looked closer. A slight smudge lay behind the word *from,* as if someone had tried to erase a previous penciled sentiment and written over it.

She stood and held the letter up to the dim attic light, squinting through the old, wrinkled paper, and could just make out two smudged, tightly scrawled capital letters.

T.R.

The paper fluttered from her grasp back to the attic floor. Her chest constricted. The room tilted, and she sank back, the beanbag catching her before she fully collapsed.

Those weren't her father's initials.

"I'm sure you're just misunderstanding, dear." Mabel poured Bri a second cup of coffee and nudged her breakfast muffin closer to her on the table. "People erase things all the time."

She stared at the blueberries dotting the whole wheat muffin. She'd gotten up that morning in a trance, still hungover from both the lack of sleep and the surge of emotions from her discovery the night before, and had somehow stumbled into the bakery on time — sans makeup, back in her *Wanderlust* sweatshirt that she wasn't sure was clean or dirty, and cutoff jeans with flip-flops.

She hadn't realized her feet were cold until she was halfway through baking the morning's orders. Then Mabel and Agnes had come in, a little earlier than usual, and started mothering her after realizing something was wrong. Mabel had even gone out to her car and gotten her pair of hot-pink slippers she'd left in her trunk. They had glittery unicorn horns on the toes.

"Sure, people erase things. But they don't typically erase their initials from love letters." Not unless they had something to hide. Bri picked a blueberry from the muffin and popped it in her mouth, unable to taste the tartness.

On that note, she probably shouldn't have baked this morning — the dozens of macarons and petit fours and sugar cookies waiting to be frosted had probably all suffered from her distracted state. Casualties of war.

"I'm sorry, I can't even focus with those ridiculous slippers in my line of sight." Agnes leaned against the counter of the empty bakery, arms crossed. Her no-nonsense, elastic-waisted khaki pants were hiked up a little higher than usual, her feet shod in black loafers. "Mabel, why do you even own those?"

"Because floral patterns are so boring. As are navy and cream. Those were the only options in the store, so I ordered these online instead." Mabel smiled. "And they matched my new lipstick."

Bri didn't even care. "I'll take them off." She started to slide her foot from the warmth of the slipper, but Mabel grabbed her arm.

"Of course you won't. Agnes, don't be ridiculous. She's in shock." She frowned at her sister.

"Because of a smudge on a letter?" Agnes

let out a *tsk.* "Don't cater to her fantasy, Mabel. I'm sure it's nothing."

"You're just grumpy because Mr. Hansen hasn't been by in a few days." Mabel rolled her eyes.

Agnes huffed and her neck flushed red. "Poppycock."

"How do you know it's nothing?" Bri's voice cracked and she hated how frail she sounded — how frail she felt. Especially in front of Agnes — who possibly had a point. Everything was speculation right now, and she was very possibly jumping to huge conclusions.

But what explanation was there? Bri crossed her arms, unable to get warm despite the bulky material of her sweatshirt.

"Clearly, your father was starting to write something else, then realized he should stick to the usual." Agnes shrugged. "Like I always say — if it isn't broken, why fix it?"

"But they were initials. T.R."

Agnes crossed her arms. "Fine. What if he had been about to write 'truly yours'?"

Maybe. But . . . "In all capital letters?" The explanation didn't ring true.

Mabel nodded eagerly. "Cursive is different — and remember, this was years ago. Maybe he was trying something new. Or maybe he was tired and started writing the

227

wrong word. He'd just poured out his heart, after all. I'm sure that's emotionally draining."

Finding out her mother had potentially been receiving love letters from another man was also incredibly draining.

Mabel took a sip of her coffee, leaving a smudge of lip color on the edge of the mug. "People are allowed mistakes."

True. After all, didn't Bri make a mistake every time she attempted to re-create her mother's macaron recipe? Or every time she allowed Gerard to stir her frustration and lashed out verbally?

Wait. Was Mabel talking about the mistake of writing the wrong word or the mistake of an affair? That made a difference.

She really didn't want to think about this anymore.

Bri stood up, took a bite of the blueberry muffin, and tried to shake off the melancholy that clung like static. "You're probably right. Both of you."

Agnes nodded, as if to agree that of course she was. Mabel offered a sympathetic frown. "You're just tired, honey. You said you were up late reading — everything looks worse when you're exhausted."

Also true. Her "aunts" were pretty wise — and they had known her mom well. If they weren't worried, why should she be?

Yet as Bri headed to the kitchen to resume her baking activities, she couldn't shake the feeling that somehow everything had just shifted.

And it might never shift back.

Gerard figured Bri would be back at Taylor's again Friday morning for pizza, and his journalist instincts were correct. Someone didn't eat pizza for breakfast without it being at least a semi-regular tradition.

He needed to get a few more quotes from her for the second part of the feature and confirm a few of the specifics for Casey's wedding. He would much rather ask Bri than the bride-to-be. After their false alarm and truce in the bakery last night, he looked forward to seeing her.

He also needed to prove to himself that last night's mash-up of feelings was nothing more than a bad combination of a late-night sugar rush and platonic bonding over family drama. He found her in the back-corner booth, facing the wall. Her golden hair, normally cascading over her shoulders, was tucked into a messy ponytail. He frowned. Were those shorts — in November? He averted his eyes from her long legs and slid into the booth across from her — platoni-cally.

She met his gaze with red-rimmed eyes, not even a flicker of surprise registering. "Hey."

He tucked his laptop bag on the seat beside him. "You look like you got as much sleep as I did." Then he looked closer. Untouched pizza. Bags under her eyes. Pale face.

And that *Wanderlust* sweatshirt.

What could have happened overnight to merit this? His resolve not to care too much wafted away like the smell of burnt bacon. "Are you okay?"

She nodded, looking back at the single slice on her plate. She poked at a pepperoni.

"Is it Charles? Are you losing the war?" Maybe he'd launched a media sneak attack overnight. He'd been waiting for Charles to pop back up with a new scheme, but aside from a few posters stuck around town advertising the potential of the upcoming chain, he'd laid relatively low.

Which was good, because Gerard still needed to swing by Charles's office to give him back that cash he'd slipped him — and he didn't want any drama. But it was also bad, because how was he going to write an exciting conclusion to his two-part series in

Trek if there was no drama or exciting conclusion?

"No, it's not Charles." Bri rubbed her hands over her face, which was free of makeup except for something glossy on her lips. Freckles he'd never seen before dotted her nose. They just added to her charm and innocence. "I'd almost forgotten about him."

Gerard's eyebrows shot up. Forgetting about Charles? He had been her priority since the moment he'd met her. Something was way off. "Okay, level with me. What's wrong?"

"Nothing. Maybe. Hopefully, anyway." She pulled a pepperoni free of its cheesy prison. "You wouldn't understand."

He leaned back in the booth, crossing his arms over his chest. "Well, it doesn't sound like you fully understand either, Cupcake."

She glared at him as she popped the pepperoni in her mouth. "Quit calling me that."

Relief flooded his veins. *There* was the Bri he knew. The one who was going to get him in trouble if he didn't put up a guardrail. He'd never been this invested in an article subject before. He'd interviewed shark cage divers, restaurant owners in Fiji, hula dancers, mountain bike designers, YouTube hiking experts, you name it — and never once

231

had he checked on one having a bad day.

Nor given one a nickname.

A band of something suspiciously like fear tightened around his chest. Maybe last night had been exactly what he thought it'd been.

Gerard opened his mouth, but words wouldn't come. The noise of the diner — the clanking of silverware, the buzz of low conversation, the screech of chair legs sliding across the floor, the fuss of a toddler two tables back — faded to a low murmur. His heartbeat roared in his ears, and his mouth dried.

She watched him, as if she could sense his fear. Blood in the water. He'd never had a weakness around women before. Not since Kelsey, especially.

He couldn't afford to start now.

But the way she stared at him was almost his undoing. Vulnerable and seeking, as if he held some kind of answer. As if he could bring her hope and fix all her unspoken problems if he only knew which questions to ask. He sort of wished he could.

And that terrified him more than anything else.

She kept her blue-eyed gaze riveted on him, lips parted slightly. He was suddenly overcome by the urge to see if that pale pink gloss tasted as sweet as it looked.

He swallowed. "Bri —"

"There you are!" Casey appeared at their table, sliding into the seat beside Bri and bumping her over with her hip. "I had to tell you first. Well, second, because I had to tell the preacher first." Her face flushed, and her eyes shone under the lid of her red ball cap. "We moved up the wedding."

"Up? As in, sooner?" Bri's gaze shifted from Gerard to Casey, surprise pitching her previously monotone voice.

"Yes! Nathan had a scheduling conflict with another guy at the fire station — long story." Casey flipped her hand dismissively, as if the details weren't important. As if this wasn't her actual wedding day she was talking about rearranging. Gerard wasn't sure if he was concerned or impressed at how chill she was about it — the exact opposite of a bridezilla. Interesting.

Casey crossed her arms on the table and leaned forward, bouncing a little in the booth. "So, to help make it easier on everyone, we're getting married Sunday."

"Sunday." Bri's face paled a shade lighter. "As in, this Sunday?"

"Yes!" Casey beamed.

Uh-oh. Gerard glanced at his watch. "You mean, the day after tomorrow?"

"Yes!" Casey grabbed Bri's arm and shook

it. "You'll still be able to get the petit-four tower ready by then, right?"

"Of course." She didn't hesitate, but Gerard saw the flicker of doubt in her eyes. Whatever was going on with her was still attempting to take priority, but being Bri, she was going to push past it for the sake of someone else. He'd never met anyone who was such a pushover. He frowned. Or was it just plain selflessness on her part?

Maybe both. There had to be a balance, though, and Bri teetered precariously toward the extreme. Did she always get taken advantage of in Story?

"You're the best." Casey squealed and hugged Bri before popping back out of the booth. "I'll come by tomorrow and help get stuff cleaned and set up outside by the wall."

"You better not." Bri pointed at Casey. "You better be getting your nails done and pampering yourself, like every other bride the day before her wedding. I can handle the setup. Just have the chairs and tables delivered ASAP, and I'll get everything in place. In fact, I'll start this afternoon."

She was going to decorate the grounds *and* bake all the petit fours? Fat chance. "I'll help." The words cleared his lips before he could take them back or fully consider their repercussions.

Casey's eyebrows raised a notch. "Really?"

"Of course." He glanced at Bri, but his mimicking of her own words didn't seem to register with her.

"Awesome." Casey leaned over and slapped him a high five. "You guys are the best! It takes a village, you know?"

Apparently.

"I'll see you soon. Text me if you want to tag along for a pedi." She hugged Bri again before dashing off, humming "Here Comes the Bride."

Like Bri would have time for something like doing her nails in the midst of all this sudden chaos. How in the world was she going to manage to pull this off?

He glanced back at her, but she wouldn't look at him, keeping her eyes trained on her pizza instead. Good thing — she'd made him way too vulnerable earlier. Casey interrupting had been divine intervention, saving him from doing something stupid. Like admitting his misplaced, misunderstood attraction to Bri.

Or leaning over the syrup-sticky table and pressing his lips against hers.

He'd been uncharacteristically emotional, that was all. He was tired, ready to go home, and worried about his mom. He'd spent way too long in this romance-saturated town.

Bri finally looked up. This time, he was ready. He kept his expression neutral.

"That was really nice of you to offer to help." She pulled off another pepperoni and this time, at least, nibbled on it. "I know weddings aren't your thing."

"Sure, no problem. I'll be writing about this for part two of the article, anyway, so it's all good. Might as well write it from an up-close, hands-on perspective." He hoped his casual tone convinced Bri he was doing this for himself and the sake of the feature — and not to save her.

She nodded, averting her eyes.

He still didn't know what was wrong with her but couldn't ask a second time. That had been close — too close. He couldn't risk getting that up front and personal again. In fact, he'd better stay as far from Bri as he could for the next week.

Except he'd just volunteered to help her set up a wedding.

CHAPTER SEVENTEEN

Bri stretched taller on the chair she'd dragged outside, straining to wrap the second layer of purple gauze around the arch Casey had convinced Jimmy from Johnson's General to let her borrow for free. The kind old man with a penchant for plaid shirts had delivered it an hour ago, and the chairs and tables were supposed to be coming soon. Casey's last-minute request had everyone in town eager to help — and had served to distract Bri from the gloomy cloud that had enveloped her since her attic discovery last night.

She tugged the material around the curve of the arch, wobbling slightly in her ankle boots as she rose to her toes. She probably should have taken her shoes off, but it was too cold.

Her mind raced with the seemingly never-ending to-do list as she adjusted the sheer fabric around the white wood, which would serve as a backdrop and parameter of sorts for the reception. She couldn't let herself forget about the cakes cooling on the counter for the petit fours. Once they were ready, she'd torte them and spread on the lemonberry filling that was still chilling in the fridge. By then the other round of cakes should be ready to come out of the oven. Then she could come back outside and arrange the chairs, if they'd arrived yet. If not, she'd sweep off the stepping-stones leading to the fountain before she had to go back and ice the petit fours.

Thankfully, Mabel and Agnes were inside the Puff, keeping the coffee fresh and taking care of customers while Bri handled the wedding prep.

She wondered briefly if Gerard would actually show up to help as he'd mentioned at Taylor's, but then decided she shouldn't care. She could handle this — Casey deserved it, and she'd offered, after all. It was just a matter of multitasking and keeping a close eye on her watch. She'd set a phone alarm just in case, to prevent anything from burning.

Although, on second thought, that proactive attempt might have been more successful if her phone was actually in her pocket, not inside on the bakery counter.

Bri smoothed the fabric over the curve of the frame. Almost done, and she could go check on the cakes and grab her phone. But a piece snagged on a nail, and she reached higher to free it. It wouldn't budge — and she couldn't risk ripping it. She didn't have more material.

She blew a stray strand of hair out of her face, then rose on her tiptoes, fingers anxiously grasping for the steel culprit. She held her breath as she attempted to wrestle the fabric free. Almost . . . there . . .

She stretched too far, and suddenly there was no more chair. Just air, and the rapidly approaching, sparse winter grass. She squeezed her eyes shut and threw her arms out to catch herself — but her fingers grasped fabric instead of dirt.

She opened her eyes, and her gaze collided with a becoming-too-familiar broad chest, covered in a hunter green, long-sleeved T-shirt. Her reluctant knight in shining armor, once again.

"Easy there, Cupcake." Gerard lowered her to the ground, his hands lingering on her waist a moment longer than necessary. Or did they? Wishful thinking?

No. They definitely lingered.

Her hips burned at the contact, and her heart lodged somewhere up in her throat.

She coughed, and he quickly let her go, his fingers flexing twice as if shaking off an electric current. He'd felt it too.

She straightened her sweatshirt and quickly reached up to tighten her ponytail. "Good timing." Or the worst. Maybe hitting the ground would have been better. A lot less confusing for her heart, at least.

He eased backward a few steps, his eyes guarded. "You won't be a very good maid of honor if you're on crutches."

"There isn't a wedding party. It's going to be just them and the two little girls." Thank goodness. She could only imagine trying to add maid-of-honor duties to her already overflowing wedding plate. Though it would have been a little fun to see Gerard's reaction to her in a nice dress.

She blinked. What was wrong with her? She hadn't even hit her head.

"Can I help you finish whatever you were doing before you tried to play Superman?" Gerard extended one hand in the air, one that could easily reach the knotted fabric. "Some of us don't need stilts."

"Very funny." She planted her hands on her hips. "Can you fix that piece there on the end that's bunched? It snagged on a nail."

"And you thought that was worth face-planting for?" Gerard freed the gauze, and it fluttered perfectly into place. "What else have you done to take one for the team?"

She frowned. "What do you mean?"

"I mean, all of this." He gestured to the arch and the lovelock wall, and she tried not to notice the way the sleeve of his shirt clung to his bicep. "You basically just volunteered to single-handedly put together this entire wedding."

There he went again. Butting into her life, trying to analyze or criticize every move she made. "Well, then, lucky for me that someone like you *volunteered* to help." Though clearly not for her sake. "Remember? For the article?"

He raised his eyebrows. "I thought I was writing a travel feature. Not a tragedy."

"Look, do you want to help, or do you want to judge me?" She crossed her arms over her sweatshirt. "I don't have time for should-haves. Hand me that broom."

She'd do the whole thing herself if she had to. The drive to prove herself — and to run from the possibilities that haunted her attic trunk — loomed large, and she swallowed hard. She didn't need Gerard's approval. She needed to get to work. To keep moving.

He handed her the broom she had brought

outside on her last trip. "Glad to see you're back to your old self, Cupcake."

She snatched the broom and started brushing off the stepping-stones. "What old self? The one that's impatient with you? Or the one that's annoyed by your attempts to control everything I do?" Dirt powdered through the air, and she coughed.

He smirked. "All of them. Do you hear their voices in your head too?"

She wanted to laugh. And cry — because there was still so much work to do. She chose to do neither and instead swept harder — maybe a little intentionally toward him.

He stepped back. "What can I do to help?"

"Stop bugging me." She turned, leaning on the broom handle. "If you're going to truly help, no more criticizing the fact that I volunteered. Casey is a good friend, and she's been through a lot. She deserves a special day." Her voice shook, and she wasn't sure from which emotion. Too many were roiling around. Frustration. Fear. Stress.

That annoying zing of attraction still jolted through her midsection.

Gerard held up both hands in surrender. "Fair enough. I said I'd help, and I will. No more analyzing."

"Great." She breathed a sigh of relief.

Both that he was backing off — and staying. Being alone with her racing thoughts felt like too much to handle, even with the distraction of the wedding preparations at large.

"The delivery truck with the chairs and tables should be here any minute." She swept the next stone, then moved to the next. "On second thought, we should probably put the tables and chairs in storage and not actually set them out until Sunday morning. So, you can help the guy unload and carry them to the shed out back."

"That's not more expensive? We should just tell them to come Sunday morning."

"No, she got them for the whole weekend, for the same price as one day."

"Nice. I guess the business owners in Story don't like to make money." Gerard hiked an eyebrow.

Bri gripped the broom handle tighter. "More so, the people in Story like to help each other out." She glanced up. "You could try mentioning that in your feature."

"Roger." Gerard saluted. "Why don't you let me finish sweeping, and you can work on the petit fours."

She gasped and the broom clattered to the ground.

The cakes.

Hopefully this wasn't an omen for the whole wedding.

"Bon appétit." Gerard extended a fork to Bri in her near-fetal position on the kitchen floor.

She sat up slightly, her head resting back against the island. Once she'd removed the ruined cakes from the oven and deposited them on the stove top, she'd sunk to the floor and had yet to find the energy or motivation to stand. Mabel and Agnes had flipped the "Closed" sign on the front door and left, probably to head out for a quick lunch break during the lull, and hadn't been there to hear the timer going off. Of all the times for them not to tell her they were leaving. Another sign of their memories slipping?

She'd been with Gerard, though . . . maybe it was another attempt at matchmaking.

She couldn't take much more of this.

Gerard shook the fork at her, breaking into her thoughts. "What are you doing?" She reached up and reluctantly accepted the fork from him.

"Come on, Cupcake. There's got to be

some perks to managing a bakery. Scoot over." He lowered to the floor beside her, stretching his jeans-clad legs across the tiles, and plopped the ruined cake in his lap. He'd transferred it from the scorched pan to a serving plate, and it lay in broken chunks.

Sort of like her crumpled plans. Now she was going to have to bake an entire extra batch of petit fours, which would put her over an hour behind schedule. On top of that, worry about her parents' letters still clung to the frayed edges of her thoughts.

Or were they just her *mom's* letters, and not her parents', after all? Her stomach knotted.

"Try it." Gerard nudged her.

She stared at the carnage on the plate. "Are you crazy?"

"It's good." He chewed slowly. "Surprisingly moist — once you get past the charcoal exterior."

Bri groaned. She didn't have time for this. And yet she couldn't convince herself to get up and start the next batch of batter.

She plucked a piece free with her fingers, not even bothering with the fork. She flicked off the crusty, black top layer and took a bite. He was right. It was still pretty decent on the inside. Not bad for comfort food.

"Still convinced you're not overstretching

yourself on Casey's behalf?" Gerard forked off another bite.

Not that she'd ever admit, especially to him. "I can handle it."

"Clearly."

She wiped crumbs from the corner of her lips. "I just need to torte the cake that didn't burn and spread the filling."

"Uh-huh. And remake this last batch."

"Right."

"And finish sweeping outside. Oh, and ice all the petit fours."

She nodded, stomach clenching. "Right."

He speared another bite of cake, calmly, as if this pending wedding wasn't a pending disaster. "And set up all those chairs and tables."

"Okay, I see your point. Hand it over." She reached for the plate.

"Now you're talking." He nudged the crumbly graveyard closer to her.

"I feel like we just reversed roles. Wasn't I the one talking *you* into desserts just a week ago?"

He rolled his eyes. "My sweatpants and I thank you, my jeans do not."

Like he'd gained an ounce of fat. He was all muscle.

Not that she'd noticed.

She leaned her head back fully against the

246

island, eyes closed. This might be her last break or still moment until after the wedding on Sunday evening. Maybe she could clear her head completely. Ignore the acrid tang of smoke hanging in the air and the rush of her adrenaline-shocked heartbeat and actually relax for just a —

"What was wrong this morning?"

The cake dried in her mouth.

She shook her head.

"Not ready to talk about it?"

She shrugged.

"Well, I'm not going to guess."

"I wasn't going to ask you to."

He shrugged.

She rolled in her lower lip. She wanted to blurt out the entire situation, all of her fears — wanted reassurance from someone not as close to her as Mabel and Agnes to tell her she was overreacting, that it was all going to be okay. That nothing would change. That her history and family legacy would remain intact and nothing was tarnished.

But she couldn't force any of it out between her dry lips.

"You don't have to talk about it." Gerard set his fork on the plate. "But whatever it is, don't let it consume you."

She swallowed. "I can't stop thinking about it."

"Is that why you jumped at the chance to become a one-woman wedding act? To distract yourself?"

Probably. She couldn't bring herself to agree out loud, but it was true. She was running, had been ever since she found that smudge.

It didn't matter whether she voiced her agreement. He had her figured out anyway. "I get it." He nudged her side with his elbow. "You're just trying to keep moving. I seem to remember the other day you called me out for doing the same."

She stared at the burned remains on the plate. "I used to always hope my mom would burn my birthday cake because I wanted her macarons instead." A slight smile tugged at her lips, and she permitted it with relief. Positive memories were better than the fear of this terrifying unknown. "But she never did, of course. She was too good a baker."

"Would you believe I've actually never had a birthday cake?"

Bri shot him a glance. "No way."

"Nope."

She tilted her head toward him. "Not ever?"

"Maybe when I was really little. And my mom made a pie a few times, I think. But nah, we usually just grilled burgers or something. She wasn't much of a baker, remember?"

That was sad. Every kid deserved birthday cakes. It was a rite of passage. The shaded guard in his eyes made Bri wonder if he thought it was sad too. Maybe Gerard had a softer center than she realized. Sort of like the ruined petits — just had to get past the crusty exterior.

She pressed her lips together. "Well, whenever your birthday rolls around, you should treat yourself. Get one of those grocery-store cakes with the thick icing that turns your teeth blue for hours."

He forked another piece of cake from the pan. "My birthday is actually next week. On Monday." Regret instantly filled his eyes. "But don't tell anyone. Last year my coworkers tricked me into going to lunch, and the waiter made me wear a sombrero."

The image of him standing by a pile of chips and salsa, grouchy-faced under a rainbow-patterned sombrero while waiters clapped around him, made Bri laugh — hard. "Oh no. I'm taking out an ad in the paper. Or better yet" — Bri snapped her fingers and grinned — "I'll call Sandra."

"Now I know you're joking." Gerard shuddered. "That woman is terrifying."

"You don't understand the half of it. You should read her old gossip column articles."

"I'm glad that's not a thing anymore — gossip columns." Gerard shook his head. "What a waste of newsprint."

She couldn't stop the erupting giggle building in her chest. It felt so good to not feel emotionally bogged down, she couldn't rein it in. "Your secret is safe . . . old man."

"Very funny."

"Hey, if you can't dish it out, then —"

Gerard smashed a piece of cake in her face. "Eat it?"

She blinked as petit four crumbs dusted her cheeks. Flakes clung to her chin and lips and fluttered in her eyelashes. "That's *not* what I was going to say."

"I'm the writer, remember? Let me stick to the happy endings."

"Sure." She grabbed the remaining hunk of cake from the pan. "But I prefer plot twists."

He blocked her desperate dive with his forearm, and the momentum pushed him backward, half-reclining against the wall.

She collapsed against his sturdy chest, laughing, maneuvering her fistful of cake toward his face, to no avail. She tried to push herself up in defeat, but her cake-crusted fingers skidded on the slick tile floor and she landed hard against him.

Their faces were inches apart.

Gerard's gaze caught hers and held. Her breath hitched. He smelled like evergreen and petit-four batter and something deeper and muskier. Something uniquely him. His hands supported her waist, keeping her weight from bearing fully on him. His fingers, coated with cake and calluses, barely grazed under the hem of her sweatshirt as he braced her, but she felt their heat to her core.

His eyes lowered to her lips, then darted back to her eyes, as if seeking permission.

Her stomach dipped, and her gaze followed the same path, noting the stubbled dimple in his jaw. A small scar she'd never noticed before barely clipped the edge of his chin.

His fingers flexed around her hips, and she couldn't breathe. Couldn't push herself up. Couldn't decide if she wanted to.

She wanted him to kiss her.

No, she didn't. It would change things. Change was scary.

But something about being this close to Gerard didn't feel scary at all.

His head rose toward her, closing the narrow distance between them. She closed her eyes in anticipation, heart pounding an unsteady beat in her chest. This was it. He was going to kiss her. His hands gripped tighter.

And propelled her up and off of him.

Her eyes flew open as she sat upright on the tile beside him. Their gazes collided, and she wondered if he could see the myriad questions racing through her mind. Wondered if she could even put words to them if she tried.

Agnes popped her head through the swinging kitchen door. "We thought we heard a commotion back here. What's going on? What's that smell?"

"Bri, is that you?" Mabel's head appeared beneath Agnes's in the doorframe, and a slow smile spread across her overly lipsticked mouth as she took in the scene before her. "Hush now, Agnes. It looks like everything is exactly as it should be." She winked before disappearing back into the storefront. Agnes followed suit with a grumbled protest.

Gerard stood and offered his hand to Bri to help her up. She accepted it, knees trembling, and avoided eye contact.

Nothing was as it should be.

CHAPTER EIGHTEEN

That had been a huge mistake.

Which part, he wasn't sure. But somewhere, there had been a mistake — plenty of them. Telling Bri about his upcoming birthday. Opening up about running from the hard stuff. Almost kissing her.

Not kissing her.

Gerard shoved one hand wearily through his hair as he peered up at the steeple atop the nondenominational church. He'd offered to help with the wedding and hated to go back on his word, but he couldn't stay in the kitchen with Bri any longer. He needed fresh air. Bri must have gotten the hint — or maybe she wanted space as badly as he did — because she'd given him the task of delivering Casey's wedding vows and updated order of ceremony to the minister, who apparently didn't have a functioning printer.

Only in Story.

Gerard hesitated in front of the small brick chapel. Late afternoon clouds billowed above, shadowed with the threat of rain. Hopefully it wouldn't downpour, since Bri already had the arch decorated and a dozen tables set out. They'd stored the seventy-five folding chairs in the shed. He could just see Bri asking him to wipe everything down with a towel tomorrow if it rained.

And he'd probably do it.

Because something had shifted in that kitchen. He felt like he was holding his breath, careening around a mountain bike trail on a seaside cliff, balancing precariously on two fast-moving wheels. One false move and he'd tumble straight off the rocks and into the breakers. He refused to stop and breathe — or acknowledge what exactly was shifting.

It was easier to just keep moving.

He pulled open the solid door of the church. Muted green carpet muffled his steps as he crept inside. A long hallway led to the right, with several shut doors that were probably offices. To the left was another set of oak double doors. One was propped open with a small wooden triangle.

He peered inside. The sanctuary. "Hello?"

His voice echoed in the dimly lit room. He turned a full circle in the lobby, but

254

there was no answer. Did they not lock their doors here either? Or maybe the staff had already left for the day.

On second thought, how big of a staff could a small church in Story, Kansas, even have in the first place?

He pulled the folded papers with Casey's vows and instructions out of his back pocket and hesitantly moved inside the sanctuary. "Mr . . . Pastor John?" His church lingo was rusty — too rusty. His mama would be disappointed in him.

Not that she'd gone to a service either in the past twenty years. And who could blame her, after the judgmental comments about her slipping lifestyle made their way from the choir loft to her ears, until they finally landed in print on a Wednesday night prayer list.

Gerard ambled down the aisle between the rows of simple wooden pews. A pulpit stood on the stage, atop a carpeted altar. A stained-glass window took the place where the baptistry typically was, back in the church he grew up in, anyway.

When was the last time he'd walked an aisle like this? The travel-writing life didn't leave much room for a home church. Or a home at all, for that matter. He'd visited several of the cathedrals on his last venture through Europe. Had taken communion in Rome two years ago.

None of those churches had felt quite like this one, though. Quiet. Unassuming. Peaceful.

Or maybe he just hadn't been still long enough to feel it those times.

Gerard stopped at the end of the aisle by the second pew and slid onto the empty bench. The serenity of the room calmed the churning emotions in the pit of his stomach, and he inhaled his first deep breath since coming to Story. Maybe he should start going back to church — if he could find one in Chicago like this.

Put down roots.

The late-afternoon sun spilled through the stained glass, sending shards of rainbow-speckled light across the carpet.

He swallowed and glanced down at the papers in his hand, brushing off the imposing thoughts. Church was a thing of the past for him — he didn't need a building full of hypocrites to point out his sins. He knew them well.

Gerard leaned forward, pressing his fingers against his throbbing forehead. He shouldn't be stalling. He needed to get these documents to the preacher — wherever he was — and get back to the Puff to help Bri. Or maybe he needed to get on his motorcycle and forget the whole thing.

Yet the thought of leaving Story didn't bring the respite it had a few days ago. In fact, it brought only confusion.

His shoulders tightened, and he massaged the base of his neck. What had this town done to him? Here he was, stressed out and exhausted, helping set up a wedding, of all things — and hiding in a church from a blonde he couldn't stop thinking about.

Peter had no idea what he'd sent him into.

Or had he? Suspicion pinched, and he frowned.

"Peaceful, isn't it?"

Gerard jerked upright as a baritone voice filled the silent room.

A man in a blue running shirt and track pants strolled down the aisle toward him, his smile bright against a tanned face. "Sorry, man. Didn't mean to startle you. I'm Pastor John."

Interesting. He'd expected a suit — and someone taller, more imposing. Definitely grayer. This guy didn't look much older than him.

Gerard stood and shook the pastor's hand. "Gerard Fortier. I'm supposed to bring you some stuff for Casey's wedding Sunday."

"Oh, right, the vows and ceremony order."

John, his smile easy and genuine, took the papers Gerard held out. "You're the travel writer, aren't you?"

He nodded. "Word gets around in Story, doesn't it?"

"It doesn't take much." John crossed his arms, his laid-back manner easing the knot in Gerard's chest. The man wasn't a day over forty. "I'm looking forward to reading your article. The Pastry Puff has been a staple around here — and we all love Bri and Mabel and Agnes."

Gerard's guard edged up, and the knot tightened. So, he was another local with an agenda, only wanting to discuss the feature. "I'll make them sound good, don't worry." He started to sidestep his way out of the pew.

"Oh, I had no doubt. I'm sure you know what you're doing."

He thought he did. But maybe not. Not with Bri looking at him with those trusting eyes and Charles slipping him undisclosed cash. He risked a glance at Pastor John, who stood unmoving, arms still crossed, eyes accessing.

"Where you headed next?"

Gerard rested one hand on the back of the pew, simultaneously ready to both flee and settle down for more of that peace he'd glimpsed. "I'm not sure, Pastor. Wherever the next assignment is, I guess."

"Call me John. And that sounds pretty exciting. Always on the move." John eased down on the pew.

Gerard sank back onto the end of the second row, facing him. "It can be." And exhausting. But it kept him moving toward his goals. Lead writer. More voice. More impact. More money. "This assignment isn't like the others, that's for sure."

"Not as adventurous, I'd imagine." John quirked an eyebrow. "Though if you're staying in the B&B, it might be." He chuckled, and the knot in Gerard's chest eased completely. "Red room?"

Finally. Someone in this town who got him. "Why does that room even exist?"

John tilted his head back and laughed. "Sometimes I think Mrs. Beeker is playing us all."

He smiled, but it didn't linger. The pastor was too close to the truth. Story did seem like a game lately — a chess game, and Gerard felt like the pawn. He refused to get caught up in Charles's manipulative moves or Bri's strategic plays with her vulnerability and innocence.

But she wasn't playing, was she? Bri was different. Different from Charles, by far, but also very different from Kelsey. Kelsey was a knight — complicated, sneaky moves with swift side attacks.

Bri was a queen — straightforward, no matter which direction she moved.

Maybe it could be okay, loving someone like Bri.

Not that he did. Or was even sure he was capable of it anymore. Not after watching his mom and her train-wreck of a love life. At least he knew he got his lack of skill in that department honestly.

Enough. Gerard abruptly stood.

John followed suit and held out his hand. "Nice to meet you, man."

"You too. I guess I'll be seeing you at the wedding." Gerard shook his hand, then edged into the aisle.

"Absolutely." John gestured with the printed vows, his analyzing gaze once more sweeping Gerard's face. It wasn't as unsettling as it was convicting.

Gerard lifted one hand in a wave and started up the aisle toward the double doors. He needed air. Needed something he couldn't really name anymore yet couldn't stop wanting since the moment he'd ridden into Story.

"Is there anything I can pray about for you as you're leaving town?"

Gerard stopped in his tracks halfway up the aisle. This definitely wasn't John's first rodeo.

He started to shake his head on default, then hesitated, the true answer burning in his heart. He only half turned to deliver his response. "My mom."

He waited for the barrage of questions, the curious prompts hidden under the guise of caring. Of wanting to "pray specifically," which in his experience, was just code for "tell the entire church." No one gossiped like a bunch of parishioners holding weekly prayer sheets, standing in line for sheet cake and coffee.

But there was nothing. Nothing except John's firm nod and quiet, assured answer. "I'm on it."

And then he left the room first, leaving Gerard standing on frayed carpet and wondering if maybe there was something to the whole church thing again after all.

She hadn't even kissed him, and yet somehow, she knew Gerard was an amazing kisser.

Bri piped yet another pink flower on top of yet another petit four and wondered how many she could complete before she actually went insane. Or maybe it just was the pent-up frustration that had yet to dissipate after that almost-kiss.

Had he pushed her away because of the interruption from Agnes? Or was it something else?

Was it her?

She squeezed the bag too hard, and a glob of icing tainted the next cake. She scraped it off with a plastic knife and tried again. She had to focus. Her friend was getting married in two days, and she still had many petit fours to make again. Thankfully Gerard had taken the paperwork to the church, saving her one errand and removing his distracting presence from the bakery while she tried to gather her thoughts.

Which was a little like herding cats.

"Bri, why don't you take a break? Work on something else for a bit." Mabel popped back into the kitchen, her eyes darting to the spot on the floor where she'd caught her and Gerard just an hour earlier.

Bri knew, because she kept staring at it too.

"It's okay, Mabel. I got it." She would do this, somehow. All of it. Casey would have the best wedding ever, if it killed her. The only kiss she needed to be thinking about was Casey and Nathan's at the altar.

"These arthritic hands aren't done for

262

completely — yet." Mabel held out her purple-veined hands, her bright orange nail polish catching the bakery lights. "Come on, now, hand over that piping bag."

Bri reluctantly relinquished the icing. She really did need to call Casey, make sure she wasn't forgetting something that her friend needed before Sunday. Had they talked at Taylor's only that morning?

Her chest tightened. Had it been only two weeks since Gerard rode into her life? Since he'd stirred up dormant feelings, upped her blood pressure, and made her feel more irritated — and alive — than she had been in years?

Had it been only a day since Bri discovered the giant question mark hanging over her parents' legacy?

Her heart thundered in her chest, and she grabbed a bottle of water from the mini-fridge. She hated to look incompetent or overwhelmed — what if that showed Mabel and Agnes she couldn't handle the bakery alone, nudging them toward selling it? She should just talk to them about it — but she wasn't ready for their answer. The only thing worse than wondering about the future was realizing her greatest fears were actually heading her way.

She needed a break. "I'll just walk over to

Casey's house and check on a few things, then be right back." Maybe if she caught her breath for a moment, and a little of her friend's pre-wedding excitement, she could get refreshed and come back to knock out the remaining tasks.

Mabel continued piping, without looking up. "Take your time, dear. This will all get done." She'd already completed three flowers. "Agnes will hold down the fort up front."

"Thank you." Bri grabbed two to-go coffees with cream before she could change her mind, then escaped outside. The November air chilled her cheeks and cooled the flush that came from working around a hot oven. If Casey was even half as overwhelmed and exhausted as Bri was, then she would also appreciate the afternoon caffeine pickup.

She rounded the corner of Maple toward Casey's house and glimpsed a tall figure strolling toward her. She squinted, trying to make the person out. The saunter and sway of his shoulders was familiar.

Gerard.

Her heart rate increased, and she clutched both coffees, halfway debating if she should duck behind the big oak tree to her left. He must be heading back from the church.

Had he seen her yet?

She squared her shoulders. She wouldn't hide. This was her town, and like it or not, he was going to be leaving it — very soon.

The thought brought relief and disappointment in equal measures.

She'd sort that out later. Right now, she had other emotions to conceal. She refused to let Gerard know how he'd affected her in the kitchen. Until she knew exactly what had happened between them — or rather, had almost happened and why he'd stopped it — she would have to keep her own reaction stuffed down.

Besides, she felt totally incapable of deciphering anything romantic with her parents' love story on the line. Clearly, she wasn't the best interpreter, after all. The thought knotted her stomach. She was refusing to let herself think about so much at this point, she wished she could just clear her brain completely.

Bri pasted on what she hoped was a casual smile and raised her mug at Gerard. "Mission accomplished?"

He nodded, removing his sunglasses and tucking them into the neck of his shirt. His eyes were a little drawn at the corners, as if he'd missed sleep the night before. Or maybe it'd just been as long a day for him as it'd been for her. "Everything's been delivered to the pastor."

Bri took a sip of her coffee. "Thanks for doing that."

He ran a hand through his slightly rumpled hair as he nodded. "No big deal." There were definitely creases by his brows too. Had something happened at the church? Or was he feeling the effects of their connection at the bakery too? She sort of hoped for the latter.

"How'd you know I'd be heading back right now?"

She raised her eyebrows. "I didn't." If she had, she'd probably have chosen another route. "What do you mean?"

He pointed to the second cup of coffee in her hand.

"Oh!" She hesitated, then held it out to him. "But you don't like my coffee."

"I told you last time — it's growing on me." He gently pushed her hand away, and the connection of his fingers on her wrist sent sparks down her spine. "But I don't want to be a coffee thief."

"It's okay, Casey won't care. Besides, you look like you need it more."

"Thanks." He took the cup, then rolled his eyes at her, a humorous spark temporarily lifting the tired lines. "I think."

She looked worse, guaranteed. Thankfully he didn't confirm that fact. "I really appreciate your help." She didn't want to get vulnerable, but he was going out of his way to assist her — and she still didn't really understand why. He didn't owe her anything. Did that mean he cared — about *her*? Or just felt sorry for the situation she'd gotten herself into?

The wind shifted, ruffling his hair. "It's no problem. I have the time, which is something you're pretty short on."

That was considerate. Hope blossomed. Hope for what, exactly, she wasn't sure, except when he was sweet like that it made her —

"Besides, like I said, it gives me an up-close-and-personal angle for the second part of this article."

Hope smashed into a dozen broken pieces. The article. Right. They were back to that.

She shoved aside the threat of disappointment. She already knew the truth — confirming it shouldn't sting like this. He wasn't interested — which was clearly why he'd pushed her away before they kissed. She'd misread those moments in the kitchen, bonding, connecting.

Besides, who cared? Her emotions were just raw from the hectic day and the long lineup of tasks still before her. Gerard Fortier was still the last guy in the universe who would be her type, and she needed to remember that.

Even if he was staring at her over the lid of his to-go cup with a steady gaze that made her legs morph into something resembling lumpy cake batter.

"I'm sure the wedding will help give the article a great extra layer." She started to step past him. "I better go check on Casey and compare to-do lists. We're burning daylight."

"Do you think Charles will show up to the wedding?" A glint tinted Gerard's eyes, one she couldn't decipher and passed too quickly before she could try.

Bri shrugged, hoping to seem unconcerned, but that particular fear had crossed her mind a few times over the last few days as well. "I don't think so. He's got to feel a little like public enemy number one right now."

"Maybe." Gerard didn't look as convinced.

Her heart stammered. "So, you think he might?" That'd be the last thing they needed on Casey's big day. The wedding was going to be hard enough to pull off as it was — Charles showing up would put such a damper on their success. Still, Casey had technically invited the whole town. He was within his rights to come.

"Honestly?" Gerard pointed his cup at her. "I think everyone in Story is a little unpredictable."

Bri started to argue, then shut her mouth. Lately, that was true. Even of herself, and she'd had the same safe, comfortable routine for years. Now here she was, stressed out, prepping for an entire wedding in one weekend, and almost kissing near strangers on the kitchen floor.

"You'd be okay, you know."

She blinked, trying to dial back into the conversation and catch up. Hopefully Gerard couldn't read where her thoughts had been. "Okay how?"

"If the bakery sold to Charles. Or folds, or otherwise goes away." Gerard shrugged.

"What do you mean?"

"You're more than the Pastry Puff, Bri. You're not fulfilled whisking icing and piping cake."

She squinted. "Reverse that."

"You know what I mean."

She didn't. She crossed her arms, waiting.

"You're happy there because you're serving the people of your town. Caring for the elderly and discounting goods for those struggling and holding babies for stressed out moms so they can drink their coffee in peace. Handing out cupcakes to homeless men on bicycles. Remembering people's orders and making them feel special. Listening to everyone who's willing to talk. *That's* what fills you up."

Her defenses bristled. Now he was psychoanalyzing her?

The frustration burned fresh. Was he switching sides? Why the sudden fascination with Charles and his next move, anyway — was he somehow cheering him on? She narrowed her eyes. Gerard had never been fully on her team in the first place. He just wanted to write his story and get out of town.

Did he *want* to see her fail? She'd trusted him — almost kissed him. But she couldn't blindly accept something he hadn't fully given. "How do you even know all that?"

His voice lowered, sincere and husky. "Because I've watched you. I've seen it."

And just like that, her defensive wall toppled. He conjured all her feelings at once, then left her reeling in the wake of them.

Still, one giant factor to his current argument remained. She needed the Puff. He didn't understand the bakery's connection to her parents, the tangible memories that held her steady on days when the car wreck seemed so fresh.

She pointed out the obvious. "I can't exactly do any of those things without the Puff. If Charles gets it, those opportunities vanish."

Gerard shrugged, hands up. "Hey. I'm just saying what I'm seeing."

And yet somehow, everyone remained so blind about this very topic. She bit back the retort begging to leave her lips and forced another smile, this one obviously missing the casual mark. "I've really got to get to Casey. I'll see you around."

"Bri." Gerard reached out and touched her arm as she started past him. "Wait."

She stopped, turning, her emotions balling in her chest until she thought she might scream. And yet somehow, she didn't even know what she wanted. Wanted to be left alone. Wanted to be done with this hectic weekend.

Wanted him.

He watched her, unspeaking. The glint was back in his eyes, the one that mirrored . . . regret. Guilt? Definitely remorse.

Over their shared moment in the kitchen, or something else?

"What?" Her gaze jumped from his eyes

to his lips — darn those lips — and back again, tension piling up between them like concrete bricks.

His lips parted, as if about to speak, then closed. They tightened into a thin line, and his hand dropped to his side. "Let me know if I can help with anything else."

"Sure." She nodded, disappointment welling as she turned back toward Casey's house. She exhaled slowly, hating how out of control her heart felt. *Help.* Right.

He could start helping by kicking her poor heart off this roller-coaster ride she hadn't bought a ticket for.

CHAPTER NINETEEN

Saturday. The wedding was now about thirty hours away. Despite the petit fours being ready to go, Bri still had a dozen little things to do for Casey — and yet there was only one task on the forefront of her mind. She'd argued about it in prayer for most of the morning, attempting to convince the Lord this couldn't possibly be a good idea, but she couldn't shake the urge from her heart.

Even now, sitting on an upholstered backless bench, watching Casey twirl in front of the seamstress in her wedding dress, her fingers itched to complete the one task dominating her mind.

But she couldn't do that from the dressing room of Sew Awesome Alterations.

"What do you think?" Casey half curtsied for Bri, the shiny, fitted bodice giving just enough to accommodate the motion.

Bri smiled at her friend, hoping she didn't

pick up on her distraction. She owed Casey her full attention. "I think you look like a princess."

"Thanks! Hmm. Maybe make that a mermaid princess." Casey smoothed her slim hips, the fabric of the dress hugging tight until halfway down her leg, where it cascaded into a mass of snowy white fabric onto the platform where she stood. The gown was gorgeous on her, and perfect for her narrow frame. "Hair up or down?" She bundled her brunette tresses up in one hand and pursed her lips.

"Down," Bri and the seamstress said at the same time.

Mrs. Bonnie, who'd been doing alterations in Story ever since Bri needed her first smocked Easter dresses hemmed, fluffed the fabric of the short train and stood back to assess. She fisted her hands on her ample hips and gave a brisk nod. "Yes. Down will balance the flare at the legs. Maybe some curls?"

"My hair hasn't held curl since my high school prom." Casey wrinkled her nose, then pulled the sides of her hair back and squinted into the giant gold mirror. "Wait. Maybe like this?"

"Perfect." Bri held her hands up like a camera and viewed Casey through her "finger lens." "That'd be really pretty. Elegant but still looks like you."

"Good." Casey let her hair go and twirled one more time with a satisfied smile. "I definitely don't want Nathan to feel like he's marrying a stranger."

Bri watched Mrs. Bonnie fuss over the dress, her unease growing — both from Casey's comment and her own hesitations over her friends' fast-developing romance. It wasn't just the timeline — people got married after knowing each other only a few months all the time. It was more the concern of what did Casey and Nathan really know about *true* love yet? Wasn't romance a lot more than messy dinners with kids and rushed weddings because of tight work schedules? Didn't Casey want more than that? Bri did.

But perhaps Casey felt like time was passing, and she was giving up on the dream. Settling, in a way. Not that Nathan was a bad guy, but maybe it was more like wanting to make sure she got her chance before she — and her kids — got any older.

She could certainly understand that kind of pressure.

Casey performed a little test cha-cha on the platform to see if her dress allowed room to dance. Her eyes shone and her skin glowed with happiness. No, more like giddiness. "He's going to love it, isn't he?" It was a statement more than a question, but Mrs. Bonnie murmured her agreement anyway as she secured one of the tiny buttons on the back of the dress.

Bri swallowed. Who was she kidding? Casey wasn't settling in the least. Nathan was her dream guy, the perfect fit for her family. She was happy for her friend.

Maybe her doubts were just projecting from inside her own heart.

Casey's phone trilled, and with an excited shriek, she hiked up her dress and rushed to grab it from her purse in the dressing room stall. Bri scrambled to help her, holding up her train on one side as Casey plucked the cell from her bag. Mrs. Bonnie, frowning, held the rest of the material off the ground.

"Hello?" Casey's breathless voice hitched with hope. Then her eyes lit. "Hey, babe." She started to pace a slow circle as Bri and Mrs. Bonnie followed. Then Casey palmed the receiving end and tucked the phone briefly under her chin. "He misses me." She squealed before going back to the conversation.

Yeah, they were going to be fine.

Bri shook her head with a smile and

maintained Casey's train as her friend absently stalked the dressing room, whispering mush into the phone. Humility was a tough bite to digest. Bri had always thought she was the know-it-all in romance, riding the coattails of her parents' legacy — an expert by default, a student of the greatest teachers in their generation.

Until that letter in the attic.

She sobered. One smudge, and everything Bri thought she knew now hung by a thread. That wasn't Casey's fault, and if Bri wasn't careful, she'd let this funk she found herself in mar her friend's perfect day.

She watched a blush crawl up Casey's cheeks as her friend whispered something privately into the phone. Maybe Casey was onto something. Maybe romance wasn't as flawless as Bri had always assumed. Casey and Nathan were in love — and wasn't that the most romantic thing of all? Spaghetti stains and toddler fingerprints and messy proposals included?

Motorcycles and sarcasm and hard truths included?

Her arms holding the train lowered. Her idea nudged again, this time growing in appeal, like cake batter slowly rising in a warm oven. Maybe she didn't know what romantic love really was yet, and maybe some of her hopes in that department were a little ideal-istic.

But she did know neighborly love, as Gerard had pointed out to her yesterday. The idea, now fully baked, buzzed like an oven timer, and the decision was made.

She had a special delivery to make.

A knock sounded on his bedroom door.

Gerard swung his legs off the side of the bed with a sigh, discarding his open laptop on the red comforter.

Another knock, more urgent.

"Hold on." He tripped over the red rug on the floor and bit back frustrated words. It was probably Mrs. Beeker again, offering more sweet tea or some other excuse for conversation. He'd chatted amicably enough for as long as he could stand, then he'd told her he really needed to work on his article before he went to sleep.

Not that he had anything to write about until after Casey's wedding — and possibly after Charles's next move. Maybe the two would coincide — maybe the prissy lawyer would get the guts to show up and create something worth writing about. He really needed to hit a home run with part two of the feature, or he couldn't guarantee that Peter would promote him.

He swung open the door, ready to reject whatever beverage Mrs. Beeker was forcing on him, but his eyes landed on someone else.

Bri.

She held a bakery box in her arms and wore a shy smile — and a different sweatshirt this time. Aqua, which lit up her makeup-free eyes like a firecracker. "Surprise."

It certainly was.

"Now you're making deliveries that people didn't even order? That's got to be good for business." He leaned against the doorframe, crossing his arms over his thumping heart. What would she think if she knew he'd been so distracted by their recent interactions that he'd finally typed her name over and over on his computer, just to get her out of his head? Apparently it'd conjured her up instead.

Then he straightened abruptly. The laptop was open on his bed — and he couldn't remember if he'd minimized the Word document.

"This is more like a special delivery." Bri started to step inside, but he instinctively blocked the way. She raised her eyebrows. "Can I come in?"

"Yeah, I mean. Sure." His chest knotted.

He wasn't trying to be weird, but he had to shut that screen ASAP. Thankfully it was facing toward the headboard, away from where they stood. Maybe she'd leave quickly. Or maybe Mrs. Beeker would come back any minute, and he could send them both away before his computer outed his confusing feelings.

Except he didn't want Bri to leave.

And it had only a small part to do with the rich aroma drifting from the box she carried. He edged closer. "So, what is it? Bedtime snack? Some kind of petit-four taste test?"

"Not exactly." She set it on the desk — across the room from the bed, to his relief — and started to open the cardboard flaps. Then she stopped, her cheeks tinting pink. "You open it."

Okay, now she was being weird. He hesitantly moved to the box, part of him still desperate to shut his laptop. But she wouldn't stay long, and besides, she had no reason to get near his bed.

The thought made his own face hot, and he quickly lifted the cardboard flaps.

A cake stared back at him — chocolate. Elegant gold script dipped and swirled above a piped motorcycle. *Bon anniversaire.*

He sucked in his breath. Not just a cake.

A birthday cake.

"Bri . . ." A hundred conflicting emotions skittered across the surface of his heart. No one had ever done something like that for him before. A dozen memories from his childhood cascaded over him, blurring his vision. His mom had tried, she really had.

But this.

He turned to Bri, afraid of what might be in his eyes, but more afraid not to look at her. And only a little afraid of what he'd see. "Thank you." The words felt petty and insufficient. He was a writer, for crying out loud. He could do better.

But his tongue felt thick and seemed glued to the roof of his mouth.

"No problem." She tucked her hair behind her ears, then crossed her arms over her sweatshirt. A smile teased her lips. "Sorry it's not red."

"That's the best part." He grinned, grateful for the comic respite from the uncertainty hovering over him like an anvil. He should say something more. He should hug her.

He should see if her glossy lips tasted like icing.

"Want to try it?"

His gaze locked on hers as his heart clambered in his chest. Yes, he did. Then he remembered she couldn't read his mind.

She meant the cake.

He drew in a long, deep breath, chasing away the sudden and unwelcome rush of desire. "Yeah." Anything to switch gears.

She dug in her oversized bag and produced two paper plates, two plastic forks, and a serving knife.

Nothing she did would surprise him at this point. "You travel prepared."

She shrugged and cut into the cake. "You want the motorcycle?"

"Did you have to ask?"

She sliced into the thick black wheel and cut off a sizeable square, then deposited it onto a plate. "Bon appétit."

He forked off a piece, his hand shaking a little beneath the plate. And he'd rejected all of those teas, so he couldn't even blame it on too much caffeine.

She reached back into her bag and pulled out a thermos of coffee.

He almost choked on his cake. Maybe just a little caffeine wouldn't hurt.

She poured some of the dark brew into the thermos lid that doubled as a mug and handed it to him. "For the birthday boy."

He took a sip. Still warm, and just a little bitter. Like always. "I still can't believe you did this."

She leaned her hip against the edge of the desk. "I had some spare time."

Hardly. He leveled his gaze at her over the rim of the mug.

She laughed — did it sound a little nervous? "Okay, so I had to make the time."

For him. He wasn't sure how to take that gesture — even less sure how he *wanted* to take it. He set his mug on the desk to pick his cake back up. He had to keep his hands busy or he'd get his answer sooner than he was prepared for. His fingers itched to tangle in her hair. He tightened his grip on his fork.

Thankfully, she ambled away from the desk as he chewed, roaming over to the bookshelf on the far wall and running her finger over the dusty titles he'd already examined.

"No Austen, sorry." There actually had been one volume, but he'd started reading it the other night and hid it under his nightstand.

She shot him a wry grin over her shoulder. "Then what on earth are you and William going to discuss at the wedding tomorrow?"

"Easy. *Motorcycle Weekly.*"

This time her laugh rang genuine. And everything in him wanted her to do it again. He eased closer to her, following like a reluctant magnet, stuffing another bite of cake in his mouth on the way. "See anything else good over there?"

"You mean you haven't looked for yourself?" She pulled a book halfway from the shelf, tilted her head to read the title, then slipped it back into place. "Mrs. Beeker has good taste."

"Not in color schemes."

She wrinkled her nose. "I take that back. She's got Charles's favorite book here."

"What's that? *War and Peace?*" He licked his fork, taking the opportunity to stand closer behind her and peer over her shoulder. She smelled like vanilla.

"Exactly." She held up the thick volume.

He winced. "Oh man. I was joking."

"Unfortunately, I'm not." She replaced it on the shelf.

Guilt started to slowly seep into his thoughts. *Charles.* He kept forgetting to go by his office and give that money back. He hated to think what Charles assumed by his keeping it. If that money had been in Gerard's pocket, it'd be burning a hole right now — especially standing this near to Bri. She'd never understand.

But it was safe in his wallet atop the nightstand, and his jeans were safe in his suitcase. He'd refused to fully unpack on this trip, refused to get comfortable or pretend he had any reason to stay a second longer than necessary.

Except now he really wanted to put his jeans in the red-lined dresser drawer.

Gerard swallowed, the last bite of cake drying out his mouth. One fact remained — playing Switzerland was growing more and more complicated. He still didn't fully realize why it would be such a big deal if Bri lost the Puff. Who cared if Charles stuck a chain in its place? She could thrive anywhere in Story — heck, anywhere in the United States. Smart, gifted in the kitchen, beautiful, relatable. Caring. Kind. Generous.

Maybe she needed the push of losing the Puff to extend herself. Could it be that the sisters selling to Charles — weaselly as he was — could be a blessing in disguise for her? She'd never see it that way. But it could be true.

He wanted the best for her. He *knew* that was true.

He turned and set the crumb-ladened cake plate on the desk. When he turned back around, Bri was perched on the edge of his bed, thumbing through one of the books she'd plucked from the shelf.

Uh-oh. Not good.

He cautiously approached. "What's that?"

Hopefully she couldn't hear his heart threatening to pounce out of his chest — and hopefully she wouldn't turn to the open laptop screen behind her. His fingers itched to grab the machine.

She held up the book with a smile. *"The Notebook."*

Oy. He fought the urge to roll his eyes. "Is that next on the book club list?" He sank down next to her and took the volume.

She smirked. "Why, are you going to come crash that session and argue everyone's interpretation too?"

"If it's on this, I sure will." He wiggled the book at her.

She snatched it back. "This is a good story. True love, against the odds."

"Hardly."

She bumped him with her shoulder. "How can you argue the romance of *The Notebook,* of all things? It's a new classic."

"How is it romantic? They cheated."

Bri opened her mouth, then closed it as his logic dawned in her eyes. "I suppose they did. But Allie wasn't married yet."

"Engagement isn't enough of a commitment?" It sure hadn't been to Kelsey.

Gerard rubbed his hand down his face, determined not to tread that path. Not tonight. Not when Bri was three inches to his left, all glossy-lipped and smelling like vanilla and reminding him of all the reasons why a relationship could be a very good thing.

But the memories taunted, begging to be remembered. The voices whispered — he wasn't enough. Wasn't enough to earn her. Wasn't enough to keep her. He fell back on the bed and covered his eyes with his bent elbow.

Bri's voice sounded above him. "I'm sorry. Hit a nerve?"

He lowered his arm, staring at the ceiling. "My fault." He was slipping. He gritted his teeth.

She flopped down next to him on her side, propped on her elbow. "Sometimes the past sucks."

"Only when it doesn't stay where it belongs." He shook his head. "Something about this town — something about . . ." His voice trailed off before he could say "you," and he realized how weary he sounded. Weary, and sort of old. His birthday loomed, and the joy of the cake she'd made faded a little. He hadn't accomplished nearly what he'd wanted to by thirty. What if he never did?

What if he ended up alone like his mom?

The thought churned his gut, and he

briefly closed his eyes. This wasn't him. He wasn't sappy. Romantic. Yearning.

Bri's vulnerable voice pierced the throbbing in his head. "Something about me?" Her words lingered barely above a whisper.

Desire to kiss her warred with desire to gain back control — to have, and keep, the upper hand. He didn't need her. Or any woman. And he had to draw the line in the sand now.

"Did I say that?" He pushed himself onto his side, turning toward her and meeting her gaze full-on. The boldness of the move seemed to affect her newfound confidence, and she faltered at his proximity just like he'd expected she would.

"You — you almost did." Her eyes dipped to his lips and back, and a pink tint coated her cheeks. "I thought you almost did, anyway. So, what about this . . . town?"

She meant what about *her*. But he could answer both at the same time. "It's like a spell. Makes me think about things I haven't thought about in forever. Makes me want things." As if on its own, proving his point, his hand reached out and traced the line of her jaw. So much for his battle for control.

She closed her eyes, her voice growing husky. "What do you want?"

To kiss her. Her parted lips practically

asked him to, and boy, he wanted to —
every fiber of his being demanded it. He
smoothed back a lock of her hair, tracing
the curve of her shoulder. Against his own
volition, he eased an inch closer, his hand
finding her hip and tugging her toward him.
She tilted her chin up, eyes closed.

But his mind was too jumbled. The last
two weeks had been messy — he and Bri
were too messy, for that matter. She'd
conjured up all kinds of old longings and
emotions, had reached down and soothed a
scarred-over sore spot with that cake she'd
baked for him. If he kissed her now, he
would just be acting on impulse and desire.

That wasn't right.

Heat thrummed through his veins, but he
reined it in. No more games. Bri deserved
better than that, and he wouldn't touch her
again until he knew he was doing it with
the right motive — until his heart was as
convinced as his body.

Besides, they were alone in his room. Talk
about a bad idea. He needed to shut that
door, quick — and probably open the
tangible one across the room.

It took every ounce of willpower he could
muster, but he pulled back, letting his hand
drop to his side despite it itching to clamp
back on her hip. He rolled over onto his

back. "Thanks again for the cake."

"You're welcome." A thousand question marks danced in her eyes, and he hated leaving her that way. She sat upright. "Gerard . . ."

"I know." This was their second almost-kiss, and he'd yet to explain either. How could he explain sheer terror, like when he'd stared into the eyes of a black bear in the Colorado wilds or parachuted out of an airplane? Yet she terrified parts of him he didn't know existed. "It's that I don't — it's not you —"

"It's her."

Statement, not a question, and that hurt. Because Bri had it all wrong. She thought he still had feelings for Kelsey, and she couldn't be more incorrect. Yet how could he argue when he couldn't tell her the real reason?

"It's okay, I get it. Old relationships die hard." Her voice cracked as she scooted toward the edge of the bed and braced herself on the mattress to stand up.

He might not be able to explain himself yet, but he definitely couldn't let her think *that.* "No, you don't get it. Can you just trust me on this one?" He sat up just as Bri's hand knocked into his laptop.

Before he could react, she straightened

the tilted monitor she'd bumped, her eyes dropping to the screen. To the document full of her name, some in caps, some lower-case. Some spaced. Some ran together.

Oh no. Heat gripped his chest in a vise.

She met his gaze, the question marks turning into something undecipherable. The corner of her lips tightened. A frown? A smile?

He couldn't tell, couldn't stop his heart from racing a marathon. "Bri —"

"Well, you certainly spelled it right."

He closed his eyes, embarrassment threatening to drown him in waves. "Bri."

She set the copy of *The Notebook* on his nightstand and strode toward the door. She lifted her hand in a wave, her face a neutral mask he couldn't interpret. "See you at the wedding."

He flopped back onto the bed and covered his face with his arm as the door clicked shut behind her.

CHAPTER TWENTY

He'd doodled her name. As much as one could doodle on a computer, anyway.

But why?

Bri tossed on her side, squishing her pillow under her head for the tenth time since her failed attempt to sleep an hour earlier. If she didn't know better, she'd assume it meant something — sort of akin to a woman drawing hearts and squiggles around her boyfriend's name. Not that Gerard was a hearts-and-squiggles kind of guy. But he wasn't the kind of guy to type someone's name without a reason either.

Apparently she'd gotten in his head. Was that what he'd meant by there was "something about this town"?

Something about her?

Bri abruptly sat up, straightening the twisted neck of her long sleep shirt. She couldn't lay there any longer, playing their second almost-kiss in her mind over and over like a scratched record. Nor could she figure any reason for her typed name. She knew what she wanted it to mean — which only proved how exhausted she was. She wasn't Gerard's type, and him *not* kissing her — while embarrassing — was a blessing in disguise. She couldn't afford to get any more emotionally tangled up than she already was right now.

Especially not with someone a week or less away from roaring out of town on his motorcycle and never looking back.

No more gifts and special treatment. The article would be what it would be — she didn't need to waste any more time buttering Gerard up. She had to start focusing on what really mattered. Like saving the Puff and finding out the truth behind her parents' story.

But even as she climbed the stairs to the attic, she knew that wasn't fully accurate. She hadn't been buttering Gerard up. She wasn't bribing him into writing what she wanted — she cared. A little more than she wanted to admit.

That urge to bake him the cake had been divine, she was sure of it. She had never felt so prompted by the Lord to give something away — more so even than the times she'd discounted baked goods for single moms and snuck Mr. Mac extra macarons and gave coffee to the homeless guy passing through town on his rusty bicycle.

That cake had been for a purpose — evidenced by the look in his eyes when he'd lifted the cardboard lid.

But her role in that purpose had to come to an end.

Bri grabbed the letters from the trunk and settled into her typical spot. She curled her bare legs up beside her and shivered, wishing she'd thought to haul a blanket up there with her. Maybe the answers wouldn't take long to find.

But as she flipped through the worn letters, nothing jumped out at her. No more clues, no more smudged letters. No more erased mistakes.

Had she imagined the whole thing?

She wanted to think that was true. She wanted to carefully tuck the packet of letters back into the depths of the trunk and cling to her memories. And leave them untarnished.

But Gerard's voice, nudging her toward the truth about her view of Paris, the truth about her heart for the people of Story, the truth about her book club friend's marriage, urged her forward.

What if there was more unwelcome truth

here to discover?

She ran her finger over the flap of the letter open in her lap. And suddenly a new memory surfaced, of her mom doing the same. Standing at the Formica counter in their kitchen, her expression unreadable — almost sad — as she held the envelope along with the rest of the stack of mail. Sunbeams streaming behind her through the kitchen window lit her hair like a halo. The memory was vague, fuzzy — but real.

Wasn't it?

Bri remembered that light halo. Remembered how stray hairs from her mother's hastily swept back braid shone silver in the sun. She thought her mom had looked like an angel.

The memory was real — as real as the foreign stamp on the back of the envelope. But if Bri was old enough to remember, then she must have been at least five years old, maybe six.

Her father had been back for years by then.

She stared at the letter — the one with the smudged initials — until her eyes blurred. T.R. The initials didn't ring a bell. She closed her eyes and racked her brain for any explanation other than the one she feared, but she came up empty.

Until another memory surfaced. Her father, yelling. A slammed bedroom door. Her mother's whispered pleas from the hallway into the wood. Mascara smears on her cheeks. Her expression transforming into a forced smile as she caught Bri watching from the bathroom doorway down the hall. She remembered those mascara smudges, just as vividly as she remembered the light halo.

Why hadn't she remembered until now?

She had to be mistaken. Her parents didn't fight. Her dad could get tense sometimes, but her mother always worked her soothing magic on him. Besides, that was never personal. It was over work or their tight finances. Of course he'd get stressed out at times, carrying the responsibility of a family and dealing with grief from the loss of his dad. No one was perfect. They'd loved each other fiercely — until the day they died. Together.

So why the sudden memories of foreign mail and smeared makeup?

Bri gathered the letters together and stood, not wanting to look further. She must be projecting her emotional state onto her past. Those memories weren't real — she was probably just imagining them to explain her fears. Her parents' love story was one for the books. She refused to let one little smudge change that.

Relieved the unnecessary burden was now behind her, Bri knelt before the trunk and tucked the letters carefully back into place. She probably shouldn't come up here again for a while. She needed to give her mind a break, get past Casey's wedding and the fate of the Pastry Puff — and Gerard's pending departure — and leave history alone for a bit.

Bri squinted into the trunk. To avoid the temptation to pull the letters out again soon, she really should bury them deeper. If they were harder to get to, maybe she wouldn't bother with them for a while — or at least it'd give her the chance to change her mind if she opened the trunk.

She quickly pulled out a folded patchwork quilt and a handful of books, then two worn shoeboxes. She'd stick the letters in the shoebox for protection, then put everything else on top.

Bri slid off the lid of the shoebox — the one containing her mother's old handkerchiefs and lace table doilies — and shifted the contents to make room for the stack of bundled letters. A faded, yellow photograph — an old one she'd never noticed before — lay in the bottom of the box.

She picked it up. A man in a brown suit stared back at her, only half smiling. He had dark, slicked-back hair, a strong jawline, and a thin mustache. Her heart rate accelerated, and she licked her dry lips. It was just a picture. Maybe one of her father's extended family members? An uncle she had never met?

That had to be it. She closed her eyes and turned it over, her heart thrumming desperate with hope. *Please* . . .

Bri opened her eyes, and a familiar cursive script mocked her.

From Paris, with love
T.R.

Gerard would typically rather face a fire-breathing dragon in a dark cave than a bride on the day of her wedding. He knew better. But regardless, he needed quotes for the feature, and he'd be more likely to get them earlier that morning than right before — or right after — the ceremony.

Besides, Casey had seemed pretty chill thus far. It shouldn't be that bad.

The early Sunday sun shone on his bare forearms as he knocked on the closed door of the little townhouse Mrs. Beeker had directed him to. He stepped back on the covered porch, nearly knocking over a mini tower of pumpkins, and turned to squint toward the unseasonably blue sky. At least she'd have great weather for the event.

If he ever got married, the sky was bound to start churning black clouds.

A series of thuds sounded against the door, hard and loud. Gerard flinched. What in the world? He knocked again. "Casey?"

Another thud followed an angry wail. "I told you to forget it!"

This felt like one of those defining moments, where he could turn away whistling and pretend like nothing had happened or knock again and possibly get sucked into a bridezilla vortex he could never escape.

He took two steps away, then sighed and knocked again, hard enough this time to bounce the bronze and gold wreath against the door. No answer. Just a steady stream of muffled thuds against the frame. *Thump. Thump.*

He took a chance and tried the knob. Open. "Casey?" He stepped into the house, halfway shielding his eyes with his hand in case she was in a pre-wedding preparation state of undress.

A red beanbag narrowly missed his head. He ducked.

"I don't even know you anymore!" Casey appeared in a fuzzy bathrobe around the corner of what seemed to be the kitchen. Her dramatic wedding makeup was already in place but smeared around the eyes like a raccoon. Curlers dotted her dark brown hair. She looked like a grandma from another era. Or maybe an alien.

Gerard held up both hands in defense at her raised fist, loaded with a blue beanbag. "What do you mean *anymore*? You barely know me at all."

She blinked. "You're not Nathan."

He shook his head in agreement. Thank goodness.

Casey wilted against the doorframe of the kitchen, lowering the beanbag to her side in defeat. "I thought you were Nathan. Back to finish our fight."

He approached, cautiously, like one might an injured boar. Not that he had a lot of experience with wild pigs, but it seemed like it'd be similar. He tripped over a stuffed animal on the ground and caught himself before stepping on some sort of preschool board game. "Can I have that?"

She handed over the beanbag.

"Glad it wasn't a ninja star."

She smirked, but the smile didn't make it all the way to her eyes. "They're from the girls' cornhole game. Harmless."

"Unless you're throwing with an arm like

Nolan Ryan." He crossed his arms over his chest, stepping backward toward the dining room table. He stopped just short of planting his jeans-clad butt in what looked like a heap of grape jelly. "Should I ask if you're okay, or ask if you need a glass of water?"

"Neither."

Apparently what she needed was a maid. He'd probably be standing around crying too if his apartment looked like this.

Not that he was ever home long enough to notice.

He eased past her into the kitchen, which was littered with paper towels and dirty dishes, to the fridge. He squinted at the meager contents and finally pulled out a bottle of water. It was half-empty, and there were some kind of sticky-looking fingerprints on the label, but moms didn't care about germs, right? He handed it to her.

She took it without meeting his eyes and twisted off the lid. "What are you doing here?"

"Needed some quotes on the wedding for my feature."

She rolled her eyes. "What wedding?"

It felt like the beanbag landed directly center on his gut. "Nathan bailed?" Anger flared. What a jerk. He ought to —

"No. I did." Casey's voice broke, and her

hand trembled as she took a sip of water.

Gerard pinched the bridge of his nose. Women. Still making zero sense. "So why are you reaming beanbags at travel writers if it's your own choice?"

"Because it's stupid. All of it." Casey sniffled, reaching up to wipe her eyes. Her fingers came away black, and she stared at them as if they weren't hers.

Weddings were dumb. He'd give her that. But she and Nathan . . . that didn't add up. "Did he do something?" He hoped she'd know what he meant so he wouldn't have to spell it out.

"No." She shook her head quickly, her curlers shaking. "He'd never cheat on me."

Never say never, but thankfully that wasn't the issue today, at least. "Where are the kids?"

"With my family, running last-minute wedding errands. They were trying to give me a break before everything started this afternoon so I could get ready in peace. But Nathan came by, and we started arguing . . ." Her voice trailed off.

Gerard shifted his weight to his other leg. He should get Bri. He really didn't know how to fix this — or if he even should. He suddenly had the urge to go back to the church and snag a slice of that peace he'd left behind. Guess that had been a useless errand. There wouldn't be vows to exchange from the looks of it.

Unless . . .

He sighed. "Okay. Give me the Cliffs-Notes." He couldn't believe he was actually inviting details from an alien bride. But something about those makeup smudges tugged at his empathy. Maybe he could re-assure her that she was making the right decision to call it off.

Because at the moment, she didn't look all that convinced.

Her eyes filled with instant tears. "We just don't even know each other. It's never going to work."

He nodded slowly. "You're right."

Her brow furrowed. "I thought you were trying to help."

He shrugged. "Odds are, it might not work. You haven't known each other that long. I'm sure there are stats on that kind of thing, right?" Stats. Data. Those were always the things he could depend on. Feelings came and went, but facts were hard and true. The sooner Casey learned that, the better.

"I didn't even know what flavor cake he wanted."

He blinked twice. "Cake?"

"For the groom's cake."

He waited. But she didn't explain any further. "Okay?"

Casey rolled her eyes, as if it was his fault he wasn't tracking with her. "Bri is handling the petit-four tower, which is technically the bride's cake, right? Well, the chief at the fire station offered to do a fireman-themed cake as a wedding gift and asked me what flavor Nathan wanted." Her eyes welled again.

"And?" It was like pulling teeth. From a dragon.

"And I told him strawberry." She bit her lower lip, looking more vulnerable than he'd ever seen her look before. In their few interactions, she'd been confident, beaming. In love.

He was still missing a step. "And he wanted . . . what? Chocolate?"

"See! Even you knew and I didn't!" She railed back her water bottle with that Nolan Ryan arm of hers.

"Easy there, Zilla." He pried it from her hand before she could release it and set her back against the doorframe. "It's just cake."

"Zilla?"

"Bridezilla."

She narrowed her eyes.

"Better to be mad at me than the groom." The poor groom. What in the world was

Nathan thinking right now? The bride bailing a few hours before the ceremony because of *cake*?

He ran his hand over the scruff on his chin, a dozen thoughts vying for first place in his mind. Maybe it would be best to call off the wedding. Save her — and her girls — some heartache later on. And Nathan too, for that matter.

An image of Kelsey shot through his mind, and this time, the residual wave of anger and regret didn't follow. In fact, all he could think about was Bri.

His mouth dried. "Hear me out, okay?"

Casey nodded, her red-rimmed eyes averted.

"I don't go for this kind of thing. Love, romance, weddings." He shuddered. "It's not my game. I'm the first one to say, 'Hey, don't do it.' "

Her gaze darted to his, hope and despair warring in her eyes. "You think I made the right decision?"

"I'm telling you, I'm not usually the guy to ask. I'd steer people away from marriage in a heartbeat. It's just not realistic for today's society." Hadn't his mom shown him that? Hadn't Kelsey? Hadn't every headline in Hollywood?

Casey started to tear up again. He grabbed

her shoulders and looked her straight in the eye, cutting her off. "And what I'm telling you is — marry Nathan."

Hope flooded her weary, makeup-streaked face. "You really think?"

"That's part of the fun of a relationship, right?" If relationships should be classified as such. Then he shook his head briefly to clear the temptation to dive into the past. This wasn't about Kelsey, this was about Casey. And she and Nathan were different — anyone could see that. "Taking time to discover someone is a good thing. You guys are just going to be doing that while you're married, is all."

"Maybe." She gnawed on her lower lip, relief dotting her expression. "So, it's just cake, right? One more discovery?"

"Exactly." He released her, giving her an awkward, obligatory pat on the arm. "Don't worry. You guys put the stats to shame."

Before he could stop her, she flung herself against him in a tight hug. "Thank you," she said, her voice muffled. "I think I just needed someone to tell me it was going to be okay. It's been so overwhelming." Her tears soaked his sleeve. "I can't wait to tell Nathan."

"Yeah, looks like it."

Gerard looked up at the agitated male

voice sounding to his right.

Turned out he wasn't as good at dodging fists as he was beanbags.

CHAPTER TWENTY-ONE

Bri sank into one of the few empty folding chairs, the arches of her feet throbbing in her high-heel pumps she'd worn for the better part of the evening. Her lower back ached, too, along with a tension headache forming behind her eyes. But it'd been worth it. The ceremony had gone off without a hitch. Pastor John had led a moving ceremony that had everyone dabbing their eyes. The announcement kiss had been a wolf-whistler, and the toddler girls had behaved themselves perfectly — short of one mini-tantrum during the unity candle lighting.

Now, Casey glowed as she danced in Nathan's arms, the fabric of her dress swishing like a bell over the top of her shoes. At the side of the dance floor, which had been formed to the left of the gazebo where they'd said their vows, her daughters painted each other's faces with cake icing, giggling as they clutched their mini-bouquets in their free hands. Guests milled about in their Sunday dresses, sipping golden punch from the table set up under the decorated arch. The entire fire department had shown up in uniform to support their brother, some with radios strapped to their belts to keep an ear out for calls. The fire truck was parked in front of the bakery on the street, ready to go just in case — which had been a big hit with the kids.

So far, the night, decorated with sheer fabric and twinkling stars and tiki torches, couldn't have gone any better. But Bri still couldn't shake the constant edge of nausea gnawing at her stomach. Every time she started to enjoy the evening, the mental image of that yellowed photo in her mother's trunk took center stage, and she was right back to reminding herself to breathe evenly. This wasn't the time to process her discovery. This was Casey's night, and she deserved for everything to go perfectly.

Speaking of which . . . Bri snuck a harried peek over her shoulder at the dessert table. The petit fours were being consumed at a steady pace, but it didn't look like she needed to grab any refills from the kitchen yet.

"Stop it."

Bri looked up in surprise as Gerard dropped into the chair next to her. He filled the space with authority, the broad width of his shoulders filling out a gray dress shirt that lightened his eyes.

She swallowed, hating his proximity and the way it affected her, yet overwhelmed with the urge to lean into his strength. She crossed her arms instead. "Stop what?"

"Stressing. It's over. You did it — she's hitched." He angled toward her in his chair, hooking his arm over the back. "Now, breathe, Cupcake." He shot her a wink, and her stomach tripped.

She looked away, back at the happy couple twirling on the dance floor. Nathan leaned in close to hear something Casey said, then tilted his head back and laughed. The joy in his expression made her want to cry happy tears for her friend.

Or maybe they were more like tears in general.

She forced a smile. "I'm keeping an eye on the petit fours."

"I know. Like I said, stop it." He was watching her, she could feel it, his eyes boring into her profile.

A random bout of self-consciousness hit her, and she tugged slightly at the hem of her dress — a pale pink sheath that hit right above her knees and went perfectly with the cream pumps currently threatening to murder her toes one by one. She hadn't stopped long enough earlier to decide if she felt pretty, but with Gerard staring at her like that, she suddenly really wanted to know.

These waters were way too dangerous to tread in her condition. Maybe she'd go grab those petit fours after all and squeeze them into the half-full trays.

Which reminded her. She twisted in her seat and squinted at Gerard. "How many petit fours did you eat tonight?"

Now he stared straight ahead, refusing to meet her gaze. "Two."

She quirked an eyebrow at him.

"Okay, four."

"Gerard." She lowered her tone in warning.

"Fine, I lost count after six. Don't judge."

A reluctant grin escaped, along with a bit of tension from her shoulders. Here she was, in the most romantic setting possible, depressed over love, and Gerard of all people was the one cheering her up. She'd definitely fallen into some kind of rabbit hole. Alice would probably appear in a moment, flanked by two playing cards and a giant teacup.

The DJ hired for the night turned on a new song, a slow country ballad. She swung her foot to the beat, determined to salvage the evening as best as possible and keep all intruding thoughts at bay.

Gerard glanced at her, and the remaining teasing light from their petit-four banter faded into something different. Something slightly more somber but just as genuine. "Would you like to dance?"

Her foot stilled. Dance. With Gerard?

She pressed her lips together, tasting the lingering remains of her cranberry gloss. "Sure." Did he hear the hesitation in her voice? Did he have any idea what might happen if Mabel and Agnes saw them? Or Casey, for that matter.

Or what might happen if she allowed herself to wrap her arms around those broad shoulders?

They stood at the same time, and she breathed a prayer as she followed him onto the dance floor, her eyes trained safely on the back of his dress shirt.

But no, that wasn't safe at all, was it?

He stopped toward one side of the floor, where they could participate but be some-what more inconspicuous. Maybe he was thinking about Mabel and Agnes, after all.

He opened his hand to her, and she slowly

placed hers in his, wishing she'd had time to touch up her nails in the frenzy of the weekend. Then she realized Gerard wouldn't notice anyway, and why did she even care if he did?

Then they were swaying, the music competing with her own heartbeat pulsing in her ears. The scent of evergreen wafted over her, mixed with the slight tang of cinnamon on his breath. She willed her palms not to sweat, unable to help but notice how calm Gerard seemed. Like he wasn't having any reaction to her at all.

Disappointment knocked, but she refused to answer. It was better that way. Just keep things nice and platonic. Simple. He'd almost kissed her twice yet hadn't, which was more than enough evidence of where he stood — and where she should be standing. Love was an illusion anyway. Her parents were showing her that with each passing memory she revisited.

Her throat tightened. She had to change the subject, fast. Forget her dreams for the future, forget the feel of his hand lightly grazing her lower back. She should focus on Casey, a few couples away, laughing with Nathan. Focus on the squeal of children running for yet another petit four, on the upcoming garter toss, on Mr. Hansen pouring a glass of punch for Agnes, who fussed over the spilled drops on the white tablecloth.

Focus on anything except the dimple in this man's jaw. "I heard how you saved the wedding."

His lips tilted up in the corners. "That I did."

She couldn't let him get too prideful. "And how Nathan almost gave you a black eye."

Gerard nodded again, slower this time. "That he did."

She risked looking closer. Faint hints of purple lingered in the edges of his eye and in the corner by his nose. That could have been a lot worse. "He felt awful after, I'm sure."

"Yeah, it just looked bad, him walking in on a hug with no context. We've shaken hands. It's all fine."

"Casey said it was pretty heroic."

He smirked. "Who? Me or Nathan?"

"Both of you." She tilted her head to the side, remembering Casey's enthusiastic reenactment of the event, complete with accents and hand gestures. "In fact, she said you were sweet."

He winced. "I'll make sure to get my publicity manager on that right away."

Bri laughed, another layer of tension sloughing off her back. "Don't bother. No one would believe it for a minute." But it had been sweet, him stepping in like that. Sweet — and totally out of character.

Which begged the question. "Why'd you do it?" She lowered her voice as the song switched to one of her favorites, a slow number about magnolias and near kisses and a man watching his true love get married to someone else. "I mean, that was your chance, right? To beef up the army on your side of the line?"

He continued to sway with her. "What line is that?"

"The 'love is a sham' line."

He spun her out in a slow circle and drew her back. His hand settled comfortably on her hip, warm through the thin material of her dress. "I never said it was a *sham.*"

"Love is a lie?"

"Okay, I might have said that."

"Well, you'd have been right."

The pressure of his fingers intensified as he adjusted his touch. Chills cascaded up her spine. "Come on, now, Cupcake. You don't mean that."

She opened her mouth, then closed it. Did she? She didn't know what she felt anymore, except hurt. Confused. Betrayed. The lyrics pulsed around her, a heartbreaking poem of love never acquired. "I think I do."

"What happened? Did someone ask for a refund on their love lock?"

She rolled her eyes, even as her fingers tightened involuntarily against his bicep. "No."

He lightly spun her away from him, and her thoughts whirled in unison with her legs. He pulled her back in and she took a shaky breath. "It's my parents."

He spun her again, double this time. "Your parents?"

"I think my mom had an affair." She collided back hard against his chest.

"What?" His eyes widened and his grip tightened around her. "When?"

She shook her head, emotion balling in her throat. Tears pricked and she clung to his shirt like a life preserver, staring at the button smushed between her fingers. No. She couldn't break down here.

The scent of laundry detergent and evergreen drifted over her like a cologne. Gerard's cologne. Dancing couples and tiki torches dimmed in her peripheral, and suddenly she was aware of only him. Of his heart thumping under her hand. Of his cinnamon breath and the dark scruff on his jawline and the thrill of his hands around her waist, holding her as if they belonged there.

As if she belonged with him.

A few painful heartbeats passed, then he lowered his head, his breath warm and his words low in her ear. "Come on, Cupcake. Don't lose it."

Lose what? Control? Dignity?

Her mind?

She looked up at him, questioning, their faces inches apart. She needed to breathe but forgot how. Their swaying all but stilled as the music and the joyful wedding crowd continued around them.

"Don't lose the best part of you. Your faith."

Faith. In God? In love? Were they connected at this point? She didn't feel connected to anything anymore.

And then it hit her, another memory. Of her parents, slow dancing in the kitchen while tears streamed down her father's cheeks.

Her chest tightened. No. That couldn't be real. But more details flooded her mind, convincing her otherwise. The crack in the cabinet behind her father's head that looked exactly like a lightning bolt. The feel of the cool tile under her thin shorts as she spied from the corner of the kitchen, hidden by the doorframe. She'd always loved to watch her mom twirl, as she'd called it. But they weren't twirling this time. Just holding each other and swaying.

Like Gerard was doing with her now.

Bri tensed, the sights and sounds of the reception morphing into one big blur. Anxiety took over, filling her mind and her mouth with cotton. She felt Gerard's arms still holding her close, firm yet gentle, but it was like looking through a distorted mirror. All reflection, no contact.

An overwhelmingly lonely sensation washed over her from head to toe. She was falling for Gerard. Her prince had finally come — on the same night she discovered love didn't exist.

She couldn't breathe. Needed to scream. Wanted to hide.

She tore free of his grip, hating how easy it was to do so. He didn't fight to hold on, which only proved her greatest fears. "I've got to go." She stepped backward, farther from his outstretched hand. If her parents' love hadn't been real, maybe there was no such thing.

"Go?" Gerard frowned, moving a few steps toward her. Confusion pinched his features. "Bri. Wait!"

She left him alone on the dance floor.

He'd never understand women. He never had before, and the odds of him figuring them out now at thirty years old were pretty slim. Nonexistent, to be exact. And yet here he was, patching up strangers' weddings and chasing after crying pastry chefs.

"Bri! Where did you go?" The music trailing from the dance floor all but drowned out his voice. She'd run in the direction of the love-lock wall and the fountain, which was to the left of the gazebo where the wedding reception was underway. Thankfully, it seemed like no one had noticed her dramatic exit. Or his.

A pair of light-colored pumps lay in the grass just ahead of him. He scooped them up and kept walking, following the scattered leaves that trailed toward the fountain. The trickle of water let him know he was close, even before his foot landed on the first stepping-stone. He saw the one marked "Wanderlust" as he neared, and his heart hitched in memory. "Bri! I know you're here."

The lights from the reception didn't stretch this far, even though the moon above offered a bit of assistance. He stepped carefully from stone to stone, her shoes hooked on two fingers. These were the same ones she'd been tottering around in the first day he met her, when she showed him the love-lock wall and the fountain. He couldn't believe he remembered that.

He *shouldn't* remember that. Shouldn't have danced with her. It was too dangerous. But his time in Story had become exactly that.

Man, she'd looked gorgeous — stunning, even, in that pink dress. All big eyes and flushed cheeks looking up at him, something withdrawn and haunting under the surface. This thing with her parents — what had she said, an affair? — had apparently cut her deep.

He didn't get it. Her parents weren't even alive. How had she found out? And why had it shaken her so thoroughly?

A frantic splashing of water sounded a few yards away, and his eyes finally adjusted to the shadows. Bri was standing knee-deep in the stone fountain, pawing anxiously through the water.

Was this what had been bothering her for the last several days? He cleared his throat. "Come on, Cupcake. Out of the fountain."

She ignored him, water splashing up onto the hem of her dress. "It has to be here

320

somewhere." Her gaze remained riveted on the small waves she was creating.

"Unless you're looking for a goldfish, I don't think it is." He took a few steps closer so he didn't have to speak quite as loudly. If the wedding guests saw their beloved pastry chef swimming with her clothes on . . . Charles could have a media heyday with that one if word got out. Revenge would be easy. Thankfully he hadn't shown up to see for himself.

Bri dove into the water up to her elbows, and the clang of metal hitting rock made him squint to decipher through the shadows. "What are those?"

"Keys."

"Keys." Nope. Repeating it didn't bring clarity.

"To the love locks." She brushed damp hair back from her face, her expression a twisted mask of hurt and panic. "I have to find my parents' key."

Oh no. His heart stammered a sympathetic beat. "There's probably a hundred keys in there."

She stirred the waters again. "More than that by now."

"Are you familiar with the phrase 'needle in a haystack'?"

She ignored him, or maybe didn't hear

him. "I have to get their lock off the fence."

"Why?"

She shook her head, refusing to answer as she scooped up another handful of keys.

He tried a different route of reason. "How are you going to recognize it?"

"I hung it up there after they died. It's gold and has their initials stamped on one side." She held a key up to the moonlight, then tossed it back into the fountain. Grabbed another handful from the fountain floor. Checked. Tossed.

Checked.

Tossed.

He crossed his arms over his chest. "This is going to take you all night, Bri."

"Then help me!" Her voice cracked as she looked up, fully focusing on him for the first time since their dance. Wet hair straggled down her shoulders, and dark makeup ran under her eyes. From water? Or tears?

Something surged in his chest. Irritation. At her, for her foolish mission. At himself, for getting mixed up in it. But mostly at himself, for not being able to fix it. For not confronting her earlier, when she'd been so down at Taylor's Sushi Barn. He should have tried to get to the bottom of it then, or during the other half a dozen opportunities he could have since.

But the last-minute wedding prep had taken over, and she'd soldiered through — apparently to her detriment. There was only one thing to do.

He toed off his loafers and cuffed his pants.

The water was cold — almost unbearably cold. Chills raced up his bare calves as the water lapped at the bottom of his pants. He set his jaw, reached down, and felt for keys. He came up with three. All silver. He tossed them back, then realized the better approach was to discard the already examined keys onto the side of the fountain so they wouldn't keep picking up the same ones.

No. The better approach was to find out what exactly was going through that head of hers so they could get out of the fountain and into some dry socks.

He waded toward her. "What are you doing, Bri?"

She shuffled through the keys in her palm. "You know what."

He gently took her wrist. "How long has their lock been on the fence?"

"It was the first one up." She rolled in her bottom lip but wouldn't look at him. The moonlight cast a shiny glow on the top of her damp blonde head.

"Then shouldn't you leave it there?"

She pulled her hand free of his grip. "It's a lie." Her voice shook, and she tossed the rejected keys back into the water before grabbing another handful. When she stood, she straightened so aggressively, he had to step back to avoid her headbutting him.

"Because you think your mom had an affair?"

"You were right all along. Love isn't real."

"I never said it wasn't real."

"Don't backpedal now because you want to argue, okay?" She waved her hand. "Your vibe was clear all along. Crystal clear. And you were right."

His heart clenched. That wasn't what he'd wanted to do. Bri was light and goodness and faith. He hadn't meant to let his bitterness snuff out her spark. Those were his issues, his past — not hers. She'd had her mom on such a pedestal — he couldn't bear to see her knock her down. Not like this. "Bri —"

"Don't. It's fine. I just want to take their lock off the gate." Her voice was level, controlled. Too controlled. A muscle worked in her jaw. "I thought they had a solid relationship, but apparently they didn't. I thought they were an example, but they weren't." Her tone wavered slightly. "I thought they were an inspiration to aspire to, but —"

"Love isn't a farce." He interrupted before she could finish her depressing monologue. She was running on straight emotion right now and would probably feel silly tomorrow.

Just like he would for standing in this fountain.

He tried to catch her eye, but she was too busy examining more keys. "Look, just because your parents might or might not have had some issues doesn't mean their marriage wasn't genuine."

"You don't understand."

No. He didn't. He stabbed his fingers through his hair. "Do you even know for sure?"

"There's a photo." She moved farther along the circular fountain, reaching for more keys.

He raised his eyebrows. "Of her with someone?"

"No."

"Then what?" He fought back an annoyed sigh. "I can't read your mind, Cupcake."

And it was a really good thing she couldn't read his. Frustration and confusion warred for first place in his train of thought. But silencing both of those was the acute, almost painful realization of how beautiful Bri looked — smeared makeup, damp dress, ragged hair and all. Her vulnerability from the dance was gone, shut up behind this defensive wall she'd concocted of assumptions and keys.

He wanted to tear it down.

He wanted to light her spark again.

He wanted to fix it.

So he sloshed through the water toward her, grabbed her around the waist, and tugged her hard against his body. Her hands gripped his arms with surprising strength. Keys splashed into the water at their feet. He wasn't sure whose lips found whose first, but suddenly they were kissing, lips melding into one. She tasted like petit-four frosting and fruity Chapstick.

And hope.

His grip tightened around her as her fingers dug into his biceps. He broke away for a quick breath, and she moaned in the back of her throat before pressing her lips back against his. Heat surged through his chest.

He'd gone for a spark.

And created an inferno.

Shouts rang from the reception. Gerard instinctively jerked backward — or had Bri pulled away first? They looked at the tent, then at each other, as they slowly stepped away. Reality began a slow descent, and the water he'd almost grown numb to crept up his legs with an aching chill.

"I think Casey and Nathan are leaving." Bri's gaze flickered from the reception to him, then to her feet. She took a ragged breath before meeting his eyes once more. Her gaze, impossible to read, looked as convoluted as he felt.

Raucous laughter sounded from the party, and a car engine started up. The moment was over, and there was way too much to say. He swallowed hard, wishing he was better at verbal words than written ones.

Bri pulled her skirt from the water and bunched it in one hand. "I guess you should probably go —"

"I guess I should probably go —" He laughed, but it sounded forced to his own ears. "Right. Duty calls."

He grasped Bri's arm and helped her out of the fountain, then climbed out beside her, suddenly unsure of everything. Unsure what she was thinking. Unsure how he was supposed to dry off his feet with nothing but leaves for a towel.

Unsure if that kiss had been a mistake — or if the real mistake was in letting Bri walk back to the reception with so much left unsaid.

CHAPTER TWENTY-TWO

Bri had kissed Gerard.

She'd kissed him like she was drowning and he was a lifeboat. And she had been drowning — in emotion, in confusion, in anxiety. His kiss had quieted the storm yet awakened a different one.

But right now, she just felt calm, serene. Almost too tranquil — like the eye of a hurricane.

She had a feeling the rest of the storm was imminent.

Bri tugged her fuzzy socks higher up her leg. She hadn't been able to get warm since her fountain dive, despite the robe wrapped around her and the space heater blaring beside the sofa in her townhouse. It was as if the chill had reached all the way inside to her core.

Yet every time she relived that kiss, she melted a little. She gingerly touched her fingers to her lips, remembering how Gerard had stood there with her shoes like something from Cinderella. He was no Prince Charming, but seeing him pursue her, her pumps dangling from his masculine hands, had stirred something deep. She couldn't pretend anymore. She was falling for him.

And it was the worst timing possible.

Her parents' letters — well, her mother's letters — lay in her lap, like a weight she couldn't shake. She ran her finger over the flap on the top one, then closed her eyes. The events from the evening played in her mind on repeat — in fast-forward, then slow-motion. All the feelings Gerard had conjured in her with that kiss twisted around and knotted up until she couldn't separate fear from elation.

After she'd seen to the closing reception duties, packed up the remaining petit fours, and waved her friend off into her new future with a handful of lit sparklers, Gerard had been nowhere to be found.

Her stomach twisted at the possibilities. Was he avoiding her? Regretting the kiss? Or just giving crazy Cinderella some space? She'd led him on quite the wild goose chase. But he'd come after her to the fountain in the middle of her breakdown. That meant something.

Right?

She adjusted the heat blowing on her legs and tightened the belt on her robe. What if it didn't? What if he'd just been caught up in the romance of the evening and acted on impulse?

Ugh. She shouldn't be sitting there, reliving it piece by aching piece. It was a dead end, anyway. Who cared what he felt? He was leaving in a matter of days.

And this feeling she had? This alleged falling in love? It was an illusion. She had to remember that — or she might end up like her parents.

Rejection was better than betrayal. It had to be. She was probably lucky that Gerard had changed his mind post-kiss.

Embarrassment tapped her on the shoulder as she leaned her head back against the soft material of the sofa. She couldn't believe she'd climbed into that fountain in the middle of a wedding party — in a dress, no less — to find her parents' key. It could have waited. She hadn't even found it.

It shouldn't be so important.

She picked up the packet of love notes. Their lock had been the first one on the wall, and now it all felt like a mockery.

She felt like a mockery.

A knock sounded on her townhouse door. Bri jumped, knocking over the space heater.

She set it upright and turned it off, heart pounding as she checked her phone for the time. Almost eleven.

Had something happened to Mabel or Agnes? Fear pricked. They'd seemed fine at the wedding — Mabel had applied fresh lipstick between dances and Agnes had pretended not to putter around Mr. Hansen and all the desserts — but you never knew with women their age. Maybe all the excitement had been too much for them.

She set aside the letters and hurried to the front door, clutching her robe closed at her throat. She peered through the peephole, and her heart hitched.

Gerard.

She turned the lock, then hesitated. Was he coming for more kisses? Or to tell her it'd all been a huge mistake? Both thoughts make her borderline nauseated — for entirely different reasons. Regardless, she had to play it cool.

She opened the door, halfway. "Hey." Her voice sounded more like a Muppet than the calm, normal vibe she'd been hoping for, so she cleared her throat and tried again. "Hey." Now it was too low, like she'd been a whiskey drinker for a few decades. She groaned inwardly.

"Warming up, I take it?" Gerard nodded

toward her getup — fleece robe, socks pulled up to her knees, and fuzzy slippers. He was still in his dress shirt, sleeves rolled up, revealing his tattoos. His pants weren't cuffed anymore, but the damp marks were still evident up his calves.

"Trying to." She opened the door to allow him in, her stubborn heart refusing to return to a normal rhythm. "That water was pretty cold."

"I remember." He stepped inside and stood by the door she shut behind him. "I'm not staying long, don't worry. I know you must be exhausted."

She nodded, unable to meet his eyes, afraid she might break down again or worse — blurt out how she felt. When she didn't even understand how she felt. And she'd probably do it in the Muppet voice again. She pressed her lips together.

He leaned against the wall. "I just wanted to make sure you were okay."

He was being sweet again. She had no idea what to do with that. She nodded a second time, still averting her eyes and swallowing any attempt at words.

He shifted his weight, his proximity warming her much faster than the space heater's feeble efforts. "So, you're okay."

She nodded a third time. Swallowed. "I

will be."

"It's not as bad as you think, Cupcake. It never is." His hands were tucked loosely in his pockets, and she realized how badly she wanted his touch again. How comforting it'd been — and how distracting. For those few glorious moments, she hadn't thought about her parents' love story or Charles or losing the bakery. She hadn't felt the slow erase of her entire identity and security fading away. She'd just been herself.

With him.

"I need to ask you a question." His eyes grew serious, and her chest tightened. Here it came. He was going to ask her to keep their kiss quiet. Because he regretted it. Because he didn't want to sully his columnist reputation by getting involved with a source. A crazy source, no less, who dove into fountains during weddings and rambled about love letters.

She lifted her chin, determined not to let him see any more vulnerability. She had to redeem what little shred of dignity might still be lingering. He hadn't come to find her after their kiss, and now she knew why. "I won't tell anyone, if that's what you're worried about."

He frowned. "I wasn't worried."

"Don't be. I know it was just a high-emotion night." Her hands shook, so she crossed her arms over her robe. "You're not obligated to anything here."

"I wasn't going —"

Her wounded pride wouldn't hush. "Weddings are romantic, and you got caught up in the moment. I totally get it."

He flinched. "That's not —"

"You're leaving soon, so that'd be ridiculous to even think that we could be —"

"That's enough, Cupcake."

She snapped her mouth shut. Then had to ask. "Why did you come?"

His eyes were unreadable now, guarded. He reached into his pocket. "I came here to give you this." He held up a key.

A golden key.

With initials stamped on the side.

Oh. She took it with trembling fingers. "Gerard . . ."

He didn't look at her. "Good night, Bri." He let himself out, shutting the door behind him.

She sagged against it, the metal cold in her hand. He'd gone back for it. All that time he'd been gone while she told Casey goodbye and finished the wedding responsibilities, all that time she'd thought he was avoiding their kiss — he'd gone back to the fountain. Alone. In the cold.

For her.

And she'd just babbled on, rejecting him before he could reject her. She was such an idiot. Now she'd never know what he thought or felt.

But wasn't that for the better? He was leaving — and they were as opposite as opposites could be. Even Mabel and Agnes had backed off on the matchmaking attempts, not making a single peep or giving them a single glance during their shared dance at the wedding. It was as if they, too, had realized the inevitable end.

There was, however, one thing she had to know.

She flung the door back open. "Gerard, wait!"

He turned, already halfway down the walk. The night breeze wafted against her face and chilled the small patches of skin showing above her knee-high socks.

Heat flushed her cheeks, despite the cold. "What were you going to ask me?"

"Oh, yeah." He shrugged, then offered a half smile. "I was just wondering what you did with the leftover petit fours."

Monday had never felt more like a Monday — and this was most likely his last one in Story.

And it was his birthday.

Bacon sizzled in the kitchen of Taylor's Sushi Barn as Gerard typed his next sentence, deleted half of it, then tried again. He'd never had writer's block like this before. Trying to highlight the bakery's charm and small-town appeal, all while keeping the report balanced, was exhausting — especially when he believed more and more that Charles was right. Not that the love-lock wall was an eyesore, necessarily, or that Story needed a coffee chain in its stead.

More so, it was what Bri needed.

He took a sip of coffee and glanced up from the corner booth, where his back was planted firmly against the wall. At least this time he didn't have to worry about running into her — unless she suddenly traded her Friday pizza treat for a Monday one.

That was just one of the many unique facts — or maybe quirks — he had discovered about Bri.

Another being how well the woman could kiss.

His stomach dove remembering their encounter in the fountain last night. In hindsight, he wondered how in the world he'd made it this long without doing so. When he'd held her in his arms, she fit so perfectly, it was like he'd discovered a piece of himself he hadn't realized was missing. It had lit and stoked a fire he'd effectively doused since Kelsey. It had felt . . . right. Natural.

It had felt a lot like setting down roots.

His stomach knotted again. He didn't do roots. He did wandering much better. So it was good that she'd put him off at her door last night before he could mutter any mumbo jumbo about home and puzzle pieces and macarons for the rest of his life — even if it'd stung pretty bad. She'd saved him from a big mistake. It was his own fault, anyway. He'd crossed the line and was paying the consequences for it today with an emotional hangover.

He pinched the bridge of his nose as his head pounded. Travel features had never been this personal before — and not just because he'd made out with the main subject. He was firmly wedged between the proverbial rock and a hard place, and his writing was suffering for it.

It wasn't like public opinion mattered here, since the decision ultimately lay with Mabel and Agnes, but if he slanted the article toward Charles's potential plans at all, Bri would be crushed. The feature had the potential to draw a lot more business to the Puff — which could possibly convince the sisters not to sell and silence Charles's persistent offers once and for all.

He hated to admit it, but Charles had had a bit of a point when he'd alluded to the power of the pen.

Gerard drummed his fingers on the table beside his laptop. He just wished Bri could see what he saw. That her identity wasn't in the bakery. It wasn't even in her parents and their story — she had her own to live out. Her strengths and talents lay far outside baking petit fours and macarons in the same place her mother had.

But she was too close to the situation to see it. Literally too close — she'd never even left Story besides a four-hour jaunt to Nashville. The woman needed to cut the apron ties — and see the world. See *Paris,* for crying out loud.

Maybe he could talk to her later today, friend to friend. Help her see reason — not for Charles's sake, but for hers. And for the sake of his finally writing "the end" once and for all on this feature. If he was going to spin it as a "goodbye to one of this small town's charms," he needed to know ASAP how it was going to go down.

The door opened across the diner, and Charles walked in. Speak of the . . .

He refused to finish the thought, however accurate, as the lawyer placed his order at the counter. The older woman in overalls working the register handed him his change and receipt, and Gerard winced. Crap. That cash he'd been intending to give back to Charles was still in his room. This would have been the perfect opportunity to end whatever alliance Charles thought they had. Regardless of Gerard's take on the Puff, he refused to accept money on the job — especially from someone as slimy as Charles. Bri's ex, for that matter.

He stared at the blinking cursor on his screen, willing Charles not to see him. He didn't want to engage with this guy and try to interpret his next move. He wanted the man to just grab his coffee and whatever grease-ladened item he'd just purchased and keep walk —

"Gerard. Always a pleasure." A hand extended into his line of vision, in front of his computer screen.

Gerard shut the laptop and shook his hand briefly, the smile he forced feeling faker by the moment. "Charles."

The stuffy lawyer didn't sit, thankfully, but leaned his khakis-clad leg against the table — probably in an effort to tower over Gerard, since he clearly couldn't while both men were standing. "I hear you had a run-in with my intern at the Puff after that news segment."

"Yeah, I set him straight." Gerard crossed his arms over his chest. "Low blow, sending a spy, don't you think?"

"Nah, just good fun." Charles laughed. "It was all in the name of research."

"Research." Gerard nodded slowly. "Is that what they're calling entrapment now?"

His smile faded as he adjusted his glasses. "Lighten up, man. It's all a big game, and you know it. A game that Bri started, remember? She went to the media, not me."

True.

"Besides, we both know it doesn't matter. Those crazy sisters are close to selling. They won't be able to resist my offers much longer — they're old and tired. Who cares what the town prefers?" Charles smirked. "Once they get some real cappuccinos and flavored mochas, they won't care about ancient macaron recipes and bitter coffee."

Also true. But the way Charles described it was so callous — like the bakery wasn't Bri's job and clearly a beloved staple in the community. No wonder she was so defensive. Still, the point remained — Bri didn't need the Puff to be Bri. To be *Abrielle.*

But she'd do a lot better seeing that fact

on her own thanks to Gerard than against her will because of Charles. He had to convince her — before Charles's plan worked and she was embarrassed in front of her entire town. From the looks of her last night, she was in no place to withstand that kind of a blow.

"I guess we'll see." He wouldn't commit to further verbiage than that. Besides, who knew? If business kept up, especially after the feature ran, maybe Mabel and Agnes wouldn't be tempted to call it quits. That is, if he ever finished it.

And if he could make himself promote a place that he knew would end up robbing Bri of adventure.

He turned back to the computer and opened it. The answer wasn't there, but maybe Charles would take the hint to leave.

"How's the article coming?" Charles pointed to the laptop.

Wrong hint. Gerard scooted the monitor a few inches away from his greasy finger. "It's coming." While Charles was lurking, Gerard really needed to clarify that the jerk's cash hadn't accomplished anything. "Hey, what are your office hours? I'll come by —"

"Well, if this isn't a meeting of the minds."

What's her name — Sandra? — appeared

at Charles's elbow, her platinum hair so shiny it was almost white under the diner lights. "And the biceps." She squeezed Charles's arm, her hot-pink talon nails bright against his white button-down shirt, then looked at Gerard like he might be next.

Gerard picked up his coffee as a shield. "Morning." He didn't say "good," because it wasn't.

"I would have grabbed you a coffee if I'd known you were coming." Charles pulled his arm free of Sandra's grip, then looped it around the top of her shoulders. Friendly hug? Or defensive move to keep her at bay? Theirs must be one exhausting friendship.

"You know I can get my own coffee." Sandra batted her hand at Charles and shot Gerard a wink. "I'm more independent woman than damsel in distress."

Hopefully that wasn't supposed to impress him.

Gerard watched over the rim of his coffee mug as Charles's arm subtly tightened around Sandra's shoulder. Jealous of the flirting? He was no threat. She would probably flirt with the potted fern on her way out the door.

Regardless, this was more than he could stomach on just a coffee and a bagel. Gerard picked up his laptop and slid it into his bag.

"I've got to go. The written word waits for no man." Or something like that. Whatever could get him out of this suddenly claustrophobic environment.

"Yes, the power of the pen, indeed." Charles raised his eyebrows pointedly at Gerard.

Sandra's overly made-up eyes darted between the two of them. "Oh, talking in code." She purred in the back of her throat, and Gerard's coffee threatened to launch from his stomach. "Come on, boys. I want in."

"Chill out." Charles nudged her side. "It's business."

"As in, none of mine?" She winked again. "That's not how that works in Story. You know you'll tell me later."

Gerard tried to slide out of the booth while they argued, but Sandra was blocking him. "Excuse me."

"Right this way, darlin'." She moved aside, but only about an inch so he'd have to brush against her. "I'll get out of your way anytime."

Gross. The woman could make the Gettysburg Address sound like a come-on. Gerard didn't even try to smile as he squeezed by. Charles's hand on his shoulder stopped him — but only because he was itching to grab the guy's wrist and fling him over his shoulder in a standard self-defense move.

Charles lowered his voice, his urgent tone implying he might not be as confident about public opinion as he let on. "We're on the same page, right? You know what to do."

Gerard shrugged off his hand, fighting the urge to tell the selfish doofus and his crazy sidekick exactly what he thought of them. But that'd be just what the lawyer needed to start some sort of slander lawsuit against him — or worse, against *Trek*. "I've got an article to finish. You two have a good day."

Gerard strode out of the diner before he could give in to his impulse. He'd return Charles's money tomorrow and get the entitled shark off his back. For now, he had to convince Bri to do what was best for herself — and he knew exactly the way to do it.

Unfortunately, that would also mean convincing his heart to stay out of it.

CHAPTER TWENTY-THREE

Mabel propped her elbows on the display counter at the bakery and leaned forward, a twinkle in her eyes. "So. Have you heard from Casey since the wedding?"

"Mabel, it was just last night." Bri gave the eager woman a playful eye roll as she poured decaf coffee into Mabel's pink-striped mug. She never drank leaded after 4:00 p.m. "I'm giving her time to settle in before bombarding her. Since they aren't getting a real honeymoon yet, there's no way I'm calling her the next day."

She slid the mug across the counter to Mabel. If the older woman only knew what had transpired between Bri and Gerard over the last twelve hours, she'd be switching gears faster than the teenagers who always raced off the line at 3rd and Oak.

"I'm so proud of us." Mabel beamed at Agnes across the room, who crossed one sensible shoe over the other from her perch on one of the nearby chairs. "Married! We really did it."

"Yes. We did our civic duty." Agnes offered a brisk nod in agreement before leaning down to buff a mark off her left shoe.

Bri couldn't resist the opportunity to tease. "So, are you and Mr. Hansen next?"

Agnes jerked upright. "Well, I — I never . . ."

"Maybe *that's* why she's so grumpy." Mabel took an intentional sip of her coffee.

Agnes narrowed her eyes. *"Mabel Pauline —"*

"I'm just saying, it wouldn't hurt you to try one of my lipsticks some time. Or wear a blouse that's actually a color." She set down her mug with a clank.

"I don't know. Mr. Hansen doesn't seem to mind beige." Bri shot a smile at Agnes, who looked equal parts miffed and giddy. "I saw how he was looking at her at the wedding. Crowding the dessert table."

She straightened her shoulders. "He just likes petit fours."

"He thought something was sweet, that's for sure."

Agnes pursed her lips. *"Abrielle —"*

"Okay, okay." She held up both hands, grateful the matchmaking attention was elsewhere for once, especially with everything brewing between her and Gerard. Or was that *brewed,* past tense? She sobered. It'd been her own fault, verbally shoving him out the door without even hearing him out.

The door chimed, and all of their heads swiveled toward it.

Gerard.

There he went again, barging into her world unannounced every time she thought of him. Acting like he fit into her cozy little town, sauntering inside wearing that same leather jacket that smelled like evergreens, and carrying . . .

A picnic basket?

He grabbed the chair opposite Agnes at the table and spun it around backward before plopping down into the seat. The giant wicker basket settled on the floor between them. "Ladies, I need to borrow your head chef."

Bri's heart stammered with confusion. Mixed with excitement. Mixed with dread. What in the world was he . . .

Agnes and Mabel locked eyes across the room, trying — but failing — to hide matching smiles. "Of course," they responded simultaneously.

Ah. Understanding dawned. Bri shook her head.

347

She hadn't escaped their matchmaking efforts completely after all.

The gazebo by the love-lock wall, where just hours ago Casey and Nathan had pledged their vows, was still draped in sheer gauze and twinkle lights. Though the sun hadn't quite set, the coming dusk provided a sufficient RSVP to the shining strand's beckoning invitation.

"Have a seat." Gerard pointed to the blue plaid blanket spread on the middle of the gazebo's platform floor, and Bri obediently sat down, crossing her legs. Thankfully, she'd worn jeans to work.

"What is this?" She tried to keep the skepticism out of her voice, but this was clearly a setup. It had Mabel and Agnes written all over it. The question remained, though, why was Gerard succumbing to it? Surely he saw through the attempt too.

It had to be related to the article. He was probably trying to pacify Mabel and Agnes, get the rest of what he needed from her to complete the feature, and break the ice she'd created between them. She would like him to leave town on friendly terms too — even if that amazing kiss had made it more complicated.

"I thought you could use an authentic

French picnic." Gerard knelt next to her and began to unpack the wicker basket.

Her throat knotted. He'd packed all that — for her? Had Mabel and Agnes suggested it?

"For tonight's dinner, we have your choice of bread — baguettes or croissants." He pulled out a long, flat tray and unwrapped the aluminum foil covering the top. "And of course, charcuterie."

She squinted. "Cured meats?"

"Pâté and ham, to be exact. And salami, because what's a picnic without salami?" He set the tray on the blanket between them and reached back inside the basket, pulling out a bowl of grapes and a giant block of cheese. "And *Tomme de Savoie.*"

She'd never heard of it but felt embarrassed admitting as much — especially since it was clearly French. It would just further prove his theory that she didn't know nearly enough about Paris as she'd always assumed. "Sounds good."

"It is. Trust me." He passed out utensils and paper plates, then handed her a bottle of water before settling on the blanket. "I'd debated bringing wine, but I don't really drink anymore."

Anymore. Interesting. She toasted him with her bottle of Evian. "Cheers."

"Cheers." He tapped his bottle against hers before opening the lid and taking a swig.

They ate in silence for a moment, Bri still desperately trying to make sense of the last twenty-four hours. The discovery of that telltale photo. The wedding. Her embarrassing meltdown at the fountain. Their kiss. Their conversation at her front door that had been two parts genius in sparing her heart but three parts agonizing in never getting to hear his.

Yet Gerard seemed at ease across from her, popping grapes into his mouth and stacking various meats between two slices of bread. Was it that simple for him to set aside what had transpired between them and just eat carbs?

If that was the case, she was envious. Men had it so much easier. Fewer emotions clouding up every action, every thought. To them, it was just: Kiss? Check. Potential relationship voided by porch brush-off? Check. Delicious dinner? Check, check.

Bri nibbled on a slice of *Tomme de Savoie,* and the nutty flavor burst across her tongue. Gerard was right — as usual, which was only half as annoying as it used to be. The cheese was amazing. But despite the desire to keep shoving cuisine into her mouth, the urge to know the truth beckoned louder. "Come on, be honest. Why did you do this?"

Gerard propped himself up on one elbow in his reclined position and grinned. "Because cheeseburgers are American?"

She rolled her eyes. "You know what I mean. Not this." She held up her slice of cheese. "I mean, this." She waved her hand to indicate the entire spread. "Especially after . . ." She couldn't bring herself to say it.

He didn't particularly look like he wanted her to, thankfully. "You've been pretty down the last few days. I thought this would cheer you up."

She blinked slowly. *"You did?"*

"Well, yeah. Who isn't cheered up by food?" He ate another grape.

He had totally missed her point, but now she knew. It wasn't a matchmaking ploy. This was *his* idea — not her aunts'.

She swallowed, her tongue still tangy from the cheese. This picnic was perhaps the most thoughtful thing anyone had ever done for her. It was the most thoughtful thing a man had ever done. Her dates — rare as they were — usually consisted of pizza at Taylor's Sushi Barn, fries at the fast-food drive-in, or occasionally, the bowling alley. Fun but average. Not specified to her tastes or interests.

Gerard had taken the time to get really specific.

"You've lost your spark." Gerard's tone grew serious, despite the fact that he'd sat up and started juggling grapes. "I couldn't take it anymore. I mean, I can't exactly write an award-winning article to convince people to come visit the Midwest's most charming bakery and its most sullen chef, now can I?"

She grunted a halfhearted protest but couldn't be offended. He was right — she'd been really grumpy lately. But that didn't change her new reality. It didn't change her mother's potential secret or the fact that her solid foundation had crumbled.

Bri reached out and snatched a grape from his jerky juggling cycle. The other one bounced off the tray of meat and the third dropped into his lap. "Hey. No fair."

She popped the grape into her mouth. "True confession time."

He raised his eyebrows at her. "You're an avid juggler?"

"No." She slid a few pieces of ham inside a croissant. "I've never heard of *Tomme de Savoie.*"

He nodded. "I figured." She chucked another grape at him, and he laughed. "Tell me something you do know about France."

She tilted her head to the side. "They didn't invent French fries."

"What about French toast?"

She swallowed a bite of bread, not as confident in the answer but determined to wing it. "Nope."

"Very good." Gerard leveled his gaze at her, and the look reminded her of the feel of his lips against hers the night before. Her stomach cartwheeled twice. "Now tell me about your mom."

There it was. The weight she'd been carrying threatened to land squarely back on her shoulders. She'd carried her mother on a pedestal all these years, and now . . . it was as if she teetered precariously on the edge. If the truth fully emerged and her mother eventually fell — what did that mean for everything Bri had ever believed? About her parents? About love?

About herself?

Gerard must have noticed her hesitation, because he reached toward her across the blanket. "I mean, tell me something good. Something from her time in Paris."

Bri drew a deep breath and closed her eyes. The good. Not the unknown . . . the bad . . . the incredibly ugly. But the good. Paris. "That would be when my mom met my dad." That part would forever be un-stained, regardless of how the rest of their love story played out.

It had to be.

He leaned back on his elbows, his gaze fully fixed on her. "Tell me."

She tucked her hair behind her ears. "For the feature?" She wasn't sure how much of this she wanted included in the article. The backstory of her parents' relationship might help encourage reader interest, which could mean more potential customers — but it felt wrong to flaunt that part until she knew the whole story.

What if she'd been wrong about all of it?

"No." He shook his head. "Tell me for you."

The woman was painfully beautiful in twinkle lights.

Bri relaxed as she talked, as he'd hoped she would. She'd wrapped up in the extra blanket he'd packed to ward off the evening air, and the bright green stripes made her eyes shine.

Gerard snagged another slice of cheese as she chatted about her mother daring to leave her small town and learn from a professional baker in Paris, where she met Bri's father — the baker's son.

This was good. He'd needed to level her defensive wall so she'd hear him when he talked about the sisters potentially selling the Puff. Plus, she'd been wound so tight ever since she found whatever evidence she thought she had on her mother, that it seemed like she might actually crack. That wasn't the way to go into this last round of war with Charles — if she decided to keep fighting, that is.

Hopefully that would change tonight.

Gerard finished his last bite of sandwich. "How long did it take your dad to ask your mom out?" Probably not as long as it'd taken him to ask Bri out — although technically, this still wasn't a date. Was it? He didn't really know the game anymore. Didn't want to play it even if he did.

Bri was different, though. Despite their kiss, despite the awkward conversation at her front door, and despite the unofficial status of their current dinner, here they were, relaxed and having a good conversation.

It was just hard not having permission to lean over and kiss her senseless again.

She wiped her fingers on the napkins he'd remembered to stick in the basket at the last minute. "Six days."

"Where was the bakery, anyway? By the Seine?"

"No, it was on *Boulevard Fleur Rouge.*" She smiled. "I've always loved that name."

"Red Flower Boulevard." Gerard sat up. "Wait a minute. Is that a few blocks from *Rue de Vaugirard*?"

"Yes, I think so." Bri twisted the cap back on her bottle of water. "She talked about walking that particular road often with my father after work while they were dating. Why?"

"Hang on. I think I might have a picture." He tugged his phone from his pocket and pulled up his photo album. He distinctly remembered having a conversation with Remy on that particular road — a conversation before the one that eventually led to warning Gerard off women and small towns.

"What?" Bri's eyes lit, and she scooted closer on the blanket to lean over his shoulder. She smelled like vanilla, as always. "You've seen the bakery where she interned?"

"There are so many bakeries in Paris, I'm not sure I went to that one or would remember if I had." He scrolled through his iPhone photos until he found the album marked "European trips," then "Paris." "But I'm pretty sure I've walked past it. That street

356

name rings a bell."

Bri's short intake of breath over his shoulder reminded him how big of a deal this was to her. He'd stood on the street where her mother had met her father. Hopefully this visual would be more sweet than bitter for her.

The picture he'd been looking for finally appeared on his screen. "Here it is." He surrendered his phone to her eager hands.

Remy had offered to take his photo — just so Gerard's starry-eyed self could say he'd had a picture taken by *the* famous travel photographer. In hindsight, he could see the humor in how he'd fawned over his idol. Travel photographers didn't typically have a cult following. But the man had humored him, like an uncle figure, and let Gerard shadow him all afternoon. It wasn't until later that Remy's bitterness emerged in the form of a life lesson for Gerard — one he'd taken to heart.

Until Kelsey, anyway.

Bri gasped. "That's you. And that's the bakery in the background! *Brioches Croisées.*"

Hot Cross Buns. Catchy. He tilted the phone to see the photo again, his hand brushing hers. The bakery had been unintentionally included in the back. Half of the store's low-hanging wooden sign was clearly visible to the right of the photo, its white cursive print beckoning pastry lovers inside.

"I can't believe you've stood where my mother spent her early adulthood." Bri shook her head, wonder etched across her face. Then her expression dampened.

"Hey."

He waited until she looked up, meeting his eyes. The vulnerability in them made him desperate to soothe the ache. "You'll get there one day." If she didn't stay glued to the safety of the Puff, anyway. He opened his mouth to say as much — it was the perfect opening for his message. But it didn't feel right. She was too raw.

She offered a half smile as she handed back his phone. "Who took the photo?" The flicker in her eyes made him briefly wonder if she was jealous it might have been a girl.

"A travel photographer idol of mine, actually. Remy." Gerard shook his head. "I'd tell you how obsessed I was with this guy at the beginning of my career, but it'd be really embarrassing."

"Tell me anyway." Bri shifted positions on the blanket, settling in for the story.

He would. But only because he wanted to keep that achy look out of her eyes, even if it was at his own expense. "Well, he's not usually a typical twenty-one-year-old's hero, but he was mine. Remy's the reason I got into this job in the first place." He still remembered that particular glossy photo. *Submerge Magazine,* page 29. It'd been a full-color shot of a man standing on a sailboat, wind whipping the sails, ropes pulled taut as he fought for control — man against ocean. Gerard could almost feel the mist from the waves, and in that moment, he knew what he wanted to write about.

Bri tugged the striped blanket up to her chin. "How is that?"

Gerard plucked another grape from the bunch and rolled it between his fingers. "His photos are art. They let people travel without ever leaving their living room." He shrugged. "It made me realize I wanted to be on the other side of that page."

Remy's warning against roots, against love, against anchoring oneself down at the expense of life had settled deep, right alongside that oceanic action shot. It'd shaped who he was for most of his twenties. Had shaped the way he'd treated Kelsey once they got serious. He'd always resented her a little for it. Was that why she'd sought attention elsewhere?

The sandwich settled like a rock in his stomach.

He knew he'd played a role in their difficult relationship — after all, it took two to fight. But it only took one to leave, and he'd been prepared to stay. Kelsey had wanted otherwise.

Maybe she had sensed his commitment was halfhearted. Remy's words had always stayed in his mind, a constant tension between the glittering diamond on Kelsey's left hand and his fear of losing himself — his dreams, his goals, his career — for the sake of love.

Roots were bad. And Kelsey had wanted roots that extended clear down to Middle-earth. Gerard's chest tightened.

Now here he sat on a picnic blanket, having to constantly restrain himself from falling for a woman who had never even left her hometown.

He quickly changed the subject to travel expenses and the absurd price of cab fare in other countries. Cracked a joke about how much he hated escargot. Shared a story about white-water rafting that made Bri's eyes widen two notches. But despite his storytelling skills, there was an unfinished story lingering in the back of his mind every time he let his gaze linger on her lips.

Theirs.

She sat with the blanket wrapped around

her shoulders, chin resting on her bent knees, laughing at a joke he'd just told and didn't remember. Bri was a threat to the security he'd wrapped himself in all these years. He felt a little like Linus from *Peanuts,* suddenly, desperately clutching at the frayed fabric he needed.

But every moment with Bri, his grip loosened just a little.

"Tell me more about your mom." Bri plucked off a corner of a croissant with her fingers and nibbled a bite. "Besides that she wasn't much of a cook."

Gerard took a tight breath. He owed Bri more information — she'd shared plenty about her own parents. "I think my mom is probably the polar opposite of yours."

"Maybe not. She raised you, right?" Bri gestured with the bread. "And you turned out alright."

He didn't fully agree, but he also didn't want to be the guy who argued a compliment. "Mom does her best, I'll give her that."

Bri kept her steady gaze on him, not allowing the out his instincts wanted to take. He exhaled slowly. "But I'm pretty sure she's abusing alcohol." *Again.*

Sympathy lit her eyes. She set down the

remains of her croissant. "That's got to be hard."

He nodded.

"For both of you."

He raised his eyebrows at her.

"You want to take care of her, and something like that makes it more difficult. It's out of your control."

A knot formed in his throat, and he didn't even try to swallow it down. Just nodded. Avoided her gaze, the one that suddenly saw way too much. She'd nailed it.

His proverbial blanket slipped further from his hands, and he steepled his fingers together in an effort not to grab it back. "After my promotion, I'll have more opportunities to help her."

Bri hesitated, reaching over and gently laying her hand on his wrist. "Can I say something hard?"

"It would be unfair for me of all people to say no."

She offered a tentative smile. "Just remember, there's a difference between helping and enabling."

The truth rolled around in his gut a moment before settling. She was right. If he started shipping his mom more money, what would that accomplish at the end of the day? He couldn't control what she bought with it. But if he helped pay for her to attend a rehab facility . . . His thoughts churned before his hope crashed. She'd never go for it.

And that wasn't in his control either.

He looked at Bri and inhaled deeply. Inhaled her. Inhaled the memory of their kiss. Of leftover cheese wafting in the cool air around them and the scent of contentment. He returned her touch, turning his hand over to lace his fingers with hers. He squeezed. "Thank you."

She squeezed back before easing into her blanket cocoon. "Of course." She nestled under the cover, then offered a corner to him. "Need this?"

He studied the striped material, then shook his head. Peace welled for the first time in months. "Nah, I don't think I do."

CHAPTER TWENTY-FOUR

Gerard was romantic. Who knew?

Bri scrubbed the bakery floor with her wet mop as if she could scrub away the memories of that evening. Of the soft blanket tucked up by her neck and the aroma of French cheese saluting her senses and the warm timbre of Gerard's voice lilting over her as they talked for hours. Despite his opening up and sharing about his mom, she'd only shared the good memories she could remember of her parents — she couldn't handle any more bad, those stealthy ones that kept creeping in from nowhere. Were they even real?

Her gut knew what her heart didn't want to accept.

Bri scrubbed at a stubborn sticky spot on the tile floor, her arms burning with the effort. She still didn't know how to reconcile the aged photo with the rest of what she knew about her parents' relationship. But the signatures and the handwriting and the initials all matched up. She couldn't ignore it any longer.

Her frantic mopping slowed. But for a minute, while she had been talking with Gerard under leftover twinkle lights, it almost hadn't mattered. It was as if the past had been momentarily suspended, and she was so caught in the present that the hope of the future actually seemed within grasp.

She tightened her grip around the blue wooden handle. She wanted something with Gerard. Wanted more than a stolen kiss during someone else's wedding and a clandestine twilight picnic. Terrifying as it was, she wanted *more* slow dances. More food fights. More kisses.

Except he was leaving in a matter of days. And she was so jaded at this point, she'd be tempted to slap Cupid in the face if he dared fly past.

If she wanted to move forward — if she wanted to even have a *chance* at determining her real feelings for Gerard — then she had to find a way to reconcile that photo.

And she wouldn't find the answer by cleaning an already clean bakery.

Before she could change her mind, she returned the broom to the utility closet, turned off the lights, and locked up. She'd go back to the photo and start there. Embrace each memory as they came, as painful as they were, and see where it all led. She owed it to her parents — and truly, she owed it to herself.

Back at home, the stairs trembled — or was that her legs? — as she climbed to her familiar spot in the attic. The spot that once brought such comfort and now brought only trepidation. Bri took a deep breath, unlatched the trunk, and dug the photo from the depths of where she'd stashed it.

The same startling sensation swept over her from head to toe as she looked back into the dark eyes of a man who was a complete stranger to her, but clearly not to her mother. She swallowed hard, turning the photo over and examining the scrawled signature. The initials. The smudge of the aged ink. The crinkled lines from bent corners.

The photo had been through a lot — and apparently so had her mom.

Bri rocked back on her heels in front of the trunk, sending a dust bunny skittering past like a tumbleweed. She let out a slow breath. There had to be more here. If her mom had saved a photo, maybe there was an explanation somewhere else.

But where? Bri frowned. She'd thoroughly gone through all her parents' belongings after the funeral and saved what she wanted for sentimental value. The rest was donated. No way anything had slipped past her and Mabel and Agnes during that teary time. No, this kind of memory would be hidden.

Hidden. She narrowed her eyes and reached back into the trunk, carefully removing the familiar contents piece by piece. The hardback books. The lace doilies. The quilt. She sneezed from another rogue puff of dust and kept mechanically removing items until her hands braced flat against the bottom.

She felt around, then rose on her knees to peer into the dim shadows. It was solid. Plain wood. Nothing fancy. But what was she expecting — a panel to open into a secret chamber? Maybe next she'd find a winter wonderland and a lamppost behind a rack of fur coats.

This was ridiculous. "You're looking for something that doesn't exist." She spoke out loud, the sound of her own voice echoing in the silent attic, giving her new appreciation for how crazy she must look. First, she had splashed around in a fountain at night in her best dress to find a key, now she was groping around a trunk in the semidarkness for clues that weren't there.

Maybe that was all there was. Just some letters. Just a photo. Just a memory better left in the past. A story untold.

Her heart thundered in protest as the ache of unanswered questions demanded to be soothed.

She began returning the items to the trunk, carefully, knowing this would be the last time she'd be back. For a while — maybe forever? At least until she moved out one day. She couldn't take the reminder of the uncertainty.

And that was the worst part of all — not knowing. Did her mother have an affair? Had it been one-sided? Was it relegated to letter-writing only, or had it been physical?

Had her father ever known? Was her mother a decades-long liar? Was it possibly all a horrible misunderstanding?

It was a lot easier to bury mementos than the past. Her stomach cramped as she piled the stacks of books on top of each other, then nestled the doilies down beside them. The faded navy, purple, and green quilt went on top last, covering the rest of the items. And there they'd stay. Protected from the truth.

Maybe that's how it was meant to be.

Bri stood reluctantly and shut the trunk,

but the quilt caught the corner and wedged between the hinges. She raised the lid and tucked the edges back down.

Something hard crinkled under her fingers.

Her breath hitched. She ran her hand between the folds of the quilt and a semi-sharp corner pricked her finger. She winced and tugged it free. An envelope.

Sealed and addressed.

Monsieur T.R.
27 Rue Pasteur
Paris, France

The letter quivered in her hands, and she willed strength into her fingers. This was it.

This was the truth. All this time, hidden inside the quilt she'd refused to wash because it still carried the faint scent of dried roses from the trunk. The faint aroma of her mom.

She stared at the letter. She should go to Mabel and Agnes and open it with them for moral support. This was the final evidence — she knew it. She hadn't been crazy. She hadn't been imagining the worst. It was here, tangible proof. Whatever the letter contained, they'd help her figure out how to process it.

But strangely enough, she didn't want to go to them. She didn't want Mabel's well-meaning coddling and Agnes's well-meaning suspicion.

She wanted Gerard.

Dear T.R.,

I used to be young, and foolish. Now I'm older and even more foolish to allow a door to stay cracked that never should have opened in the first place.

Newlywed life was hard, and living in a foreign country was even more difficult for me all those years ago. Hard to learn the language, hard to be separated from my hometown and all things familiar . . . hard to trust a man. When I met you that day on the Seine, I should have nodded and kept walking.

But you drew me in, with your passion and your photos and compliments. My husband was never a natural at those things — at finding beauty and making a woman feel beautiful. He was always working, always pursuing the next financial goal instead of my heart. But you were a natural at those things, and it was to my detriment.

The letters you sent were nice, I admit. My sinful heart knows that well. It was comforting, in the turmoil of a new marriage, to have a plan B, a "just in case"

370

for myself if marriage proved too difficult. But you deserve more than a plan B, and my husband and daughter deserve much more than a halfhearted wife and mother.

So I'm going to confess it all. I almost did years ago, when I first moved back to the States and cut you off. Those years of silence from you were the best for all of us as I healed and moved forward. I never should have allowed you to start sending letters again years later. But I was selfish and prideful and scared as my husband's stress and temperamental outbursts grew stronger. I clung to a backup possibility again, even though I never responded to you.

The last several years of my marriage have been so fulfilling that I hated to cast a long shadow on something brimming full of light. But it's time. Starting with you and what should have been said long ago. I'm going to burn all of the letters.

You may no longer contact me. I know that what we shared was real to you, but I'm choosing a reality that you can't understand. I'm choosing love. Not frothy affection, nor secret meetings, nor forbidden letters, but love. Real love. It's hard. It's often messy and loud and full of grit. But it's also kindness, patience, and forgiveness, which I have no doubt my husband will extend to me. And even if he doesn't, my faith will no longer allow me to hold this secret close. I long to be rid of it.

What happened in Paris will no longer stay in Paris. The truth will emerge, for better or for worse. Love is a choice, over and above a feeling. My heart — and my choice — is forever with my family. I do hope one day you find the same grace.

Please do not respond to this letter.

Sincerely,

Julia Duval

"Wow." Gerard leaned forward against the back of the chair he'd straddled at the desk under his B&B window as Bri finished reading. So heavy — and it made sense now, the emotional turmoil Bri had been under the past week. He had known her only a short time and had immediately recognized the respect and admiration she carried for her parents. No wonder she'd been so shaken.

Bri paced the floor between him and the red-draped bed, her high ponytail swinging with every faltered step. "Right?"

"It sounds like there were more letters than the ones you read all the time."

"I think so too. My mom must have gotten rid of those." She started to fold the letter in her hands, then stopped. Then folded it in half and replaced it inside the envelope. She looked like she was torn between burning the entire thing and preserving it. He didn't blame her.

When Bri had first knocked on his bedroom door about fifteen minutes ago, his instinct had been to joke about Mrs. Beeker starting rumors about these late-night pop-ins. Then when he saw her red-rimmed eyes and pale face, his next instinct had been to pull her close, to protect her from sadness, to right whatever was wrong. Which was sort of terrifying.

Though not as terrifying as the fact that in a few days, he wouldn't see her anymore. His open laptop sat on the desk behind him, cursor blinking a steady reminder that he was almost done with part two of the article.

Almost done with Story.

"Who knows how off-again, on-again the letter part of their correspondence was once Mom made it back to the States. But I would imagine the bulk of it took place when I was a little girl, during that year my dad was in France dealing with his family inheritance." Bri shook her head, a sad smile turning the edges of her mouth. "I had the time frame of the letters right, but the author wrong."

"This should make you feel better, though, huh?" Gerard braced his arms on the back of the chair. "She did the right thing. She shut it down."

"I guess. I just still hate that it happened at all." Bri closed her eyes briefly, and when she opened them again, she looked . . . older. Wiser. And a little more exhausted.

But that spark, that glimmer he'd missed these last few days — it was there. Barely smoldering, but there.

He exhaled in relief. Part of him didn't want to leave Story at all. But no part of him wanted to leave with Bri not her perky, romance-oozing, love-obsessed self. She contributed to the people of Story in that way, and he hated to see it end. She was chiseling her gift into something beautiful, and he'd gotten to watch the masterpiece develop. Despite his own cynicism, he'd felt something growing beneath the surface. Like long-buried seeds finally exposed to sun.

Great. This town was making him sappy. *Bri* was making him sappy. And he almost didn't mind anymore, which was the scari-

374

est element to it all.

He rubbed his hands down his face, then looked at Bri. "Sometimes the truth is better than the wondering — even if the truth isn't pretty." His own words shot an arrow of conviction deep. Wasn't he doing that with his own mom? Avoiding the issue of her alcohol consumption rather than confronting her with the truth?

"I'm starting to agree." Bri pulled in her lower lip, worry furrowing her brow. "The one thing that really grates on me still is that she didn't send it. If she never mailed it, does that mean she changed her mind? Why was the letter in the trunk?"

"Maybe she just needed to vent. People write stuff they never send all the time." Gerard shrugged. "People should do that more often, actually, especially on social media."

"Maybe." Bri didn't look convinced. "But if the whole point of the letter was to cut off any future communication, then he would have had to have received it to know to do so. I don't think that's it."

"May I see it?" He held out his hand.

Bri hesitated, then slowly placed the envelope in his palm.

He carefully removed the letter and studied the loops and swirls of her mother's handwriting. History breathed off the page. This paper was important — not just morally, or spiritually, though it was that — but important for Bri. For generations to come, this paper mattered.

Why *hadn't* her mother sent it?

His eyes zeroed in on the date, expecting to see fifteen to twenty years in the past. But it was only about ten years ago. A hunch tapped on his shoulder, and he held his breath. "Bri? What day was your parents' . . . accident?"

She didn't hesitate. "October 12th, 2010."

That's what he thought. He held up the date for her to see, and her eyes widened.

"October 10th, 2010." She collapsed on the edge of the bed, gripping the fabric in both hands. Wonder filled her voice. "She never had a chance to mail it."

"Sounds to me like she wrote it, then stashed it in her trunk until she could make it to the post office alone."

"But she never did." Sorrow immersed her expression. "I don't even know . . ."

It was a lot to process. He wanted to sit next to her, to comfort her, but wasn't sure that was wise — for about a dozen reasons. One being that if he got that close, he'd also want to press her back against the bed and kiss her senseless. He'd almost done so a dozen times during their picnic but had restrained. It hadn't been about that — and tangling up their ties before he rode out of town wouldn't be beneficial to either of them.

She sniffled and pressed her fingers under her eyes, dabbing at the remains of her makeup.

Well, maybe just a quick hug wouldn't hurt.

He moved to her side on the bed and wrapped his arm around her shoulders. She leaned in automatically and fit so perfectly into the curve of his arm that he shivered. He tucked her in close and held her, breathing in the vanilla scent of her hair even as his heart thudded a warning.

He'd never been one to appreciate red lights.

He turned toward her, tilting her chin up with one finger, and grazed the curve of her jaw. Her skin was painfully soft, her breath warm. Her tear-filled eyes closed and her lips parted.

That was all the motivation he needed to close the distance.

The kiss was shorter than their last one, but it fanned a flame a dozen times hotter. His lips moved against hers as he pulled her in closer. She sagged against him, filling any remaining space between them with soft sighs and fingers clutching the folds of his shirt.

He kissed her as if he wasn't leaving. As if her life wasn't in turmoil. As if either of their futures weren't up in the air. He just kissed her, as easily and naturally as he breathed.

She pulled away first, sucking in a gulp of air and dabbing the corners of her mouth. "Gerard."

He wanted to pull her back in but didn't. He didn't trust himself or the gallop of his heartbeat. "Hey."

Her hair was mussed, and her eyes were bright with leftover tears and a shining emotion he couldn't quite name. "Thank you."

He laughed. "Thank *you,* Cupcake."

She blushed, and he loved that he could make her do so. "I meant for listening. And for the hug. And — you know."

Boy, did he. "I know."

"But you're —"

He sobered. "I know." He was leaving. And she was staying. And that was most likely the end of their story in Story.

A careful guard took over her expression. "I never showed you the picture."

Dodging the new subject worked for him. "Show me." It didn't really matter to him to put a face with a name, but it seemed important to her — and offered a distraction from the mass of feelings trying to talk him into kissing her again.

Bri stood and went for her purse across the room, and he immediately missed the warmth of her presence at his side.

She returned but didn't sit, just stood in front of him and extended the slightly crinkled photo. "This is him."

He took the photo, glanced down, and started to nod. Then his grip tightened and his heart accelerated. "Wait. This is who?"

She crossed her arms over her chest. "T.R."

He stared down at the dark swoop of slicked hair, the thin mustache, the camera strap slung over one shoulder.

Remy.

CHAPTER TWENTY-FIVE

Her mom always baked when she was upset.

Bri remembered that now, the way her mother's anxious whisks around a mixing bowl slowly turned into careful, therapeutic strokes. The way her tense shoulders eased as the warmth of the oven filled the kitchen, the way her expression softened as she slid her hands into pink, checkered oven mitts and withdrew delicious-smelling trays.

Bri stirred with that same anxiety now, another halfhearted effort at matching her mother's famous macarons. She was a glutton for punishment, wasn't she? Attempting an impossible recipe for the hundredth time. Developing feelings for a man who would be leaving any day now. Trying to hold on to a bakery that her ex was determined to steal from her.

Her grip tightened around the whisk as the hands on the clock above ticked closer to noon. Charles couldn't succeed. He might have backed off for now, but she wouldn't relax until Mabel and Agnes specifically told her that they would never sell to him. That they planned to die of old age in another decade or longer and leave the bakery to her.

That nothing else would change.

Her cell phone on the bakery counter buzzed with an incoming text. It was Casey, texting a selfie of her new family of four with a dozen heart-eye emojis. Bri smiled, grateful her friend had found her happily ever after — one that wasn't quite as complicated as the chapter Bri found herself in.

The memory of Gerard's lips on hers last night shot a tingle up her spine, and her smile faded. How long until he left Story? After she'd shown him the picture last night, he had acknowledged it with less interest than she'd imagined he would have and soon after ushered her out the door to finish his article. She would have been concerned at the abrupt change of mood if that kiss hadn't held such . . . well, everything. Passion. Gentleness. Comfort. It'd been even more genuine than the kiss at the fountain. It'd been *real,* no doubt.

But those kisses couldn't lead anywhere other than to the trail of exhaust from Gerard's motorcycle.

The door to the bakery opened, and a brisk wind swept across the room ahead of Mr. Mac. Bri set aside the whisk and brushed her hands on her apron. Mabel and Agnes were grocery shopping, so she'd brought her mixing bowls up front to help customers while she experimented with the macarons.

"Well, aren't you a welcome sight." Her smile begged to return, and she granted allowance. "I was just itching to make a decaf soy latte, and here you are."

"I know you're lying, but I'll believe you because I want it." Mr. Mac shuffled toward the counter, his eyes twinkling beneath his trademark bushy eyebrows. "You got anything new for my sweet tooth?"

He patted the front pocket of his hunter-green button-down and retrieved his wallet with slightly shaky, darkly veined hands. Hands that once fought as a Marine and had held the same woman for over sixty years. A true hero.

"I'm working on a new recipe, but it's not ready yet." She glanced dubiously at the bowl. "It might not ever be, honestly."

"You're the best baker I know, Miss Bri."

"I do have plenty of these Parisian cookies." Bri tapped the display. "Buttercream frosting and Eiffel Towers."

"I'll take three." The edge of his Marine insignia tattoo peeked from the rolled-up cuff of his shirt as he pulled out a handful of bills.

Jill, his nurse who waited by the door, cleared her throat pointedly. "I'm assuming two of those are for Betty? You know you can't have all three, sir."

"I was going to give one to you, you old nag." He winked at Bri and lowered his voice. "Make it four."

"No one tries to sneak extra sugar on my watch, Mr. Mac." Jill grinned, crossing her arms over her dark scrubs. "I know you're anxious to rejoin your bride, but we don't want you bailing out of here too soon, now."

He grumbled back good-naturedly as Bri bagged his purchase — three cookies — and started working on his latte. The door opened again, and Jill stepped aside as Gerard entered.

Bri's breath hitched and her hand stumbled on the steamer handle. It sputtered — sort of like her heart as he strode toward her, nodding to Mr. Mac before locking eyes on Bri. She fought to regain control of the machine. They'd just seen each other last night — and his article was all but wrapped up. Why was he here?

Mr. Mac's thick brows raised and furrowed. His wiry gray mustache couldn't begin to hide the mischievous grin that spread across his weathered cheeks. "I'll be. Finally!"

Heat climbed up Bri's neck as she reached for a lid. "It's not what you think." She kept her voice down, hoping he'd get the hint to do the same. But Mr. Mac continued to look back and forth between her and Gerard like an awed spectator at a professional ping-pong tournament.

"Oh, I think it is." Mr. Mac took his bag of cookies and stole a bite of one with a furtive glance over his shoulder at Jill. Crumbs dusted his mustache, and the twinkle in his eyes took over as he slid the evidence back into the sack. "But it's never what we think it's going to look like, is it?"

She snapped the lid securely onto the latte cup, but then her hands stilled. Never what you thought it was going to look like. That perfectly described Casey and Nathan. Perfectly described this new revelation about her parents.

Perfectly described her and Gerard? She swallowed.

"Me and Betty overcame more than one obstacle in our day." Mr. Mac shrugged. "And we have a pretty big one keeping us apart right now." A shadow of sadness battled the light in his wise eyes. "But it's a temporary long distance. Everything can be overcome eventually, my dear."

Emotion balled in her throat and Bri nodded, unable and unwilling to speak past the lump. Her parents had overcome their obstacle, too, hadn't they? It hadn't been all peaches and cream, as she now knew — but they'd made it. They were still together and still loved each other the day of the wreck.

Could she and Gerard overcome long distance? And his commitment issues? And her fears of repeating the past?

Was that even a choice she had the liberty to make?

She shot Gerard a glance across the room. He'd remained a polite distance back, as if sensing the importance of the conversation. Or maybe he just remembered the last time he'd put his foot in his mouth about the kind old man.

"Maybe." She fiddled with the lid on the jar of coffee grounds perched next to the coffeepot, screwing it on and off again. Her heart raced. "But what about in the meantime?" Open. Shut. Open. Shut.

"In the meantime . . ." Mr. Mac released a slow breath, his eyebrows dipping as he thought. "You make every moment count. You pray. You sneak sugar past your warden, bring flowers to the ones you love, even when they're no longer with you — and look forward to the next time you get to see them." He shot his gaze to the left, where Gerard lurked. "Whether that's in this world or the next."

Finally, she gathered herself and sniffed. "Don't you dare pay me for that latte, Mr. Mac."

He shoved the bills across the counter and picked up his cup, voice pitched with humor. "Don't you dare refuse to let me."

She bit her lower lip to catch her smile. "Give Betty my best."

"I always do." He offered a slight salute, reminiscent of his former glory days, then turned and shuffled toward Jill, goodies in hand.

Then he paused in front of Gerard. Bri held her breath. He looked him up and down, inches from his face. Gerard didn't move, just straightened to attention. His eyes flicked to Bri, then back to Mr. Mac, where he held the older man's gaze.

Mr. Mac nodded briskly, then shot Bri a wink over his shoulder. "Definitely not what you'd think."

Her cheeks warmed another degree hotter. Gerard gestured over his shoulder as the door shut behind Mr. Mac and Jill. "I'm a little confused. Did I pass inspection?"

"I'm pretty sure." Bri wiped up a spill of steamed milk with a dish towel, emotions still spinning. She gripped the towel tighter.

"Didn't know that was up for debate." He closed the distance to the counter, but to Bri's surprise he didn't stop on the other side. He came around the back straight toward her.

"Hey, now. This is highly against regulation." Bri turned to face him, a nervous laugh bubbling in her chest at his proximity. She tossed the damp rag aside. "I mean, if you wanted a macaron that badly, I could have just handed you one."

"That's not what I want."

She licked her lips as he drew closer. "I thought they were your favorite."

"Second place, currently." The heat in his eyes burned hotter than the oven in the next room, and Bri's stomach began a salsa dance.

He planted his hands on the counter on either side of her, trapping her between his corded forearms. She stared at the muscular lines extending from his biceps instead of looking into his eyes, where she knew she'd promptly melt into a pat of butter.

She fought to keep her voice evenly toned despite her racing heart. "So, you prefer the petit fours, then?"

He hovered over her, a teasing grin breaking up the thick stubble on his face. "Third place, currently."

Bri's mouth dried. "Is that why you came over?" Man, she wanted the comfort of nestling into his arms. Wanted the luxury of asking him for ridiculous things, like not driving away in the next twenty-four hours. Wanted the right to kiss him anytime she wanted.

Turned out she didn't need it.

Immediately, his hands were tangled in her hair, his warm body pressing against hers as he backed her fully against the counter. Her hands gripped the sides of his T-shirt, her head spinning in a blissfully dizzy cloud as their lips and breath mingled.

"I didn't come for petit fours." He whispered the words against her cheek, his jaw endearingly scratchy on her face. "Or macarons." His lips grazed near her ear and she shivered.

"Well, I know you didn't come for the coffee."

He chuckled low, and the sound vibrated through every fiber of her being. She pulled him in closer, tucking herself against his chest like she'd wanted to do since the moment he strode inside the bakery.

He rested his forehead against hers, bracing their joined weight against the counter with his other arm. "I actually came because I wanted to tell —"

A clattering of glass broke them apart.

Bri straightened with a gasp and turned. The jar of coffee she'd been playing with earlier lay turned on its side. Dark coffee grounds dusted the dry ingredients inside her mixing bowl and spilled along the counter.

Gerard winced, pulling back from her. "Was that another attempt at your mom's recipe?"

"Yeah. It's okay, though." Thankfully, the glass hadn't broken. Bri righted the jar. "I'm sure it was another wasted effort, anyway. It's been years of attempts." She struggled to control her runaway heartbeat, struggled to convince the rest of her body to relax as she began to clean up the mess. It was just a kiss. Just a kiss with an incredibly attractive, soon-to-be-leaving man who —

"Wait." Gerard's hand gripped her wrist. "Hold on. You said you've tried everything?"

"Ten times each." Bri blew out her breath. The list over the years was never-ending. "Milk chocolate, cocoa powder, dark chocolate, white chocolate, almond extract, extra vanilla, less vanilla, extra cinnamon, so yes, everything."

"But maybe not *everything.*" He released her wrist as he nodded toward the spilled coffee grounds.

Bri's eyes widened.

"I can't believe it." Crumbs flaked to the table between them as Bri took another bite of the last batch of macarons. The first batch she'd ruined had way too many grounds in it, but she could sense they were on the right track. They'd made another mix with about a fourth of the coffee, and she'd nearly wept with relief when they'd come out of the oven. "Who would have ever thought?"

"I guess that's why it's a *secret* ingredient." Gerard couldn't stop staring at Bri. At the way her eyes lit with joy over the discovery, at the way she kept wiggling her shoulders back and forth in a little happy dance as she ate. The way her lips curled in victory.

He'd kissed those lips about six more times while she'd mixed and poured and baked. Longer while they'd had to wait on the oven. Then Mabel and Agnes had come back to put away their recently purchased eggs, flour, and sugar, successfully cutting off any further attempts at making out.

Though knowing those love angels, they probably wouldn't have minded.

Now, all Gerard could do was shred a napkin between his fingers and stare at Bri and wonder how on earth he was going to drive away tomorrow. He'd come to tell her that his article was complete. He had no reason to stay.

But watching her, glowing behind the counter as she tended to one of her favorite people in town, well — he had started wondering if maybe there was a reason he *should* stay. She'd lit up the entire bakery and those dark, inaccessible corners of his heart with her innocence and genuineness and bitter coffee.

Turns out the bitterness was just what the macarons needed.

Just what he needed.

"Mom would be proud." Bri studied the macaron in her hands, her thin brows furrowed as if convincing herself. "I hope."

"Of course she would." Gerard leaned away in his chair, rocking back on two legs. He needed to tell her about Remy. He'd been so shocked last night when he saw the picture, he couldn't get the words out. He'd had to process the impossible first.

But he wouldn't dare burst her bubble now and bring up the tainted past during a moment of victory. How could he tell her that the man who very nearly destroyed her parents' marriage was the same man who once steered him away from love? It was too small a world. It would rock hers again.

His chair legs hit the ground with a thud. "Bri, I finished the feature."

Her eyes darted to his, acknowledging what he refused to say: *I'm leaving.* "I'm sure you did the Puff justice."

"I did my best." And he had. But it'd been hard — he'd had to force some of the words of praise onto the page, despite his instincts to the contrary. Not because of Bri. Not because of the bakery's uniqueness and quality desserts. Rather, because he knew she needed more than this. Her wings were clipped, and he wanted her to soar. Charles wasn't the anvil holding her down.

The Pastry Puff was.

"Good." She dusted crumbs from her fingers. "Maybe that will finally hush Charles up."

Blast. That money was still in his room. After Sandra interrupted them at Taylor's the other day, he'd forgotten to ask Charles when he could swing by his office.

"Maybe." Gerard shrugged, tearing the napkin into smaller pieces. His leg bounced beneath the table, and he realized that this was the longest he'd gone in years without some sort of adrenaline rush.

Unless he counted kissing Bri. Which he did.

She smiled. "I can't wait to read it."

He could. Because once it was in print, that meant he was back in Chicago or on to his next adventure.

Alone.

His leg jiggled harder.

"Here." Bri handed him the last half of her macaron, and he ate it. It was good — surprisingly good. She'd nailed the recipe this time, no doubt about it.

Bri frowned slightly, holding up another macaron an inch from her face and peering into the filled middle. "Do you think it's missing something?"

"No. I think it's exactly as it should be." He couldn't hold back any longer. They had to talk about the inevitable. He reached across the table for her hand. "Look, Bri — about last night."

She set the dessert down and laced her fingers through his. The simplicity of that natural motion nearly destroyed him. He fought to focus. He had a plan. He was about to be handed his dream job at *Traipse Horizon* — lead writer. He'd get to write things people truly wanted to read. His opinion — his voice — would matter. His paychecks would increase. He could get his mom the help she needed. He had to leave.

But that didn't mean that whatever was sparking between them had to die.

She raised her eyebrows. "Do you mean the picture?"

That too. He took a deep breath. Which to divulge first?

"Or do you mean this?" She gestured between them with her free hand. The blush tinging her cheeks was almost as adorable as the hesitant pitch in her voice.

Oh man. He'd just thought the word *adorable* in a non-sarcastic way. This town had changed him.

Bri had changed him.

A sliver of fear pricked. Did he want to be changed?

It was far, far too late for that to be relevant. And just like that day on the rocky cliffs of Hawaii overlooking the turquoise waters, he took a deep breath and dove in. "What are you doing for New Year's?"

CHAPTER TWENTY-SIX

For the first time in four years, Bri had a date for New Year's Eve.

Unless you counted two years ago, when Mrs. Beeker's grandson bought her pizza at Taylor's Sushi Barn while she was out drowning her non-festive holiday sorrows with a gallon of sweet tea and denial. But she didn't count it.

She couldn't stop smiling, which drew a few curious stares from the stay-at-home moms and elderly gentlemen in suspenders standing in line around her at the bank. Gerard was leaving, which dimmed her smile a little every time she let it soak in. But he was coming back.

For a date with her.

Her smile widened automatically, and her stomach flipped in anticipation. She eagerly swung the bank bag of receipts and cash between her fingers as she waited for her turn at the teller counter. Everything was

looking up. The bag in her hands was full
— which meant business was solid —
Gerard wasn't permanently roaring out of
her life, and she'd finally figured out her
mom's oldest and best recipe. Nothing
could bring her down.

"Well, well. Fancy meeting you here —
again."

Not even Sandra.

Bri turned, smile still easily in place.
"Hello, Sandra." The heater in the vents
above shuddered off, as if sensing the need
for less hot air at her arrival.

"You still haven't come by the consignment shop, I gather." The woman's heavily
made-up eyes flitted over Bri's outfit, dusted
in flour and coffee grounds. She smoothed
the tailored lines of her hot-pink blazer and
sniffed her disapproval.

Bri halfheartedly brushed at the stains on
her sweater. "Been a little busy." She
couldn't help the smile that twitched on her
lips at the thought of what — make that
who — she'd been busy with. Gerard wasn't
leaving for two more days, so he'd promised
tonight they'd get some dinner and have a
picnic at the B&B. She planned to absorb
and appreciate every minute she could with
him and make it last until December 31.
After that . . . Her smile faltered for the

first time that day.

"I assume business has picked up?" Sandra pressed a little too close and gestured to the zippered pouch in Bri's hands.

Bri only nodded, unwilling to divulge more specifics to Charles's right-hand man. Woman. Whatever. She inched up a few steps, hoping Sandra would get the hint. But she hadn't gotten a hint for as long as she'd known her.

Still close on her heels, Sandra made a *tsk* sound under her breath. "Looks like the Puff didn't even need that article, then." She let out an amused cough. "Good thing."

Bri frowned. "What do you mean?" She instantly regretted engaging — Sandra was clearly up to something, and it wouldn't be anything Bri would want to be involved with.

"Just that I can't imagine that feature having gone in your favor." Sandra placed a cool hand on Bri's arm, her matching hot-pink fingernails shockingly bright. "Even if you are sleeping with the enemy." She wiggled her eyebrows.

"Sleeping with — no one is sleeping anywhere." Bri's chest heated, and she swallowed against the knot taking up residence in her throat. "Sandra, what are you talking about?"

"I'm talking about Charles and Gerard being all chummy." Sandra leaned in, glancing over her shoulder as if checking for eavesdroppers. But she would have been the only one. "They had a deal, if you know what I mean."

Bri's heart stammered a beat. The line moved forward, but her feet felt stuck to the tile floor. Instead of giving Sandra the satisfaction of her glance, she focused on a young boy ahead of them in line licking a Dum Dum sucker.

Don't ask. Don't ask. Don't — "What deal?"

"Gerard has been playing devil's advocate, sugar. Wasn't it obvious?" A slow smile spread across Sandra's face. The woman lived for gossip and clearly felt she had an inside scoop, reminiscent of her glory days. "He was playing both sides, trying to keep the fires of competition burning for the sake of the article."

"You're not even making sense." Why had she even entertained this crazy woman for so long? Bri held the bank bag in a white-knuckled grip and willed the line ahead of them to move.

"Listen to me. Gerard is a writer — a businessman. He's in it for the entertainment value. Drama sells, especially in print." Sandra squared her shoulders with

398

authority. "Trust me, I know."

She did know. But Gerard wouldn't do that — he wouldn't side with Charles after everything they'd been through. After everything he'd coached her through.

Running off Charles's intern.

Helping her navigate the press interview.

Assisting with Casey's wedding.

Encouraging her to keep trying her mom's recipes.

Impossible. She shook her head. "You must be confused."

"I'm a lot of things, honey, but confused isn't one of them." Sandra rocked back on her high-heeled boots and crossed her arms over her chest. "Why don't you ask him where he got that two hundred dollars cash?"

"That's ridiculous." Bri's temper flared as they finally shuffled forward in line. Her voice pitched and cracked, and the young boy with the sucker stared at her, wide-eyed. She attempted to lower her tone. "Gerard isn't like you. He cares about the Puff — and me. And while we're asking questions, why don't you ask *him* who he's coming back to see for New Year's?" She hated falling prey to Sandra's games, but she refused to let the nosy woman ruin her day with slander.

"I'm not concerned about your New Year's plans. Except I highly suggest you come by the consignment shop before your night out." Sandra rolled her eyes. "I'm telling you, I came across Gerard and Charles talking at Taylor's, all secret-like. Charles wouldn't even tell me right away what it was about." She smirked. "I got him to talk later."

"You're going to have to gossip somewhere else, Sandra. I'm not falling for this." A spike of adrenaline, mixed with a shot of indignation, flowed through Bri's veins. Just wait until she told Gerard at dinner about Sandra's latest scheme. She was probably just jealous that Gerard hadn't given her attention. "The article is in favor of the Puff."

"So, you've read it?"

Bri's mouth snapped shut. She hadn't.

And he'd never offered.

Why hadn't he ever offered?

Sandra stepped forward, cutting Bri in line, and tossed a smug smile over her shoulder. "I'm guessing that's a no."

Dread started a slow descent into Bri's stomach. The little boy peered around Sandra's leg at Bri and loudly crunched the remains of his Dum Dum.

Now who was the sucker?

Bri's excitement over their evening picnic morphed into a paralyzing sense of worry. She alternated between convincing herself there was no way Gerard had played her that way and believing maybe there was some truth to Sandra's explanation, after all. Then again, Sandra had a bitter streak against Bri as long as Main Street. She had plenty of motivation to lie if she wanted to — especially if she'd been jealous about Gerard.

It was the heavy "what if" she couldn't shake.

Bri hesitantly climbed the porch steps of the B&B, mini-cooler in hand. She'd insisted on bringing some goodies of her own this time, but her heart hadn't been in it as she'd packed fresh fruit, flaky croissants, and newly baked oatmeal-raisin cookies.

She shifted the cooler to knock on the door. She'd feel better after she talked to him. Surely it was all one big misunderstanding, and they'd get a good laugh and eat cookies and —

"Over here, Cupcake." The porch swing creaked, and Bri tightened her grip on the plastic blue handle as she spun to face Gerard.

"You scared me — again." She forced a laugh that sounded hollow.

"Do you ever look to your right?" He grinned, and unlike their last porch visit, he stood to greet her. Bri couldn't contain the butterflies taking flight in her stomach as he closed the distance between them.

"When there's a good reason to." She tried to smile back, but even her flirting felt awkward, forced. She had to know his side of the story or she'd never be able to relax.

He opened his arms, and she stepped into them on autopilot. His strong grip shut around her, his heartbeat steady in his chest, calming her racing one. She rested in his embrace.

"I've been waiting for this all day." He pressed a kiss against her forehead.

"Me too." And she had. There was no reason to believe anything had changed. In fact, the longer she stayed in his arms — inhaling his unique scent of evergreen and coffee and earth, feeling his muscles beneath her fingertips — the sillier she felt for having given Sandra's gossip a second thought.

"I hope you're hungry." Gerard broke away from the hug and began opening containers of sliced deli meat for the croissants. "This isn't as authentic as our last picnic, but I didn't want to be distracted by details." He caught her hand as she set the cooler on the table. "I'd much rather focus on other things."

"So, I'm a thing now, huh?" She shook her head with exaggeration as she began pulling containers from the cooler. "Agnes always warned me, once you let a man kiss you, it's all downhill from —"

Gerard cut her off with an intentional press of his lips against hers, and suddenly she was having dessert before dinner. She kissed him in return, Sandra's petty accusations now all but a fleeting memory as his hand warmed her back through her thin sweater. This was Gerard. This was them. This was real.

He drew away slowly, fingers grazing down the length of her arm and tugging at her fingers. "Downhill, you were saying?"

"Like a roller coaster." She rose on her tiptoes and kissed him once more before forcing herself to step back. Two steps, to be safe. "We do have to eat."

"Eating is overrated." But he obediently began assembling sandwiches while she set the fruit on paper plates. "How are the love angels today?"

"Tired," Bri answered before fully thinking through the ramifications of what that could mean. She pulled in her lower lip. "Probably just from the busy weekend of Casey's wedding, though. They're not used to being up that late. I'm sure it takes a few days to recover and get back into their routine."

"Maybe so." Gerard nodded, but his tone didn't sound convinced.

Just like at the bank, a piece of her security separated from the whole and began floating away. Bri hastily plucked grapes from the bunch, one after the other, desperate to prove her own point. "You know, Mabel was dancing for half the reception, and Agnes was flirting with Mr. Hansen most of the night." *Pluck. Pluck.* "That's a lot on tired legs." *Pluck.* "Even if they are in compression hose." *Pluck.*

Gerard stilled her hand with his, and she released what was about to be her twentieth grape. He laughed and gestured for her to sit at the wicker chair by the table. "Come on. What gives?"

"Sorry, I'm just a little on edge." Bri released the sigh that had been building all afternoon and rolled her eyes as she popped a grape in her mouth and sat. "It's stupid."

Gerard sat in the chair across from her. "Tell me. Let me be the judge." He took a bite of a meat-laden croissant.

She needed to tell him about Sandra. Get it over with so they could go back to the good part of the evening — like kissing. She really didn't want to waste her last few hours with Gerard worrying over nothing. Nothing was changing. Not with them, not with Mabel and Agnes. Not with the Puff.

She was probably just riding the tails of the discovery of her mother's letters. "It's nothing, really."

"That's not what the grapes said."

Bri stifled a laugh. "Fine. I ran into Sandra at the bank while making deposits."

"Say no more." Gerard set his plate on the table and held up both hands. "I totally understand."

"You're hilarious."

"Seriously, though, that woman can ruin anyone's day in a heartbeat. It's a gift." Gerard frowned. "Or maybe a curse. What'd she do — insult your dog?"

"Only my wardrobe. But that's probably just because I don't have a dog."

"You don't care what Sandra thinks of your clothes." Gerard leaned to the side and made an exaggerated show of looking her up and down, waggling his dark eyebrows. "I think you look nice. Really nice. In fact, come here, and I'll show you I mean it."

She swatted at his outstretched hand. "I'm being serious."

"How can you? It's Sandra. Shake her off." Crumbs from the croissant flaked into his lap, and he brushed them away.

Sort of like he was doing with the conversation. Bri frowned. "You don't want to know what she said?"

"If it's that upsetting to you, then yes. Tell me." He speared a strawberry with a fork and leaned back in his chair.

"She said you and Charles had a deal."

Gerard choked. He quickly sat upright, pounding his chest as he coughed. "A *what*?"

"A deal. That you were egging on both sides, so to speak, for the sake of the article." Bri shook her head. "She even said it was a good thing business at the Puff had picked up, because she knew the feature wasn't going to be entirely favorable."

Gerard guzzled half a bottle of water.

"That's crazy." She looked down at her hands, then back at Gerard, who dabbed his mouth with the back of his hand. "Right?"

"Isn't she the town gossip?"

"Unofficially. Used to be officially."

He scoffed. "Like I said, babe. Shake her off."

Babe. Not Cupcake. Bri's frown deepened. "So, there's no deal with Charles, then."

"Define deal." Gerard busied himself with making another sandwich.

The dread that had been ballooning in her stomach all afternoon, and slowly deflating over the last hour, swelled back up to twice its size. "It's true, isn't it?"

"I didn't agree to anything, Bri. Charles is a manipulating scumbag who's used to getting what he wants." Gerard shrugged. "I turned the tables on him, is all."

"You let him believe the feature was slanted against the Puff?" Bri stood, her hip knocking the table. Gerard's half-empty bottle of water shook precariously. "But you didn't really do that, right?"

He opened his mouth, but she didn't let him finish. "Can I read it? Let me read it." She looked frantically around for his laptop, which never seemed to be far from him. She headed for the swing and began riffling through the pile of notebooks and books stacked on the end.

Gerard was instantly behind her. "I already turned it in." He rubbed her arms. "You've got to calm down."

She turned to face him, panic lodged in her throat. "Email it to me, then."

His brow furrowed, frustration tightening his jaw. "You don't trust me? Why would I make the Puff sound bad? My job is to make it sound worth coming to!"

The disdain in his voice wasn't lost on her. Bri slowly stepped out of his grip. The hands that felt so safe and familiar just a few minutes ago now felt like a stranger's. "Do *you* think it's worth coming to?"

He didn't, did he? He never really had, though she thought the petit fours had finally won him over. All the conversations they'd had about her possibly losing the Puff began to play back like a movie reel.

His pointing out her obsession with the Puff but that she'd had no problem selling her parents' house — so why the big deal?

His butting into her book club, her friend-ships, her advice. Always having to be right.

His cocky assuredness that she'd hate Paris — that she was only hanging on to the Puff because it was a safety net.

She shuddered and stepped back, away from him. Away from the obvious. Away from what she'd been refusing to see all day.

He wasn't for her.

"Bri." Gerard rubbed his hands briskly down his face, his hands scraping against stubble. "Look, please just sit down. I can't talk to you when you're like this."

He hadn't answered a single question directly yet. The balloon swelled another size as he turned to sit. There was only one way to know. "Sandra said there was money."

Gerard froze halfway to his chair.

Bri crossed her arms over her chest, hugging herself against the evening breeze. But a deeper chill started from within. "Two hundred dollars."

He turned, his features pale and pinched. "Bri, I can —"

"You used me, didn't you? You used me for the story. Entertainment sells, right?"

Sandra was right. She couldn't believe it. Anxiety stabbed at her chest, begging for freedom, and she stood stoically in place, refusing to give it the release it demanded. "Were you playing devil's advocate with me and Charles?"

"It wasn't like that." Gerard winced. "Okay, maybe a little at first. But not the whole time."

The balloon burst, filling her to the brim with despair. "So, during which time, exactly? When you were kissing me in the fountain? Or when you were kissing me in the Puff? Or kissing me on the porch?" Her voice cracked and she hated it. She covered her mouth with shaky hands. Everything was changing, after all. And she had no one to blame but herself. She'd trusted him. A complete stranger on a motorcycle. She'd fallen for all of it. Believed they could have a love story to rival her parents'.

But theirs hadn't been entirely real either, had it? A sob hiccupped free.

"Bri, please. You're overreacting." Gerard stepped toward her, anguish in his eyes, but she jerked away before he could touch her.

"And you're dodging all my questions! Answer me." Heat flared, warming her chest and neck and bringing a surge of confidence. "Do you or do you not have cash from Charles in your possession at this moment?"

Gerard raked his hands through his hair and groaned. "Technically, yes, but —"

"But nothing. We're done here." Tears blurred her vision as she grabbed her cooler and stalked down the stairs. She needed a petit four. Needed the wisdom of her wisest and oldest friends. Needed the Puff.

She needed something that would never change.

CHAPTER TWENTY-SEVEN

"What's the rush? You were due to come home day after next." Peter's pen clicked on and off in the background as he presumably gave half his attention to Gerard's fit. "What's one more night?"

A lot. Gerard pressed his lips together in an effort to keep from unleashing on his boss as he paced the B&B's front porch, cell clenched in his fist. He almost didn't care who saw him or heard his conversation at this point. Bri was gone — long gone — back to the bakery or wherever she'd stormed off to, and she'd taken all of his good mood with her. He wanted to get out of Story. ASAP.

"I wasn't asking. I was telling you I'll be in the office a day sooner than scheduled." He gritted his teeth. "If that's a problem, I'll take a detour on the way home and kill twenty-four hours elsewhere."

"Calm down. I was just curious." The pen

clicked in double time. "What happened?"

"The blonde happened." Gerard paced the other direction, eyes sweeping the windows of the house for any signs of Mrs. Beeker or other guests. Maybe he cared a little if he was overheard. That would be just his luck — word getting back to Sandra about his and Bri's fight.

Sandra. If that busybody had just kept to herself, their fledgling relationship wouldn't have been ruined. How dare she accuse him of catering to Charles, like he'd accepted that money without the intent of returning it? He'd been bamboozled, which was possibly Charles's play all along. If he couldn't have Bri, he'd make sure no one could. Gerard should have seen it coming, should have stayed on guard when it seemed like Charles had laid low in the bakery standoff — but he'd gotten distracted.

By Bri.

"You're finally admitting your feelings for Bri, huh?" Peter chuckled, half-amused, half-smug. "It's about time."

About time? Gerard slowly lowered his phone and looked at it, as if his boss could give him answers to the questions running through his mind.

Peter had given him this assignment. Peter had conveniently demanded he turn the piece into a series and stay longer. And Peter was one of the only humans alive who knew the things Remy had told him.

"Always travel, never land."

"You know what love does, son? Love prisons you in a Podunk town in mid-America, that's what it does."

"You keep moving, boy, you hear me? Chase after the story. Don't let it catch you."

Gerard's hand tightened around the phone as the pieces clicked into place. Peter had been on him for the past ten months about moving on from Kelsey and dating again. He'd seen an opportunity for this assignment with Bri and forced it on him.

His jaw tightened. He'd been played. All this time, he'd been on guard about the love angels' matchmaking schemes, and all along, it'd been Peter.

He interrupted his boss's ramble about the assignment and his next bonus and profit margins. "Dude. You sent me here on purpose."

"I know." He didn't even bother denying it.

Gerard ran his hand through his hair, grasping the longer strands in desperate need of a cut. He tugged hard, wishing he could throat punch his obnoxious best friend/boss through the phone. "That would

413

have been good to know a heck of a lot sooner." The man who never, ever bluffed had just stacked the deck — against him.

His anger flared.

But Peter's voice remained calm, even. "No, because you'd never have gone if you'd known."

Gerard narrowed his eyes. "Would my job really have been on the line if I had resisted?" He'd been set up. Played for a fool. By his boss. By Sandra. By Charles. By Bri.

Not Bri. Bri was genuine. That's what hurt the most. She'd been the realest part of all this. And he'd been the one to screw that up with his secrets. Sandra hadn't been right to say what she did, but Gerard hadn't been totally blame-free either. Hadn't he entertained the idea initially of keeping the feature interesting by playing both sides?

But that changed when he got closer to Bri, and it became a matter of wanting what was best for her. And blast it, if he still didn't think the Puff wasn't best for her.

His stomach balled into a knot. It didn't matter — she hadn't given him a chance to explain. Just accused him of lying and using her, then stormed off before he could even offer reassurance. Now his pride throbbed. But the anger was a good thing — it'd make the goodbye a heck of a lot easier. He had been getting way too close. Way too vulnerable again.

It was safer this way.

"I never lied to you about any of this." Peter cleared his throat. "I just — nudged. Hard. I'm a nudger, Gerard."

"You're a something, alright." Gerard pinched the bridge of his nose. "So, you sent me on a blind mission to fall in love in Kansas?"

Peter paused. "It worked, didn't it?"

His heart thundered with indignation. "This is my life, man. Not a game." But if it were a game, it would be found on the back of the clearance shelf at the discount store. Hardly worth hiking it to the checkout counter. He groaned.

"Right. *Your* life, that you're wasting away. Wasting valuable talent —"

"Then why didn't you give me lead sooner?" He threw one arm out in frustration.

"To everything there is a season." Peter clicked his tongue. "A time to rend, a time to sow . . ."

"A time to kill," Gerard growled.

Peter carried on, unfazed. "A time to keep silent and a time to speak."

"What are you getting at?"

"It's your time to speak. I want you to

415

have more of a voice — I always have. But you weren't ready. You were too . . . chiseled."

He had a feeling Peter wasn't referring to his gym regimen. "Quit waxing poetic and get to the point."

Peter sighed. "You were stony, man. You were hard as rock, and that's not the voice we need at *Traipse Horizon*. We need someone passionate but clear-minded. Genuine but open to new ideas and concepts. Someone who knew what it meant to truly live."

"I said to stop waxing poetic."

"You don't even know what you're living for anymore, do you? Not since Kelsey." Peter's tone gentled, and Gerard despised the pity lingering around the edges. "I was hoping you'd get to Story and put that Remy guy's lousy love advice aside, and maybe find out."

"Well, Remy is back, so that notion is shot."

"What do you mean?"

He filled his boss in on the connection between his inspirational hero and Bri's mother.

Peter whistled. "Wow. Small world." He hesitated. "You know, that would make an amazing tie-in to —"

"Don't even go there. I'm not writing

416

about it."

"I know. Too soon." A long pause hovered over the line. "I'm a man of my word, Gerard. Lead is yours — if you think you're ready for it."

Gerard opened his mouth, then snapped it shut as he realized Peter had already hung up. He shoved his cell in the back pocket of his jeans and began packing up the remains of the abandoned picnic.

Blast it — Peter nailed two things.

He *was* falling for Bri.

And he didn't know if he was ready at all.

Bri had always been able to count on Mabel and Agnes. They had consistently been there for her — teaching Sunday school, sneaking her snacks on the way home from school, babysitting when her parents went out of town. Ever since her parents died, they'd also been there, as close as family, filling in as many gaps as they could — sitting in the front row of her college graduation, being a shoulder to cry on after breakups, taste-testing new recipes.

Bri needed them now. Except, she didn't want to cry this time. She felt too numb to generate tears. Gerard's words circled in her mind as she knocked lightly on the door of the sisters' shared townhome, hoping they were still up. It was only eight o'clock, but the way they'd seemed so worn out lately . . .

She knocked a second time, more timidly than the first. Emotions balled in her throat as she fought to process all the if-onlys crowding her thoughts. If only her parents hadn't died, she wouldn't be here right now, so needy. If only her mom hadn't kept those letters, she wouldn't have suffered the loss of her favorite memories. If only Gerard hadn't betrayed her, she wouldn't be trying to figure out how to mend the fissure in her heart.

If only she could still cling to the security of her parents' relationship, then maybe this fight with Gerard wouldn't have stolen all her hope . . .

She knocked a third time, her anxiety and frustration pounding into the wood.

The door opened to reveal Mabel, sporting a robe and bright yellow curlers in her hair. Agnes was right behind her with a baseball bat, a green facial mask smeared across her cheeks and forehead.

Mabel rolled her eyes at her sister. "I told you it wasn't a burglar. What kind of burglar knocks first?"

"The smart kind, to see if you're home before breaking your window." Agnes tapped the bat in her palm. "Don't you watch crime TV?"

"No. I watch *I Love Lucy* and *Saved by the Bell* reruns like a normal person."

Agnes huffed. "You couldn't be normal if your —"

Bri cleared her throat.

Mabel's eyes widened. "So sorry honey, are you okay? Come on in." She ushered Bri inside, shutting the door behind her. Their townhome, as always, smelled like cinnamon rolls and cookie dough, but it was just from the scented candles Mabel insisted on burning year-round. "Is everything alright? Did something happen at the bakery?"

Bri started to answer, but Agnes cut her off.

"I thought you were going to Gerard's tonight. Wait a minute." Agnes narrowed her eyes, brandishing the bat. "Did he hurt you?"

It was too much. The sight of Agnes, alien-green, holding a bat in her thin-as-spaghetti arms as if she could actually wield it against someone did Bri in. She started to giggle. Then the giggle turned into a cough, then into a hysterical guffaw, then a wailing sob. She choked, and tears streamed down her face.

"Oh dear." Mabel put her arm around Bri's shoulder and guided her toward the couch. "Sit down. Agnes, get her some water."

"Don't be ridiculous. When someone is upset, you offer a hot beverage." Agnes leaned the bat into the foyer closet and shut the door. "I'll put on the teakettle."

Mabel sat next to Bri on the couch and picked up her hand. "You're freezing." She grabbed the crocheted afghan from the back of the floral-patterned couch and draped it around Bri's shoulders. "There."

Bri gripped the blanket with both hands, the warmth soaking into her back and soothing the burst of hysteria. She hated how scattered her emotions had been lately. Mabel and Agnes had always been steady and constant in her life — she owed it to them to return the favor. She wasn't a hormonal teenager anymore.

But something about Gerard made her feel like a high schooler with a crush — out of control, uncertain, and slightly desperate. Was that love? If so, maybe she was better off forgetting about it. Forgetting about Gerard altogether and focusing solely on the Puff. Maybe they could expand the menu this spring and find a way to branch into national sales. That would bring in a

420

lot of extra profit, if the shipping could be factored in cheaply enough. She could even create a website and a whole new marketing plan.

Feeling better now that she had a new goal, Bri snuggled deeper into the blanket. "I'm sorry I scared you two."

"Don't be silly." Mabel waved her hand to dismiss the thought. "We don't frighten easily. Agnes just likes an excuse to wave that ridiculous Loony Toon Sluggard around."

Bri wiped under her eyes, checking her finger for mascara streaks. Then Mabel's words registered. "Loony Toon what?"

"She *means* Louisville Slugger." Agnes appeared with a mug, the tea bag string dangling over the side. She handed it to Bri before taking a seat on the adjacent armchair. "And that is why Mabel never played sports a day in her life."

"I preferred to cheer for the handsome players instead." Mabel wiggled her eyebrows at Bri. "And they enjoyed my cheering for them, trust me."

Agnes pursed her lips. "I believe Bri came to us, Mabel. We should hear what she has to say."

"She's just jealous." Mabel elbowed Bri in the side. "Pay no mind."

Bri sipped her tea — green, with a touch

of honey — and relished the familiarity of this moment. Their bickering was one of the more comforting elements in her life — it reminded her that some things really didn't change. She took a calming breath. "I feel better already, just listening to you guys."

"Is that so? Maybe we should start a counseling service on the side, along with the matchmaking." Mabel tapped her chin. "Instead of the love angels, we could be the wise old owls."

"Poppycock." Agnes crossed one flannel pant–covered leg over the other. "You're not so much wise as you are lucky."

"Sure I am." Mabel cinched her robe belt tighter and squared her shoulders. "I'm wise enough to know why Bri's here. Duh." She stuck her tongue out at her sister.

Agnes's slipper-clad foot bounced a rhythm. "She doesn't know yet. We haven't told anyone."

Bri frowned. "Told anyone what?"

Mabel's face whitened. "About the Puff." Her voice shrank a size. "Isn't that why you're here?"

Bri shook her head. "I came to tell you that Gerard is leaving — and we got into a big fight." Her stomach clenched as she set her mug on the end table. "What about the Puff?"

"Oh no." Mabel reached toward Bri. "I didn't know, I just assumed —"

"You know what happens when you assume, Mabel." Agnes stood up, glowering. "Now you've upset her again, and we're out of tea."

"Thank you, but I don't want any more tea." Bri sat up, tossing the blanket onto the couch. She asked again. "What about the Puff?"

The sisters stared at her, the answer evident in their gaze. A rock settled into her gut, paralyzing her. She tried to swallow and couldn't. *No.*

"It's for the best, sweetheart." Mabel touched her shoulder.

"How? How can it be best? Best for who?" Bri jumped up. Her legs trembled and the room tilted. She didn't want to fall apart in front of them. Didn't want to make them feel guilty. But she couldn't stop the storm brewing in her chest. First her parents . . . then Gerard . . . now the Puff.

She was going to be sick. "I have to go."

"Oh no. She's mad." Mabel wrung her hands. "This didn't go the way I'd planned."

"No, I'm not mad. I'm just . . ." Unshed tears ballooned inside and begged for release. She didn't want to hurt them, but she couldn't believe it. They'd betrayed her too. Why didn't anyone care about what she cared about? Why did everything have to change at once?

It was too much. She wanted to hide. Wanted to feel safe. She wanted to go *home.* But that was the Puff, wasn't it?

Her home was going to be demolished — along with the last remaining pieces of her mother's pedestal.

Bri sat surrounded by tissues and Coke cans and stared at the plane ticket in her shopping cart, her mouse hovering over the "complete purchase" button. Paris was almost hers. Her mouth dried, and her finger trembled. What did she have to lose?

Nothing. She'd already lost it.

She closed her eyes and inhaled deeply. *Just click it.* She should go. Prove Gerard wrong — show him that she'd love the authentic City of Light, and that she didn't need a man by her side to appreciate it.

Her heart sank. But he would never know if she went, would he? Their relationship, as quickly as it'd started, was over. She had no reason to tell him. If she did this, if she pushed that button — she had to do it for herself.

Which she was most definitely not ac-
customed to doing. She was used to doing
for others. Discounting treats and handing
out coffee and offering a listening ear and a
warm hug and a word of encouragement —
which always went down better with a fresh
petit four. She had no problem doting on
others — so why the hesitation to do something for herself? She deserved this. Right?

She took her hand off the mouse and
fiddled with the miniature Eiffel Tower
figurine on her desk. What would it be like
to finally see it in person?

A wave of anxiety, maybe even fear, rushed
over her, and she quickly pulled her hand
away. She swallowed hard and crossed her
arms over her chest — away from the
mouse. Where was the fear coming from? It
was as tangible as her heartbeat. Maybe if
she figured that out, she could just click the
button already.

Bri tapped one foot against the side of her
desk as she ran through the possibilities.
She wasn't afraid to fly. That wasn't it. She
wasn't afraid to be alone in a foreign city,
though she felt somewhat unprepared.
Nothing a little research couldn't help,
though. And she wasn't afraid of the expense — she'd been able to afford it for
years now, as Gerard had not-so-tactfully

pointed out.

Nothing jumped out at her as the obvious answer. So why the heart-pounding adrenaline rush holding her back?

Everything in her wanted to go. Wanted to see the place where her parents fell in love. Wanted to taste fresh croissants and stroll the Seine and all the cliché things Gerard had made fun of — plus the not-so-cliché list he'd mentioned. As much as she hated to admit it, that list sounded incredibly appealing.

She just wanted to do it with *him* now.

That was it, wasn't it? The fear holding her captive. All these years, she'd held herself back to take care of the Puff, to sustain it and her mother's memory.

Now that it was soon to be gone, she had no reason to stay.

And was terrified to go.

She groaned as the obvious sank in. Gerard lived fast to avoid planting roots — she clung to her roots to avoid living. What a pair they were. No wonder it hadn't worked out. Well, that, and the small detail that Gerard had betrayed her. And yet she couldn't turn her heart off long enough to see the truth. He'd played her for his story.

Against her own ex-boyfriend.

For cash.

It didn't get much lower than that.

An ad for his and hers matching luggage sets popped up in the sidebar of the airline's website. She stared at the happy couple toting their black rolling suitcases, the woman laughing as she half turned toward her clean-shaven guy. Bri snorted. She bet that guy hadn't betrayed his woman — with her perfect ringlets — like Gerard had her.

Then again, the guy on the screen probably hadn't made that girl an authentic French picnic, kissed her in a fountain during a wedding, or wrestled her on a kitchen floor over burned petit fours.

A smile tugged at her reluctant lips. Gerard, for all the bitterness he'd carried into town, had somehow represented a more genuine love than she'd ever had in any past relationship. Not by sweeping her off her feet with grand gestures, but with honesty, truth, and even confrontation — all when she'd rather live in denial. Over Paris. Over her parents.

Over love.

The fear knotting in her stomach began to unravel. He'd never been afraid to tell her like it was. To challenge her, to call her out on her blindness or her bad advice to friends and people she loved. He never avoided conflict for the sake of peace-keeping, like she did. All those uncertainties she'd had about Casey and Nathan's engagement — had she ever voiced them to Casey? No, she'd hidden them. Gerard, however, who had nothing invested in Casey at all, immediately spoke up that day in the bakery and put her to the test — one Casey immediately passed.

Which was more loving? Suppressing concern to avoid awkwardness or delivering honesty in love?

She rolled the Eiffel Tower between her fingers. Gerard had stayed right next to her during the journey through her parents' love story, and yet somehow, at the same time, he'd refused to let her stay in the misguided fantasy. He had shown her how beauty was found in reality rather than in an illusion. He had pointed out the depth of her parents' love in her mom's choice to stay and make it right rather than focusing on how it shouldn't have happened at all. That spoke of grace. Restoration.

Would a man like that really hurt her on purpose?

The knot unraveled another inch. No. Gerard had been honest from the beginning — painfully honest, actually, about not liking her coffee and thinking her interpretation of *Pride and Prejudice* was all wrong.

She smirked. A man who was forthright enough to confront her in a book club wasn't sneaky and manipulative. She *knew* that.

She hadn't even heard him out. She'd taken the few pieces of information he'd partially explained and held on to them instead of the whole truth.

Regret pinched hard. She had to make this right — or she'd always have that "what if" hanging over her head.

Bri jumped up from her computer, her heart racing. She had to find him — now, before he roared out of town and officially out of her life. She grabbed her jacket from the back of the dining room chair and launched toward her townhome door.

Time to run, for once.

She started to flip the dead bolt behind her, then stopped. Oops. Almost forgot. Jaw set, she rushed back to her computer.

Click.

CHAPTER TWENTY-EIGHT

He wanted a petit four.

Gerard stared at the rows of packaged candy bars and chips, debating his options. This town had created a stress-eat reaction in him, and since it had no twenty-four-hour gym like in Chicago to fight it off, he had no choice but to hit up the only gas station still open at nine o'clock at night and scrounge for sugar instead.

He picked up and discarded a chocolate bar, frustration welling in his chest. Before Bri, he'd have just grabbed a Snickers and been on his way. Actually, before Bri, he hadn't had much of a sweet tooth at all. Now, none of the options on the shelf looked appealing, yet the craving remained. None of them were petit fours or macarons.

None of them were made by Bri.

"Sometimes too many choices are a bad thing."

Gerard turned at the sudden voice over

his shoulder. Pastor John. He sounded his agreement. "Especially when you know you don't actually need any of them."

"Hey, that's pretty good. I should work that into a sermon." John grinned. Even this late in the evening, he looked energetic in a hoodie and track pants. "Personally, I can recommend these here." With a wink, he reached out and snagged a package of Double Stuf Oreos.

They actually sounded pretty good. Gerard picked up his own pack. "Are you a sermon-writing snacker?"

"Sometimes, when I get stuck." John shrugged. "Tonight, though, just had a hankering."

Gerard nodded. "Same here." More like he was eating his feelings.

"Did you finish the feature? Or is this supposed to help?" The pastor gestured toward the cookies.

"It's done. I'm done." He and Bri were done. But then again, John never knew they were together in the first place. And the last place Gerard wanted to vent that entire story was in the candy aisle of a gas station.

Or at all.

"I'm glad to hear you met your goal but sorry to see you leave." John easily held his gaze, his confidence more inviting than off-putting. "So, where to next?"

"Home for now. Chicago." Gerard studied the cookies in his hand, wary of John reading the unsaid in his heavy, scratchy eyes. "I'm up for a promotion, so I'll stick around there for a bit."

"Congratulations." John tilted his head, stepping aside briefly to make room for an older man passing down the aisle. "Right?"

"Absolutely. It's what I've been after. I'll have a voice. More opportunities to help my mom. Deeper topics to write about."

John nodded slowly. "That sounds good."

It did. So why the gaping hole in his heart suggesting otherwise?

Gerard squeezed the package of cookies. This had been a bad idea. He should have started for home already instead of making the wiser decision to head out at first light. He needed the wind on his face and the roar of his motorcycle in his ears to drown out the doubt. He needed the distraction of an adrenaline rush.

He needed to *move*.

"Staying in one place has its perks, you know." John flipped and caught the package of Oreos, over and over, as casually as if he hadn't just somehow read Gerard's mind. "There's something to be said for security." *Flip, catch.* "For roots." *Flip, catch.* His eyes locked with Gerard's. "For relationships."

"So, you know about Bri." Figured.

John grinned wide. "It was obvious at Casey and Nathan's wedding, man. The two of you . . ." He shook his head, letting out a low whistle. "Gives new meaning to 'opposites attract.' "

"Well, they might be repelling now, if you ask her."

"What do you think?"

Gerard shrugged, his throat knotting up. "It doesn't matter, unfortunately. I'm heading out tomorrow, and she made it clear how she feels."

"One thing I've learned in my years of pastoral counseling is that it's never too late." John pointed at him with his cookies. "But it's hard to talk when you're driving away."

"You think I should stay longer?" The thought both appealed to and repulsed him. Plus, *Trek* was waiting on him. His mom was waiting on him . . .

John shrugged. "I don't know what the Lord has planned for you and Bri. But I know you won't find out if you're afraid to try."

Gerard scoffed. "I'm not afraid of anything."

John raised his eyebrows, as if waiting for

elaboration.

He had plenty to give. "I've cliff-dived. Bungee jumped. Swam with sharks." Gerard's heart pounded even now at the memories. He pushed up his shirt sleeves. "I've gotten more tats than I can count. I've never turned down a dare or a challenge. I'm a straight-up adrenaline junkie, man. You're preaching to the wrong choir on that one."

"That's impressive. I couldn't do half of those things." John nodded slowly. "But tell me this. Have you ever sat still?"

No. Gerard clenched his jaw. And he clearly didn't need to speak it for John to know the truth. How did this man keep doing that — keep reading him with the familiarity of a used paperback?

"I jog a lot." John plucked at the front of his hoodie. "My wife teases me about having more athletic gear than she does, but it's what I do. I run. Run when I'm hungry, when I'm stressed, when I'm bummed out. Run when I'm mad." He paused. "I've come to realize that staying still is often hard because it means we have to face ourselves — and our inadequacies."

Gerard started to protest. "But you're —"

"I've got them too. Don't think that just because I'm a preacher I have it all figured out." John shook his head. "I still sin. I have flaws and baggage. I need the Lord daily."

Gerard's rebuttal died in his throat. He'd never heard a pastor admit to even half of that.

"I don't know what kind of church background you have, and I can't fix old hurts, but I *can* tell you that you'd probably have a different experience in our congregation." He winked. "If you stick around, that is."

Gerard clamped his mouth shut. The pastor had a point — as much as he hated to admit it. He'd been running. Bri had seen it. He'd even felt it but refused to acknowledge it. He ran to hide from his mom's addiction. Ran to evade rejection. Ran to avoid the truth about his feelings for Bri.

All it'd gotten him were sore legs and loneliness.

"I've been talking to the Lord about your mom." John lightly tapped Gerard on the shoulder with his Oreos. "Wouldn't hurt for you to take a minute and do the same about your future."

Bri flipped on the bakery lights at the Puff, wincing against the sudden glare. Her eyes, which had been red-rimmed and glazed when she dared peek in the mirror that morning before heading to work, felt as dry and lifeless as she did.

She had been too late. She hadn't found Gerard. He hadn't answered his cell, and when she ran by the B&B, Mrs. Beeker admitted she hadn't seen him all evening.

Now, it was after 6:00 a.m. He was probably halfway back to Chicago — if not already all the way home. She'd googled the distance last night while lying in bed, kicking herself for her emotional knee-jerk reaction and losing him. Over eight hours.

Maybe a clean break was for the best. Rip off the Band-Aid and all that.

But it didn't feel like the best.

In fact, nothing felt right anymore. It was like she'd awakened from a dream, and now everything felt . . . a little false. Tainted. Different.

She was different.

Bri planted her hands on her hips and turned a slow circle around the empty bakery. In a matter of weeks — maybe sooner, if Charles had his way — the Pastry Puff would be gutted and a uniformed barista would be standing in that same spot her mother used to stand. But instead of humming and creating delectable art, this barista would be pouring brand-name coffee and pushing brand-name muffins across the counter.

The door chimed, and Mabel and Agnes shuffled in. Agnes's coat was buttoned to her neck, and Mabel had a mink — hopefully fake — scarf draped around her neck.

"Good morning." Bri forced her best smile, but Mabel shook her head.

"No need for the fakesies today. We know you're upset."

"That's not even a word, Mabel." Agnes rolled her eyes as she dumped her purse on one of the nearby tables and began to unbutton her coat.

"It's a word now, because I said it. *Fakesies.*" Mabel repeated it louder as she undraped her scarf with a dramatic flair. "And Bri knows what I mean. Don't you, honey?"

Before Bri could answer, Mabel pointed to the chair across from Agnes's coat. "Sit."

Bri sat.

"We couldn't let you go a minute longer without hearing the whole story." Mabel took the chair next to Bri and reached for her with her gnarled, wrinkled hand. The deep purple of her fingernail polish matched the veins running across the top of her hand.

Bri clung to her — to the same hand that had wiped her tears, hugged her tight, and swatted her when she was being ridiculous.

"Are you mad at us?" Agnes sat down in

the third chair, leaning forward and bracing her weight on her elbows. Her gaze, while always serious, held a tinge of genuine concern Bri hadn't seen in a long time. "It's okay if you are."

"Not mad." Bri shook her head, not fully trusting her voice. "Just — confused." To say the least. After all this time — why now? Why at all? Had she failed, somehow? All the questions she couldn't voice without collapsing into a pile of tears.

Mabel nodded. "It was a hard decision. I know we act like spring chickens, but we're getting older, and honestly, I don't think we can keep up this pace."

"Don't get us wrong, you're an amazing help around here. You run the place and do most of the baking." Agnes patted Bri's arm. "But you can't be a one-woman show forever."

"You have a gift, Bri." Mabel's voice dropped to a whisper, as if she were sharing a secret. "You bake like your mother."

The compliment ricocheted off her guarded heart. She couldn't let it fully sink in. Couldn't take the praise she so desperately wanted to hear. She'd wanted it for so long, she didn't know how to receive it. "You mean because I finally figured out her secret ingredient?"

Agnes raised her chin. "Speaking of which, that was the most random secret ingredient ever —"

"No." Mabel shot Agnes a look with a capital *L.* "Because you bake with love, honey. You put yourself into those desserts. It matters to you — because the customers matter to you."

The compliment wiggled through the brick guard and embedded deep. Slowly, her wall began to dissolve. Mabel's words reminded her what Gerard had said on the street that day she'd run into him on her way to Casey's house. *"You're happy because you're serving the people of your town. Caring for the elderly and discounting goods for those struggling and holding babies for stressed out moms so they can drink their coffee in peace. Handing out cupcakes to homeless men on bicycles. Remembering people's orders and making them feel special. Listening to everyone who's willing to talk. That's what fills you up."*

Her mom had done the same — baked with love, with intentionality. She used desserts to calm anxieties and develop friendships and offer encouragement. She'd brought back her recipes from Paris to create masterpieces in her little town, ones filled more with joy and hope than cream or

439

compote.

Tears pricked for an entirely different reason. Was she really like that? She wanted to be.

"You're capable of more than this." Mabel gestured around the Puff. "You have so much to offer. We knew if we held on to the Puff, you'd never leave. We want you to fly."

"Why is leaving such a good idea?" Her pulse thudded in her ears, and she thought of her plane ticket to Paris. She was about to fly, literally — ready or not. "What's wrong with home?" With security. With familiarity.

"It's never truly leaving when you have a home. And you always have a home here. With us." Mable gestured between her and Agnes, who nodded. "Nothing else will change."

But Bri knew it would. The Puff would change into a chain. Charles would be in charge. She'd have to make an effort to go by Mabel and Agnes's house to see them regularly. Their tight dynamic would shift a little, because that's what happened when you stopped seeing someone every day. And one day they wouldn't be there at all — many years down the road, hopefully.

Somehow, Bri had to be okay with that.

She took a deep breath. She couldn't

control it — couldn't control her parents' decisions. Couldn't control the sisters'. And couldn't control Gerard's. She could only control her own.

"I understand. Thank you, both. I'm sorry I didn't take the news better last night."

Agnes waved her hand in the air dismissively. "It was late, and honestly, that tea was pretty bad."

"We wanted you to have this." Mabel handed Bri a piece of paper.

A check. Bri stared at the numbers in the dollar field and blinked. Then blinked again. "How can — this is —"

"Let's just say Charles was a desperate man." Agnes winked.

Mabel giggled. "And Agnes here knows how to strike a deal."

"Seriously." Agnes shook her head in disgust. "You should have heard what Mabel was going to accept. Someone had to step in."

"I can't take this. It's too much. You guys need it." Bri slid the check across the table, heart thudding. There was no way she was accepting that much money from two elderly angels.

Mabel immediately slid it back. "If you have one single ounce of respect for either of us, you'll put this in your purse right now,

441

young lady."

Bri opened her mouth to protest.

"Use it to take a risk." Agnes reached over, clamping her warm hand on top of Bri's.

Bri looked up in surprise at the unusual show of affection.

Agnes's gaze riveted to hers. "Your mother took a risk going to Paris — and look how that turned out for her. You need to live too."

"Yes. Don't be afraid to try." Mabel put her hand over the two of theirs.

Agnes yanked her palm free. "Stop getting so mushy."

Mabel bristled. "That's not mushy. Mushy would be *Agnes and Mr. Hanseeeen sitting in a tree . . .*" She broke into sing-song.

Agnes glared. "His name is Carl."

Bri tuned them out, tucking the check inside her pocket. The sisters were right. Gerard had been right. All this time, she'd been so focused on romantic love, she'd never realized how much she was showing love to others in different ways. Never realized how fulfilling it was despite her single status. Real love was sacrifice. Serving.

God was love. And she had to find her identity there. Not in Paris. Not in her parents' relationship.

And not in her relationship with Gerard.

The door opened, and a gust of wind

swooshed in. Mabel grabbed for her mink. Agnes turned abruptly in her chair, and Bri's heart stuttered.

He hadn't left.

Gerard stepped just inside the threshold, as if unsure he'd be welcomed.

Bri slowly stood, also unsure if she should welcome him. Her heart and her fears played tug-of-war in her chest.

"Come on, Mabel. Let's go turn on the ovens." Agnes grabbed Mabel's elbow and pulled.

"That's hardly a two-person job," Mabel protested as Agnes dragged her away. "How am I supposed to eavesdrop from the kitchen?"

Their voices faded as the kitchen door swung shut behind them.

Gerard approached her cautiously, wearing the black leather jacket he'd worn the first day she saw him, backpack slung over his shoulder. As Agnes had asked on that first day, Bri followed suit. "You needing directions — or a cup of coffee?"

Recognition flickered in his eyes and a half smile tugged at his lips. "I don't know. Is it any good?"

She shrugged, unable to stop the hope blossoming within. "I hear it's pretty awful. But I can vouch for the macarons."

"I can vouch for their baker." Gerard stopped directly in front of her, and the heat from his body warmed her all the way through, despite the inches separating them. "I'm sorry, Bri. I was wrong." He winced. "I don't say those words often enough."

"No, I was wrong. I should have heard you out." Bri wrung her fingers together. "I let Sandra get to me, and when you didn't immediately correct what she'd said, I panicked and assumed the worst."

"It wasn't totally inaccurate — but the motivation was. Charles swindled me." Gerard pushed his hands through his hair. "I figured it out. He knew I wouldn't keep that money, but he wanted to make sure you eventually found out that I took it. It's obvious now."

"That's why he backed off for that long in the media war, wasn't it? He had a new strategy to get to me." Bri shook her head. Dismay filled her chest. "What a rat. And now after all that, he got what he wanted."

"What do you mean?" Gerard frowned.

"They sold the bakery." The words still felt foreign on her tongue. "Charles won."

"Oh man." Gerard sank into the chair Agnes had vacated. "I'm sorry, Bri."

"No, you're not." She sat in the chair across from him.

"I'm sorry you're hurting, but you're right. I do think this is good news. Hard news, but good."

"That's what Mabel and Agnes said." Bri released a slow breath, trying to garner the courage that had carried her this far. "They said I have more to offer, and that I need to fly." She pulled out the check she'd tucked into her pocket. "Apparently now I have the wings to do so."

Gerard's eyes widened. "I'd say so. What are you going to do with it?"

"I don't know yet." Bri shrugged. "It's all still a little . . . surreal." She bit down on her lower lip. "I really thought you'd left already."

"I did." Gerard smirked. "I got about an hour down the road last night, then decided to take Pastor John's advice and quit being a coward. I came back to the B&B around midnight and prayed until I crashed." He looked down at his hands. "Also hard, but good."

"Sounds like it." Bri's pulse started a runaway gallop. "Why are you here?" Her voice sunk to a whisper as her fears rode shotgun. Afraid of him leaving. Afraid she already cared too much if he did.

Afraid of the giant unknown future staring at her from all fronts.

"Because I needed you to know that I started off caring more about the feature and my promotion than I did about you and the Puff. But that changed — quickly, I might add." Gerard reached for her hand, waiting until she slowly opened her palm to him before threading his fingers through hers. His touch warmed the leftover chill inside. "I should have let you read the feature, but I was afraid of how you were going to take it."

"Is it bad?"

"No. But it's not what you were expecting."

"I've learned recently that it's better to just have zero expectations."

"Great. Then you'll love it." Gerard reached into his pack on the floor and pulled out his laptop. "Here." He booted it up, hit a few keys, and turned the screen for her to see. "This is the final part two, save any edits my boss feels led to incorporate."

Bri adjusted the screen to compensate for the glare of the overhead lights and started to read.

Not all who wander are lost — but in Story, Kansas, not all who stay are found.

She raised her eyes to meet his.

"Keep reading."

That said, there's much to be found in the

Pastry Puff, a Parisian-themed café tucked into the middle of the Midwest — somewhat bitter coffee, exceptional service, and one of the best macarons this world traveler has ever tasted.

"You had to mention the coffee."

"I'm a man of honesty. Keep going." He tapped the computer.

She skimmed through the recap of their menu offerings, more fully described in part one, along with the joint ownership between Mabel and Agnes.

The Puff is best known for its love locks and matchmaking schemes — but perhaps the Puff's greatest treasure isn't found in its celebration of traditional love. Perhaps it's found in the heart of the service behind the management.

A popular TV show once thrived on the theme of belonging, of coming where "everybody knows your name." At the Puff, not only will your name be heard and remembered, it'll become part of the establishment.

This seasoned traveler has purchased goods from remote corners of the world — from tents surrounded by camels, from huts composed of mud and straw, and from modern stores dripping in diamonds — and not once have I encountered such a genuine desire by the management to connect with and make a difference in the community.

Bri's eyes misted over and she kept reading. *The number of days the Puff has left are unfortunately quite possibly numbered. Mid-America cafés aren't always suited for longevity and are hard to sustain in the ever-changing retail market. Throw in a few wealthy sharks circling live bait, and the end is often inevitable.*

She snickered at the accurate allusion to Charles.

But one tale I suspect will live on forever in Story is the one that began in a tiny, Midwestern bakery. A story of once upon a time, of a beautiful woman with a great deal of courage who left her home to journey to a faraway land. A story where a woman fell in love, made choices both good and bad, and birthed a miniature version of herself, whom she taught to carry on her legacy.

That lovely blonde legacy still bakes at the Pastry Puff today. And it's my suspicion that, come what may to the brick and mortar, this particular legacy will continue to do what she does best — serve with love — wherever she goes.

Bri blinked back tears, a hundred thoughts vying for attention first. She licked her lips, wanting to speak, unsure where to even start. "I don't know what to say."

His gaze held hers, steady and intentional. "Say you love me too."

Her heart cartwheeled and her mouth dried. "You haven't said it first."

"Oh, yeah." He smiled and stood, then took her hand, tugging her up beside him. "I love you, Abrielle. I love your bitter coffee and your heart for people and your courage." He tucked her hair behind her ear, his finger tangling into her thick strands. "I even love your blonde hair."

"What do you mean, *even*?" She pulled back an inch to meet his gaze and frowned.

"Long story. Tell you later." He grinned, then his eyes grew serious once more. "My boss sent me here because he hoped I'd find something to get my writing back on par — he hoped I'd find you."

Bri swallowed hard.

"And after talking with Pastor John and then after an even longer conversation with God, I realized that the Lord was the one who actually sent me here." He gently rubbed her arms. "When I first met you, I thought you were a romance-obsessed, head-in-the-clouds kind of girl. A woman stuck in a fantasy."

"You've never done this before, have you?" Bri squinted at him.

"Hang on. I'm not done." He drew her

449

close. "Turns out I was wrong — again. You had the wisdom I needed all along. You called me out for running — so when Pastor John did the same last night, I was able to hear it. You were right. I've been hiding. Scared of roots and what would grow if I stood still long enough."

"And are you standing now?" She held her breath, afraid to hope. Afraid not to.

"A little wobbly, but I'm up." He pressed a kiss to her forehead. "I see now how many people tried to love me with little acts of kindness. They offered me a place to stay when Mom vanished for days or tried to give me home-cooked meals when she was on one of her benders."

She squeezed his hand. She couldn't even imagine dealing with that as a kid — especially as a young boy trying to shoulder the responsibilities that should have been on a father. Her childhood had been perfect. Maybe some of it had been an illusion, in hindsight, but her parents' love for her — and clearly for each other — had been a constant. Despite the recent discovery of the letters, she'd never had to doubt her security or her family's name.

Gerard continued. "I was so guarded, I thought the church members were just being nosy or pitying me. But watching you love the people of this town showed me how much genuine heart goes into those kinds of gestures. Then when I met Remy and heard all his negative talk, it sunk in even deeper."

"What do you mean?"

Gerard hesitated. "There might be one more thing I haven't had a chance to tell you yet."

And here they went again. She tried to brace herself and hang on to her new no-expectations policy. She took a deep breath. "What?"

"Remember the photographer I idolized for years, Remy? The one who took the photo of me on the street near the bakery where your parents met?"

She nodded.

"That's T.R."

Bri's legs wobbled, and she pulled away, dropping into her chair. Blood rushed from her face, and she clenched her hands into a fist. What? No. "That's impossible."

"When you showed me the picture, I couldn't believe it either. But it's definitely him."

Her brain raced to connect the dots. "Your idol had an affair with my mom?"

"I guess that's one way to put it." Gerard hesitated. "I have a better way, though."

She raised her eyebrows, not trusting her voice.

"I like to think of it as God using a man who interfered negatively in both of our lives for an overall good. It connects us in a way that sort of feels meant to be, doesn't it?"

Maybe. Bri rolled in her lip. How could so much have changed in just a few weeks' time? Gerard had roared into town and upset everything she'd ever known. But she couldn't find the room to be even remotely resentful about it. He was right. It was like it'd been meant to be. All of it. Her mistakes. His.

Her parents'.

"I put Remy on a pedestal, and he fell off — hard. You did the same with your mom."

Ouch. But true.

"Remy spoke negativity into my life, and it came out in my relationship afterward. I was so guarded, always assuming the worst about my fiancée — and eventually, that self-prophecy was fulfilled. She became the worst." Gerard pulled the empty chair closer to Bri and sat down, their knees brushing. "Remy was broken and hurting because your mother dumped him for your dad. She did the right thing — but he couldn't handle it. He stayed bitter. He kept running from one location to another and had me convinced I had to do the same. Avoid love — avoid heartbreak. I thought he was onto something."

"Wow." Mabel's voice echoed across the room from the bakery counter. "Now, that's a small world."

"Mabel!" Bri jerked around just in time to see Agnes hissing the same. She grabbed her sister's sleeve. They briefly scuffled in a flimsy slap fight, then the two sisters disappeared back into the kitchen. But not before Mabel's desperate voice pierced through the still-swinging door. "Kiss him, Bri! Fly!"

Bri closed her eyes, torn between her desire to laugh and sob. It was like living in a cartoon lately. Nothing made sense, nothing was as it seemed to be. But maybe that's what she'd needed all along. Picture-perfect wasn't real. This was.

And real was pretty romantic.

She opened her eyes. "You were saying?"

"My boss reminded me the other day that there's a time — and a purpose — for everything. Ecclesiastes." Gerard sighed. "The last few years, I've sort of been in a permanent state of 'time to refrain from embracing.' " He rubbed one finger over her jeans-clad knee. "Until you."

"And now?"

"I'd like to think I'm in the 'time to love' portion of the Scripture." He clasped her hand. "You still haven't said it, you know."

"Said what?" She couldn't resist teasing him a little.

He kept a deadpan expression. "That your coffee really does suck."

She playfully slapped his shoulder. "It's not *that* bad."

"Am I still incorrigible?"

"Apparently some things never change, after all."

"Some things do." Gerard sobered.

"And some things do." Bri hesitated, then remembered her wings. Time to fly. She scooted over into Gerard's lap, perched on his knee, and wrapped her arms around his neck. "You live in Chicago." Speaking of wanting facts to change.

"For now. Lucky for you, I work for a *travel* magazine." Gerard lifted one shoulder. "Seems like there's some good possibilities there for relocation."

"*You'd* move to Story?"

"There's a blonde there I hear makes it a pretty appealing place."

"You're going to have to explain the blonde thing eventually, you know."

Gerard's arms hooked around her waist.

"Thankfully, I've got plenty of time."

Joy ballooned in her stomach. Still so many unanswered questions, but hope rose high. They'd figure out the details, somehow. Right now, she needed to celebrate. "You know, I've been instructed to kiss you, and it's never wise to disobey love angels." Her heart stammered in anticipation.

"I really hate that phrase." His gaze darted to her lips then back to her eyes.

"I can live with that." She pressed her lips against his. "Are you always going to tell me like it is?"

"Always." He kissed her again, longer this time, and her stomach applauded. "Are you gonna love me even when I do?"

She searched his gaze, then breathed a new kiss onto his lips. "Always."

One year later . . .

"We're out of macarons."

"Again?" Bri slid the next tray of petit fours into the display and turned to Gerard in surprise. "How many did you eat?"

He avoided eye contact and shrugged. "Not as many as you and Junior."

"For the tenth time, you don't know that this is a boy." Bri touched her rounded belly under her apron.

Gerard sidled up to her, tugging at her

apron ties. "You don't know that it's not. And, hey, I'm just being a good husband and trying to gain sympathy weight." He patted his own flat stomach with pride.

"Try harder. But not with my macarons. You're stealing them from the customers." Bri waited until he stepped up to help the next guest at the counter — old Mr. Peters from the shelter across town — then snuck a bite of a petit four. Junior — or Juniorette — sure loved them, too, during this second trimester. Sweets were almost all she'd eaten. Thankfully, they'd left the pickle-chip stage behind in the first trimester. She almost turned green at the memory.

"Have I mentioned I love that you're a baker, and you have a bun in your oven?" Casey popped an apple slice into her mouth from her spot at a nearby booth and grinned.

"Only nine times. Maybe thirteen." Bri grinned back. Casey and Nathan had had their own surprise a few months ago, who was now nestled in the carrier at her feet, snoozing away in the muted sun streaming through the café's beveled glass windows. "Why didn't you tell me pregnancy was this exhausting?"

"Because you forget that part after realizing how much more exhausting the actual tiny humans are." Casey snorted. "Want the horror stories yet?"

"Not yet. I prefer my naive 'baking' stage." She rubbed her belly. She couldn't believe everything that had happened in the past year. Marriage. A whirlwind honeymoon. An unexpected but most welcome surprise a few months later. And the grand opening of her very own nonprofit ministry café.

The café door opened, and Mabel and Agnes strolled inside. Mabel was walking with a cane now, but it barely slowed her down. In fact, Bri had seen her swing it like she was in a Broadway production more than once.

"We're not late, are we?" Mabel hobbled across the tile floor. "I was wanting one of those legendary grilled cheese sandwiches."

Bri headed for the refrigerator. "You're right on time. And I might have stuck one back for you." Turned out she was better at cooking more than just sweets. Who would have thought? It was funny what one could do with a hefty check, a heartfelt dream to serve, and the perfect location a few blocks down from the Puff. Well, the former Puff, anyway.

She heated the sandwich for Mabel and slid it across the counter to her on a paper plate — pink, of course.

"Have we mentioned that we're proud of you?" Agnes's voice grew slightly raspy as she braced her forearms on the counter.

"Yes." Mabel nodded solemnly. "That, and we want a souvenir from Paris."

Agnes elbowed Mabel, and she huffed. "Well, it's true. You know you do too."

"She's right. We do." Agnes nodded. "Preferably something purple."

"I'll see what I can do." They were leaving the next morning for a week in Paris before her third trimester hit, when it would be more dangerous to travel.

"And for the record, I'm proud of us too." Mabel held out her hand to Agnes, who reluctantly slapped it a high five.

"We knew the truth about you two the minute he roared into the bakery last year, you know." Mabel gestured with her sandwich.

Agnes nodded. "Obnoxious motorcycle and all."

"I know." Bri smiled across the counter at Gerard, who was leaning against the display, strong arms crossed over his broad chest, talking earnestly to Mr. Peters. Gerard gave him his full attention and respect — just as he did the other homeless, poverty-stricken, or simply "having a bad day" folks who ambled through their doors every week.

She'd married a man who'd not only helped her recognize her dreams but helped carry them out. "There's no one I'd rather go to Paris with. It'll be a fun trip."

"Who ever heard of going to Paris twice in a year? You two didn't get enough on your honeymoon?" Agnes huffed.

"Clearly they got plenty." Mabel gestured to Bri's rounded stomach.

Agnes elbowed her again, harder.

"Don't make me whack you with my cane." Mabel slapped at her with the hand not clutching her sandwich.

"You already do. Quit pretending like it's always an accident." Agnes rolled her eyes as she ambled to the table next to Casey's booth.

"We're just trying to make the most of our time before Junior comes." Bri followed, handing Mabel a napkin and gesturing for her to wipe cheese off her chin.

"Aha!" Gerard pointed at her from across the room, interrupting his own conversation. "You said Junior. So you *do* know it's a boy."

Now it was Bri's turn to roll her eyes. "He's still incorrigible, you guys. Not even marriage can fix that."

"Hey, did you hear business is pretty slow down at Charles's franchise?" A wry grin slid across Casey's lips as she reached down and offered her now-waking baby boy a pacifier.

"Is that so?" Bri kept a neutral expression as she ambled over to the counter and began to wipe up bread crumbs. Charles sure hadn't wasted any time tearing down the love-lock wall — save the portion with her parents' lock that Gerard surprised her with in her own front yard a week later — and remodeling the Puff into a well-known chain.

Casey blew out her breath in a short laugh. "Oh, come on. Quit acting like you don't care."

"I genuinely wish Charles the best." She could say that honestly now, as she took in the blessings around her. Love. Family. Friends. An opportunity to live out her heart's desire. Charles was the one to be pitied — manipulative and alone.

Unless you counted Sandra, which Bri most often did not.

Bri pulled her purse from under the counter and slung it over her shoulder. Hard to think in a few months it'd be a diaper bag. At least she had Casey to help guide her through this next adventure. She nodded at her friend. "Thanks for coming to lock up for me. We're heading to put flowers on Mr. Mac's grave before the sun sets."

"And Betty's?" Casey leaned forward in her seat and raised her eyebrows.

"Of course." Bri grinned. "I'm sure I'd hear about it somehow otherwise." A bittersweet twinge plucked, the way it always did when she considered the sweet man's recent absence. But he and Betty were whole now, and together with their Lord. Yet another love story for the books.

Speaking of . . .

She held out her hand for Gerard, who came to her side. She twined her fingers through his, smiling up into the face of the one who knew her best and loved her anyway. They'd helped each other unlock their fears and insecurities — and guided each other toward the One who held the key to true love. There weren't Parisian streets or kitchen slow dances or keys tossed overboard in the Seine. There weren't heavy burdens and secret recipes and financial stress.

After all this time, her story sure hadn't turned out like her parents' at all — it was better.

It was theirs.

ACKNOWLEDGMENTS

Writing a novel is sort of like raising a child — it takes a village. Special thanks to my talented tribe, including but certainly not limited to my awesome agents, Tamela Hancock Murray and Steve Laube, and to my brilliant editors, Kelsey Bowen and Amy Ballor. You guys make me look good!

Additional thanks to the marketing and design teams at Revell — Brianne, Gayle, Mackenzie, Karen, Michele, and Erin. I knew I liked you all from that first sip of coffee during our meeting at the 2019 ACFW conference, but wow — you guys are the best! Thanks for your hard work and heart work.

To my former assistant and current friend, Bri McMurry — I'll forever remember you jamming out with me to Taylor Swift in that little oil and gas office on the fourteenth floor, where the idea for this book was born many moons ago. I still remember telling you the heroine was going to be named Bri, and here we are. You're welcome.

To Allen and Jim — I'm honored to be on this journey with you brothers in Christ. Thanks for walking me through all The Things. Pass the salsa.

Georgiana — I couldn't do this writing thing without your encouragement and critiques. Rachel — thanks for always harassing me to keep writing because you want more to read. Lori — you're always one Vox away from a totally on-point brainstorming session that saves the day. Ashley — how were we ever NOT friends? Thanks for being you. Casey, Anne, Cat, Melissa, Katie, and Jenn — thank you for prayers, texts, salads in bed, pillow talk, counseling via text, random trips to monasteries, and other daily contributions to help me keep my sanity. Love you guys!

Last but never least, to my husband, Topher — I'm so glad neither of us canceled that first coffee date. You're the best thing to ever come from a nonfat, white-chocolate mocha. I love you!

ABOUT THE AUTHOR

Betsy St. Amant is the author of more than fifteen inspirational romances and a frequent contributor to iBelieve.com. She lives in north Louisiana with her husband, two daughters, a collection of Austen novels, and an impressive stash of pickle-flavored Pringles. When she's not composing her next book or trying to prove unicorns are real, Betsy can usually be found somewhere in the vicinity of a white-chocolate mocha — no whip. Learn more at www.betsystamant.com.